The *Wicked* Truth

The Wickeds: Dark Knights at Bayside

Melissa Foster

ISBN: 978-1-948004-71-8

Cover Design: Elizabeth Mackey Designs
Cover Photography: Wander Pedro Aguiar

WORLD LITERARY PRESS
PRINTED IN THE UNITED STATES OF AMERICA

A Note to Readers

Madigan Wicked has been one of my favorite characters since I first met her in TAMING MY WHISKEY (The Whiskeys: Dark Knights at Peaceful Harbor). She is feisty and confident, and having grown up with a gaggle of brothers and male cousins, she knows how to hold her own. But she's suffered loss and heartbreak, and although she believes in love for others, she isn't looking for it for herself. I knew her hero would have to challenge her as much as he adored her and connect with her in a fiery way in order for her to really open up to him. Tobias Riggs is strikingly handsome, broody, intelligent, and mysterious. Madigan Wicked has met her match, and I hope you love them as much as I do.

Music plays a large role in many of my stories, and as a musical storyteller, music plays a large part in Madigan Wicked's life. I am forever grateful to my son Jake Foster (aka musician Blue Foster) for not only allowing me to use his lyrics in my stories but for also performing Madigan Wicked's song "Kiss Off" so I could share it with readers. You can find "Kiss Off" on my website, Spotify, and all major music-streaming services, listed by (fictional) artist Madigan Wicked.

The Wicked novels are set on the sandy shores of Cape Cod Bay and feature fiercely protective heroes, strong heroines, and unbreakable family bonds. All Wicked novels may be enjoyed as stand-alone romances or as part of the larger series. On the next

page you will find a character map of the Wicked world. You can also download a free copy here:
www.MelissaFoster.com/Wicked-World-Character-Map.html

The Wickeds are the cousins of the Whiskeys, each of whom has already been given their own story. You can download the first book in the Whiskey series, TRU BLUE, and a Whiskey/Wicked family tree here:

TRU BLUE
www.MelissaFoster.com/TheWhiskeys

WHISKEY/WICKED Family Tree
www.MelissaFoster.com/Wicked-Whiskey-Family-Tree

Remember to sign up for my newsletter to make sure you don't miss out on future Wicked releases:
www.MelissaFoster.com/News

For information about more of my sexy romances, all of which can be read as stand-alone novels or as part of the larger series, visit my website:
www.MelissaFoster.com

If you prefer sweet romance with no explicit scenes or graphic language, please try the Sweet with Heat series written under my pen name, Addison Cole.

Happy reading!
~ Melissa

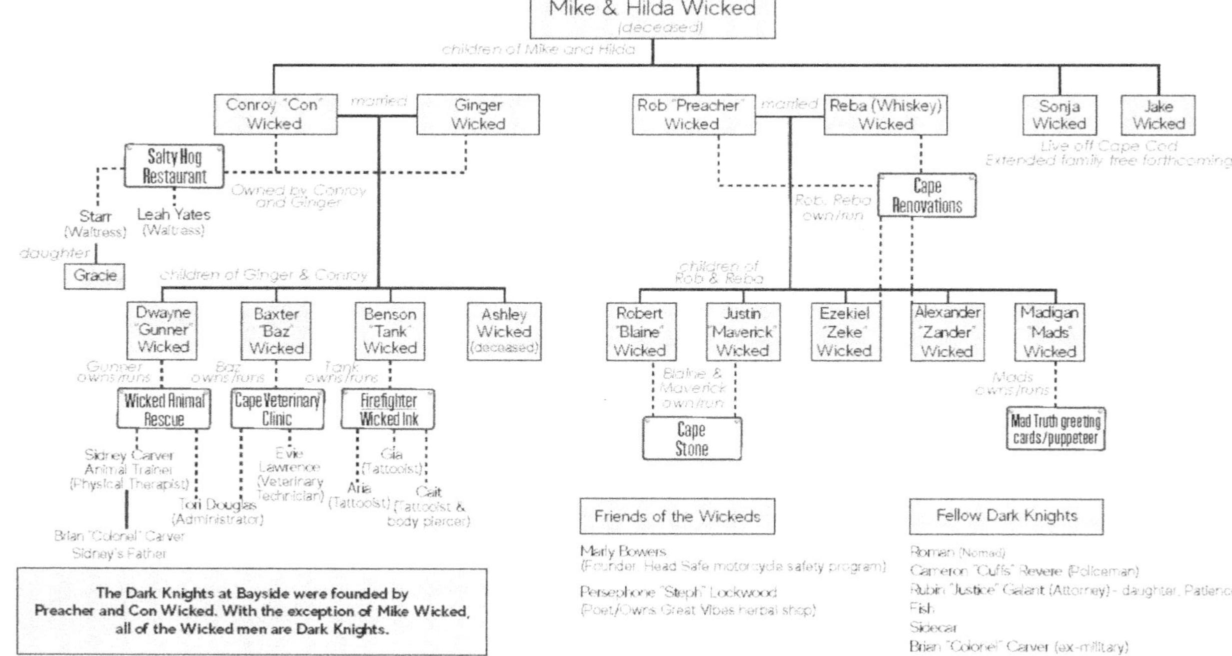
THE WICKED WORLD
DARK KNIGHTS AT BAYSIDE
Mike & Hilda Wicked
(deceased)
children of Mike and Hilda
Conroy "Con" Wicked
married
Ginger Wicked
Rob "Preacher" Wicked
married
Reba (Whiskey) Wicked
Sonja Wicked
Jake Wicked
Live off Cape Cod
Extended family tree forthcoming
Salty Hog Restaurant
Owned by Conroy and Ginger
Starr (Waitress)
Leah Yates (Waitress)
daughter
Gracie
Cape Renovations
Rob, Reba own/run
children of Ginger & Conroy
Dwayne "Gunner" Wicked
Baxter "Baz" Wicked
Benson "Tank" Wicked
Ashley Wicked (deceased)
children of Rob & Reba
Robert "Blaine" Wicked
Justin "Maverick" Wicked
Ezekiel "Zeke" Wicked
Alexander "Zander" Wicked
Madigan "Mads" Wicked
Gunner owns/runs
Baz owns/runs
Tank owns/runs
Wicked Animal Rescue
Cape Veterinary Clinic
Firefighter Wicked Ink
Blaine & Maverick own/run
Cape Stone
Mads owns/runs
Mad Truth greeting cards/puppeteer
Sidney Carver
Animal Trainer
(Physical Therapist)
Tori Douglas
(Administrator)
Evie Lawrence
(Veterinary Technician)
Gia
(Tattooist)
Aria
(Tattooist)
Cait
(Tattooist & body piercer)
Brian "Colonel" Carver
Sidney's Father
The Dark Knights at Bayside were founded by Preacher and Con Wicked. With the exception of Mike Wicked, all of the Wicked men are Dark Knights.
Friends of the Wickeds
Marly Bowers
(Founder, Head Safe motorcycle safety program)
Persephone "Steph" Lockwood
(Poet/Owns Great Vibes herbal shop)
Fellow Dark Knights
Roman (Nomad)
Cameron "Cuffs" Revere (Policeman)
Rubin "Justice" Galant (Attorney) - daughter, Patience
Fish
Sidecar
Brian "Colonel" Carver (ex-military)

Playlist

"You and Your Pain" by Blue Foster

"Unwritten" by Natasha Bedingfield

"The Sounds of Silence" by Simon and Garfunkel

"In My Blood" by Shawn Mendes

"Craving You" by Thomas Rhett and Maren Morris

"Elderly Woman Behind the Counter in a Small Town" by Pearl Jam

"InUrLife" by Blue Foster

"Tonight" by Blue Foster

"OCD Destroyer" by Blue Foster

"Like a Virgin" by Madonna

"Paint It, Black" by the Rolling Stones

"Kiss Off" by Madigan Wicked, performed by Blue Foster

Chapter One

TOBIAS RIGGS THOUGHT time had passed at a snail's pace in prison. But while those three years had felt like ten, they had nothing on the pace at which time moved in the free world after he'd lost everything he loved.

He climbed off his motorcycle, planting his leather boots on the ground as he took off his helmet and looked up at the Salty Hog. He'd stumbled upon the rustic restaurant and bar several weeks ago, when he'd first come to the nondescript town of Harwich, Massachusetts. The bar catered to people from all walks of life, making it the perfect place for a guy like him to blend in. Helmet in hand, he headed up the wooden steps to the second-story bar. When he'd gotten out of the pen, he'd thought he'd never be able to smell anything but the rancid stench of hate, anger, and oppression, which had hung in the prison air, coating his lungs and seeping beneath his skin. It had taken a while for new scents to push past his mental armor. The salty air coming off the harbor brought bittersweet memories of his youth with a family who had adored him.

And now, with the exception of his grandfather, those who were left couldn't even look him in the eye.

He wore those memories like a shield as he walked into the

crowded bar. A dozen or so guys wearing black leather vests with Dark Knights motorcycle club patches on the back eyed him skeptically, just as they'd done every other time he'd been there. At six three, pushing two hundred and thirty pounds, he stood out, but he stood out less with big guys like them around, and that suited him just fine. He kept his eyes trained on the bar as he made his way through the crowd, but a sultry voice drew his attention to the stage, where the gorgeous mahogany-haired chick who had been tossing him flirtatious looks for weeks sat on a stool playing guitar and singing. He'd seen her perform a few times. She sang *stories*, not songs, and she looked hot as sin in a black miniskirt and gold-and-black strappy top that bared her stomach. One black leather boot was propped on the foot ring of the stool. The other tapped the floor as she played, and a taunting smile graced the sexiest mouth he'd ever seen. Those plump lips had fucked with his head since the first time he'd walked into the bar and had seen her watching him, but it was her curious, and somehow also challenging, sky-blue eyes tracking his every step that stirred a primal desire he'd kept locked down for years.

And that was exactly where it was going to stay.

He tore his gaze away and stepped up to the bar. The hot strawberry-blond bartender, who looked to be in her late forties or early fifties, offered a warm smile, nudging her tortoiseshell glasses to the bridge of her nose. "Haven't seen you in a few days. What can I get you, darlin'?"

Her warm demeanor was comforting, which was another reason he liked being there. She reminded him of his mother, whom he'd lost when he was thirteen and whose absence felt even more pronounced without his sister, Carrie, chattering in his ear. "Beer's good. Whatever's on tap. Thanks."

"Comin' right up."

As she got his drink, he watched Blue Eyes onstage. Her glossy hair hung past her shoulders, brushing the edge of her guitar, which looked too big for her petite frame. He listened a little more closely to the words she sang.

"I hate the feeling of just lying in bed
With my stomach so heavy it feels like I'm falling to my death
Too complicated to just give it a rest..."

Her voice was a captivating mix of huskiness and silk, but *damn,* that story was dark. Could such a pretty thing feel that way, too, or was she just making shit up for entertainment purposes?

"Here you go." The bartender set his drink down in front of him and glanced at the girl onstage with admiration. "God, she's good."

"Yup." He paid for his drink and went back to listening to the story.

"When you realize you're the source of your pain
Will you make enough adjustments to make a change?"

Blue Eyes looked directly at him as she sang, stoking the embers he was trying to snuff out. Christ, those eyes and that voice were a lethal combination. But she was singing too fast, and the next few lyrics were lost to her speed. Tobias cringed, embarrassed for her, and turned away, wondering why she was rushing through such a powerful song. As he did, she slowed down again, and her gorgeous voice sailed into his ears.

"The lie is in the omission, my memory is in remission
Probably a mechanism to pretend whatever happened didn't really happen
Well, whatever happened, happened anyway."

She could have been singing about his life. He gritted his teeth as she strummed the last chord, and applause rang out. A cute brunette hollered, "*Go, Mads!*"

Blue Eyes inhaled deeply, her shoulders lowering just a fraction as she pushed to her feet, as if she were relieved to have gotten through the story. Tobias wondered if anyone else had picked up on that, but from the cheering crowd, he doubted it. If he hadn't been through his own hell, he might have missed it, too.

"Thanks so much," she said to the crowd. "That was called 'You and Your Pain.' Who's going to see fireworks for the Fourth this weekend?" There was another round of cheers. "Be safe. I'll be playing at the Rusty Anchor on Tuesday night. I hope you'll come out and see me."

Her gaze landed on Tobias again, only this time there was no taunting smile. She looked mildly annoyed. He had a feeling those luminous eyes could see right through to a person's soul, and that was the last thing he needed. He turned away, focusing on his beer as she announced, "Now, let's give it up for Carnal Beat."

Applause rang out, and a minute later she strutted over to the bar, guitar in hand.

The bartender set a glass of water down in front of her. "That was great, sweetheart."

"Thanks. But I don't believe *he* thought so," she said pointedly.

Tobias glanced at her out of the corners of his eyes.

"That's right. I'm talking about *you.*" She planted her hand on her hip. "What was that look for?"

"I don't know what you're talking about."

"Did you hear that, Aunt Ginger? The broody stranger *speaks.*" Blue Eyes smirked. "I told you he wasn't a caveman."

Cute *and* feisty. In another life, he'd be buying her a drink. He shook his head and guzzled his beer, catching her aunt's amused expression. No wonder Blue Eyes was there nearly every time he came in. Did she have a thing for being around family, or was Harwich *that* small a town?

"Come on. Spit it out," she pushed. "I know a distasteful expression when I see it. I can take criticism. I'm a professional."

If he'd learned one thing in his twenty-eight years, it was that when women asked for criticism, they didn't really want to hear it. Responding usually caused an argument, and there was no winning an argument with a woman. They had a knack for dredging up everything a guy had ever said or done, as if they'd not only kept notes but were being fed information by osmosis from acquaintances and exes. Or worse, they gave the silent treatment, and after the argument was over, when they said they were cool, they usually weren't. Women tucked away that shit like ammunition for an automatic weapon and pulled it out when you least expected it.

He finished his beer and set down his empty glass. "I got nothing to say."

"You come in here and never talk to anyone; then you *cringe* when I'm onstage but refuse to tell me why. A big guy like you shouldn't be afraid to speak his mind." She stared him down with the confidence of a lioness sizing up her prey.

Sexy as sin.

And lethal as cyanide.

Her aunt glanced over from where she was making a drink for another customer and arched a brow.

Great. He'd look like an ass if he refused again. Clearing his throat, he turned to the pushy sexpot with her too-short flouncy skirt and bare stomach, which was just begging to be touched and licked, and…*Fuck.* Biting back those thoughts, he gave her what she'd asked for. "That was a powerful story. Slow it down and your words will have a bigger impact."

Her eyes widened, then instantly narrowed as another sexy smirk slid into place. "I think I *know* how to tell a story. I've been doing this for years." The humor bled from her voice. "Nobody else thought it was too fast. Didn't you hear the applause? What do *you* know about music? You sure don't look like Simon Cowell to me."

This chick was a triple threat, as tough as she was cute and feisty, which spelled his favorite kind of trouble. Trouble he couldn't afford to get mixed up with.

"Sorry I said anything. It won't happen again." He pushed to his feet and pulled a twenty from his pocket, nodding to Ginger as he put the money on the bar. "Her next drink is on me."

"I don't need your money," Blue Eyes snapped.

"Sounds like somebody struck a nerve." Ginger winked at him and went to help another customer as two dark-haired bikers strode up to Blue Eyes, openly sizing up Tobias.

"What's going on?" the taller of the two asked, setting a serious stare on him.

"He giving you trouble, Mads?" the heavily tatted one asked, puffing out his chest as two more guys in black leather vests with enough ink on their skin to fill a novel strode over with icy stares.

Fuck.

Tobias readied for a fight, muscles flexing, feet shifting, mentally choreographing how it would play out. He was no stranger to unfair fights, no matter how he tried to avoid them. He'd take a few hits, but he'd pummel them in the process, taking at least two down with him. Memories impaled him—the crack of bones against his knuckles, the thud of his best friend landing on the floor, and the agonizing hell that had followed. Clenching his jaw tighter, he unfurled his fists. He was *not* doing this. Not tonight. Not ever again.

Tobias held his hands up. "Nah, man. I was just leaving." He reached for his helmet and turned to leave, but the two latecomers blocked his way.

"*Mads?* What'd he do?" the tallest one seethed.

She rolled her eyes. "I *don't* need your protection, Blaine. He didn't do anything. He just didn't like my performance."

"No shit?" another asked, eyeing Tobias. "Why not? Mads is a killer storyteller, and she's my songwriting partner, so if you got a beef with her, you're gonna have to deal with me."

"Just let it go, Zander." She pushed past them, stalking toward the table where the cute brunette who had cheered her on was sitting.

"Stay away from our sister, or we're going to have trouble," the guy she'd called Blaine ordered, and motioned for the other guys to step aside.

"*Boys,*" Ginger warned. "Leave that man alone. He didn't do anything wrong."

Tobias appreciated her support, but Blaine was right. That blue-eyed firecracker was *exactly* the kind of trouble he'd like to get into, which was why he headed for the door.

MADIGAN THREW HERSELF into a chair beside Marly Bowers, one of her besties, watching the broody bastard stalk out the door. "Can this day get any crappier? This morning my Vespa started acting funny, then a kid threw up at my puppeteering gig, and I stopped for coffee on the way here, only to spill it all over myself. I had to run home and change, which is why I was late, and now I have to scratch that hottie off my fantasy list. It's a shame, too, because he's even hotter up close, and he's got that gruff, gravelly voice that you *know* sounds freaking hot in the dark. I could really use some of that in my fantasies."

"In real life too, Mads. It's not like you've been dating much since you moved back to the Cape."

Wasn't that the truth? She and Marly had never been jump-in-the-sack kind of girls, no matter how much they talked like they were. Madigan had tried no-strings-attached hookups a couple of times since she'd stopped traveling and had moved back to the Cape about two years ago, but she hadn't enjoyed them. Still, she hoped she could enjoy it with the right guy, because while Marly was looking for a long-term relationship that would lead to love, Madigan had been in love once, and she had no interest in opening herself up to that kind of heartbreak again. But she was still a twenty-five-year-old woman, and she had needs battery-operated boyfriends couldn't satiate, like toe-curling kisses and a set of strong arms around her.

"Why do you have to scratch Mr. Mysterious off your list? There were serious sparks flying between you two when you were singing. I was like, *You go, girl.*" Marly could have any guy she wanted. She was fun, easygoing, and flat-out gorgeous, with long dark hair, olive skin, and almond-shaped eyes. She was also the founder of Head Safe, a national motorcycle helmet program she'd developed after losing her brother to a reckless motorcycle accident. She'd been the first one to spot *Mr. Mysterious* several weeks ago, but she didn't date men who drove motorcycles, and she'd said he was too broody for her.

Broody and a little closed off *worked* for Madigan. She'd grown up in a biker family, and some of her favorite men were that way, including the broodiest of all, her cousin Tank.

"I thought so, too," Madigan admitted, although she'd never been one to spill all of her secrets. She didn't tell Marly that she'd felt an unfamiliar hum of something deep and undeniable between them. A connection that went beyond two strangers catching each other's attention across a crowded room, as if they were supposed to meet. Was that even possible? Or was her mind playing tricks on her? It wasn't like she was *looking* for a connection, but she'd watched the sexy stranger listening intently to her story, and she'd seen pain in his brooding eyes. Pain caused by *her* words, and she wanted to know why.

"Then what went wrong?" Marly urged.

"He made a face when I was performing, as if I were massacring the story." The truth was, she *had* rushed through the story, but she hadn't thought it was noticeable. It was a difficult story to tell, and she shouldn't have even tried when she'd had such a frustrating day, but it just came out, and with that gorgeous broody guy watching her, she'd gotten a little nervous and had tried to get through it even faster.

"That jerk. He *should* be off your list. Is that why your

brothers looked like they were going to rip him apart?"

Madigan's older brothers, Blaine, Justin—who went by the road name Maverick, except at work and with his wife—Zeke, and Zander, could be a *tad* overprotective. She loved them for wanting to keep her safe, but at twenty-five, she was perfectly capable of taking care of herself.

She gave Marly a deadpan look. "*No.* He has a penis; therefore he doesn't belong anywhere near their baby sister."

Marly giggled. "It's a good thing they're hot, because they're the *worst* cockblockers."

"Clamjammers," Madigan corrected her.

"*Ew.* That sounds gross."

"Really? I heard some girls say it at one of my gigs the other night, and I kind of like having our own saying."

"Can we *not*?"

"Whatever. I'm too annoyed to argue," she said as their friend Starr, who also happened to be their waitress, set a fruity drink down in front of Madigan.

"I've got you, girl." Starr was a single mother to an adorable toddler named Gracie. She had one nostril pierced, her kinky blond hair lay like a thick mane down her back, and the colorful tattoos on her arms were on display in her Salty Hog tank top. "It's sweet enough to make up for the sour shit I just witnessed. I don't know what went down between you and that guy, but be careful. He doesn't seem like he's looking for company, and he sure pissed off your brothers."

"Yeah? Well, he pissed *me* off tonight, too." Madigan took a drink. "You guys *know* how long it's been since a guy has piqued my interest enough to make me consider hooking up, and Mr. Mysterious had definitely piqued my interest." He'd piqued a lot more than just her interest. Thoughts of him had pulled her through many long, lonely nights. "It figures I'd be attracted to the one guy who thinks my performance sucks." Although she still couldn't shake the feeling that he was right, or that his noticing the imperfection seemed important. Like it was part of that connection she felt.

Or maybe I'm just losing it at the end of a stressful day.

"He obviously doesn't know what he's talking about," Starr said.

"She's right," Marly agreed. "You were amazing up there."

"No, I wasn't." Madigan sighed. "I was a little off my game, but he didn't have to make a face."

"If I were you, I'd make Dante your new hookup destination." Starr gazed up at the shaggy-haired guitarist playing his heart out onstage.

"He's got that whole edgy musician thing going on," Marly said.

Madigan's friend Dante Dubois had devilish dark eyes that melted panties by the truckload, and surprisingly, he *wasn't* a womanizer. He was a great guy, a talented musician, picky as hell, into smart, down-to-earth women who wouldn't freak out at dog slobber. He had three dogs, which was why Madigan had tried to set him up with her friend Sidney before she and Madigan's cousin Gunner had gotten together. "I should."

"But you won't." Marly looked at Starr. "He's not broody enough for her."

"Uh-oh. There's double trouble heading this way." Starr nodded in the direction of Blaine and Zander making a beeline for their table. "I've got customers. Good luck."

As Starr walked away, Madigan said, "I'm not in the mood to listen to their bullshit." She stood, pulling Marly up with her. "Come on. Let's go dance off my bad mood."

Chapter Two

MADIGAN DIDN'T LIKE to sit still, which was why she loved to travel and had three very different professions. In addition to musical storytelling, she was a puppeteer, and after a devastating breakup while she was in college, she'd started the Mad Truth About Love greeting card line, which made light of the harder aspects of relationships. Her Mad Truth social media accounts had blown up over the last few years, and sales had spiked higher than she'd ever thought possible. That success had carried over to her storytelling gigs and puppeteering.

She could work on her cards from anywhere, and she'd been living the high life, traveling around the world, doing puppeteering and storytelling wherever she landed. But after her grandfather had taken a few falls, she'd realized she might not have a lot of time left with him, and she'd put traveling on hold to spend time with family. She felt good about her decision, but she hadn't counted on having so much downtime in the evenings or watching Maverick and Chloe, Tank and Leah, and Gunner and Sidney fall in love. She was happy for them, but their couplings, and all the things that went along with them—secret smiles, furtive touches, inside jokes—sparked emotions she'd been too busy to think about before, like loneliness. She missed the rituals of being part of a couple even if she didn't want to be in a relationship. To combat the unwanted feelings, she'd been gearing up to expand her Mad Truth brand, and her interaction with Mr. Mysterious the other night had underscored the reasons she needed to focus on work, *not* men.

Friday afternoon, determined to get the big, broody music critic off her mind, she presented her idea of expansion to her friend and Mad Truth client Jules Steele. Jules lived on Silver Island, just off the coast of Cape Cod, and she owned the Happy End gift shop.

"I'm thinking about expanding the Mad Truth into a line of wearable merchandise, like hoodies, T-shirts, and tanks. Do you think your customers would have an interest in that?"

"They'd *love* it," Jules exclaimed. "Heck, *I'd* love it."

"I was hoping you'd say that."

"You should consider mugs, too. My customers love them so much. It seems no matter how many I order, they sell out in days. You know what else sells really well? Small things they can pick up as unexpected gifts, like key chains and wall plaques." Jules gasped. "I have the best idea! My friend Bellamy is a lifestyle influencer. We can get her to wear the clothes and pimp them out on her social accounts. She's amazing, and her posts have made clothing and makeup go viral before. You should talk to my sister Leni, too. She does marketing and PR, and she *always* has great ideas."

"Hold on, Jules," Madigan said with a laugh. "I love how excited you are, but I'm still in the planning stages. I need to talk to a few other clients to make sure there's a big enough market before I dive in, and then I'll need to work out budgets and find a distributor." The distributor she used for her cards had recommended a company to her, and Marly had a friend who worked for a reputable distributor that she highly recommended, but Madigan hadn't reached out to them yet. "I have a lot to figure out before I'm in the marketing stage."

"*Oh*, I didn't think about all that. I guess you can't use an Etsy shop with your huge following."

"I thought about that as a way to test the market, but then the distribution will fall on my shoulders, and while I have some extra time, I don't have that much. I'm lucky I get through the books for our club each month." She and Jules and several of their friends were in an online erotic romance book club that Maverick's wife, Chloe, had started with her friend Daphne, Jules's sister-in-law, who now lived on Silver Island.

"Speaking of the book club, are you *loving* the newest Nice Girls After Dark book? I've never been so thankful for Amber's LWW connections."

Amber Montgomery was another member of the club. She owned a bookstore in southern Virginia and handled the club's monthly book orders. This month she'd scored advanced reader copies of bestselling romance author Charlotte Sterling-Braden's upcoming release through her connections with the Ladies Who Write. LWW had originated as a sisterhood of women who had attended Boyer University and had bonded over a shared love of writing. Amber had been part of that sisterhood. Three of the founding members had gone on to form LWW Enterprises, a multimedia corporation, and Charlotte was a client of their publishing division.

"*Yes.* I can barely make it through each chapter without needing a cold shower. I saw Marly on Tuesday night, and she was already on her second read. She's highlighting the best parts."

Jules giggled. "I highlight the steamy scenes, too, but then I act them out with Grant." Grant Silver was Jules's fiancé.

"I bet he loves that."

"You know it. Will you be at Chloe's meeting? Daphne and I will be on the video chat."

The book club had members all over the world, and although the forums were online, every month a member was chosen to host and pick a location for an in-person meeting. The member who was hosting this month lived on the West Coast, but since Chloe and Daphne had founded the book club, they also coordinated local meetings with themes that went with the books. The meeting was in two weeks at Skaket Beach in Orleans, and because the heroine in the story owned a gentleman's club, the theme was sexy outfits, and every member had to wear or bring something leather.

"I wouldn't miss it with a book this juicy. I hate to cut this short, but I'd better run. I've got a puppet therapy class at six thirty." They talked for another minute, and after ending the call, Madigan put on her backpack, grabbed the keys to her Vespa and her helmet, and headed out. She worked part time at the Lower Cape Assisted Living Facility (LOCAL) and kept a case with most of her puppetry supplies there.

She was halfway to work when the Vespa started sputtering every time she accelerated. Damn it. She didn't need another crappy day. She'd hoped to make it through work and drop it off afterward at a shop close to home, but she couldn't afford to get stuck on the side of the road. She pulled into a gas station/auto repair shop on the next block and went to find someone who worked there.

In one of the open bays, she saw jeans-clad legs and scuffed work boots sticking out from under a car. "Excuse me." She waited a minute, but the guy didn't respond. *"Hello?"* She tapped the bottom of his boot with the toe of hers. "Hey. Are you awake under there?"

As the guy rolled slowly out from under the car, she couldn't help but admire his thick thighs and the way his torso flared into a broad chest. Her day just got a little brighter.

Her hope deflated when his head cleared the car. It was the ex-star of her dirty fantasies. Well, he was *supposed* to be an ex, but she hadn't been able to get him out of her head the last three nights, and he'd continued appearing in her dreams, his sexy voice coaxing her into all sorts of erotic things.

Her cheeks burned with the memories as he pushed to his feet, wiping his enormous hands on a rag. *You know what they say about men with big hands. Or was it feet?* She looked down at his feet. It didn't matter what the old saying was—he had them both covered.

"You stalkin' me now?"

"No." Her gaze snapped up to his, and she tried to ignore the heat blazing from his intense and guarded dark eyes. The same eyes that had promised so many sinful things in her dreams. He was even taller than she remembered, broader, with a chiseled jawline covered in scruff the same warm caramel color as his hair, and lips she wanted to feel against her skin.

"You sure of that?" he asked, pulling her from her lustful stupor. He arched a brow with amusement.

"Do I *look* like I have to stalk men? I'm not saying I'm a ten, but I'm smart and I'm easy on the eyes. Being a little taller might be nice, but I'm small boned, so it could make me look awkward, like Olive Oyl. My brothers got the height in our family. But I think I'm a solid eight and a half. Not that I'm even looking for a man. Been there done that, and I'm *not* going there again. I mean, maybe for a little fun, but relationships aren't on my to-do list."

He was looking at her with slanted brows, as if she were speaking a foreign language. "Are you always like this?"

"Like what?"

"Never mind." He scrubbed a hand down his face. "What're you doing here?"

"My Vespa is sputtering when I give it gas, and I'm afraid it's going to die. Is there anyone here who can fix it?"

"You mean like a mechanic?" He glanced at the car he'd just rolled out from under, a reluctant smile spreading across his face. It softened his rough edges but did nothing to lessen the intensity of those brooding eyes.

"*Yes.* Sorry. Can you fix it?"

"There's not much I can't fix, but I'm about to clock out for the night, and the other guy is already gone. Can you leave it here and we'll check it out tomorrow?"

"Sure."

"Why don't you pull it into that bay so I can lock it up for the night. Get whatever you need out of the storage compartment."

"I have everything I need." She pointed to her backpack. "Will you hold this?"

She handed him her helmet, and his brow wrinkled as he looked it over. "It's *pink.*"

"Yup. To match my ride." The heat of his stare followed her as she moved the Vespa. When she climbed off, he held out his hand. She stared at it. Did he want her to take it? Her mind tiptoed down a curious path, wondering what his hand might feel like.

"The *key,*" he said gruffly.

Way to go, Mads. She handed it over, and he gave her the

helmet.

"Come into the shop and I'll get your information. You got a name?"

"No. My parents were wolves," she said, following him in. "They just growled at us and we all came running."

He chuckled, and it was so genuine, light flashed in his eyes. But it disappeared as quickly as it had come.

"I'm Madigan. *Mads.* What's your name?"

"Tobias." He went around the counter and typed something into the computer. "What's your last name?"

"Wicked."

"I bet you are," he said under his breath as he typed. "Okay, Blue Eyes, I need your home address and phone number."

He'd noticed her eyes? A thrill skated through her as she gave him the information. "Will you call me tomorrow?"

"I don't think your brothers would like that." He headed out of the shop.

She followed him. "I meant with an estimate."

"*Sure* you did."

She liked his sense of humor, and his guardedness made her feel special, as if he didn't let many people see that side of himself.

"But the answer is no, I won't be calling you," he said evenly. "I'm off tomorrow. The other mechanic will call after he takes a look at it."

She tried to ignore the pang of disappointment that brought. "I hope it's nothing too bad. What do you think is wrong with it?"

"No way of knowing until we check it out."

"But what do you *think* it is?"

He looked at the Vespa. "Could be your carburetor or a

vacuum leak, fuel leak, tuning issue, damaged spark plugs." He met her gaze. "Or maybe it just doesn't like being pink."

She tried to give him an incredulous look, but her smile broke through. "I can assure you, it *loves* being pink."

"If you say so."

"What do you have against the color *pink*?" She emphasized the word *pink* with a poke to his chest.

He flattened his hand over hers, holding it there. "Careful, Blue Eyes. You don't want to get yourself in trouble."

His piercing stare, the roughness of his hand, and the feel of his heart beating against her palm brought memories of last night's fantasy. She could still feel his rough hands groping and caressing, his chunky silver rings and thick chain bracelet cold against her skin, the thinner leather bracelet warm and soft as he drove her wild with that growly mouth of his.

As if he'd read her mind, flames flickered in his eyes, and his muscles tensed. With a gaggle of brothers and male cousins, if anyone knew not to poke a bear, it was her, but she couldn't help it. She lifted her chin and said, "Maybe I *like* trouble."

"I have no doubt."

The air between them thickened with sexual tension, the intensity of their connection sparking hot, greedy desires. She'd never felt anything so *dark*. It felt taboo, wanting a man she knew nothing about. She swallowed hard, trying to resist the lust pooling inside her, but the way he was looking at her, like he was fighting it too, made it that much more exciting. In the next second, his brows knitted, and as if he caught himself getting sucked into whatever this wickedness was between them, he released her hand and went to close the bay doors.

"Don't worry. The other guy will get your Barbie ride all fixed up for you."

"You really do have something against pink, don't you?"

"Not on things that are *supposed* to be pink, like blush on your cheeks or a bunny's nose."

"A bunny's nose?" She laughed. "That's a funny thing for a guy to say."

"Can't a guy like bunnies?"

"Yes, but most guys I know would say Playboy Bunnies."

He cocked an arrogant grin that made him impossibly hotter. "I didn't know you wanted specifics. Do you want to know which cheeks I meant, too?"

"*Ah*, there it is. Your inner caveman."

"You brought up Playboy Bunnies, not me. How about you worry about your ride and not my color preferences?"

"*Whatever.*" She liked his brash personality more than she should. "I hope there's nothing major wrong with my Vespa. I want to drive it to the fireworks tomorrow night. It's such a pain to find a spot for my Jeep."

"You got someone picking you up?"

"For the fireworks? No, but that's a good idea."

He shook his head. "I meant now."

"Oh, *no*. I'm going to work. I'll get an Uber."

"I doubt your brothers would want you getting in a car with someone you don't know. Give me a second to wash my hands and clock out, and I'll give you a lift."

"You don't have to do that."

"It's the least I can do after pissing you off the other night."

"You didn't piss me off."

"You shouldn't lie to yourself."

That took her by surprise. Most people didn't want to be lied *to*. "Okay, you *did* piss me off, but my crappy mood didn't help. Did you really think I sang too fast?"

He held his hands up in surrender. "I plead the Fifth."

"Come on. I can take it."

"I'm not dumb enough to go back for seconds."

"Are you always so annoyingly and refreshingly honest?"

He shrugged. "You want a ride, or what?"

"Well, I don't really know you, so I'd still be getting in a car with a semi-stranger."

"You know my name and that I work here, which is more than you know about some random guy who pulls up in a car and tells you to get in. And I don't drive a car, so you won't be getting into something you can't get out of. You can decide while I lock up the place."

He strode away, and a few minutes later he walked past her carrying a motorcycle helmet and didn't slow down as he said, "What's it gonna be, Blue Eyes?"

She caught up to him. "My brothers aren't going to find my lifeless body someplace tomorrow, are they?"

He didn't respond, his expression serious.

"I'm *kidding*."

"Death is no joke. Where are we headed?"

"LOCAL."

His brows knitted.

"The Lower Cape Assisted Living Facility."

"I know the place. Off Route Six, by the church. Put on that Barbie helmet, and let's go." He put on his helmet and straddled the bike, looking like sex on wheels.

As if sex on *legs* wasn't enough.

She really was losing her mind. She pulled on her helmet and climbed on behind him, wrapping her arms around his broad body. Heat seeped through their clothing, making her nipples tingle with desire. He slid his hands around her legs just above her knees, tugging her closer, and then he grabbed her hands, pulling until she was pressed so tightly against him, not even air could fit between them, and placed her hands just below his chest. "Hold tight, Blue Eyes."

As if she'd move from the most enticing place she'd ever been?

TOBIAS WAS ALREADY going straight to hell for things he'd done in his life, and his thoughts about the blue-eyed firecracker pressing her sweet, soft body against him would only ensure that door was locked behind him. But he'd thought about her, and that pain-filled story she'd told, for two and a half days. He liked her feisty banter and the way she said whatever was on her mind, and she felt fucking fantastic plastered against him. He clung to the desire stacking up inside him, willing himself to fight off his demons for just a little longer, but memories invaded like cancer, sneaking in through fissures and taking root.

He'd only had one other woman on the back of his bike, and he'd thought she'd be his back warmer forever, but she'd walked away and had never looked back. Three grueling years had numbed the pain of losing her. He wasn't stupid enough to let himself get tangled up with another woman and let whatever was brewing between him and Madigan go anywhere. But he was going to enjoy the hell out of this moment and revel in the feel of her and the ferocity of wanting and being wanted.

When he pulled up in front of LOCAL and cut the engine, he was fully prepared to shut this shit down. To drive away, have the other mechanic at the shop fix her vehicle, and never give Madigan Wicked another thought.

They climbed off the bike, and she peeled off her helmet. As she shook out her hair, tipping her face up to the sky, she was so fucking beautiful, he knew he'd replay the stunning sight too many times to count.

"Thanks for the ride." She cocked her head, her hair falling in front of one eye, giving her a seductively innocent look.

With those sweet, smiling eyes watching him, he suddenly didn't want to say goodbye, and hell if he knew why. "What do you do here?"

"I'm a puppeteer. I do puppet therapy with the residents."

He couldn't hide the amusement rising inside him, and she must have seen it on his face, because her expression turned serious.

"Why is that funny?"

He shrugged. "I don't know. You drive a pink Vespa, wear a Barbie helmet, and you're a puppeteer. You tell me."

"I guess if you put it that way, it kind of makes me look like I'm living out a childhood fantasy."

"Are you? Because I've got to tell you, I can picture you as a plucky little girl telling her brothers off and planning some sort of revenge with your puppets."

"They're not voodoo dolls." She laughed. "Although that's probably a good thing, because having four brothers can be trying. But I didn't get into puppets until after high school, and I take this part of puppetry very seriously. What I do helps with fine motor skills, and encouraging the residents to use and make puppets helps with social interaction and stimulates their brains."

"Really?" Thinking of his grandfather, he said, "Any chance

it helps with middle-stage Alzheimer's?"

"It can't cure it, but it can help trigger memories and break down communication barriers that can go hand in hand with dementia. It can help with depression, too." She glanced at the building. "I'd better get in there so I'm not late. My grandfather lives here, and I want to see him before I start work."

"Really?" He couldn't stop himself from asking, "Do you see him often?"

"Every week. I used to travel a lot, and after he suffered a few falls, I decided to take a break and come back home for a while."

"How's that working out for ya?"

"It was hard at first, readjusting to life under my family's watchful eyes, but it's fine now. My grandfather pretty much saved my sanity."

He knew a little something about the healing power of grandparents. "What time do you get off?"

"In a little more than an hour. The session starts in half an hour, and it's forty-five minutes long."

"I've got something to do nearby. I'll give you a ride home afterward." He told himself he was just doing the right thing, making sure she got home safely. It was true. It just wasn't the *whole* truth. But he'd buy it in order to get a little more time with her.

Her gaze softened. "You don't have to do that. I can—"

"Take an Uber. I know. We already covered why you're not doing that. I'll be here waiting when you get out."

"Are you *sure* you don't mind?"

"I don't say things I don't mean."

"Okay. Thanks." She headed for the doors but turned back with a tentative expression. "I guess that means you really *do* think I sang too fast."

Shit. He hated being the cause of the disappointment in her eyes. "I…" He couldn't bring himself to lie. *"Sorry."*

"You shouldn't lie to yourself. See you when I'm done."

He cursed himself as she went inside. Could he have fucked that up any worse? He paced, giving her time to get wherever she needed to be, before moving his motorcycle to a parking place and heading inside. He took the elevator to the second floor and went down the hall to his grandfather's apartment. Pushing thoughts of Madigan aside, he took a moment to rake a hand through his hair and brush the dirt from the front of his shirt and jeans. Not that his grandfather would care how he looked. His grandfather returned his affection in droves, but the disease was slowly stealing more of him, and there was a good chance the old man wouldn't even recognize him. But Tobias would never forget the gruff but kind and loving man behind those sometimes vacant, sometimes frightened or angry eyes, and he feared the day he'd lose him altogether.

But as he did at the start of every visit, he held on to the hope that he'd catch his grandfather in a moment of lucidity. With his heart beating at the excited pace of the young boy who used to follow his *Nonno* around, he knocked on the door.

"Coming," Elsa Cohen, his grandfather's live-in nurse and their family friend, said cheerily. The door opened, and she gasped. "*Ah!* My boy! What a lovely surprise."

"Hi, Elsa." He bent to hug her, dwarfing her petite frame.

Elsa was in her late fifties, with a mass of shoulder-length dark wavy hair, apple cheeks, and enough love to fill the hearts of all the lonely people on the East Coast. She had taken care of Tobias's mother before his mother had followed in his grandmother's unfortunate footsteps and passed away from ovarian cancer. Elsa's mother had grown up with Tobias's grandfather in the nearby town of Orleans, and her mother had helped his grandfather care for his wife during her last arduous months, more than a decade ago.

"Sorry I didn't call first. I was in the area, and I knew today was a free day." Elsa was aware of what had gone down with Carrie and his father, and she knew better than to try to talk with him about it. But when he'd come back to town, she'd told him that Carrie and her daughter, Carolyn—*Lynnie*—named for their mother, had moved back to Bourne last year, and they, and his father, visited his grandfather often. She'd given him their visitation schedules, which rarely changed, and had called the unscheduled days *free* days.

"Don't be silly. You're always welcome. Come." She took his hand, pulling him into the foyer. The scent of brisket hung in the air, his grandfather's favorite and one of Elsa's specialties. "Have you eaten?"

"No, but I'm good, thanks. How is he?"

"Testing my patience, as always," she said lovingly. His grandfather had been the kindest man he'd ever known, but the disease often made him frustrated and angry. "He thinks I've hidden his fishing pole."

"I'm sorry." Tobias was grateful for Elsa's patience and for her forgiveness. His grandfather had moved to the Independent Living wing of LOCAL after his grandmother had died, but a few months after Tobias had gone to prison, his grandfather's cognition had declined. Elsa had moved him into the assisted care wing and had been caring for him ever since. She'd written to Tobias every week with updates, and through those letters, he'd watched his grandfather slowly slip away. He'd held on to hope that Elsa had painted the worst picture when in fact his grandfather was doing well. But of course that hadn't been the case. It was strange how easily his mind had held on to that hope in order to pull him through the worst of times.

Elsa waved her hand dismissively. "I raised three ornery boys. I can handle your grandfather."

"I know you can. Before we go in, do you know anything about the puppet therapy program they offer here?"

"Funny you ask. I wasn't sure what to think about it at first. But some of the other caretakers have had very good things to say about the program and the woman who runs it. Apparently she has the gift of patience and knows just how to get through to the residents she works with."

The way Madigan had pushed him for an answer about what might be wrong with her Vespa made him wonder about her patience. But as a man who shut out most people and would bend over backward for his grandfather, he knew how a person projected themselves wasn't always consistent. "Would you mind talking to his doctor about getting him into it?"

"I'd be happy to."

"Great, thank you. You won't forget?"

She gave him a *don't be silly* look. "What's important to you and your grandfather is important to me. I won't forget."

As they walked into the living room, his grandfather barked, "John, it's about time you got here." He waggled a shaky finger at Elsa. "Mom hid our fishing poles again."

John was his grandfather's younger brother, whom he also sometimes called *knucklehead*, to which John had always replied, *Want me to give you a knuckle sandwich?* John had passed away several years ago, and while it cut Tobias to his core that the one living relative who had always loved him unconditionally had also forgotten him, he'd learned not to correct him. He tucked away the sadness that brought and looked at the withering man on the couch, with his wispy white hair, sagging jowls, and angry eyes, baring almost no resemblance to the Henry "Hank" Pettazzoni he'd once been, with jet-black hair, a barrel chest, and a booming voice that had only been outdone by his deep, contagious laughter. But Tobias knew that beneath the disease was the biggest heart known to man. As Tobias had grown from a teen to a young adult, his father's adoration had turned to disappointment, but his grandfather's love had made up for the ridicule his father had so often dumped on him.

"That's okay, Hank. We'll find them," Tobias reassured him, glancing at the picture of Carrie and Lynnie on the end table, wishing for the millionth time that he could turn back the clock.

But wishing was for innocent kids who still had their heads in the clouds, and reality always came crashing in.

A while later, he paced the parking lot as he waited for Madigan. He considered every visit with his grandfather a gift, but that didn't mean they were easy. They always left him trudging through a swamp of memories of the people he'd loved and lost, figuratively and literally, unleashing his demons to swarm like alligators snapping at his heels, trying to drown him in their murky water.

He'd only come back to the Cape to be near his grandfather while he figured out his next step. Soon he would climb on his bike and leave his demons and everything he'd ever known and loved behind.

"Hey there!"

He spun around at the sound of Madigan's chipper voice and felt a smile tugging at his lips. She waved, looking adorable as she hurried over in her dressy floral shorts and blouse. "I just had the *best* session…"

She was talking a mile a minute, going on about the progress her clients were making, and she was so passionate, so happy for them, he got swept up in her excitement. Just like he felt after a great workout, even in the pen, when the endorphins kicked in, and everything looked brighter. He hung on to her every word, wanting that feeling to remain, to understand what made her so elated.

That was when reality hit like a blow to the chest. Her world was bright. His was dark and would never be light again. He sure as hell wasn't going to take her down with him. He'd been a fool to offer her a ride home, to hang on to time with her as if he were a normal guy with no demons waiting to pounce.

He needed to nip this connection in the bud.

"Hey, I have a great idea," she said excitedly. "Let me take you to dinner for giving me a ride, and we can get to know each other better."

"No thanks. I'm good." He straddled his bike to avoid the hurt in her eyes. "Where am I taking you?"

The pep in her voice was replaced with confusion as she rattled off her address and directions to her house. "Did something happen while I was in there?" she asked tentatively.

"*Nope.* I got things to do. Climb on, Blue Eyes. Let's get you home." He pulled on his helmet, feeling like a prick, and waited for her to get situated. When she did, gone was the tight grip of a woman hoping for something more. It took everything he had not to haul her closer and apologize for dimming her light. But what would that accomplish?

Absofuckinglutely nothing.

They came from different worlds. Severing their budding ties was the right thing to do, even if it made him feel like shit.

He tried to get his head on straight as he drove her home, hating himself for the things he'd done and the man he'd become. But that was the point, wasn't it? He'd become someone a woman like Madigan, with her open nature and shiny pink thoughts, didn't need hanging around.

When he turned down her narrow, tree-lined street, he noticed her cottage was tucked away on a private lot. His protective instincts had him driving slower, checking out the surrounding area like he'd always done for his sister. He pulled into the driveway of her quaint cottage and cut the engine as she climbed off. He couldn't help but make sure she was safe. "You got roommates or someone waiting for you?"

She shook her head. "Just me. Do you want to come in for a drink? We can talk about whatever's bothering you."

He'd love to pretend he was just a regular guy without a prison record or a family who had disowned him and just get to know her better. A guy who could seduce her with words, not make her feel bad for singing too fast, and when the feeling struck, haul her into his arms and kiss her until she pleaded for more. *Christ.* He wanted that really fucking bad.

"Nah. I've got to go."

"'Kay," she said dejectedly.

As she walked away, his conscience got the best of him. "Hey, Blue Eyes."

She turned, a gut-wrenching mix of confusion and something tougher looking back at him.

"I wasn't lying to myself earlier. Lies cause irreversible damage, and I try not to choose that route. I *was* sorry that I hurt your feelings. I *am* sorry. Even if you did sing too fast."

A small smile appeared, but that gut-wrenching mix of confusion and strength were still there as she nodded and headed inside.

He started his bike, channeling the frustration eating away at him into his grip as he revved the engine, craving the freedom of the open road. But as he drove away, leaving the residential streets behind, and picked up speed, her tormented expression burned into his mind, and freedom was nowhere to be found.

Chapter Three

MADIGAN LAY ON her bed late Saturday morning listening to music, watching her curtains sway in the breeze, and thinking about Tobias. She'd never met anyone named Tobias before. It was a good name for him, as strong and mysterious as he was. But she couldn't say she'd never met anyone like *him*, because the way he'd gone hot and cold was all too familiar, sending red flags waving. She'd fallen for a guy like that before, and he'd broken her heart.

So why can't I stop thinking about Sir Broodiness?

It should be a no-brainer. She was no longer a grieving college student getting over the death of Ashley, her best friend and cousin, fiercely determined to live out the dreams they'd had of traveling and making something different and exciting of their lives. She wasn't that naive girl who had been caught up in the excitement of being overseas for the first time, away from her hawk-eyed brothers and cousins, enraptured by a man finally treating her like a woman instead of a girl. She'd left that starry-eyed girl, and any silly notions about falling in love, behind, and as Tobias had so eloquently put it, she wasn't dumb enough to go back for seconds.

She'd given up on relationships, focusing on making something of herself, and she'd done a damn good job of it. Wanting to make her late cousin proud, she'd traveled all over the world, doing puppetry and musical storytelling, while building a six-figure career with her greeting card line. But even now, with all that experience, knowing better than to ignore the red flags, as she closed her eyes, willing herself *not* to think about Tobias, it was his face that appeared behind her closed lids. Those guarded eyes, the lips that had slipped and curved into a smile for only a few seconds, giving her a glimpse of... *Who?* The man he'd once been? The person he could be? She didn't know, but she knew there was more to him than just a hot, broody guy. She'd felt his pain when he'd shut down. The same way she'd felt Ashley's older brother Tank's pain when he'd shut everyone out all those years ago.

Ashley's death had impacted everyone differently, and while Ashley's other brothers, Baz and Gunner, had been devastated, too, Tank had literally walled off his emotions, keeping everyone at arm's length. He was the one who had found Ashley after she'd accidentally overdosed, and he'd never forgiven himself for not being able to revive her. Nobody thought he would ever allow himself to be happy again, but Madigan had always believed he'd find his way out of the darkness at some point. She'd tried to draw him out of his pain, and although they were close, she was never able to do it for more than a few minutes. But that didn't stop her from believing that someone would eventually scale the walls he'd erected and ease that pain. It had taken a decade and the love of Leah Yates and her two young girls, Junie and Rosie. Tank would never be the same person he'd been when Ashley was alive—none of them would be—but he was happy with Leah, who was pregnant with their baby, and the girls, who adored their Papa Tank, and *that* was everything.

Madigan's phone rang, startling her, and Marly's name appeared on the screen. *Finally.* She had left Marly a message last night after Tobias had dropped her off. *Guys suck. Want to boy bash with me? I have ice cream.* But shortly thereafter, another of their close friends, Sidney, Madigan's cousin Gunner's fiancée, had called and invited her over for pizza with their friend Steph, whom Gunner and Madigan had grown up with.

Gunner and Sidney had served in the Marines together, and now they ran Wicked Animal Rescue and lived in a farmhouse on the premises. Steph owned an herbal shop and volunteered at the rescue. The three of them wouldn't be at the July Fourth festivities. They would be staying with the animals, so Madigan had joined them last night, expecting to have a girls' night and talk about Tobias. But Gunner had stuck around. She loved her cousin, but she didn't need him getting on her case about a guy who she would probably never see again after she picked up her Vespa, so she hadn't mentioned Tobias. When she'd gotten home, she'd left another message for Marly, hoping that talking about the way Tobias had acted might put an end to thinking about him.

But once again, he was the star of her every naughty fantasy.

Madigan sat up, answering on speakerphone. "Hey."

"Hi. Sorry I didn't call you back last night. I was out with Blaine."

"All night?" Marly and Blaine hung out often. Madigan wondered if there was something going on between them, but Marly denied it, and if there was, that was a secret Madigan didn't want to keep, which was why she quickly said, "*Wait.* Don't answer that."

"Would you *stop*? He was in a bad mood over something that happened at work." Blaine and Maverick owned a stone distribution and stonemasonry company. "We took his boat out and decided to spend the night on the water."

"I *don't* want details."

"That's good, because there are none to give. Baz and Evie were with us." Madigan's cousin Baz and his best friend since childhood, Evie Lawrence, worked together at Baz's veterinary clinic, on the same property as Wicked Animal Rescue. Baz lived above the clinic. "I'm sorry I didn't see your messages last night. We started playing Cards Against Humanity, and Evie brought wine. You know how that goes. But I would *love* to boy bash with you. Who are we bashing?"

"I don't want to boy bash anymore, but maybe you can help me figure something out. You won't believe what happened yesterday. You know how my Vespa was acting up?" Still in her pajamas, she padded out to the kitchen to make coffee as she told Marly about her encounter with Tobias. "I don't get it. Why do you think he turned me down like that?"

"Can I just say I love that he calls you Blue Eyes? That's *so* sexy."

"*Marly.* Focus."

"Sorry. Maybe he has a girlfriend and he got caught up in all your hotness, then realized he didn't want to be a cheating dick after all."

"I didn't think of that. He did say he had to go someplace nearby when I was at work. Maybe he went to see someone."

"Or not," Marly said casually. "He *is* a guy, and half the time they don't even know why they do things."

"That's true, but what you said doesn't seem far-fetched. So, why am I still thinking about him? He's obviously not interested, and I need a guy with secrets about as badly as I need a hole in my head."

"I don't know, Mads. Maybe because he's got thick, delicious thighs, a perfect ass, and eyes that say he screws like a sex God *and* he's a little broken. I think you like that mystery, and *if* he's looking, I doubt he wants anything more than a good time, which makes him perfect for you. That's why you can't stop thinking about him. And we both know everyone wants what they can't have, so the more you think about why he turned you down, the more you'll want him."

"So what you're saying is that I'm totally screwed?"

"According to the laws of attraction…"

As Marly went on about the laws of attraction, Madigan glanced out the kitchen window, and for a moment she thought she was hallucinating. Her Vespa was *in* the driveway. "Holy shit."

"I know, right? If the energy of our thoughts attracted people or experiences with the same energy, couples would never break up."

"Not *that*. He dropped off my Vespa."

"At your *house*?"

"Yes. It's in the driveway."

"Now, that's what I call service. I guess you know why he didn't come in last night. I like a guy who gets shit done. Too bad he drives a motorcycle."

Madigan's heart raced as she hurried out the front door and saw an envelope sticking out from under the mat on the porch. "Hold on. He left a note."

She felt the hard form of the key as she withdrew the note, and Marly said, "*Dear Blue Eyes, I don't like to leave things unfinished. Now that your Vespa is fixed, want to screw?*"

"It's not an invitation to a mattress party," Madigan said with disappointment. "It's a receipt for the work he did. The labor is zeroed out, and it looks like he paid for the parts."

"You've got to like that. What else?"

She looked inside the envelope again. "Nothing. What the hell? This was really nice of him, but how am I supposed to take this?"

"Maybe he realized he was a jerk and wanted to make up for it."

"Why wouldn't he leave a note? Should I go by the shop and pay him back, or at least thank him?"

"You could do that, or you can kill two birds with one stone. You want to stop thinking about him, right?"

"Kind of. He has red flags written all over him."

"*And* she waffles." Marly giggled. "You could pay him with sexual favors and screw him out of your system."

"That's like asking for trouble." His voice trampled through her mind. *Careful, Blue Eyes. You don't want to get yourself in trouble*, and on its heels, her response *Maybe I like trouble.* Her stomach flip-flopped at the prospect of getting into that kind of trouble with Tobias.

"Then leave it. Don't go see him, and forget about him. A gorgeous man fixing your vehicle and dropping it off is *not* a bad problem to have."

"Wait, I just remembered I can't go see him. He's not working today."

"Problem solved. Out of sight, out of mind. Let's meet for breakfast and go shopping for something cute to wear tonight. Maybe you'll get lucky and meet a hot guy at the fireworks who'll make you forget all about your moody mechanic."

Tobias had been out of sight since yesterday evening and he

was still on Madigan's mind despite the red flags, which made her feel like that naive college girl lusting after someone she shouldn't. That was a sobering reality. She wasn't about to let another man steal one more second of her sanity.

"You know what? I don't need to meet another guy to forget Tobias. I just fell off the never-again wagon for a little while. But I'm back in control. Consider him *forgotten*."

AFTER A DAY of shopping and trying to convince herself that she wasn't *still* thinking about Tobias, Madigan met her family and friends at the beach just down the road from the Salty Hog. They'd been going there to watch the fireworks instead of the more popular beaches where locals and tourists went to celebrate since she was a kid. But over the years, more people had discovered their secret, and tonight there were dozens of people there. Giggles and shouts rang out, competing with the sounds of waves crashing against the shore, as families sat on blankets and chairs, children darted across the sand waving miniature flags, and couples strolled by the water's edge. Teenagers gathered in groups down the beach, too cool to throw Frisbees and footballs, while twentysomethings sat around bonfires drinking and talking loudly.

Madigan loved getting together with her family, and tonight most of her cousins and closest friends had joined them. She sat by their bonfire, between her parents and Chloe and Maverick, soaking it all in. Chloe was sitting between Maverick's legs, her back against his chest. Marly and Evie shared a blanket and a pizza. Tank's wife, Leah, sat in a chair with a bag of dill pickle chips balanced on her very pregnant belly. Zander was sitting in the sand playing his guitar, and just down the beach, Blaine and Baz were chatting with two women. Tank and Zeke were digging for buried treasure by the dunes with Junie and Rosie. Little did the girls know that their uncle Zeke had come to the beach earlier and buried elaborate treasure maps and goodies for them to find.

"Whoever came up with these should win some kind of award," Leah said with a slightly Southern drawl as she popped another chip into her mouth. She was uniquely beautiful. Her mother was white, and her father was black. She was petite, with a wild mass of brownish-red corkscrew curls, thick dark brows over soft hazel eyes, a slightly flat nose, heavily freckled fair skin, and full lips, which Tank was always kissing.

"I don't know how you can eat those." Evie, a vivacious brunette, wrinkled her nose.

Leah snagged another chip and made a show of biting into it. *"Mm."*

Evie pretended to gag, and Madigan and the others laughed.

"You do have funny cravings," Madigan pointed out. "Last month it was peanut butter on oranges."

"It's not *me*. It's this mammoth child I'm carrying." Leah rubbed her belly. "I swear it has Tank's appetite."

"When I was pregnant, I ate everything in sight and then some," Ginger said as she and her husband, Conroy, joined them by the fire. "I gained a lot of weight, but it was worth it."

"And every pound looked and felt stunning on you." Conroy flashed a dimple-revealing grin and lowered himself into a chair. Ginger looked at him adoringly as he took her hand, pulling her into a kiss.

"Enjoy it while you can, honey," Ginger said to Leah.

"Once that baby is born, you'll be so busy feeding and changing it, you'll forget to feed yourself."

"Tank won't let her starve," Madigan's mother chimed in, tucking her shoulder-length mahogany hair behind her ear. "He dotes on Leah the way Preacher doted on me when I was pregnant."

Madigan's father went by the road name Preacher. He was tall, broad shouldered, and in excellent shape from working at their family business, Cape Renovations. Tattoos covered most of his body, including his hands, and he wore his short black-and-silver hair slicked back. His pitch-black brows, ice-blue eyes that were always assessing, studying, ready for anything, and trim beard gave him an authoritative presence, but inside that tough, serious biker was a warm heart that treated friends like family.

"I wanted to reap the benefits of those pregnancy hormones," her father said with a wink, which her mother ate up.

"I don't need to know that about you, Dad," Madigan said.

"Neither do I," Conroy said, and everyone chuckled. Her uncle was also tall and fit, but that was about as far as his physical similarities to her father went. Conroy had an easy nature and Hollywood good looks, with wavy collar-length silver hair, blue eyes that usually glittered playfully, and a bright smile that brought out deep dimples, which his sons had all inherited.

Zander started playing "Let's Get It On" by Marvin Gaye, causing a round of chuckles.

"All kidding aside, pregnancy is a beautiful thing," her father said. "There's nothing like bringing life into this world." His thoughtful gaze trailed to Blaine as he and Baz joined them around the bonfire. It lingered on Blaine for a moment before moving to Zeke, Zander, Madigan, and finally coming to rest on Maverick. "I take that back. There is something just as special as bringing life into this world. Being gifted a child who becomes your son." They'd fostered, and later adopted, Maverick when he was a teenager.

"And *our* brother," Blaine said as he sat beside Marly, and Baz took up residence next to Evie.

Maverick nodded, emotions brimming in his eyes. "I'm glad you guys feel that way, because Chloe and I are working on bringing another baby into our family." Chloe looked lovingly up at him, and he pressed a kiss to her lips.

"Oh, *honey*, that's wonderful news," their mother exclaimed. "But I thought you'd decided to wait. What changed?"

"I was nervous about being a mother," Chloe said. "But Serena just found out she was pregnant, and something inside me clicked. Suddenly I knew it was the right time, and Justin was ready." Serena was Chloe's younger sister.

"I sure am." Maverick hugged her.

"Yay. More babies!" Madigan cheered, and everyone talked at once, sharing their excitement, which led to the topic of Leah and Tank's baby and Leah's baby shower, which was taking place next month.

"Mama! Look what we found!" Junie was sprinting toward Leah. Red ringlets bounced around her adorable fair-skinned face, in stark contrast to her younger sister, Rosie, who was trying her hardest to catch up. Rosie's thick brown curls were a shade darker than her skin and currently pinned up in pigtails.

Tank and Zeke were right behind them, Tank's serious gaze tracking the girls' every step. Zeke was shaking his head with an easy smile. At six four with thick dark hair and a beard to match, Tank was tattooed from neck to ankles, with piercings in his nostril and ears. He was the biggest, gruffest, and most intimidating of Madigan's cousins, but he was all heart with his family. Zeke was the calm to everyone's chaos. Like all the men in their family, he was also a big guy at six one or two. He had a few tattoos and bright blue eyes that could go from amicable to deadly in a single second if the situation called for it.

Junie skidded to a stop beside Leah. "We found tweasure maps!" Her hand shot out, showing Leah the map.

"Wow. A *real* treasure map." Leah shared a knowing smile with Tank and Zeke.

"Gingy! Connie! Look!" Rosie scampered onto Conroy's lap, thrusting a map into his face.

"Careful, baby girl," Reba said gently. "You almost gave Grandpa Con a black eye."

"Papa Tank said if we find tweasure, we can keep it," Junie exclaimed.

Rosie nodded enthusiastically. "We gonna find it!"

Junie put her hand on Leah's stomach and lowered her face closer. "I'm gonna find some for *you*, baby."

There was a collective "Aw."

Leah ran a hand down Junie's back. "I think the baby would like that."

"Attagirl, Twitch." Tank ruffled Junie's hair, and Junie beamed at the nickname he'd bestowed upon her. He winked and set a serious gaze on Leah. "You doing okay, Lee? Can I get you anything?"

"Just a kiss," Leah said sweetly. "Unless you can figure out a way to carry and birth this baby for me."

"I would if I could." He leaned down to kiss her.

"I have no doubt you would," Zeke announced. "You need to have a serious talk with this guy, Leah. He's so protective of

Junie and Rosie, he was staring down the little boys that wanted to dig in the sand with them."

"Tank...?" Leah shook her head.

"What? They were getting too close," Tank grumbled.

"They were little kids, trying to see into the holes they'd dug, not into their"—Zeke glanced at Junie and Rosie—"P-A-N-T-S."

Everyone cracked up, and Rosie said, "Papa Tank's funny."

"He says boys shouldn't get too close, because if you give 'em an inch, they'll make it a mile," Junie explained, brows knitted. "But sometimes I like to play with boys and we have to be close."

"Benson Wicked," Ginger said sharply, catching Tank's attention with his given name. "You need to give these girls room to grow up."

"They'll grow up just fine," Tank grumbled.

"I feel your pain, Junie," Madigan said. "They've been telling me that since I was your age, and sometimes I like to play close with boys, too."

"I hope the little girls are better at picking friends than you are," Blaine said.

"I have *great* taste in friends," Madigan snapped. "I'm way pickier than you are."

"I think it's time to go find that treasure," Zeke said.

Junie and Rosie ran toward the dunes, chatting excitedly, with Tank and Zeke close behind.

"I heard you got into it the other night with that shady-looking guy who's been coming to the Hog," Baz said.

"What're you talking about?" Maverick looked at Madigan. "What guy?"

"I didn't get *into* anything," Madigan snapped. "And you

guys all look shady to people who aren't bikers."

"I don't look *shady*." Baz put an arm around Evie, turning on the charm, with his longish dirty-blond hair, dimpled smile, and the puppy-dog eyes women lusted after. "Tell her, Evie."

"I'm not getting involved in this." Evie ducked out from beneath his arm. "But if I were, I'd be on Madigan's side."

"Mads, who is this guy, and what kind of *shady* is he? Is he dangerous?" Maverick demanded.

Madigan rolled her eyes.

"I don't know why you boys are getting up in arms," her mother said. "Your father looked pretty shady when he rolled into Maryland when we first met, and look how great a man he is."

"Did you conveniently forget that your brothers were *not* happy about Preacher going after their sister?" Conroy asked.

"*No.* That's my point," her mother said. "We don't judge by looks alone."

"It's not just his looks," Blaine said. "He gives off a strong don't-fuck-with-me vibe."

Concern rose in her mother's eyes.

Zander put down his guitar and said, "The dude didn't like her performance. It turned out Mads was just giving him a hard time."

"Mads?" Her father lifted his chin. "Anything I should know about?"

"No." She appreciated that her parents treated her like the adult she was, rather than just taking her brothers' word for it, but she was irritated to be at the center of this discussion. "It was nothing."

Her father turned his attention to Blaine, a silent question passing between them.

"She handled it," Blaine admitted. "And then I made sure he knew we were watching out for her, that's all."

"That's not *all*," Ginger said. "You boys ran him out of there. He's a nice guy. He just keeps to himself, but it took a lot of pushing before he even responded to Mads. That's not a guy who's looking for trouble."

She was right. A guy who was looking for trouble would have taken Madigan up on the invitation to come inside last night, and he sure as heck wouldn't have fixed her Vespa and paid for the parts. If anything, Tobias was pushing her away, which was still bugging her.

"Can't say I'm sorry." Blaine held Madigan's gaze and said, "Something about that guy rubs me the wrong way."

As frustrated with her brother as she was with herself for being attracted to Mr. Red Flag, Madigan pushed to her feet. "Okay, you know what? I'm going for a walk."

"I'll go with you," Zander and Marly said at the same time.

"I'm fine by myself. Thanks." She headed down the beach and made it a good distance before her mother caught up with her.

"Honey, are you sure you're okay?"

"I'm fine." She kept her eyes trained on the sand, because in addition to intuitively knowing who needed a little extra love, her mother had a knack for seeing past lies and smokescreens.

"I know that tone, and it means you're pissed. The question is, who are you angry at? You know Blaine just worries about you." Her mother touched her arm.

Madigan stopped walking and met her gaze. "It's not Blaine. It's *me*. Blaine's right. The guy is a walking red flag, but there's something there, and I can't shake it. The way he listened to my performance was like it spoke to him, and yes, he's guarded. But he also fixed my Vespa and paid for the parts himself, and gave me a ride to and from work, and when he drove me home, he *didn't* take me up on my offer to come inside. It doesn't matter anyway. He'll probably never go to the Hog again, thanks to all of us, and you know I won't chase him down."

"I don't think you'll have to."

"What do you mean?"

"I've never seen you like this over a guy. That fire in your belly is there for a reason, and if you're feeling it, chances are he is, too."

"I don't know what that means."

Her mother smiled. "It means some fires are bigger than we are. You can try to ignore it, but if this is what I think it is, there's not enough water in the ocean to extinguish those flames."

"*Great.* Now I'm even more confused."

She took Madigan's hand, giving it a gentle squeeze. "That's okay. You're due a little confusion. You sure you don't want company on your walk?"

She nodded. "I'm sure, but thanks."

"Okay, sweetheart. Just one piece of advice. Trust your gut, even if you don't understand it."

"My gut is giving me whiplash at the moment." She laughed softly. "I'll be back in a little while."

As she headed away from the busy beach, the din of the partygoers faded, giving way to the sounds of the sea and her thoughts about the man she *shouldn't* be thinking about.

TOBIAS PLAYED HIS guitar, thinking back on the years when holidays weren't shrouded in darkness. But thinking of all he'd lost just pissed him off, so he stopped playing nostalgic songs and went for something that fit his current situation. He began playing "Paint It, Black" by the Rolling Stones, strumming quietly at first, his voice hushed, though there was no one around to hear him. But as he sang about painting everything black, the sea never changing colors, and his inability to have foreseen what had happened, anger simmered to a burn inside him. He played more aggressively, strumming and picking angrily at the strings, fury bursting from his lungs. He closed his eyes, pouring those unwanted emotions into the song, into the idea of painting everything black.

Maybe then he wouldn't feel like he'd been ripped from a world, and a life, he'd known and enjoyed and dropped into some alternate universe, where he didn't have a clue how to fit in.

When he finished the song, it felt so good to get that shit out of his head, he shouted at the moon, "*Hell yeah!*"

Applause rang out, and he whipped his head to the side. Madigan Wicked stood on the beach, bathed in moonlight, one hand planted on her hip. She looked hot as sin in skimpy cutoffs, a white sweater that hung off one shoulder, and a smirk on her very fuckable lips. He steeled himself against the flames licking at his skin.

"I guess you do know a little something about music," she said sassily, walking closer.

"You stalking me again, Blue Eyes?"

"Hardly. I'd say it's the other way around."

He scoffed and shook his head. "I've been sitting here all night. Where'd you come from? Shouldn't you be barbecuing on a pink grill or something?"

"Shows how much you know. Barbie girls use pink skewers and spatulas, not pink grills."

Touché. "Your bodyguards have the night off?"

"If you mean my brothers and cousins, they're farther down the beach with the rest of my family."

"Why aren't you with them? You probably shouldn't be wandering around alone."

"I like being alone. Besides, nobody messes with a *biker princess.*" *Biker princess* was filled with sarcasm.

"Is that a reference to your Vespa? It's cool that you drive one, but that Barbie mobile is not going to scare anyone off."

"It's *not* a reference to my Vespa. Everyone around here knows my father and uncle founded the Dark Knights and my brothers and cousins are members."

"So? Where does *princess* come in? Or is that just how you see yourself?"

Her eyes narrowed. "Is that a joke?"

"No. It's not every day a woman calls herself a princess."

She crossed her arms. "You drive a *motorcycle.* How can you not know that the president of a motorcycle club's daughter is referred to as a princess?"

"I don't run in those circles."

"*Oh,*" she said with surprise. "I guess I assumed everyone who drove a motorcycle knew about clubs."

"Guess again. What does it mean, anyway? Do people bow down to you? Because I got news for you, Blue Eyes. I don't bow down to anyone."

"*I* don't either, and I don't *want* anyone bowing to me. I hate entitlement. The daughter of the president—"

"You."

"Yes, *me*. I'm supposed to be off-limits, so the guys protect me. They protect everyone's family, really, but there's something special about the president's daughter."

"Again, something special about *you*." He said it just to get a reaction, because she was cute as hell when she was annoyed, and the scowl she sported was worth it. He already knew she was different from other women, and *special* was a good word for her. But that had nothing to do with her family's biker affiliation and everything to do with the challenging woman she was. And he just couldn't resist twisting the needle. "Does that mean you've got a chastity belt under those skimpy shorts?"

Rebellion rose in her eyes. "No, but they *wish* I did."

Yet another reason he should keep his distance. But something—*everything*—about the blue-eyed princess made him want to know more. "That's a ballsy thing to say to a guy you don't know. What if I had bad intentions?"

Those gorgeous eyes didn't show a hint of worry. "If you were planning on attacking me, you probably would have driven me out to some remote place last night to do it."

As much as he liked her attitude, he'd worry if his sister challenged a stranger like that, and his protective urges rose to the surface. But she wasn't *his* to worry about, so he bit back the urge to warn her off trusting too easily.

"Besides, I'm pretty sure guys with bad intentions don't fix and pay for women's vehicles and drop them at their door." She uncrossed her arms. "Thank you, by the way. That was really nice of you. But why did you do it?"

"You seemed worried about having it for tonight, so I took care of it. No big deal."

"It's a big deal to me." She glanced down at the sand and tucked her hair behind one ear before lifting a softer gaze, the challenge replaced with curiosity. "Why didn't you leave a note?"

He shrugged. "I figured you'd know who did it."

"Right," she said softly, as if that answer satisfied the question but not her curiosity. "Are you married?"

"No."

"Do you have a girlfriend?"

He shook his head. "Nope."

"Boyfriend?"

"*No.* Why?"

"I'm just making sure before I put any more time into talking to you."

She was smart, even if she trusted too easily, and just like yesterday, he felt himself smiling. It was a weird sensation, as if his face didn't remember how to do it properly, and he forced himself to stop. "Don't let me put you out."

"If anything, you made my life easier by fixing my ride."

She plopped down beside him like she belonged there, and hell if his temperature didn't rise. That was another thing he hadn't felt in a long damn time before he'd first spotted her at the bar. He'd been attracted to his ex, but not in the same visceral way he was to Madigan. There was something about her that brought out his base instincts and made him feel primal and animalistic.

"Look, I know you said you're not looking for a man, but after the inquisition you just gave me, I'm not so sure I believe you. *You* might believe it, but you also thought you could take criticism, so I'm just going to put this out there. If you're hoping for a boyfriend, I'm not him."

"Trust me, I'm not looking for a boyfriend. I was just trying to figure out why you didn't want to hang out last night."

"Because if I'd gone inside with you, we would've ended up horizontal."

"And what? That repulses you?" she asked teasingly.

He chuckled, loving her sass. "Yeah, that's it. I barely made it to the end of your street before puking my guts out at the thought of kissing you."

"Ah, so you thought about kissing me. *Interesting.*" That taunting smile from the other night returned with a vengeance.

"That's where it *started.*" After fixing her Vespa, he still couldn't stop thinking about her. He'd gone out for a drink at a bar around the corner from his apartment, thinking he might hook up with a random chick and fuck Madigan off his mind. He'd been with a few women since he'd gotten out of prison, trying to feel something, anything other than numb. But it hadn't helped, and last night when the opportunity arose with a leggy blonde, he didn't get that rush of adrenaline he'd gotten with Madigan that had made him *crave* or felt the all-consuming heat that had made him want to *take*. He hadn't felt anything good in so damn long, now that he remembered how incredible it felt to want a woman, he didn't want to fake it. He'd left the bar alone and had taken thoughts of Madigan's sassy mouth, challenging eyes, and killer body to bed with him.

Last night was a fantasy, but tonight, with the warm air swirling between them and the smart-mouthed beauty looking at him like she wanted to climb onto his lap and ride him home, it took everything he had to rein in the raw, greedy *want* taking root inside him.

"I'm glad you saved yourself." She tilted her head, running her fingers through the sand, eyes still fucking with his control. "I wouldn't want to be the cause of you getting sick."

They both laughed. *God*, it had been a long time since he'd laughed.

"And for what it's worth, I *can* take criticism," she insisted.

He arched a brow.

"I *can*. You just caught me on a bad night, but you were right. I rushed through the performance. I'd had a crappy day, and that was a tough story to tell. I don't even know why I told it."

"I can see that. How'd you get into musical storytelling?"

"It happened by accident. I lost my cousin Ashley when I was eighteen. She was a year older than me, and she was my best friend. Our families are really close, and after she died, I didn't know what to do with my grief, so I wrote about it."

Once again, she could have been telling his story. He'd written to handle his grief after losing his mother and had taken up the habit again when he'd gone to prison. But he'd never put any of it to music.

"I'm sorry about your cousin. I know what it's like to lose someone you care about. You must miss her."

"I do. Every day. There aren't many people who understand what it's like to grow up in a family like mine."

"What do you mean?"

"Biker families are a little different. I love my family, but they can be a lot." A pained smile appeared, as if she'd told a secret she was ashamed to carry.

"Do you have a big family?"

"I have a huge family. Everyone in the club and their families are considered our family, and I love that. I *really* do. I don't think a person can have too many people who love them in their life. But I have four annoyingly overprotective older brothers—Blaine, Maverick, Zeke, and Zander—and Ashley had three, my cousins Tank, Baz, and Gunner. That's *seven* guys watching every move we made, and then there were the rest of the Dark Knights, reporting back to each other and to our fathers. Ashley was the one person who understood what it was like to love your family so much it hurts and to also want space from them. Ash and I couldn't wait to spread our wings. We had big plans to study abroad, travel the world together, and figure out who we were apart from our families."

"I think a lot of people feel like that." There were definitely times his sister had driven him crazy and he'd had to get away from her. Conversely, when his sister had spread her wings, everything had gone to hell. He'd give anything to hear her nagging him about nonsense or giving him shit right now.

"True, but what happened with you and my brothers the other night doesn't usually happen in every family, and unfortunately, that wasn't out of the ordinary for mine."

"I got that impression. Those guys moved as if they were all cogs in the same wheel. Like they'd been doing it their whole lives." He'd never had that solidarity until he'd met Kevin Arlo, his mentor and best friend, and that had ended the fateful night when he'd seen the guy for who he really was.

"They have been, and I don't begrudge them for it. They're born protectors, and Blaine and Tank have been watching over all of us, including my other brothers and cousins, since we were kids. I can't tell you how many times our families had dinner at the Salty Hog together, and all of us kids would go outside to run around and play while our parents stayed inside to talk. Blaine and Tank were like shepherds watching over sheep."

"Were the guys backing up Blaine and Zander your other brothers, or your cousins?"

"Neither. Those were other Dark Knights. I told you they all protect me. They did the same with Ash, because my uncle

Conroy is the vice president of the club."

"It's good to have people looking out for you." Not a day passed when he didn't wonder who was watching out for his sister and niece. He worked hard to shove those thoughts down deep. He'd been doing it for years, and it never got any easier.

"I agree, but try being a teenage girl who can't go on dates because her brothers scare boys off, or a twenty-five-year-old who can't even flirt without fear of her brothers hearing and causing a scene."

"You did a pretty good job of flirting with me these last few weeks, and you never had to say a word."

She smiled a little bashfully, and that hint of vulnerability made him want to wrap her in his arms and take the protector job away from her brothers.

Shit.

He did *not* need this, and she definitely didn't need his fucked-up ass hanging around. She wasn't a girl you fucked and forgot. She was an endgame girl, even if she refused to acknowledge it. One day some lucky bastard would heal the hurt of her past and fill all her needs. He wasn't that guy. But that didn't stop him from wanting to know more and going after it.

"If you're trying to tell me that a gorgeous, strong-willed woman like you, who speaks her mind and goes after what she wants, lets her brothers stop her from going out with guys, I'm not buying it."

"They don't stop me anymore, even when they try. But I honestly don't date much."

"Because of your brothers?"

"Not really. My uncle used to call me and Ashley his starry-eyed girls, and I'm not that girl anymore."

"I got news for you, Blue Eyes. You've still got stars in your eyes."

"Not like I used to."

There were women that were pure sunshine, and he'd never been into them. They were too innocent, expecting a simple life of flowers and puppies. Then there were women who were nothing but darkness, which was too much of a downer for him. But between the sunshine and the darkness were a thousand stages, and he'd always ridden that middle lane, intrigued by the darkness but needing the light. Madigan Wicked struck that chord hard.

"Do you mind if I ask what happened that changed you?"

"Life," she said sadly. "It started with Ashley's death. She died of an accidental overdose. She'd never even tried using drugs before that night. We found out later that some jerk at college had been spreading lies about her." She paused, tension riddling her brow, and when she spoke again, her words were drenched with pain. "If she had just told someone in our family—anyone in our family—she'd probably still be here today. But she didn't. She told her friend Bethany, who did what friends do. She kept Ashley's secrets about the rumors and wanting to try ecstasy to escape them."

"Maybe she knew if she told you, you'd get your families involved."

Madigan nodded. "That's what I think too."

"Would you have?"

"I would have *wanted* to. We weren't brought up to let people talk shit about us, and I loved her. I'd want to go find that jerk and give him a piece of my mind."

He could see her doing that and getting herself into trouble. "With or without your brothers and cousins?"

"I'm tough, not stupid. I would probably have brought them."

"I'm glad to hear that."

"But I'm not sure that would have happened, because if Ashley had begged me not to tell anyone, like she did with Bethany, and if I thought I had talked her out of doing drugs, like Bethany thought she did, then I probably would have believed her, too. Ashley told Tank she wanted to talk to him the night before she took the drugs, and maybe she'd planned on telling him, but they never got around to it. He texted her later that night, and she never responded. He was the one who found her, and he tried to revive her, but…" She shook her head, tearing up.

His chest constricted. He ached to console her. He didn't want to get too close, but he couldn't sit by and do nothing. He put his arm around her, hugging her against his side. "Sorry for asking. I didn't mean to upset you."

She wiped her eyes. "It's okay. I'm fine, really."

"It's okay not to be fine. You don't have to be tough for me."

"I know. But I'm okay. It was a long time ago, and from that moment on, everything changed. I don't know how any of us survived those early days. I felt like part of me died with her."

"It did. You can't be that close to someone and go unchanged after losing them." His mother's death had stolen a piece of him. But that was nothing compared to the guilt and agony of having killed a man. He looked at Madigan's sorrowful expression and vowed not to dump that shit on her.

"I used to feel like I couldn't breathe every time I thought about her."

He swallowed hard, remembering those days all too well.

Being in prison had made it that much worse. "I'd imagine your family tried to help you through."

"They did, but it was easier for me to write about how I felt than to talk about it. That's what helped the most. It made me see her death from a different perspective. We lost Ashley, but I still had our dreams, and I was determined to keep them alive. I went to Barcelona the first semester of the next school year. I took off three weeks early to see the sights and settle in, and I met a guy and fell hard for him. I thought he was just what I needed to move forward, as if Ashley had guided me to him and was cheering me on, celebrating that I'd done it for both of us. I held on to those feelings like a lifeline. I was *high* on all of it. Being away from home, free for the first time, adored by an older, cultured man. It was everything Ash and I thought it would be. Until we broke up, and what I thought was my whole world came crashing down around me."

"What you *thought* was your whole world?"

She nodded. "I was young and stupid. I thought that guy was everything. But it turned out he was just put in my path to kick me in my ass and make me realize I never wanted to make a man the center of my life again. So I wrote and wrote and *wrote*, until the tears stopped and I felt all the broken pieces of myself coming back together. And when that wasn't enough, I put those words to music, and *that* allowed me to get all those awful feelings out. Like you were when you were singing tonight. I could tell that was cathartic for you."

He looked out at the water, contemplating her heartbreak, struggling with anger toward the asshole who'd hurt her, and fighting off the urge to share part of himself with her. He'd suffered just as bad of a breakup when he'd gone to prison, although he'd been the cause of it. But revealing a piece of his background would only lead to the ugly truth, and even Madigan, with her sexy rebellious streak and insurmountable self-confidence, wasn't strong enough to look past that.

"Anyway," she said lightly. "That's how I accidentally became a musical storyteller, and I've since come up with lots of different types of stories. They're not all about breakups."

Relieved she hadn't tried to get him talking about how the song he'd sung had affected him, he let out a breath he hadn't realized he'd been holding and said, "That breakup must have really sucked."

"More than you know. But I should probably thank the bastard. That breakup, and all of that writing, led to me starting the Mad Truth About Love greeting card line, which allows me to travel all over the world doing my storytelling and puppeteering."

His gut clenched. He knew those cards all too well. Knew their rough texture, the papery smell. The way the printed letters looked handwritten and the logo on the back had an angry face as the *a* in *Mad* and a broken heart for the *o* in *Love*, and the way reading them now slayed him.

"You're the girl behind the cards?"

"Yup. I created every one of them and have distributors all over the world," she said proudly. "Are you familiar with them?"

He nodded. "My sister is a fan." Or at least she had been. He swallowed hard and quickly tried to thwart any questions about his family. "I think you should sic your brothers on the bastard who broke your heart."

"My brothers don't know about him, because they *would* kill him."

He wanted to say *Let's hope not*, because he wouldn't wish the guilt he carried on anyone. But he kept that to himself. "It sounds like you found your calling three times over, and that's more than many people get in this lifetime."

"I know. I only wish Ashley were here to find hers."

He wished that for her, too.

"You said you knew what it was like to lose someone?" she said carefully. "Who have you lost?"

He hadn't thought she'd paid attention to that, and he wrestled with the idea of changing the subject, but she'd been so open, he decided to give her something. "My mother, to cancer, a long time ago." He pushed a hand through his hair and cleared his throat. "Aren't there supposed to be fireworks?"

"They should start soon. I'm really sorry about your mom. How old were you when she passed away?"

"Thirteen. So how'd you get into puppetry? Was it because some asshole broke your heart, too?"

"Smooth subject change."

"I guess that's a *yes*?"

She rolled her eyes. "I heard a podcast about grief, and they talked about using puppet therapy with kids. I thought it was a cool idea and went from there. What about you? You know how I got through losing Ashley. How did you get past your mom's death?"

"I didn't have a choice. I had to be strong for my younger sister."

"Ah, the plot thickens. How many siblings do you have?"

He wished he hadn't mentioned her. "Just Carrie."

"That must have been hard for both of you."

"Yeah. She was only nine, and she was a wreck. She had horrible nightmares." He didn't know why he was still talking, but he couldn't stop the painful memory from spilling out. "I'd go in and calm her down, but she was anxious all the time, worried she'd get cancer because she was named after our mother, *Carolyn*, and fearful that something would happen to our father or to me, which made her clingy. It drove our father nuts. I took her with me wherever I went on the weekends and kept her busy in the evenings, so she wouldn't bother him." He inhaled deeply, looking away to keep from saying more.

"That's really sweet. Does she live nearby?"

He nodded, trying to figure out how to redirect the conversation.

"Why aren't you with her tonight?"

"I prefer to be alone."

"Oh." She was quiet for a minute, the light in her eyes dimming. But before he could get a word out, she squared her shoulders and lifted her chin, as if she were hitching her armor into place, and said, "Don't let me cramp your style," and pushed to her feet.

He grabbed her wrist. "Sit down, Blue Eyes. You're not cramping anything." He tugged her down beside him. She was a tough bird, clearly gun-shy about getting hurt and strong enough to take control and walk away. He wished his sister had been that strong and chalked it up as just one more thing he liked about Madigan.

"You sure?"

He nodded. "I like talking to you."

"I think you mean listening."

"What can I say? I like the sound of your voice." He handed her his guitar. "Why don't you give me something else to listen to."

"You thought I messed up my last performance. You sure you want a private show?"

He wanted a private show, all right, no guitar necessary, and based on the flicker of heat in her eyes, she meant it *exactly* the way he'd taken it. "Hell yeah. Show me what you've got."

She settled the guitar on her lap, eyeing him seductively. Then her brows knitted in concentration, as if she were paging through songs in her head. He wondered which ones she was passing over and why and immediately cursed himself for caring.

A mischievous glimmer rose in her eyes, and she started playing "The Sounds of Silence." She barely made it through three lines before they both cracked up.

"What?" She leaned against his side. "You don't like that one?"

"I do now" came out before he could stop it.

Her smile brightened everything around them. "I've got one you'll like even better."

He had a feeling he'd like anything she sang.

She started playing "Unwritten," swaying to the beat, staring daringly into his eyes as she changed the lyrics. *"You are unwritten. I can't read your mind. You're totally undefined."* She laughed, still strumming. "You really are, you know that, right?"

Damn, she sure knew how to slither beneath his skin. "I like it that way."

She rolled those gorgeous eyes and began singing again. *"You're just beginning. The pen is in your hand. Is your ending unplanned?"* Her shoulders rocked to the beat, her husky, silken voice escalating as she sang about staring at blank pages, opening dirty windows, and feeling rain on *his* skin, those challenging eyes reaching right into his soul.

He was grinning again and couldn't help giving her a taste of her own medicine. When she started singing about no one else being able to speak for him and living life with open arms, he chimed in with his own lyrics. *"I don't want to feel the rain on my skin. You can let it in. I'll stay in my quiet world, with all my words unspoken."*

She smirked, strumming louder, singing, "*I'm not gonna let you, broody boy*," and gave in to her laughter, falling against him, making him laugh, too.

"I'll give you *broody boy*." He grabbed her ribs, and the guitar fell to the sand, making them laugh even harder.

"*I won't let you swallow your words*," she sang through laughter, and he tickled her again, making her squeal.

The happy sound zipped through him, unearthing a joyous part of him that he'd thought was gone forever. His laughter rang out, sounding and feeling foreign, and at the same time, addicting. *She* was an addicting mix of pushy and playful, and the way she hid her softness behind her strength made him want to peel back her layers and find out more of the words she'd written all those years ago. She felt incredible in his arms, her laughter lighting him up inside. Their eyes collided like a summer storm, hot, sharp, and thunderous, drowning out their laughter, and the world fell silent, save for the sounds of their heavy breathing. Sexual tension crackled in the air, and as a war between right and wrong raged in his head, she pressed her luscious lips to his—*Fuuck*—adding want and need to the battle. In his split second of hesitation, she pulled away, confusion and embarrassment staring back at him.

"Sorry," she said awkwardly. "I—"

"*Fuck that*, Blue Eyes." He grabbed her face with both hands. "I knew your lips would own me." He crushed his mouth to hers with an urgency he'd never felt before, as if she were the very air he needed to breathe. Their kisses were fierce and bruising. She tasted sweet and sinful, opening wide for him.

She was so fucking eager, he couldn't get enough. His tongue plunged deeper. He wanted to taste *all* of her, to explore her mouth until he knew it by heart. His hands moved over her roughly and greedily as he lifted her onto his lap. Her fingers dove into his hair, and she held on tight, rocking against his cock, sending heat scorching through him.

Hell yeah, baby. They feasted on each other's mouths. Desperate ravenous beasts intent on pleasure. He fucked her mouth with his tongue the way he ached to fuck her sweet body, so thoroughly they'd both forget their painful pasts. The *whistle* and *crack* of fireworks sounded in the distance, but he didn't give a shit. He was lost in the feel of her grinding against him, arching and moaning into his mouth. A growl rumbled up his throat, and he felt her smile against his lips. She was so damn sexy, he needed *more.* He pushed his hand beneath her sweater, cupping her breast, and squeezed her nipple through her thin lace bra, earning a lustful moan that made his dick ache. He was vaguely aware of shouting between the *hisses* and *booms* of the fireworks, but as their tongues tangled, he intensified their kisses, taking her down onto her back. She felt so fucking good beneath him, petite, feminine, and *fierce.* She spread her legs wide, and he lifted one at her knee, clutching her ass with his other hand, holding her still as he ground harder against her center. She moaned, long and low and so damn sensually, he wanted to be inside her and feel her body hum around his cock. Her hips rose, rocking and gyrating just as someone shouted, sounding closer.

Her eyes flew open, the sharp gash of annoyance breaking through the lust in her eyes, bringing reality crashing in as she said, "*Shit.* My brothers."

"*Fuck.* What am I doing?" He moved off her.

"Well, you *were* kissing me senseless," she said adorably as she straightened her sweater.

He shook his head. He'd lost his damn mind, and he'd lost it in *her*. "That shouldn't've happened."

Her brows knitted as her brothers shouted her name again from down the beach. Fireworks lit up the sky, and the colorful bursts illuminated her face. He saw a flash of hurt, but in the next second, it was erased by anger.

"Madigan, I'm sor—"

"You know what?" She pushed to her feet, brushing off her shorts. "I thought we had a connection and we were having fun, but I don't have the patience for whatever this hot-cold thing is that you have going on. See you around, Tobias."

"*Madigan*," he called after her, but his voice was wasted on another whistle and boom of fireworks as she jogged down the beach toward her brothers. *Fuck it. I'm out of here.*

Chapter Four

THE RUSTY ANCHOR was a cute pub known for its uniquely named drinks located off the beaten path about half an hour outside Harwich. It was more of a tourist hangout than a local haunt, which meant Madigan didn't usually know her audience, making it one of her favorite venues in which to perform. It was easier to relax when she didn't have her brothers or other Dark Knights watching over her, and a new audience meant there were no expectations. Nobody would know if she changed lyrics on the fly, messed up chords...*or sang too fast.* A wave of heat moved through her with thoughts of Tobias, followed by a sliver of hurt and a dose of longing. She closed her eyes against the unwanted emotions that had plagued her for the last three days.

No. I'm not doing this.

Too late. Just the thought of him brought back the luxuriousness of his rough hands moving possessively over her body, the seductive taste of his mouth, and the cruel ravishment of his kisses. She could still feel the welcome intrusion of his tongue, penetrating, searching, *claiming*, and the formidable monster in his pants that had been imprinted on her body, turning her into some sort of sex-starved nymph. Tobias's gruff voice barged into her thoughts—*I knew your lips would own me*—so real, goose bumps rose on her skin, and she opened her eyes, half expecting to see him standing with her by the stage.

Her cheeks burned, and she looked around, thankful the bar patrons were still eating, drinking, and talking among themselves and hadn't seemed to notice her momentary lascivious slip. But her thoughts lingered on that night and the man whose mere kisses had awakened something untamed inside her that she hadn't even known existed. Thank goodness her brothers hadn't spotted them on the dune. She was embarrassed to admit, even to herself, that the grief her brothers had given her for disappearing for so long had been a walk in the park compared to the sting of Tobias's proclamation that their wild kisses shouldn't have happened.

She swallowed hard as she took her guitar out of its case. Her reaction to him had been nothing short of shocking. She was no wallflower, and she wasn't afraid to let a guy know when she was interested. But the *way* she'd gone after him, making the first move, and the unbridled passion that had consumed her once he'd kissed her back, making her feel like a tigress unleashed? That was all new, and she hadn't wanted to fight it. She'd been with enough guys to know when chemistry was real, and since the first time their eyes had connected, all Tobias had to do was *look* at her, and she got fired up inside. Before she'd gone in for a kiss, she'd felt the searing heat between them, which had blazed hotter by the second, and she'd *seen* the look in his eyes. Like he'd been ready to combust, too. She'd thought he was just overthinking what she'd said about her brothers. *That* was why she'd gone in for the kiss. To bridge that gap and let him know without a shadow of a doubt that she was her own woman and made her own decisions.

In hindsight, she should have walked away when he hadn't immediately kissed her back, because now that she knew the dark, delicious taste of him, now that she'd felt his desire for *her*, Mr. Mysterious had become Mr. Unforgettable.

"Just about ready, Mads?" Bayani, the thirtysomething manager of the Rusty Anchor, was a raven-haired beauty from the Philippines. She wore her glossy hair just past her shoulders, the ends dyed white-blond, and she was model thin and looked like a strong wind could blow her over. But it was an illusion. The woman had a will of steel. Madigan had seen her go head-to-head with drunk and ornery customers, and she always came out on top.

Madigan imagined tucking her thoughts into her guitar case as she closed it, just as she'd done hundreds of other times before performances. She was determined not to sing too fast or get sidetracked by the sting of rejection by some broody, motorcycle-driving behemoth. She'd dressed in her favorite outfit, a flirty black miniskirt with a daisy pattern, a black strappy tank that bared her stomach, three gold necklaces, because she always felt flirtier with a little bling, and the black chunky leather boots she wore no matter what the weather. The outfit reeked of youthful confidence, the kind she and Ashley had sworn they'd wear into their thirties. She was playing a forty-five-minute set, and she'd stacked her playlist with fun stories that she enjoyed playing, even if a few included the sharp edges of betrayal, and she was raring to go.

"I sure am," she said cheerily.

Bayani gave a quick nod and stepped onto the stage to introduce her.

Ten minutes later, Madigan finished her second song and waited for the applause to silence, thanking the audience. "I'm glad you enjoyed that one. This next story is called 'Party Games,' and it might throw you right back to your teenage years." She began strumming and singing, "*It's been so long since it started. But I can't get you out of my head…*"

The door to the pub opened, and her heart nearly stopped when Tobias strode in, his thick thighs wrapped in worn denim, heavy boots moving across the floor. His muscular chest and biceps strained against his thin black T-shirt as he ran a hand through his hair, pushing the long strands away from his finely chiseled features, those broody eyes locking on Madigan.

Her heart thudded faster, and she played harder, sang louder. *"Do you wanna play some party games? The rule book says we have to make out…"*

The audience chuckled, and Tobias's lips quirked as he made his way to the bar, as if he were amused but refused to let that emotion break through his steely exterior.

Madigan tore her gaze away, refusing to give him the satisfaction of looking over again as she finished that story and started another, practically shouting relevant lyrics to "Sports 2." A message to the man she refused to acknowledge. *"Fuck that. I'm gonna rule this town tonight. You will never be the same when I leave your sight…"*

His gaze burned into her like a laser beam, beckoning her to look over. Her skin prickled with the urge to meet his dark eyes. The same eyes that had lit up Saturday night with his laughter and had flamed with desire, revealing a very different man from the one who gave off a slightly dangerous vibe to the public. Was that why he'd said they shouldn't have kissed? Because he'd let his guard down and then thought better of it? Or did he just get off on making women feel like shit?

It didn't matter. She refused to be toyed with.

She finished the story, and as applause rang out, she decided to give him a taste of his own medicine and tell her newest story, which she'd written Saturday night after the fireworks.

"That's a fun story to tell, and I have a feeling you'll like my next one, too. It's *new*, so if I mess it up, please go easy on me." The audience chuckled, and she slid her gaze to the towering oak standing by the bar, taller and broader than all the men around him. Everyone was watching her, but Tobias's gaze was so intense, it felt like his hands were gripping her as tightly as they had when he'd put her onto his lap and consumed her.

She lifted her chin, a smile gracing her lips, knowing it would bug the shit out of him once he realized what she was singing about. "This story is called 'Kiss Off.'" She held his gaze as she started playing.

"Intrigue, beauty, and oh, can he kiss. Now, that's a package I don't want to miss." The audience laughed. *"He talks in simple words. Red flags waving. My gut clenching. But that fire in his eyes ignites an inferno in the air, drawing me in so deep that I don't care."* She spoke the next words instead of singing. "We've all been there. Am I right, ladies?"

The women cheered, and she looked out at the crowd before returning her gaze to Tobias, his jaw tight, body tense. *"Anticipation is my drug, and staring at those lips, hell, I'm a fucking addict."* The audience laughed. *"Hold my breath and close my eyes. No time to think. Sink. Sink. Sink. Sink. Into his kiss, his arms, his insanely sexy body. My heart's on fire. Mind turns to mush, soul drenched in desire."* She paused, speaking the next few lines. "But wait. Isn't he *too* much? He's got muscles, he's got lips, but he's also got a *dick*."

More laughter rang out, and she said, "No offense, men, but *come on*. We know the games. Lips from heaven and a heart?

Well, a heart straight from hell." She played faster, louder, returning a narrow-eyed gaze to Tobias, who did *not* look amused as she sang the chorus. *"Life's too short. Batteries are cheap. I want the one who doesn't speak. So take your red flags and kiss off, kiss off, kiss off…"*

Madigan had been sure Tobias would leave after "Kiss Off," but he stayed for her entire performance, his insolent eyes impaling her every second of it. But she held her own, singing her stories at a perfect pace, the most cutting lines with vehemence aimed at him and the softest with the sweetest of tenors, aimed anywhere *but* at him. She nailed every story, and as she strummed the last chord, the audience sprang to their feet, clapping and whistling.

She was on top of the world. "Thank you all so much. You're an amazing audience, and you made it fun to play for you. If you're around next week, I'll be playing at the Lonesome Cluck in Provincetown on Thursday afternoon at two. I hope to see you there."

More cheers rang out as she left the stage and put her guitar away. She headed toward the bar, guitar case in hand, a little giddy as people stopped her to chat and compliment her storytelling.

Take that, you big broody jerk.

Tobias was watching her like a hawk, his jaw tightening as she neared the bar, making her entire body vibrate with thoughts of his ruthless kisses. How could she still want him after he'd shut her down? Her nerves caught fire, and she went to the opposite end of the bar, setting her guitar against it. The bartender had her usual glass of ice water ready and waiting. He also set a Beach Lover, a fruity sangria concoction, in front of her, and pointed to a good-looking dark-haired guy sitting at a table by the window. He was clean cut, and when he smiled, it made him a little too pretty for her liking. Why did she have to be attracted to tough, growly guys who would try her patience and offered to buy her a drink only as an apology, instead of nice guys who bought her drinks because they wanted to meet her?

The guy lifted his glass as if he were toasting her.

She lifted hers, mouthing, *Thank you*, and sipped the refreshingly cool, sweet drink. The guy rose to his feet, heading her way just as every inch of her prickled with awareness and Tobias stepped into her line of sight. His big body blocked her view, alighting flames beneath her skin. Damn him. It pissed her off that her own body betrayed her, and she lifted her chin, meeting his too-easy-to-get-lost-in gaze, seeing as much regret as darkness. "Do you mind?"

His eyes narrowed, facial muscles twitching. "Can we talk?"

"I believe I was just going to have a conversation with the guy who bought me this cocktail." She leaned to the left, trying to see around him, but the other guy had already returned to his table. "*Thanks*," she said sarcastically, and took a hefty drink. "You're as good of a clamjammer as my brothers are."

"Clamjammer?" His brows slanted.

She rolled her eyes. "The female version of cockblocking. *Jesus.* First you know nothing about bikers, and now this? Have you been living under a rock?"

His expression hardened, and for a split second he looked as though he might walk away, and she felt a pang of regret for being bitchy. But damn it, he'd rejected her, and that *hurt.*

"Come on, Blue Eyes. Give me five minutes of your time."

Hearing the nickname he'd so quickly coined for her roll gruffly, and strangely familiarly, off his tongue, as if he'd been calling her that for years, had the same effect as it had the other night, softening her resolve. But she wasn't caving that easily. She downed her drink and flagged down the bartender to bring her another. "And *why* would I do that when you basically called kissing me a *mistake*?"

"I *never* said mistake."

"Don't pull semantic bullshit on me. I'm not into games, Tobias."

His eyes drilled into her. "Neither am I."

"Then why are you here? If you're worried about my brothers coming after you—"

"Your brothers and their wolf pack *don't* scare me."

Why was that such a turn-on? "What, then? If you're one of those guys who cares about a girl talking shit about him, you're safe. I don't kiss and tell."

"No, you just write stories about it and sing them for all the world to hear."

"Is *that* why you want to talk to me? Are you worried I'll tell someone a particular song was written about you? Lucky for you, I don't reveal such things."

"Then how do I know about that Spanish asshole who broke your heart?"

She snapped her mouth closed. She still couldn't believe she'd let that slip, but the way he'd listened had been as intense as the way he'd listened to her singing at the Salty Hog, and it had just come out. And God, she was in trouble, because the way he was looking at her now, as if her words were important, magnified their undeniable connection. But he'd shut her down, and that wasn't easily forgotten.

"You know what they say. *If you can't take the heat…*" She nodded toward the door, expecting him to leave, knowing that once he did, she'd long for the heat of his stare, the fire and ice of their banter.

But he didn't retreat. He stepped closer, sucking up all the oxygen around them. "I *crave* the burn."

His rugged scent enveloped her, and her traitorous nipples rose to aching peaks as he stared at her in silence, the air between them sparking like live wires. It became harder to breathe, to think past the lust simmering low in her belly. What was it about him that had this hold on her? Just when she was sure her legs would give out, the bartender brought her drink, breaking their connection.

Tobias took out his wallet and tossed a ten on the bar.

"Trying to *buy* my silence? I can pay for my own drink, thank you very much."

"Not when I'm standing here, you won't." Tobias nodded at the bartender to take his money, and he did.

As independent as she was, she liked that chivalry. *I'm such an idiot.* "Why are you here, Tobias?"

He leaned in so close, their lips almost touched. "I don't think you want me to tell you that around all these people."

The low timbre of his voice and his proximity ratcheted up her lust to a full boil. "I've got nothing to hide."

He arched a brow. "Sure about that?"

She thought about the way she'd lost control the other night. If he would've tried to fuck her on the dunes, she probably would've done it. Brothers be damned. "*Fine.* Five minutes."

She grabbed her guitar and stalked through the crowd and out the door. When she spun around, he was *right there.* He grabbed her by the elbow, leading her around to the side of the building. "Where are we going?"

"Away from prying eyes and ears."

He released her, and a gust of cooler air swept between them. She crossed her arms against it, but he moved in front of her, smothering that chill in scorching heat. He was so tall and so close, she had to tilt her head up to meet his gaze. She opened her mouth to speak, but he beat her to it.

"Kissing you *wasn't* a mistake," he said gruffly. "I'm sorry for saying that, but I didn't believe you were cool with just having fun, and I'm not looking to put down roots. I'm taking off as soon as I get a few things figured out."

"You arrogant ass. You thought I was trying to trick you into more? Like once you fucked me, you wouldn't be able to walk away?"

"Considering I can't stop thinking about your *mouth* after just kissing you, yes."

You thought of me, too. She did a mental happy dance. She *wasn't* alone in this. Their connection wasn't only in her head. Her heart raced, and she soaked in his confession, which made it hard to keep her guard up. But she needed to, because she was never going to open herself up in that way again. Not even to a guy she couldn't get out of her head. "Maybe you should learn to take a girl at her word."

"Maybe," he said sharply. "But you've been hurt, and I didn't want to give you hope, because when I'm ready, I will drive the hell away from this place and *never* look back."

She believed him, and she couldn't miss the red flags waving. But the carnal desires billowing inside her were bigger and louder than the voice in the back of her head reminding her, *warning* her, that she'd only kissed him on the beach, and he'd plagued her thoughts so badly she'd had to bring herself to orgasm every night since just to take the edge off. But now that she'd felt that hum in her loins, that inner ache that had taken her by surprise and chained her to him, she wanted more of it.

He held her gaze, every second making her breathe harder, and at the same time, making it harder to breathe. Those dark eyes weren't windows to his soul—they only worked one way, drinking her in as they slid leisurely to her mouth, lingering there so long she had to squeeze her thighs together to dull the ache he caused. His gaze coasted lower, openly watching her breasts rise and fall, unapologetically visually devouring her. Why was that such a turn-on? Her knees weakened, and just when she was sure they'd give out, he met her gaze. The wickedness flickering in his eyes made her body burn with *want*. Her fingers curled with the urge to touch him, to dig her nails into his shoulders and climb him like a tree.

Just as his stare became too potent to resist, he said, "I'm not the guy for you, and you sure as hell aren't the girl for me, but if that offer for fun is still on the table, I want *in*."

She didn't hesitate. "I want you *in*, too."

He stepped closer, and her back hit the building. "You sure about that, Blue Eyes? You asked a lot of questions for a girl who isn't looking for something deeper."

"It got you kissing me, didn't it?" she challenged, because she wasn't going to tell him that she didn't have a lot of practice picking up guys for one-night stands. "I might not be looking for a relationship, but I wasn't going to just blurt out, *Hey, you want to get down and dirty?*"

A slow smile crept into place, and "*Hell yes*," barely left his lips before his mouth came down over hers in a merciless kiss. His hard body pinned her against the building, unleashing the desires she'd been holding back for days. She went up on her toes, holding on to his broad shoulders for leverage. He grabbed her ass with both hands, lifting her higher, her legs circling his thick waist as they ate at each other's mouths like starving castaways. When he tore his mouth away, a needy sound escaped.

"See how easy that was?" he said huskily, and squeezed her ass. "You drive your Vespa in this sexy skirt?"

"It's a *skort*, but I do wear skirts and dresses when I drive my Vespa."

"Good to know." He set her on her feet. "Let's go see how that skort looks on my floor."

Minutes later, her guitar was strapped to her back, and she was following his motorcycle toward his place, unable to believe she was going for it after weeks of wanting him. The cool air whisking over her skin did nothing to lessen the desire searing through her as she tried to calm her racing thoughts. *Am I really doing this? Following a guy I barely know to have sex with him?* She studied his broad back, remembering their moonlight make-out session, and shuddered with anticipation. Oh yeah, she was doing it, all right.

He lived in an apartment, which made sense for a guy who wasn't looking to put down roots, but her nerves got the better of her as he unlocked the door. "How do you like living here? Do you like your neighbors? I lived in an apartment in Paris briefly, and…"

He pushed the door open and took her helmet from her, setting it, and his, on the floor by the door as she babbled nervously about the places she'd lived. He took her guitar, which she'd forgotten was strapped to her back, and set it by her helmet, then began unlacing his boots. That simple act knocked her brain back into gear. She followed his lead and left her boots and socks by the door. Was that a hookup thing? Most guys she knew trampled through houses with their boots on.

She continued rambling as he led her into a sparsely furnished living room, asking questions and too nervous to wait for answers. There was a futon against the far wall and a small end table. His guitar was propped by the patio door. The living room opened to a kitchen to their right, and she noticed there was no kitchen table. As she surveyed her surroundings, she didn't see a table anywhere else, either. There was a bathroom down the hall, and just beyond, a bedroom that looked empty from her vantage point.

She looked up at him curiously. "Are you a minimalist?"

"Just temporary housing, that's all."

"How long have you been in town?"

"Few months." He closed the distance between them, eyes boring into her, causing a heat wave to engulf her entire body. "You've got a lot of questions for a girl who's just looking for some fun."

"I tend to ramble when I'm nervous," she said softly.

His eyes narrowed. "You want to call this off, Blue Eyes? There's the door." He motioned toward it.

"No," she said quickly, her heart jackhammering in her chest.

He stepped closer with a slightly softer expression and ran his knuckles down her cheek. "Then how about we put that mouth of yours to better use?"

"God *yes*." She reached for him as his mouth covered hers, hot and hungry and so deliciously, her body flooded with desire, until there was no room for nervousness.

MADIGAN'S MOUTH HAD already become Tobias's favorite destination, but as their tongues collided and his hands roamed over her body, he was eager to take an in-depth tour of every dip and curve. He lifted her into his arms and sank onto the futon with her straddling his lap. Reclaiming her luscious, sinful mouth, he intensified his efforts, kissing her deeper as he took off her top and tossed it aside. His breath caught in his throat. She was braless, her perfect breasts there for the taking, necklaces dangling in the valley between them, pert nipples begging to be tasted. Musical notes on a staff trailed down her ribs, and he wondered if those specific notes had a special meaning but forced himself not to ask.

"Christ, you're gorgeous." He pressed a kiss to the swell of one breast, and his gaze drifted up to her flushed cheeks and the sweetest smile he'd ever seen, twisting him up inside. *Fuck.* He took her in a rough, passionate kiss, trying to outrun the unwanted sensation. She returned his efforts with fervor, like she was starved for him, and that was exactly what he needed to get lost in her. Greed pounded through him. He'd spent days thinking of nothing but kissing her, touching her, and the feel of her grinding against his cock, just as she was now. He tore his mouth away and dipped his head, nipping a path down her neck, and dragged his tongue over and around her nipple, earning soft, surrendering sighs. He lowered his mouth over it, sucking hard, turning those sighs to cries of pleasure. When he dragged his teeth over the tip, she grabbed his head, holding him there.

"Don't stop," she pleaded.

He sucked, licked, and nipped, earning more needful pleas. He grabbed her thighs and squeezed and pushed his hands into the legs of her skort as he devoured her other breast. He brushed his fingers over her damp panties, groaning at the wetness, and pressed them over her clit, working her into a trembling frenzy.

"Ah. Yes. Ah."

The high-pitched, needy noises falling from her lips were so fucking sexy, he sucked harder, wanting to hear those sounds in his sleep. She rocked along his length like she was riding him, her fingernails digging into his scalp, making him hard as stone. "Give me your mouth," he demanded. She was quick to oblige, her tongue thrusting against his as he moved his thumb to her clit and pushed his fingers into her panties, sliding two into her tight heat. "So fucking wet for me," he growled against her lips, earning a whimper. His cock ached as she rode his hand. He trapped her lower lip between his teeth, biting just hard enough to earn a sharp inhalation. "Eyes on me, baby. I want to see everything you feel and watch you come for me."

She swallowed hard, her eyes trained on him. He worked her slowly, gauging her every breath and the flare of sparks in her eyes each time he stroked that magical spot that brought a gasp, a moan, or a high-pitched greedy sound that spiked through him.

"*Faster*," she pleaded.

He sank his teeth into the swell of her breast, and she gasped. "No fucking way am I going to rush this. I've thought about your sweet pussy for days." He continued fucking her slowly with his fingers, applying just enough pressure on her clit to bring her to the edge of release. "I want you so needy, when you come on my hand, my mouth, and my cock, you feel it everywhere."

Her eyes flared, cheeks reddening.

"I'm no Boy Scout, Blue Eyes. If I'm too much for you, tell me now before we go any further."

"I'd be disappointed if you were." Her eyes narrowed with challenge. "But the promise of three orgasms is big talk. I sure hope you can stand up to your promises."

He crooked his fingers, and "*Holy…*" fell breathily from her lips as her eyes closed, and her head tipped back.

"Eyes. On. *Me.*"

The scowl on her face was adorably sexy. He nipped at her lower lip, and she ground her hips, smirking.

"I look forward to fucking that smirking mouth."

"That's awfully presumptuous. You'll fuck my mouth when and *if* I want you to."

"I'd have it no other way, but trust me. You'll beg me to do it."

"We'll see about that."

"Yes, we will." He withdrew his fingers from her pussy and brought them to his mouth, gliding his tongue along the length of them. "So fucking sweet. Open your mouth." When she did, he pushed his fingers in it. "Show me how you'll suck my cock. Make me want it."

Eyes narrowing, she slid her tongue along and over his fingers, her mouth hanging open so he could watch, and watch he did, every slide, every lick, every flash of lust in her beautiful eyes. When she closed her mouth, sucking hard, he felt it in his dick, and his hips shot up, drawing a guttural moan from his lungs.

She smiled victoriously. "I'm no Girl Scout. If you can't take it, tell me now."

"I'm going to take *everything* you have to give." He fisted his hand in her hair, bringing her mouth to his as he lowered his hand, pushing his fingers into her again, using his thumb as he did before, until she was whimpering into their kisses, her lower body trembling, breasts heaving. He tugged her head back but kept her close, eyes blazing, as he took her right up to the verge of release.

Her nails dug into his shoulders. "*Tobias*," she pleaded.

"Good girl," he gritted out. "Say my name."

"Tobias, *please*."

He gave her what she needed, and as her orgasm crashed over her, his name flew from her lips like the best fucking prayer he'd ever heard. He crushed his mouth to hers, capturing her cries, and stayed with her until she collapsed, breathless, against him. Her heart raced as he stroked her back, his fingers still buried deep, soaking in the lingering pulses.

He kissed beside her ear, whispering, "You're so damn beautiful," bringing her heavily lidded eyes to his. He caressed her cheek and pressed his lips to hers as he withdrew his fingers. "I want to taste you—*all* of you." He painted her lips with her arousal and dragged his tongue along the same path, licking them clean. Her breath hitched with every slick of his tongue, and he was aching to grab her beautiful face and kiss her fiercely, but instead, he gave her the reins with one last demand—"Kiss me—" curious about what she'd do with them.

He didn't pull her to him, letting her set their pace.

She kissed him softly at first, and he followed her lead with tender slicks of his tongue and light kisses that left him hungry for more. She touched her forehead to his, her warm breath coasting over his mouth as she ran her fingers over his cheeks and beard. She didn't say a word, just touched him like she was memorizing his features, pressing kisses to his lips, his cheeks, his jaw, all the while grinding along his shaft. She kissed his neck, ran her fingers through his hair and over the muscles in his jaw. He'd never been touched so intimately, and he felt himself getting twisted up inside again. Every touch, every rock of her hips, increased his anticipation, until the emotions and sensations became too much, and he grabbed her hair, tugging her head back, regaining control.

Flames danced in her eyes as he held her there and lowered his mouth a whisper away from hers. "You're a dangerous woman, Blue Eyes." He kissed her hard, and they both went a little wild, as they had the other night, groping and thrusting. He lifted her to her feet, and they stripped each other bare between urgent, messy kisses, clothes flying, laughter ringing out when he lost his balance trying to kick off his jeans, nearly toppling them both to the floor.

Her eyes locked on his erection, and a grin lifted her cheeks. "Guess I picked the right guy. Are you sure that thing is real? I've never seen one so thick."

He grinned and hauled her to him, kissing her breathless.

"Bedroom?" she panted out.

"Futon." He went to open it, but it got stuck halfway. "Damn it." What the hell had he been thinking, bringing her home to this shithole?

She giggled. "Is that your bed?"

"Yeah. I told you, it's temporary." His ex had put his shit in storage when he was in prison, and that was where it would stay until he figured out where he was heading. "Fuck it." He grabbed the mattress and threw it on the floor, sending the throw pillow tumbling beside it.

Madigan giggled and flopped down to the mattress. Leaning on her palms and crossing her legs at the ankles, she patted the space beside her. "You coming?"

He drank in her sexy curves, the neatly trimmed tuft of hair between her legs, and those mysterious musical notes he was dying to ask about. He cocked a grin and lowered himself to his knees, crawling over her until they were eye to eye. "I'm not coming until you're thoroughly orgasmed out."

"I really *did* pick the right guy."

He pressed his lips to hers, and she opened for him as he lowered her down to her back and took his time devouring her mouth before kissing his way down her body, slowing at the spots that made her breathing hitch or a giggle slip out. Damn, that was a sweet sound. He wanted to know all her erogenous zones, and as he kissed each of the musical notes, nipping at the dip at her waist and the flare of her hips, earning sighs, moans, giggles, and sounds that were too erotic to describe, he learned every one of the spots that turned her on. At least on her front. Her backside would have to wait, because the scent of her arousal and her greedy pleas drew him in. The first slick of his tongue brought a loud, surrendering moan. He grabbed a throw pillow, sliding it under her hips, and guided her legs over his shoulders. "Watch me eat you."

Crimson stained her cheeks as she watched him lick, taunt, tongue-fuck, and suck. Her hands fisted, thighs trembling. "Lick your fingers and run them over your nipples," he said gruffly, and she did as he pushed two fingers inside her and sucked her swollen clit into his mouth.

"Ohmygod—"

Her sensual sounds filled the room as he feasted and fucked her with his hands and mouth, until she cried out so loud, it echoed around them. He didn't relent. He continued his ministrations, drinking in her arousal, reaching up to squeeze her nipples, sending her over the edge again, as "*Tobias—*" flew from her lips.

He lapped up everything she had to give, her essence seeping into his tongue, down his throat, becoming a part of him he knew he'd taste forever.

When she finally came down from her high, he grabbed his wallet, fishing out a condom, and sheathed his length. Leaving the pillow in place, he moved over her, blue eyes gazing up at him through a lustful haze. He kissed her softly. "Still want me *in*?"

"More than ever," she said in one long breath, her arms circling him.

The head of his cock breached her entrance, and he groaned at how tight she was. "Give me your hands." She did, and he laced them with his, settling them beside her head. "I don't want to hurt you. If it's too much, squeeze my hand." She nodded, and he brushed his lips along her cheek. "You feel so fucking good." He met her gaze as he pushed in slowly. Her hands tightened around his, and he stilled.

"Don't stop," she said with a laugh.

"I thought I hurt you."

She shook her head. "Feels good. I'm just holding on for the ride. Do it fast, all at once."

"With that pillow under your hips, I'm going deep. You sure?"

"Unless you're too much of a Boy Scout," she taunted.

With that, he thrust in deep and she cried out. His head dipped beside hers. "Shit. I'm sorry."

She giggled. "We might have to do this a few times so you can tell the difference between a cry of ecstasy and one of pain."

"Thank Christ." He withdrew, then drove in again. This time when she cried out, he felt like a fucking god and continued pounding into her, her loud cries like applause.

Someone banged on the wall, and Madigan's eyes widened.

"I forgot you have neighbors."

"I've never had a woman here before. I didn't know the walls were so thin."

"That's kind of rude of them."

"Maybe they're jealous."

"Or maybe they're dicks." Her eyes filled with mischief, and she shouted, "*Yes! More! Oh, Tobias!*"

Another bang on the wall rang out, and they both cracked up.

"You're a troublemaker, and I fucking love it." He slanted his mouth over hers, kissing her slowly as they began to move, gradually gaining in intensity, finding a rhythm that bound them together in a moaning, grunting, pleading tangle of limbs and cries. The banging on the wall took a back seat to the thrum of desire pounding between them as he ground his pelvis against her clit, and she shattered beneath him, crying out as her inner muscles pulsed tight and perfect around his cock. He fought against his own mounting release, riding out her climax, taking her right up to the verge of another. Madigan clung to him, those mesmerizing baby blues silently imploring him, like she was hanging on by a thread, waiting for him to go over the edge *with* her. With the next thrust, he abandoned all restraint, catapulting them both into ecstasy. Her eyes slammed shut, and she arched and bucked beneath him. He buried his face in her hair, breathing her in as he came so hard, it felt like it was ripped from his bones.

When his body went slack, he was acutely aware of her delicate body beneath him. Holding his weight above her, he pulled the pillow out from under her hips, brushing kisses to her lips and cheeks, until her eyes fluttered open, spent and sated and so damn beautiful, they hurt to look at. He'd never felt so good or laughed so much, and by the look in her eyes, she was right there with him, trying to figure out what the hell was happening between them. He dipped his head again to avoid losing himself in her any more than he already had and allowed himself to hold her for a long moment, because this was it.

Their one excruciatingly perfect night.

That thought caused a physical ache in his chest. He'd had nothing in his life for so long, he wanted to soak in more of her. All of her. Her laughter, those mischievous eyes, the snark that spilled from her lips.

But that wasn't part of the plan, so he forced himself to get up and take care of the condom. When he returned to the living room, she was gathering her clothes, her hair a tangled mess from his hands, her flawless skin flushed and marred by a few red bite marks. Clutching the bundle of clothes against her stomach, she looked at him awkwardly, and a little embarrassed, her vulnerability snapping his resolve.

Fuck what I signed up for. "Not sticking around for round two?"

"Is that an *option*?" she asked softly, as if she were unsure.

She was so fucking cute, laughter bubbled out. "Only if you want it to be."

She dropped her clothes, grinning, naked and radiant, lighting up his dingy living room. "I'll take that option, please." She touched her stomach. "But I'm kind of hungry."

He arched a brow and glanced down at his cock.

"For *food*." She sauntered into his kitchen naked, completely comfortable, like she'd been there a hundred times before, and hell if it didn't feel like it as she opened the fridge and peered inside, giving him a glorious view of her ass. "How old is this pizza?"

"I had it last night."

"Perfect." She grabbed the box and flipped it open, snagging a slice, and held the box out toward him. "Want some?"

"Hell yes." He went to her and set the box on the counter, then lifted her up, putting *her* on the counter beside it, and wedged himself between her legs.

"I'll get you a piece."

As she reached into the box, he slicked his tongue over her nipple. "You eat the pizza. I've got all I need right here."

Chapter Five

MADIGAN SAT AT her dining room table Thursday evening, putting the final touches on the digital sketch of a card she was working on, and sat back to see how it looked. SORRY YOUR WIFE WAS BITCHY was scrawled across the front of the card in black. Inside, AT LEAST SHE LOVES YOUR PENIS was written in red with a heart around it. XO, YOUR WIFE was scribbled beneath it in black.

Laughing softly, she printed it out and set it aside with the other new ideas she'd come up with, including sketches for the expansion into wearable merchandise. They were all sexual, which made sense, considering her mind hadn't climbed out of the gutter since Tuesday night with Tobias. She was still exquisitely sore in places that made it impossible *not* to think about him. She'd allowed herself to replay their dirty deeds so many times, all it took was the mere thought of his name and she shuddered with delicious memories of them both *taking* and *giving* and the vixen he had sparked in her.

She hadn't left until nearly two in the morning. She'd been a little hurt when he hadn't asked for her phone number, and that had pissed her off because she didn't *want* to care. But then he'd surprised her by following her home to make sure she arrived safely, and *that* had made her swoon. He'd climbed off his bike, and she'd asked him if he followed all of his hookups home. *Only the ones I want to fuck again*, he'd said in the same gruff voice that had turned her inside out all night. That had made her wonder if she was just one of many, but he'd hauled her into a toe-curling kiss, obliterating her ability to think about anything other than how much she didn't want that kiss to end. They'd finally exchanged numbers, and she'd spent yesterday on cloud nine, reveling in the aftermath of their electrically charged connection.

But he hadn't texted, and today she'd been obsessively checking her phone, only to be disappointed. That was a sucky feeling and a good reminder that it was only a hookup, and she needed to keep her head on straight and focus on work.

That didn't stop her heart from racing half an hour later when her phone vibrated with a text. She grabbed it, hoping it was him, and Marly's name flashed on the screen. Feeling foolish, she silently chided herself and read her message. *Any word from Sir Broodiness?*

Madigan thumbed out, *Crickets. WHY do people do this to themselves? It's torture.*

Marly's response rolled in seconds later. *You've had hookups before. You know how it works.*

She typed furiously. *I've had two, and I didn't WANT to see them again. I'm not sure I can do this.* Her phone rang seconds later with a call from Marly.

"What do you mean you're not sure you can do this?" Marly asked. "Now you want a relationship? Because you know he's not looking for one."

"No. I *don't* want a relationship, but I also don't like sitting around waiting for him to call. That's an awful feeling."

"But that's what hooking up *is*. It's just a booty call. He might call today or tomorrow, or he might never call, *but* the guy made sure you got home safely, and that's going above and beyond hookup rules. He's probably just busy."

"Or hooking up with someone else," she said with a pang of jealousy, which she *also* hated. "He's walking around with an orgasm machine in his pants, and trust me, it's loaded for all-nighters."

Marly was quiet for a few seconds. "Mads, did you catch feelings for him?"

"No." Maybe. Shit. He must have rattled her brain when he'd screwed her senseless. "You know what? You're right. We had great sex and amazing chemistry, but that's where it ends."

"You sure you're okay with that?"

"Yes. I'm *not* putting myself into a position to get hurt again."

"Okay, so if he texts you tonight, you're not going to end up on his floor?"

"We were on a futon mattress…and the kitchen counter, against the wall, and…oh yeah, the floor."

"Uh-huh," Marly said teasingly.

"It doesn't matter. I'm *not* going to end up on it again. What time is it? I'm starved." Madigan went into the kitchen and opened the fridge.

"After six. Do you actually have food in your house?"

Madigan peered into her nearly empty fridge and sighed. "No. I forgot to go grocery shopping again."

"You're probably the only woman on earth who *forgets* to buy food."

"Hey, don't judge. I was busy having amazing sex and cold pizza with the orgasm machine, okay?" She closed the refrigerator and headed out of the kitchen to put on her boots. "Besides, there are certain benefits to living close to my parents. I'll catch you later."

Twenty minutes later she walked into the kitchen of her childhood home and was met with the sweet scents of family, a home-cooked meal, and fresh-baked cookies. Three of her favorite things. Her parents were sitting at the kitchen table with her paternal grandfather, Mike Wicked. Their dinner plates were empty, and her parents' fur babies, Buster, a golden retriever mix, and Milo, an adorable fluffy brown mutt, trotted over to greet her. "Hi, guys."

As she crouched to love them up, her mother stood from her seat. "Hi, baby girl. What a nice surprise. Have you eaten?"

"No. Do you have extras? I forgot to get groceries last night." Madigan hugged her and grabbed a cookie from the white plate on the counter, which indicated cookies made with real sugar. Her grandfather was supposed to watch his sugar intake, so her mother baked sugar-free treats for him and always put them on blue plates.

Her father took her hand, tugging her closer as he tapped his cheek. "Lay some sugar on me, sweetheart. Then you can sit down and enjoy your mama's lemon chicken."

"Hi, Daddy." She kissed his cheek. "How are you, Grandpa?"

"I could be better. Get in here." He opened his arms, and as he hugged her, he whispered, "I'll give you five bucks for that cookie."

"I would if I could, but I don't need to get yelled at tonight."

"Who raised you to be so weak?"

Her grandfather winked, but she knew he was only half-kidding. He'd always been a bit of a curmudgeon with an authoritative craggy voice that even now, with his aging body, face mapped with wrinkles, gray hair, thin lips, and blue-gray eyes, made him seem bigger than life. Madigan adored him, and she didn't blame him for his disgruntled attitude. She'd be upset too if her body began failing her and people monitored her every move. She'd had a hard enough time readjusting to her protective family after she'd moved back home.

"Pop, that's enough," her father said.

"I could give him half," Madigan suggested just as her grandfather shot out a hand, stealing the entire cookie from her, and shoved it into his mouth.

"Damn it, old man." Her father shook his head. "We're trying to keep you healthy."

Her grandfather grumbled something indiscernible and waved a hand dismissively as her mother set a full plate of food and silverware in front of Madigan and took a seat between the two men, stifling a laugh.

"You've got a death wish, and I'm not ready for you to leave this earth yet," her father said to her grandfather. "I'm not done giving you hell."

"Listen here, son. It's bad enough I'm living these years without the woman I have loved since I was seventeen years old," her grandfather said. Madigan's grandmother had passed away several years ago. "You take away my sugar, and what've I got left?"

"You've got me," Madigan chimed in, putting her hand on his. "I moved back home so I could see you more."

All eyes were on her grandfather as his expression softened, and he turned his hand over, giving hers a gentle squeeze. "I know you did, Mads, and I love you, but as I've told you, I don't want you putting your life on hold for me. You're a pretty young thing. You should be out dating, having the time of your life. Going out with a different guy every week until you find the right one."

"Let's not go *too* far," her father said, giving her grandfather a stern look.

"I'm not putting my life on hold, Grandpa." Madigan took another bite of the delicious food her mother had made.

"I haven't seen you with a single young man since you moved back," her grandfather said.

"Do you blame her, with four brothers and this one breathing down her back?" Her mother motioned toward her father. "When Mads went for a walk on the beach, the boys wanted to send out a search party."

"Don't worry, Grandpa. I go out with guys." It wasn't a total lie. She often went out with her brothers, cousins, and friends.

Her mother's brows lifted curiously, and her father's brows slanted.

"I mean a guy here and there, okay? Besides, I'm working on expanding my business to sell hoodies and T-shirts and other merchandise." She told them about what she envisioned and shared pictures of some of the designs she'd put together over the last few weeks. "What do you think?"

"You never fail to amaze me," her grandfather said.

"Thanks, Grandpa."

"If anyone can make a go of it, it's you, darlin'," her father added.

"Honey, we are so proud of all that you've accomplished, but are you sure now is the right time?" her mother asked. "You're already so busy."

The last twenty-four hours had proven that she wasn't busy enough. She needed a project in which to pour her energy and brainpower so her stupid heart wouldn't have time to sneak in.

"Actually, I have more free time than I'd like, and you know how much I hate being idle. It's not like I'd be launching a business from scratch. This will be an offshoot of my existing company."

"Don't kid yourself, darlin'," her father said. "Launching a merchandise line is a big endeavor. You've already achieved more than most people will in a lifetime. You're making more money than you could ever spend, and you've managed to maintain a schedule that allows time for yourself and family. We'd just hate to see you get so wrapped up in work that you lose sight of what's really important."

"I'm not. I'll always have time for family and friends." *I just want to lock up my brain in the evenings, so when I come home after seeing Tank and Leah and their kids, or Justin and Chloe, or Gunner and Sid, or you two, I don't play with ideas of having that for myself.*

"You know, there *are* other things you could do in the evenings that are more fun than building businesses," her grandfather said.

"Grandpa, how many times do I have to tell you that I'm not looking for a relationship?"

"Who's talking about a relationship?" her grandfather snapped. "I was thinking about taking your old grandpa out to dinner, where I can get some *real* dessert."

"You really want to get me in trouble, don't you?" Madigan teased.

They had a nice visit as she finished eating. When she finally headed out the door, she put on her helmet. Her phone vibrated with a message, and she pulled it from her pocket. *Sir Broodiness* appeared on the screen. Her heart skipped, and she immediately chastised herself for it, forcing herself to take a few deep breaths before reading the message.

You up for some fun?

Her resolve was no match for the tingles chasing over her skin. She glanced at her parents' house, as if they might sense what she was up to, but the dirty promises behind Tobias's offer quickly reeled her back in. She needed to take control of this situation so she felt less like she was at his mercy and more like the badass lady boss she was.

She thumbed out, *My place your condoms. Be ready to satisfy.* She pocketed her phone and climbed onto her *Barbie mobile*, ready to show broody *Ken* just how fierce a pink-lover could be.

When she pulled up to her house, Tobias was already there, leaning against his motorcycle in the driveway. His thick hair was pushed away from his face like he'd just raked a hand through it. A black T-shirt hugged his broad chest, and his powerful legs were anchored to the concrete by black leather boots. He really was beautiful, but not in the sense of being pretty. No, Tobias's beauty was sharp and jagged, commanding attention in the same way a dangerous cliff drew spectators who inherently knew they shouldn't get too close, but the intrigue was too much for some to resist.

That was Madigan.

She was *some*.

His dark eyes locked on her as she parked beside him, and her nerves caught fire, but she was determined not to let it show. She whipped off her helmet and shook out her hair, emboldened by the heat in his eyes as he drank her in. "How'd you get here so fast?"

"It's nice to see you, too, Blue Eyes."

His hungry gaze found her mouth, making it go dry. She licked her lips, and he shook his head, making the sexiest "*Mm*" sound she'd ever heard, and continued his visual appraisal. His gaze lowered, lingering on her breasts. His wolfish grin told her he could see her nipples pebbling through the thin material of her tank top. But he didn't stop there, taking in her Daisy Dukes and every inch of her legs. She should probably be offended that he was so into her body, but as he was inspecting what was yet to come, she was taking her own visual tour, noticing the way his fingers curled, like he wanted to touch her, the enticingly formidable bulge in his worn jeans, and the slight flex of his thighs. She imagined peeling those clothes off him and running her hands over his hot skin.

By the time their eyes connected again, she was so turned on, she could barely think. But she forced her legs to move, and he followed her into her cottage. She put her keys and helmet on the table by the door, trying to pull herself together as he set down his helmet and took off his boots and socks, just as he had at his place. Why did bare feet make him even sexier? She took off hers, too, her nerves kicking up as he sauntered past the foyer, standing between the open kitchen and living room, making the cozy space feel even smaller.

She'd spent a lifetime around large men, but not men who practically oozed desire for her. As if it weren't hard enough to keep from ripping Tobias's clothes off, she wondered what he thought of her home. She'd rented the two-bedroom cottage fully furnished from Chloe when Chloe had moved in with Maverick. She'd replaced Chloe's accent pillows and decorations with pillows that were pale pink and yellow, some with messages on them like BE NICE OR LEAVE and MY PLACE, MY RULES, and had hung up pictures of her family and friends and the places she'd traveled.

She watched him taking a quick visual sweep of her off-white couches, fireplace flanked by bookshelves, and glass doors that led to a screened-in porch. His brows knitted as he glanced to his left, taking in the bright kitchen, and the dining room table littered with her designs and other work. Was he judging her pink pillows and messy work area? Or was he cataloging all the places he could bend her over and take her from behind? A thrill shot through her.

When did I become so sexual?

Tobias walked over to the dining room and picked up something she'd printed out, reading it aloud. "Fighting sucks, but I'm here for the make-up sex." He eyed her, arching a brow.

"It's a new card design."

He picked up another and read it. "Can your penis come out to play? Love, my vagina." He scanned the others. "These are all about sex."

"Yeah, well, I blame you for that." She went to the table and began gathering her papers, her nervousness taking over. "You sound surprised. My cards make fun of the difficult aspects of relationships. They're not *only* about sex. I have cards for all types of relationships. Siblings, friends, exes. I thought you said your sister was a fan of them. Does she give them to you or her boyfriend or husband? Is she married?"

His jaw clenched, and his eyes narrowed. He was silent for a long moment. "Am I making you nervous, Blue Eyes? I didn't come here to talk, and I've got better things in mind for that sexy mouth of yours."

The way he'd clammed up and tried to distract her from her question did not go unnoticed, but she was practically salivating for a taste of him. *Take control, Mads.* "Oh yeah? Well, I have better things in mind for *your* mouth, too."

She unbuttoned her shorts and shimmied them down her legs. They'd barely hit the floor before he tore off her panties and crushed his mouth to hers, pinning her against the dining room wall in a penetrating kiss, sending rivers of heat rushing through her core. His body was hard and strong, but she wasn't afraid, and there was no room for nervousness with the desire pulsing through her. She was engulfed in his hunger, enraptured by its power as it unleashed something dark and greedily dirty inside her. She wanted his fierceness and pushed up on his shirt, needing to feel his bare skin.

He broke the kiss, ripping his shirt off, eyes burning into her. "You're so fucking cute, it's hot. And that mouth…" He gritted out a curse and turned, sweeping his arm across the table, sending her papers sailing into the air.

She squealed as he picked her up and laid her down on the space he'd cleared, pulling her to the edge of the table, wasting no time burying his face between her legs. *Holy mother of magical tongues.* This man knew just how to make her body sing. Her skin was on fire, an orgasm hovering just out of reach. A flood of sensations charged up her limbs, gathering in her chest and low in her belly, pulsing and swelling, until she clawed at the table, needing something to anchor her in the dizzying room. As if he'd read her mind, he pressed his hands to her inner thighs, opening her wider and holding her right where he wanted her as he sucked her throbbing clit. His fingers entered her, stroking over that hidden detonator, setting off an explosion of fiery sensations. A loud cry flew from her lungs. She thrashed with the overwhelming pleasures coursing through her, but he stayed with her, sucking and fucking, holding her at the crest so long, she was sure her heart would stop. She couldn't see, couldn't think, could only feel *everything*—his hot mouth sucking, teeth grazing, talented tongue teasing, fingers plunging, and one big, rough hand squeezing her thigh. His beard abraded her skin, and she wanted *all* of it. The scratches she knew he'd leave just as he had the other night, the ache of her inner muscles from squeezing so tight, the obscene pleasure of his fingers going deep, and knowing his cock would go even deeper.

Just when she started to come down from the peak, he withdrew his fingers, replacing them with his mouth, licking and sucking at a slow, torturous pace as she panted to catch her breath.

"This time I want those baby blues on me," he demanded.

It took all her focus to open her eyes. Control forgotten, she put a hand behind her head, holding it up, wanting to see his mouth on her. *Sweet baby Jesus*, she could come from the riveting look in his eyes. They were just having fun, but she swore there was something deeper in the way he was looking at her. She felt something tangible and strong between them, like a cable wrapping around her, keeping them tethered.

"Good girl," he said huskily, and pressed a kiss to her inner thigh. "So fucking sexy." He brushed his whiskers along the same spot, sending ripples of sensations through her. "I want to hear my name this time."

This time? Giddy with anticipation, she watched as he pressed his fingers to her clit and devoured her again, feasting roughly and hungrily, then impossibly slowly and tenderly, all the while moving his fingers in circles with exactly the right amount of pressure to hold her hostage. Overwhelming sensations engulfed her. Her head spun trying to keep up, and every time her eyes closed, he growled, "I said *watch*," and she did, wanting to please him, to hear the lust dripping in his voice. His eyes remained trained on her as he took her to the edge, then lifted his face, sliding the tip of his tongue along her sex and over that sensitive bundle of nerves his fingers had been wreaking havoc with. She gasped and held her breath, readying for the next delicious assault.

"You're fucking perfect," he said gruffly.

His praise brought new thrills. When his fingers pushed into her at the same time as he took her clit between his teeth and sucked, heaven and earth collided and "*Tobias—*" screamed from her lungs. She was soaring, suspended above, her body riddled with heat and ice and something too glorious for words. She saw herself spread out for him as he took what he wanted with unapologetic abandon, and she *wanted* everything he gave in return. Every hot slick of his tongue, every curse of appreciation, every thrust of his fingers. She *wanted* to watch, getting as much of a thrill from seeing the lust in his eyes and restraint in his muscles as she was from his mouth and hands. Then she was floating down from her high, and he was there to catch her, kissing his way up her body, pushing her bra over her breasts.

"*Again*," he commanded, and sucked her nipple into his mouth.

A stream of sinful noises fell from her lips, and she fisted her hands in his hair, panting out, "*Don't stop.*" He grinned around his mouthful, and she knew she hadn't needed to ask. He pushed his fingers between her legs, sucking harder, until she shattered again, her body bucking, inner muscles clenching as she gasped for air. He slanted his mouth over hers, filling her lungs, riding out her climax with her, until she lay spent beneath him, limp as a rag doll.

Their lips parted on a series of feathery kisses, so light and tender, she forced her eyes open, not believing he was the same man who had just ravaged her. But there he was, in all his powerful glory, and the way he was looking at her took her breath away.

His beautiful mouth tipped up, and that gravelly voice rumbled out, “On your knees, Blue Eyes. It’s your turn.”

TOBIAS HELPED MADIGAN sit up and stripped off her shirt and bra, taking an eyeful of the most gorgeous, and adorably sexy, woman he’d ever seen. He’d always been an intense lover, but he was far more demanding with Madigan. He had a visceral urge to claim her in an animalistic way. He didn’t know what it was about her that made him want her eyes on him or need to hear her say his name in the throes of passion. But he ached for it.

She slid off the table, her delicate hands trailing over his pecs. Her touch was soft, but the look in her eyes was liquid heat as she leaned forward and her luscious mouth toyed with his nipple. His cock jerked, and he stroked her jaw. “I’ve been thinking about fucking your mouth for days.”

Her cheeks reddened, and her hands pressed harder into his chest. She stared resolutely up at him. “I’m totally into this, but I don’t know where”—her gaze flicked to his dick and back up—“has been. Do I need to worry about…Are you *clean*? Because sex with a condom is one thing, but…”

“If I wasn’t clean, I wouldn’t be fucking around with you. I’m not that big of an asshole.”

She let out a relieved breath. "Good, because you're not the only one who's been thinking about this, and I'd hate to kick you out without satisfying my curiosity."

Holy fuck, she was hot.

She pressed a kiss to the center of his chest and worked her way down his abs as she unzipped his jeans. Her fingers curled around the waist of his boxer briefs and jeans, and she tugged them down his legs. He kicked them off, and she sank to her knees, reaching for him, but the height difference brought his cock to her forehead.

She looked up at him with amusement, and they both laughed.

He pulled a chair over and sat in it, guiding her between his legs. What a sight she was on her knees, hair teasing just above her creamy breasts, pert nipples proof of her eagerness as she fisted his cock. Those pretty eyes never left his as she slid her tongue over and around the head. He groaned low in his throat, and she grinned. *Fucking grinned* like she craved his reaction. She licked the crown again, and another greedy groan escaped. He threaded his fingers into her hair as she continued driving him crazy, licking his shaft, her hand following the slick trail, slow, tight, and so fucking perfect, he gripped her hair tighter. He wanted to yank her forward, to thrust up and go deep into her throat, but he had a solid nine inches of thick, hard cock, and her mouth was too exquisite to ruin his chances of a replay.

Instead, he rasped, "*Suck it.*"

Her eyes narrowed. "I'll do what I want, when I want." She sat back on her heels.

His rumbling growl earned nothing more than a giggle. She continued licking around the broad head, across the slit at the tip, moaning and stroking, until his every muscle flexed with restraint.

"Jesus, Blue Eyes, you're killing me." Seeing her plump lips stretched around his cock nearly did him in. "Are you gonna let me come in that pretty mouth of yours?"

"I guess we'll see. But *if* I do, and you don't give me what I want"—she leaned closer, lowering her voice—"you'll never get near my mouth again."

Her confidence was as hot as that shadow of vulnerability he'd glimpsed earlier. "What is it that you want?"

"When you come, I want to hear *my* name fly off *your* lips. Got it, *Sir Broodiness?*"

"Sir Broodiness?" He grinned. "Damn, I like that."

"That's not an answer," she challenged.

Holding her steady gaze, he parroted her words. "I guess we'll see."

She started to lower her mouth over his dick but stopped, reaching up to touch his fisted hand in her hair. "*I* set the pace, but you can help me stay there."

Christ, this woman was his every fantasy come true.

She teased the crown again and took just the head in her mouth, sucking as she stroked his length. "Deeper," he demanded.

Her eyes flared, and she released the head and went back to teasing. *Fuck.* He ground his back teeth, willing her to go deeper, and when she finally did, she took him all the way to her throat, the head catching in the tight channel. A loud moan, followed by a string of curses, fell from his lips as she sucked and stroked, slowing every few sucks to tease the head, heightening his arousal to painful lengths. She went up on her knees, straightened her spine, working him faster and taking him agonizingly deep. He was afraid he'd choke her when he came, but she didn't seem worried. She increased her speed and tightened her hold with every curse he uttered, those mesmerizing, trusting eyes locked on him. He tugged her forward, in sync with her efforts, appreciation, *enjoyment*, and so much desire glowing in her eyes, he wanted to give her everything he had. He pumped faster, and she met his quickening. Heat seared down his spine, and she must have sensed it, because she cupped his balls and tugged, severing the last of his restraint. "Fuuck…*Blue Eyes*—" he said as he poured himself down her throat, every pump causing her eyes to darken, until they were midnight blue. Come pooled in the corners of her mouth as he grunted through the last of his release. But she kept him deep even as his dick jerked with aftershocks.

He hissed as she released his cock and licked the wetness running down her chin. Her eyes were at half-mast, glazed over as if she were in a blissed-out fog, too. He cupped her face with one hand, trying to get his brain to function, and brushed his thumb over her swollen lower lip. "You're too fucking sexy." He lifted her up and onto his lap, taking her in a kiss so deep, he didn't know where he ended and she began, and he didn't want to find out.

She pushed playfully at his chest, flashing a wicked smile. "You didn't say my name."

"Like hell I didn't."

"You said *Blue Eyes*."

"That's your name when you're with me." He brushed his lips over hers. "Don't even think about withholding this mouth from me. I'm not done with you yet." He nipped at her lower lip.

She giggled. "It's *my* mouth. I'll do what I want with it."

He wouldn't have it any other way. "I have no doubt you'll

want me so bad, you'll beg for my cock."

"Overconfident much?"

"You can take that back when we're done. For now we'll just have to put *my* mouth to good use again." Holding her on his lap, he leaned down and snagged his jeans, digging the condoms from his pocket, and rose with her in his arms. "Which bedroom?"

"The one on the right, but you *just*...You sure you can go again?"

He didn't bother to respond as he stood with her in his arms, her legs around his waist, and carried her into the bedroom. The room was dark save for a strip of yellow and black twinkling lights running across the headboard of the king-size bed. A half dozen patterned pillows and layers of blankets in a feminine mix of pinks, grays, teal, black, and white, covered the bed. "You always leave these lights on when you're out?"

"They're welcoming, don't you think?"

He eyed her, trying to ignore the streak of jealousy blazing through him. "You have that many guys in here?"

"*No*," she snapped. "Ever heard of self-care? It sets the mood."

"I bet it does." With one hard yank, he stripped the top blanket and throw pillows off the bed and tossed them to the floor, then lay her in the middle of the bed. Her hair fanned out around her beautiful face, and he pictured her, vibrator in hand, thinking about *him* as she pleasured herself. His cock hardened, and her gaze trailed down to it, appreciation shining in her eyes as he dropped the condoms beside her.

"Three?" She arched a brow.

"Now that I've got an image of you pleasuring yourself in my head, I'm thinking I should've brought four." That jealousy was still clinging to him, and he was determined to erase the memory of any man that had touched her before him. The need was so visceral, he went with it and didn't allow himself to think about why.

"Why do you have *that* image in your head?" she asked as he came down over her.

"Self-care." He arched a brow.

Her cheeks flamed. "I didn't mean *that*."

He rocked the base of his cock against her clit, and she sighed longingly. "Are you telling me you didn't lie in this bed last night remembering the feel of my mouth on you and how hard you came?" Her breathing hitched. "That you didn't lie here thinking about fucking me and get so wet you had to take things into your own hands?"

She swallowed hard, clamping her mouth shut.

He'd gone through the same torture. He'd been dying to see her, to touch her, to *kiss* her, eat her, *fuck* her, and it had taken everything he had not to text her.

"Thought so." He angled his hips, the base of his shaft brushing along her wetness. He dragged his tongue over the seam of her lips. "After tonight, you won't be able to forget the feel of me, and you can guarantee I'll be thinking about you naked and on your knees, that sexy mouth of yours sucking me off, for weeks to come."

Her lips parted with a needy sigh. "And will you...?"

"Fuck yeah, I will. Or maybe I'll hit you up for a little fun."

The sweet smile that earned stirred something deep inside him. He tried to shove that feeling away and regain control, but it lingered. *Fuck.* "Time to turn off your brain, and let me give your pussy the ride of a lifetime."

He lowered his mouth to hers, kissing her ravenously as he

ground against her. She moaned and rocked, her every sound making him ache to be inside her, but her mouth was so sweet and hot, he couldn't get enough. He continued feasting on her, her arousal coating his balls, her moans pulling greedy sounds from his lungs. She was so wet and ready, but as much as he wanted to fuck her, he wanted to hear her desire for *him* even more. He shifted his weight, using his hand between her legs. She moaned, her hips rocking as he teased over her wetness, tangling his other hand in her hair, knowing just how to make her come. She'd gotten off when he'd pinned her hands to the mattress the other night, and after the way she'd swallowed like a champ, he had a feeling there was a lot more to sweet Madigan yet to be discovered.

Time to test her boundaries. He held her hair against the mattress as he lowered his mouth to her breast and teased along her center with his fingers, rubbing circles on her clit with his thumb.

"*Oh God*," she panted out, her hips rising with every stroke.

He released her nipple, giving her a coy smile. "I liked Sir Broodiness, but God works."

She laughed. "Shut up and get busy."

He fucking loved her sense of humor, and getting busy was *exactly* what he did, sucking and teasing. Taunting her until she was drenched.

"*More*," she pleaded. "I need your fingers *in* me."

"No, you don't." He wanted her to come out of sheer desperation, and continued his ministrations as she moaned and writhed. "Come for me."

"I can't." Her legs trembled, her voice a shaky thread.

"Come on, Blue Eyes."

"I can't come without something inside me."

Challenge accepted. "You're not getting anything in your sweet pussy until you come, but I'm happy to put something *in* you." He moved swiftly up her body, kissing her hard, and turned around, straddling her head. "Suck me while I make you come. Then I'll fuck you good."

She grabbed his cock and sucked like she was born to do it, while he teased her pussy without entering her and sucked her clit. The urge to come was so strong it was painful, but he wanted to give her what she'd never had before and focused on making her come. He teased her lighter with his fingers, flicking her clit faster with his tongue, feeling her mounting orgasm in the tightening of her muscles, the stilling of her mouth around his cock. Hips writhing, nails clawing, she moaned, and the sound vibrated along his shaft. He used his teeth on her clit, and she cried out as her orgasm took hold. He withdrew from her mouth, feeling like a fucking king, and stayed with her, licking and sucking as she bucked and thrashed in the throes of pleasure.

When she sank into the mattress, panting, he grabbed a condom, shifting to kneel between her legs as he sheathed himself. She lay with one arm across her forehead, trying to catch her breath, as he lowered himself over her. "Still with me, gorgeous?"

"Uh-huh." She blinked up at him. "I didn't know I could do that."

"You're welcome." He lowered his mouth to hers, driving into her in one hard thrust. She clung to him, clearly getting a second wind as she met his efforts one for one. She was so tight, so greedy for him. He hiked up her knees, pounding deeper into her, and tore his mouth away with the need to see her. Their eyes connected, their bodies moving in perfect sync, and with every thrust he felt their connection deepening, *strengthening*. When she surrendered to their passion, crying out in ecstasy, she was so damn beautiful, he felt himself getting lost in her.

He needed to end that shit and fought against his release. When she went limp beneath him, he smacked the side of her ass. "On your hands and knees, Blue Eyes."

Her eyes widened with excitement, and she scrambled up on all fours, her perfect, heart-shaped ass there for the taking. She glanced over her shoulder, mahogany hair dancing around her beautiful face, eyes brimming with so much desire, it was palpable. *Fuck.* He kissed her spine, running his hands along the dip at her waist and the swell of her hips. "Gorgeous."

He brushed his palm over her supple ass as he aligned their bodies. "Keep your legs together." He pushed into her, feeling her legs squeezing, pussy tightening like a vise. "That's it." She squeezed tighter, and man, that felt good. *"Good girl."* He thrust, gradually gaining speed. "You feel incredible." Where was all this praise coming from? He wasn't normally like that. He grabbed her hair in one hand, planting his other on her shoulder for leverage as he pounded into her. Their skin grew slick with their efforts, and when she lowered herself onto her elbows, her head falling forward, he drove deeper, the pleasure agonizingly exquisite.

"*Faster*," she pleaded. "I want to feel you lose control."

"Then you're losing it with me." He wrapped an arm around her belly, sliding his fingers between her legs.

"I *can't*," she said breathlessly. "I've already come so many times."

"Yes, you *can*, and you will." He zeroed in on her clit, thrusting faster, earning more sexy pleas. The sounds of flesh on flesh rang out, the scent of sex permeating the air, and he was so close to coming, when she squeezed her legs tighter, he nearly lost it.

"*Tobias—*" she pleaded shakily.

"Come with me, Madigan. Come *for* me."

"Not without you."

"I'm ready, baby. So damn ready to explode."

She drove her hips back as he thrust forward, their bodies hammering to the same frantic beat, until they spiraled over the edge together, her pussy clamping down around him as she cried out his name, and he grunted out hers. He wished he could brand her from the inside out, claim her as his own. Ruin her for any other man. But as their lust-filled cries, moans, and curses rang out, he closed his eyes, telling himself this night would be their last.

NEARLY TWO HOURS and multiple orgasms later, the sheets damp with their sweat, empty condom wrappers littering the floor, they lay staring up at the ceiling, spent and panting.

Madigan's head rested on the crook of Tobias's shoulder, their sides touching. Her skin was soft, and hot, and even after several rounds of phenomenal sex, she was too enticing to ignore.

"Water," Madigan said weakly. "I need water. My body hasn't been contorted in so many positions since I tried doing yoga with my friend Marly last year."

He grinned at her cuteness and pressed a kiss to her temple. As he did it, the intimacy of the act struck like a blow to the gut. He needed to get the hell out of there before she cast more of a spell on him.

"I'll get you some water." He strode into the bathroom to take care of the condom and berated himself as he washed up. He should have left after the blow job, or at least after their first round of sex. But everything about her, from her cute comments and determined challenges to her sensuality and willingness to push boundaries, drew him in like metal to magnet. This had to be the last time they hooked up. Madigan was *too* exciting, too challenging, too adorable, too sexy. Too fucking easy to hang out with and get close to.

When he came out of the bathroom, she was lying on her stomach, her arms crossed beneath her cheek, pink bite marks on her ass and shoulder. The sight of those marks thrilled him more than they should. He had no right to brand her like that, but when she'd ridden him backward, all that creamy skin had called out to him, and when he'd bitten her shoulder, she'd come so hard, she'd pulled him over the edge with her.

He looked away and headed out of the bedroom, taking a look around her living room as he gathered his clothes. Everything about the place felt like her, feminine, creative, unafraid to be who she wanted to be. He pulled on his boxer briefs and jeans and gathered the papers he'd thrown off the table, skimming a few of the designs and a lengthy to-do list outlining phone calls and her puppetry schedule. Madigan wasn't just a twentysomething fumbling through life, like the few other women he'd hooked up with. She was an incredible, funny, beautiful, stable creative businesswoman with a family who went to great lengths to protect her. While he had no clue what his future held and a family that had cast him aside without so much as a backward glance.

He had no business screwing around with Madigan, no

matter how much she brightened his world just by existing in it.

Biting back the acidic taste of that reality, he headed into her kitchen and rooted around for a glass. He filled it with water, guzzled it down, and refilled it before returning to the bedroom, grabbing his shirt along the way.

Madigan was still lying on her stomach naked. So beautiful and trusting.

She had no idea she was hooking up with a convicted felon.

He steeled himself against the self-loathing swamping him. "Got your water, Blue Eyes."

"Thanks." She sat up, pulling the sheet over her chest, and smiled when she saw his shirt in his hand. "Oh *good*." She reached for it. "Do you mind?" Before he could respond, she put it on. It billowed around her, making her even more irresistible as she thanked him for the water and took a sip. "I was just thinking I should start a line of ecards specifically for booty calls."

"That mind of yours is always working, isn't it?"

"Kind of. Don't you think it would be nice to let your booty call know they're on your mind without crossing that line between relationship and hookup?"

"And how are you going to do that?"

"I don't know yet. Maybe a picture of a peach or a banana on the front of the card and THINKING OF YOU on the inside."

He chuckled. "That'll do it."

"You like that? How about this? The front of the card says COME QUICK, and the inside says something like, SAID NO BOOTY CALL EVER." Her eyes lit up. "Or, IT'S HOT AS HELL OUTSIDE. WANT TO COME OVER AND GET NAKED?"

"You're a trip, Blue Eyes." *A dangerous, entertaining trip.* "Thanks for a good time, but I've got to take off."

"I don't think that's card worthy." Her brows knitted, and he saw the moment understanding dawned on her, stealing the light from her eyes. *"Oh."*

How could two simple letters carry so much disappointment?

As if she caught it, too, she lifted her chin and said, "Actually, I can use that for a card. WHAT'S THE ONLY TIME A HIT AND RUN IS APPROPRIATE?"

He arched a brow, wishing he could play the silly game all night, just to see her smile again.

"WITH YOUR BOOTY CALL." She wiggled her shoulders and said, "*Hey*," in a singsong voice.

"You definitely have a knack for the card stuff." *And for sex, and making me smile, and…Fuck…*He wasn't going there.

"Yeah, it's a gift." She climbed off the bed and started to take off his shirt, but he stopped her. "Keep it. It looks better on you."

"You can't drive home shirtless."

"Sure I can." He took her chin between his finger and thumb, tipping her face up. "You're really something, Blue Eyes. Take care of yourself." He pressed his lips to hers, aching to take her in his arms, disappear into her, and pretend the real world didn't exist for a few more hours.

Which was exactly why he had to leave.

Now.

TOBIAS TOOK THE long way home, trying to shake off the urge to turn around and go back. He'd seen Madigan wince with his last remark. It had lasted only a second, but that was all he needed to feel it rip through his chest and to know it was the right thing to say to end whatever this was between them.

He couldn't stomach the thought of going back to his empty apartment, where he'd toss and turn all night, wrestling ghosts of his past on a fucking futon that still smelled like Madigan. Why was he still on the Cape? His grandfather didn't even remember him most of the time. He should pack his shit and get the hell out of there. He stopped at a red light at the corner of the road that led to his apartment. But when the light turned green, instead of turning toward his apartment, he sped straight ahead, took the entrance to the highway, and opened the throttle.

Wind whipped against his bare skin as his thoughts blasted from the present to the past, his sister's hateful words—*You stole the love of my life. I hope you never get yours back*—scalding him anew. He drove faster, and when he came to Bourne, he flew over the bridge, leaving the Cape behind.

Flashes of Madigan gazing lustfully up at him warred with images of his sister crumpling to the ground beside his best friend's lifeless body and his horrified ex walking away like he was yesterday's trash. He gritted his teeth against the surge of emotions pushing through his veins. Sadness, regret, and anger tangled together, twisting and knotting, making his chest constrict and his skin feel too tight. He lowered his chin, cranking up his speed, but even the roar of the engine couldn't drown out his sister's wails.

He drove until the pain wasn't deafening and the past felt a little farther away, and then he drove farther. But the draw of the sister he'd practically raised clawed at him, too strong to leave behind, and as he'd done a dozen times before, he turned his fucking bike around, driving two hours back to the Cape.

He crossed the bridge, but instead of heading for his apartment, he remained in Bourne, winding through the streets of his youth, memories impaling him, their warmth annihilated by the sharp, cold reality of what had come later. Drowning in emotions, he made his way out of that residential neighborhood, driving to the place he'd never seen in the light of day.

As the dark of night gave way to a hint of dawn, he sat in front of the cedar-sided rambler nestled among hydrangeas and tiger lilies behind a white picket fence, his heart aching for what he'd never have.

Chapter Six

TOBIAS LEANED BENEATH the hood of an old Cadillac, trying to concentrate on work, but his thoughts kept trampling back to Blue Eyes, just as they'd been doing for the last two days. He uttered a curse as the other mechanic's dog, Cheddar, a six-year-old Labrador mix, leaned against his leg.

Kent sauntered over. "Dude, did you just curse at my dog?"

"Nah, man. Coincidence." He wiped his hands on a rag and reached down to pet the mutt, who had been hanging around him all morning. "What's up with you today, buddy?"

Cheddar sat beside him, snout tipped up, and Tobias swore the dog, who always seemed to be smiling, was looking at him with concern.

"He's used to you being quiet or ornery, depending on the situation," Kent said. "But you've been giving off a pretty negative vibe the last couple of days, and I guess he senses it. Anything you want to talk about?"

Weighing the offer, Tobias took a hard look at the guy he'd worked with since he'd first come to town. Kent was ex-military, in his early twenties. He was outgoing, honest, clean cut, and a little chatty for Tobias. Or at least for the man he'd become. The first week Tobias had worked there, Kent had told him about his plight with PTSD. He'd said Cheddar had helped him through some tough times, as did a therapist, realizing too late that if Tobias had wanted to know about his life, he'd have asked. Needless to say, Kent no longer tried to push conversation on him, and he rarely asked about Tobias's life, which Tobias appreciated. But while Kent seemed to be troubled enough by Tobias's *vibe* to ask about it, Tobias saw something new in Kent that sent a streak of jealousy ripping through him.

Kent was the type of guy Madigan *should* be hanging out with. He'd handled his demons and had something to offer her, like conversation and a positive outlook. Tobias might have stuck to his guns and stayed away from her for the past couple of days, despite desperately wanting to see her again, but that didn't mean he was going to hand-feed her to another guy.

He shook his head. "I'm good, thanks."

"I've worked with you for a few months now, and if this is *good*, then I'm Mary Poppins."

Tobias hiked a thumb over his shoulder. "You want me to go get you an umbrella so you can float up to the roof?"

Kent shook his head and went into the shop. Tobias ducked under the hood again, thankful for the respite. Well, except for Cheddar, standing sentinel at his side.

A little while later two high-pitched horn beeps sounded, and Tobias peered out from under the hood just in time to see Madigan climbing off her Vespa, round sunglasses hiding her eyes. A flash of heat engulfed him, but he wondered if she'd come to give him hell for the way he'd hightailed it out of her place.

She pulled off her helmet, and he saw her shaking out her hair in slow motion, his mind sprinting back to when she'd ridden him, her hair tumbling over her shoulders, pink nipples poking out between those glossy locks. His dick jerked behind his zipper, and his mind jumped to when she'd turned around, riding him backward. But as she strutted toward him in a dressy white tank top, high-waisted blue linen shorts, and sexy-as-sin strappy, wedged white sandals, the way her smile lit him up inside had him cursing under his breath.

"Hey, *broody*." She lifted her hand, dangling a paper bag. "I brought you lunch to make up for fixing my Vespa."

What the…? Before he could form a sentence, Cheddar bounded out to her, and she crouched with open arms.

"Well, hello, beautiful. You look just like a dog I used to know." She looked up at Tobias. "Is he yours?"

"He's mine," Kent said as he came out the shop door.

Madigan pushed to her feet, a megawatt smile illuminating the whole fucking world. "Kent?"

"Yeah." Kent tilted his head in question as he closed the distance with her, recognition bringing a boyish grin, taking him from dirty mechanic to charmer on the prowl.

What kind of hell was this?

"We met at the fundraiser for the rescue, right? You're Gunner's cousin?" Kent asked.

"Yes. Madigan. *Mads.* It's so good to see you again." She opened her arms to embrace him.

Kent glanced at Tobias over her shoulder, looking so damn happy, Tobias's hands fisted.

"Cheddar looks great," Madigan said cheerily, oblivious to the hell she was putting Tobias through. "You bring him with you to work now?"

"Yeah. He's such a good boy, the boss doesn't mind."

If Tobias were a better man, he'd walk away and let them

be, but he *wasn't* a better man. Apparently he was a possessive bastard where she was concerned, and he strode out of the bay, determined to stake his claim as the *only* booty call Blue Eyes was getting from that auto shop. "You two know each other, huh?"

"Kent got Cheddar from my cousin Gunner and his fiancée Sid's animal rescue," Madigan explained, petting Cheddar.

"I haven't seen Gunner and Sid in a while," Kent said. "I really should start going to the gym in the mornings again, but I usually go for a run with Cheddar instead."

"Aw, that's so sweet," Madigan said, making Tobias wish he had a fucking dog. "I don't know how often Gunner and Sid make it to the gym that early anymore. I swear they'd never leave their bed if they could get away with it."

Kent glanced at Tobias, giving him a look that said he'd like to take *Madigan* to bed.

"So, you brought me lunch?" Tobias said, knowing Kent would get the hint.

"Yes, but I only brought enough for two. I'm sorry, Kent. I didn't know you guys worked together. You can have it, and I can eat later."

"My ass you can." Driven by something bigger than him, Tobias took her by the elbow, leading her away, with Cheddar trotting behind them. "Kent can fend for himself."

"Enjoy your lunch," Kent called after them. "Cheddar, come on, boy." The pooch doubled back to him.

Tobias knew he was flirting with danger as he led Madigan around the building to a picnic table in the grass, but the thought of her getting together with Kent screwed with his head.

"Where are we going? I hope you like what I brought. I

wasn't sure what you liked to drink, so I brought iced tea and soda…"

Her nervous babbling tugged at those feelings he was trying to ignore.

"There's a picnic table," she exclaimed. "I'm glad you can take a break to eat. I wasn't sure if you got one. Are you hungry?"

For you? Ravenous. He slid her a look that made her blush. *Fuck. What am I doing?* "I'll be right back."

"Where are you going? I brought everything we need," she said sweetly.

He leaned closer, breathing in the scent that had haunted him since they'd met. "I need a minute to get my head on straight, or I'm going to put your pretty little ass on that table and eat *you* for lunch."

"*Oh,*" she said with surprise, her gaze darting around them. "Kent might see us." She lowered her voice to a whisper. "Do you have a truck or something?"

"*Jesus.*" Now he was hard. "Give me a second." He stalked inside to the employee washroom and leaned both hands on the sink, staring at his reflection in the mirror. It had taken a solid year before he could even look at himself, and to this day, he still didn't feel like he knew the man looking back at him. He used to be the kind of guy who could hang out with anyone, strike up conversations, and joke around. Now there was a noose around his neck. Say too much or think about all he'd lost, and it tightened. Say too little, and he scared people. What a fucking mess.

He narrowed his eyes, glowering at the man in the mirror. "Get your ass out there and *end* this. Cut her off before she gets hurt."

He washed his hands, strengthening his resolve, and headed back outside, determined to do the right thing. When he rejoined her at the picnic table, she'd already set out their lunches. A cheeseburger and fries for him and fried clams for her.

He straddled the bench, facing her. "Blue Eyes."

"Yes, Sir Broodiness?" She leaned closer. "Did you take care of your not-so-little problem?"

Her gaze dropped to his crotch, and hell if his dick didn't start to rise to the occasion. *Down, you greedy bastard.* "Madigan, this was really sweet of you, but I don't think we should hook up anymore."

"I know you don't," she said with a shrug. "I got your hint the other night. This is just me paying you back for fixing my Vespa."

"You don't need to pay me back, and you certainly didn't need to bring me lunch."

"You didn't need to pay for it, and you gave me several great orgasms. This is the least I can do."

Christ, she was making this difficult. "Mads, I'm not a guy you need in your life. I'm not going to fall for you over lunches and cute conversations, and I'm not sticking around long enough for you to try to change my mind. I'm not that guy." He hated what he was about to say, but deep down he *was* that big of an asshole. "But Kent might be."

She rolled her eyes. "Kent is hot, but he's a little *too* nice for me."

"You're going to get yourself in trouble saying shit like that."

She put her hands on his thighs, leaning in so close, her breath became his as she said, "Does that mean you want to spank me?"

He bit out, "*Fuck*," and she giggled. He thrust his hand to the nape of her neck, tugging her closer. Their lips brushed, and he struggled to keep from taking the kiss he desperately wanted. "Don't say that to guys like me."

"Why not? Even if you took me up on it, I know you wouldn't hurt me."

"You don't know that." He'd never hurt a woman, but he wasn't worried about what *he'd* do. He didn't want her saying shit like that to some other asshole who might take things too far.

"*Yes*, I do. You would've already done it."

"*Madigan*," he warned.

"You know you want to kiss me," she taunted, their faces still a breath apart.

"That's not the point."

Her eyes narrowed. "There's something between us, and I *know* you feel it."

There it was, the unavoidable truth. "I'm not looking to get tied down."

"That's a shame, because it was next on my list for us." She paused as her words sank in. "My book club is reading a super-sexy book about a girl who runs a gentleman's club, and there are a few scenes I was hoping we could act out."

He was wrong. This wasn't *hell*. It was worse, and there was no stopping the grin sliding across his face.

"Come *on*, Tobias," she said, exasperated. "Work with me here. The single-guy booty-call pool isn't exactly overflowing on the Cape, and you and I have such great chemistry."

"You can have any guy you want, and you deserve more than hookups."

"No *kidding*, broody boy," she said sharply. "But I don't *want* more. I gave my heart away, and it was crushed to smithereens with lies and manipulations. I am *never* going there again. The fact that you're not sticking around makes you even *more* appealing. I'm not asking you to date me."

He glanced at the food and soda she'd brought him. "This sure looks a lot like a lunch date to me."

"That's only because, aside from when we're naked, your listening skills leave a little to be desired." She snagged one of his fries and bit off a piece. "I told you this is my way of thanking you for fixing my ride, and I meant it." She grabbed the bag the food had come in and began fishing out mustard packets, and he realized it was from Hook, Line, and Sinker, a food shack he'd gone to with his family as a child. "You'd better eat before your break is over…"

She continued talking as she put mustard on her fried clams, and he got caught up in a memory he hadn't realized he still held.

Madigan put her face right in front of his. "*Hey.* Where'd you go?"

"Sorry." An incredulous laugh fell from his lips. "I've never seen anyone put mustard on fried clams other than my mother."

"Really? Everyone makes fun of me for it."

"We made fun of her, too."

"You're smiling."

He tried to school his expression, but the good memories wouldn't allow it. "Yeah. Hook, Line, and Sinker was one of her favorite places to eat. We'd hit it a few times each summer."

She plucked a clam from the cardboard boat, waving it at him. "See? Your mom is trying to send you a message from the great beyond." Speaking softly, as if she were far away, Madigan said, "*Tobias, this girl is cute and fun, and she has great taste in restaurants. Don't push her away.*"

He shook his head, picturing his mother's big brown eyes, which had seen the world differently than most people. "As cute as that was, you've got her all wrong."

She popped another clam into her mouth. "Then tell me about her. But you'd better do it while you eat. I have a one thirty puppetry session at LOCAL, so I don't have long."

He'd spoken to Elsa yesterday, and she'd already started the process of getting his grandfather into Madigan's program. Tobias was tempted to ask Madigan if she could do anything to speed the process up, but he didn't want to owe her anything. The fewer ties, the better.

"What would your mother have said?" she asked, stealing another fry.

He thought about that for a moment before answering. "Something like, *Watch this one, Toe. She's been kissed by the moon and sung to by the stars. She's got a bit of rascal in her, so don't be actin' a fool.*"

"What does that mean? *Kissed by the moon and sung to by the stars?*"

He shrugged like he had no idea, but he knew exactly what it meant. His mother had said it about him and his sister, and he'd asked her what it meant. *The moon's kisses filled you with light, so you outshine everyone around you, and the stars sang to you before you even knew what stars were. They whispered while you slept, teaching you to spread your wings and giving you the courage to chase big dreams.*

"She was always saying crazy shit."

"She would've been right about the rascal in me, and she called you *Toe*? How cute is that?"

"She called me a lot of things." He bit into the cheeseburger.

"Like what?"

He shook his head and took another bite.

"Come on, *Toe*."

He narrowed his eyes, and she steepled her hands, eyes pleading. She had the cute thing down pat, and he hadn't talked about his mother in so long, the words forced their way out, as if they'd been waiting to be set free. "*Sprout*, because when I was ten, I grew three inches. *Pest*, for obvious reasons, and *Big Bo*, because my little sister couldn't say brother." He took another bite, looking away with the bittersweet memories.

She touched his leg, bringing his eyes back to her. "I'm good at picking up on hints. I know you don't want to talk about your sister, so don't worry, I'm not going to ask. But if you ever need an ear, I'm a pretty good listener, and since I have brothers, I might be able to share some insight with you."

He'd never met anyone like her. She made him want to take her at her word. But he'd been burned one too many times to put himself out there.

"Tell me something else about your mom," she urged. "She sounds like she was spiritual."

"She was beautiful inside and out."

"Do you look like her?"

"Are you saying I'm pretty?" he teased, finishing his burger.

"You've got too much fuck-off energy to be pretty. But seriously. I look just like my mom did when she was younger, only she had bigger boobs than me."

"Yours are perfect."

"I'm glad you think so." She ate another fry. "So? Do you look like your mom or dad?"

"I've got her eyes and nose, thank God, because my father's nose is huge."

She shook her head, amused. "Do you ever wonder what your parents were like when they were young?"

"No. But I bet my mom was a lot like you. Trouble waiting to happen."

"I think the word you're looking for is *awesome*," she said sassily. "Do you have a picture of your mom?"

He hesitated for only a second before pulling out his wallet and handing her the tattered-edged picture, watching her reaction to the scars on the right side of his mother's face. When he was a kid, everyone asked about them, even adults. He'd asked his mother once if it bothered her when people asked about her scars, and she'd said, *I don't really think about them. It's the people who don't ask that hold my thoughts.* He'd asked why. *Because they're the special ones who really see me.*

"She *is* beautiful, and she has kind eyes." Her gaze flicked to him, then back to the picture. "You do have her nose and her lips. I'm sorry you lost her when you were so young."

"Me too, but that's life." Thinking about her cousin, he said, "I guess you know all about that."

He reached for the picture, but she didn't let go. Their gazes held, that powerful and undefinable connection vibrating between them. He couldn't look away, though he knew he should. She hadn't mentioned the scars, and that tugged at him like so many other things she'd done. He didn't know how long they sat gazing into each other's eyes, but every second drew him deeper into her. When Cheddar bounded up to the table, stealing her attention, he physically ached to have it back.

He put the picture in his wallet and shoved it in his pocket, fighting that feeling with everything he had.

Cheddar stretched out in the grass as they finished eating, and their conversation turned lighter. They chatted about funny food combinations, nicknames Madigan had been called over the years—short stuff, brat, Mini Mav because she followed her brother Maverick around when she was little, and Diva for singing around the house—and more ideas for her booty call card line, which Tobias was impressed to learn she'd decided to actually launch.

The time passed too quickly, and before Tobias knew it, his break was over. He threw away the trash and tried to repay her for lunch.

"I don't want your money. But I'm playing at the Sundance Café tonight. You and me, my place afterward?" She bit her lower lip, trapping her hopeful smile.

"You're killing me, Blue Eyes. I told you I'm not the guy for you."

She poked his chest. "You also think I'm looking for forever, and I'm not, which shows you how far off your judgment is."

He was *this close* to giving in. "Mads…"

"Come on," she urged. "Don't leave your booty hanging."

He uttered a curse. "Are you always this cute?"

She shrugged. "You can tell me tonight at my place. Ten o'clock. Come prepared." She turned on her heels and strutted toward the parking lot with an extra sexy sway in her hips, and Cheddar bounded off with her. When she reached the parking lot, she loved up Cheddar, waved to Kent, who shouted, "See you around," and turned a heart-stopping smile on Tobias. She kissed her hand and blew it in his direction. "See you tonight."

So much for ending things.

He lifted his chin in acknowledgment, and she turned around, doing a shoulder-rocking, butt-wiggling happy dance on her way to her Barbie mobile.

Chapter Seven

MADIGAN SAT IN her Jeep in the parking lot of Skaket Beach on Friday evening, trying to speed-read the last couple of chapters of the book for her book club meeting. What had started as her and Tobias exchanging ideas via text for booty call cards the day she'd brought him lunch had quickly turned to sexting and hooking up every night this week, leaving little time to read. But she was having so much fun with her broody, and *reluctant*, sex god, it was totally worth it.

They hadn't planned to see each other every night, and most nights she fought the urge to reach out just as hard as she knew he was fighting it, because it was a little scary how much she liked being with him and how drawn to him she was. But resisting, wondering who would break down first and reach out, was torturous, which made it just as exciting as the hours they had their hands and mouths on each other.

Every night after their trysts, Tobias did his best to sever their ties—*Take care of yourself, Blue Eyes. Have a good life, Blue Eyes. Be good, Blue Eyes*—and knowing he couldn't resist her made her stupid, romantic heart like him even more. She knew how dangerous that was, which was why on Tuesday she'd vowed to take a two-day Sir Broodiness hiatus. She'd gone to

Common Grounds coffee shop with her girlfriends and had planned on hanging out for an hour and then going home to read. But when she'd gotten home, Tobias had texted a peach emoji. Knowing he'd remembered the first booty-call card she'd mentioned and was thinking of her had made her swoon, but she'd stuck to her guns, told him she was busy, and sent a picture of a book and a flame emoji. He'd replied with *Date with a sweaty book nerd?* She'd texted, *No* with a laughing emoji. *Fictional book boyfriend.* He'd sent a smirking emoji and *You know I'll put him to shame* and had added an eggplant and a tongue emoji. Needless to say, their texts had ignited from there, and half an hour later they were tangled up in each other, her book forgotten.

Wednesday night she'd seen him at the Salty Hog, but her brothers and cousins had joined her after church, which was what they called the meetings of the Dark Knights, and in order to avoid their scrutiny, she hadn't spoken to Tobias. Instead, she'd texted him. *Your place, half an hour?* A cute blonde had sidled up to him as he was reading the text, and he'd responded with *I'm busy* and a winking emoji. Madigan, struck with jealousy, had quickly replied, *Your loss*, and had walked out of the bar. She hadn't gotten halfway across the parking lot before she'd sensed Tobias behind her, felt his heat and frustration, like a volcano ready to blow. He'd growled, *You getting jealous on me, Blue Eyes? Because that's not part of this game.* She'd continued walking and said, *Not even a little. You're the one following me.* He'd spun her around, taking up all her personal space, his big body pushing against her, dark eyes devouring her, but before he could say a word, she'd said, *I thought you were busy.* He'd reached around her and grabbed her ass, pulling her tight against him. The feel of him had made her insides go hot as he'd said, *Thought you weren't jealous.* She'd held his gaze, refusing to admit the emotion she hated, and had said, *You can fuck anyone you want. None of them will be better than me.* She'd barely gotten the last word out before his lips had claimed hers, releasing them long enough only to grit out, *You think I don't know that?* and drag her into the woods, where they'd torn at each other's clothes, and he'd taken her against a tree.

She shuddered. The memory of that risky night just as earth-shattering as the real thing.

She blew out a breath, returning her focus to the book she was supposed to be finishing. But as she read another steamy scene, it was her and Tobias she pictured, his hands and mouth she felt on her skin, her body flooding with heat. She grabbed her yellow highlighter, circled the scene, and took a picture of it with her phone. She began thumbing out a text—*Next up on our to-do list*—nearly jumping out of her skin when someone knocked on the window.

Starr peered through the glass, her kinky blond hair curtaining her face, the diamond in her nostril glittering from the interior light. "Are you coming?"

Not yet was on the tip of Madigan's tongue. Her mind had gotten a lot dirtier since enjoying sexy banter with Tobias. Pocketing her phone, and the unsent text, she shoved the book into her bag and climbed out of the car. She took in Starr's leather shorts, long-sleeved black shirt, and leather wrist cuffs. "Girl, you look amazing. I hope you have someone to share that outfit with tonight."

"Oh, I *do*. Me and my battery-operated boyfriend will be getting down and dirty while Gracie sleeps in the other bedroom." She touched her forehead to Madigan's shoulder. "Save me, Mads. I need a real man before I forget they don't have *Off* buttons and give them up for good."

"I've got several single brothers and cousins," Madigan offered.

"Blaine's too bossy, Zander's a player, Zeke needs to get off his ass and make a move on Aria, and Baz has no interest in marriage. Thanks but no thanks." She took a step back, admiring Madigan's spiked leather collar, leather bustier, and leather miniskirt, all of which she'd bought from Leather and Lace, her cousin Dixie Whiskey's husband's clothing line. "Wow. You look *hot*."

"Wait until you see what I've got in my goody bag." She'd bought a BDSM starter kit specifically for the meeting, and *maybe* to explore with Tobias.

"Come on." Starr tugged her toward the dunes. "I can't wait to see what Chloe has in store for us."

Chloe went all out for their meetings, and every month Maverick rallied their brothers to help set up whatever his gorgeous wife came up with. Madigan might not be looking for a permanent guy in her life, but if she ever did, she'd want someone who cared about and supported all of her interests, like Maverick did for Chloe.

Seductive music floated in the balmy bay breeze as they made their way down to the beach and were greeted at the end of the sandy path by Zander. He was a few years older than Madigan and was known for being a jokester, a shameless flirt, and a hell of a skilled carpenter.

His brown hair fell in front of his eyes as he opened his heavily inked and muscled arms, like he was going to swallow them up. "Welcome to a night of naughty book clubbing, ladies. Clothes are mandatory for my sister." His bright blue eyes shifted to Starr, and he flashed the Wicked grin women went wild for. "But for you, my blond beauty, clothing is optional. Although I have to say, I'm itching to be the one that peels *that* outfit off you."

Madigan rolled her eyes.

"You couldn't handle the stretch marks," Starr retorted. She was used to Zander's antics from the Salty Hog.

Zander smirked. "I've got something that'll *stretch* you, and I'm more than happy to leave bite marks."

"*Ohmygod,*" Madigan said incredulously, but as she did, she realized if Tobias had said that to her, she'd be totally turned on. She studied Starr for some hint of a spark between them, but she looked totally unfazed.

"Save it, Zan," Starr said as they headed over to join the others. "Gracie and I need a man, not a playboy."

He fell into step with them. "You don't know what you're missing."

Starr didn't even look at him as she said, "I've heard that before, and nobody has ever lived up to their self-professed hype."

"That's because you haven't been with Zan the Man."

As Zander tried to convince Starr to give in to a night of fun, Madigan took in the tiki lights flickering around a roaring bonfire, beside which Marly and Blaine looked to be in a hushed and heated conversation. Marly was wearing a strappy leather bralette with silver spikes and a built-in collar and one of her colorful skirts that had a slit all the way up to her hip. Zeke was pacing with his phone to his ear a few feet away from the group, and Chloe, dressed in a red leather minidress, was fussing over the food table, swatting Maverick's hand away as he tried to grab her ass. Steph and Sid were assessing the goodies on the table. Madigan was excited to see Sid, since she didn't usually participate in the book club.

Marly stalked away from Blaine, heading for a cooler in the sand by the food table. Madigan headed in that direction, but Blaine cut her off.

"Hey, brat," he said playfully. His thick dark hair was as tousled as always, making him look even more like James Marsden. "I hope you've got a sweatshirt to put on over that."

"Sorry, *Daddy*, but haven't you heard? I'm a big girl now."

He chuckled. "I'm just giving you shit, but be careful dressed like that."

"Aren't I always?"

He cocked a brow, and they both smiled. "I haven't seen much of you this week. Where've you been hiding?"

"What are you talking about? You just saw me Wednesday night."

"Yeah, for five minutes before you stormed out of the bar. What's going on with you lately?"

"Nothing. Just busy."

Blaine's brows slanted. "Busy, like seeing a new guy or busy like you don't feel like hanging out?"

"Wouldn't *you* like to know? What's up with you and Marly?"

He smirked. "Wouldn't *you* like to know?"

"You know she'll tell me."

His gaze drifted to Marly. "She's mad because I went out with someone she's apparently not very fond of."

"Does she have a reason to be jealous?"

Blaine scoffed. "Marly doesn't get jealous. She's pissed."

"If you two aren't together, why does she care?"

"Your guess is as good as mine." His phone rang, and he pulled it from his pocket, glancing at it. "I've gotta take this."

He put his phone to his ear. "What's up, Preach?" His brows slanted, and he headed for Zeke.

"Mads!" Steph, a curvy brunette with hot-pink streaks in her hair, waved her over to the table with the other girls as Zander and Maverick walked past, heading for Blaine and Zeke. Steph looked sexy in cutoffs, a long-sleeved red V-neck that had CURVALICIOUS printed across her chest, and a leather harness.

"Look at you all harnessed up," Madigan said.

"I know, right?" Steph said. "Can you believe I got Sid to join us?"

"I can't believe Gunner let her out of the house in those leather pants," Madigan said. "You look hot, Sid."

"Thanks, but he didn't exactly let me out," Sid said. She was lean and fit, with wavy brown hair cut just above her shoulders. She never liked being the center of attention and preferred T-shirts and jeans to dresses or skirts. "I didn't even get out of the bedroom before he had them off me and tried to make me wear *him* like a second skin. The horny bastard."

The girls laughed.

"You love it," Chloe said.

"More than you know," Sid said. "He's at the gym right now, working off his excess energy, because Steph showed up before he could plunder me."

Steph reached for a cookie. "Sorry for the cockblock."

"Clamjam," Madigan corrected, gaining odd looks from the others. "*What?* It's like cockblocking for girls."

"I told you it sounds grosser than cockblock," Marly said.

"Fine." Madigan glanced at the table, amused that Chloe had carried the BDSM theme to the food.

There were cookies shaped like a woman's body from neck to thigh, frosted with purple-and-pink lace-up bustiers and matching panties, pink lace garters with purple panties and tassle-covered nipples, and a variety of other sexy lingerie. Miniature heart-shaped peach pies were frosted to look like women's butts with colorful thongs, and then there was cleverly labeled Dip Your Meat cheese fondue, complete with penis-shaped meats, and an Eat All Night platter of tacos. The pièce de résistance was the use of BDSM accoutrements. Leather cuffs were used as cup holders, a ball gag circled a bowl of chips, feather ticklers rose from vases like naughty bouquets, and handcuffs, whips, and other toys dangled from ropes and chains around the edge of the table.

"This is *amazing*." Madigan reached for a cookie. "Chloe, did you make these?"

"No. I had everything catered by Evie's sister Brandy. But the Dip Your Meat was Justin's idea."

"Of course it was," Madigan said.

"Okay, that's it. I seriously need a man in my life." Marly grabbed a tickler and waved it at the girls. "Do you think this thing works like a magic wand?"

"That depends on what type of magic *wand* you're talking about," Madigan said, and the girls giggled.

Marly shook the tickler up at the sky. "Make me a guy who wants me as much as Gunner wants Sid and Maverick wants Chloe."

"You might want to ask for him to be hung like Gunner, too," Sid said conspiratorially.

"And as talented in the sheets as Maverick," Chloe added.

"You guys, I do *not* want to know those things about my cousin and brother," Madigan complained, and everyone laughed.

Steph coughed to mask her saying, "*Blaine.*"

Marly shook her head. "No, thank you."

"Did you really give him shit for going out with someone?" Madigan asked.

"*Yes.* The woman he went out with will sleep with anyone who has a dick. He's too good for her," Marly insisted.

"But you don't want him?" Chloe asked.

Without answering, Marly said, "Uh-oh. I wonder what's up." She motioned to the guys walking toward them shoulder to shoulder, their expressions serious.

Maverick went straight to Chloe and put a hand on her back. "I've got to go, babe. Club business."

"Be safe," Chloe said.

"What's wrong?" Madigan asked, even though she knew better than to ask about club business, since they'd never tell her, or anyone else who wasn't a Dark Knight.

"Nothing we can't handle," Blaine said, shutting down any further questioning.

"Text me when it's cool to come back and clean up. Love you." Maverick kissed Chloe and eyed the rest of them. "Try to behave."

"Why would we do that, when it's so fun to misbehave?" Steph teased.

"Hear that, Starr? Even Steph thinks it's fun to be bad." Zander snagged a cookie and dragged his tongue along the frosted crotch.

Ever Zander's gatekeeper, Zeke grabbed him by the arm. "Let's go, Casanova, before she gives you a black eye."

As the men headed for the parking lot, Starr said, "I can't believe they're leaving. I was sure they'd stick around because of how we were dressed."

Madigan arched a brow. "Have you learned nothing about

the biker world?" She glanced at the dunes. "I'm willing to bet there are no fewer than four Dark Knights camped out up there with binoculars."

AN HOUR LATER, their bellies full and their minds filthy, they were deep into their book chat with members from other locations joining via video chat. There were several conversations taking place at once, and Madigan tried to keep up, but as they discussed the erotic nuances of the story, she had to ask, "Is anyone else curious about trying out some of the sexy things they described?"

"Not anymore," Jules chimed in over video. "Grant and I already acted out all the spicy scenes, and I give them five stars."

Daphne, the cute blonde on the video with Jules, gasped, her eyes widening. "You *did*? I can't even get up the guts to ask Jock if he wants to."

"Ohmygosh, really? You totally have to. I'll babysit and you can seduce my brother." Jules winced. "Okay, that sounded weird. You should still do it, but don't give me the details."

Daphne blushed. "I wasn't going to."

"Has anyone else done a little kink exploration?" Madigan asked.

"I plead the Fifth," Chloe said with a giggle.

"Jace and I did," Dixie said via video from Peaceful Harbor, Maryland. "But I'd give my man *ten* stars."

"*Wait.* I can give more stars?" Jules asked. "Grant deserves a zillion."

There was a round of laughter.

"I bought a BDSM starter kit for anyone who's interested." Madigan picked up her bag, holding up the items as she named them. "Cuffs, a tickler, nipple clips, a collar and leash..." When she finished, she said, "Any takers?"

"I can't resist." Sid held out her hand. "Give me that collar and leash. I'll use it the next time Gunner's in the dog house."

"You go, girl." Madigan handed them to her. "Knowing Gunner, that'll get a lot of use. Anyone else want something?" After a few seconds of silence, she said, "More for me, then."

"If I were there, and I had a guy, I'd take some," Mia Stone, Jace's sister, a cute brunette from New York City, chimed in via video chat with her sister. "But I have to ask what everyone thought about that freaking hot dining room scene."

"That was a *hands-free* reread for me," Izzy Ryder said, chiming in from Maryland with Dixie. "I've never been so happy to have an ereader holder next to my bed."

"I need one of those," Starr said.

Or a booty call guy. Madigan remembered the scene she'd taken a picture of in the parking lot and the unsent text, *Next up on our to-do list.* She took out her phone and sent them to Tobias.

"I think we can all agree that the spice was top tier in this one," Amber Montgomery said, joining via video chat from Oak Falls, Virginia. "But the hero's backstory was heartbreaking, wasn't it?"

Murmurs of agreement rang out.

"Well, not everyone is blessed to have good parents or an easy life," Chloe said.

Madigan wondered if she was thinking about her absent father and worthless mother, or if she was thinking about Maverick, whose father was a no-good thief and his mother had died by suicide when he was just a boy.

"It was sad, but I thought it was an empowering story that proved there's nothing that can't be overcome if someone wants it bad enough," Steph said. "I gave my copy of the book to Bethany as a little more motivation to stay on the straight and narrow."

"I hope you gave her a vibrator, too," Madigan said with a giggle.

"I think the heroine saved his life," Sid said. "He was in such a dark place…"

Madigan's phone vibrated, and as the girls talked, she glanced at Tobias's response. *Noted. Want to know what's on my to-do list?*

She thumbed out, *Yes.*

Her pulse quickened as she stared at the phone, gripping it tighter with every passing second as she waited for his response. When it finally came, it was a hand-drawn picture of two stick figures in a shower. The female, complete with breasts, was standing with her hands on a wall, legs spread, and the male stick figure stood behind her, his enormous cock aimed between her legs. Madigan's body flamed. They had been getting creative, having sex on nearly every surface in her house and his apartment, but they hadn't made their way to the shower yet. She was imagining his hard, wet body when another text rolled in. A drawing of a male stick figure straddling a motorcycle and a woman straddling him.

"*Yes, please*" fell breathily from Madigan's lips, and she thumbed out the same.

Chloe cleared her throat, jerking Madigan back to the moment.

Everyone was staring at her with amused expressions. She

pressed her phone to her chest. "Sorry."

"Is there something you'd like to share with the class?" Starr asked.

"Uh-uh. Nope. No sharing. Nothing to see here. Just a work text." She shoved her phone in her bag, but that was all just a knee-jerk reaction. She'd told Marly about hooking up with Tobias, and she was dying to talk about him, but she was also worried because someone might mention him to her brothers or cousins.

"Real smooth, Mads," Sid said.

Steph cocked her head. "What are you hiding?"

"She's a Dark Knights princess, so the real question is, *who* is she hiding?" Dixie corrected. Her father, Biggs Whiskey, was Madigan's mother's brother and the president of the Peaceful Harbor, Maryland, chapter of the Dark Knights. All three of her brothers were members.

"Do tell, Mads," Evie urged, glancing at Marly.

Madigan wondered if Marly had already spilled the beans, and she glanced at her, too.

Marly held her hands up. "This one's on you, girl. You've got *sexting* written all over your face."

"You don't have to worry," Chloe reassured her. "Nothing other than book-related comments will leave this group, right, girls?"

Everyone chimed in, in agreement, and Jules said, "Girl code!"

"Okay," Madigan said. "I've been hooking up with this amazing sex god of a man, and it's…" She looked up at the sky, searching for the right words, before blurting out, "Dirty and delicious and *so* much fun!"

Several of the girls squealed.

"Details, please," Steph urged.

"Do we know this mystery man?" Sid asked.

"You don't know him, but you know *of* him," Madigan said. "His name is Tobias, and he's the strong, silent type. He's big, probably about six three, with thick brown hair that I *love* putting my hands in. Is that weird? I've never liked to do that before."

"No. I love Justin's hair," Chloe said.

"Hair is a synonym for *handle* when a guy's going down on you," Izzy said, earning giggles.

Yes, it is.

"What's his last name?" Sid asked.

Madigan thought about it for a second. "You know what? I don't think he ever told me his last name. I'll have to ask him."

"The sex must be out of this world if you didn't even get that far," Izzy said.

"Where did you meet him?" Amber asked.

"At the Salty Hog. Marly and I used to call him Mr. Mysterious, because he'd sit at the bar, have a drink or two, and never talk to anyone. He obviously goes there to unwind, or rather, went there, because lately we've been unwinding together." She wiggled her shoulders.

Steph and Sid shared a glance.

"This isn't the guy who didn't like your performance, is it?" Sid asked.

"How did you hear about that?" Madigan glanced at Marly and Starr, both of whom shook their heads.

"The guys were talking about it on the Fourth," Sid explained.

"Right before they went looking for you," Chloe added. "Was that Tobias?"

"Yes, but you should know he was right about my performance. I'd had a bad day, and I rushed through the set."

"Blaine said that's the same guy you and Marly were checking out several weeks ago. The night you and Marly were dancing and Blaine planted himself between the dance floor and that guy at the bar. Is that the same guy?" Steph asked.

Madigan would never forget that night. It was the first time she'd seen Tobias, and her heart had practically stood like a silver-backed gorilla and pounded on its chest, wanting to stake a claim on him. "Yup, that's him."

"He looked very hands-off," Sid said, worry lacing her words.

"He's just a private person, and I can assure you, he's very *hands-on*." Madigan grinned. "It's not like I'm marrying him. Neither of us is looking to get tied down. At least not *figuratively*."

"You go, girl," Dixie said. "But watch it. Jace and I started as a hookup." She held up her left hand, showing off her wedding ring.

"Don't worry. I'm in no danger of ending up in a committed relationship, much less married. He's not even staying in the area. We're just having fun."

"So, you don't care if he hooks up with other women?" Daphne asked.

"I didn't say that." Even though they'd been together every night lately, Madigan knew there would probably come a time when she had to face that uncomfortable situation. But she wasn't going to think about it until she had to.

"Of course she cares," Marly said, coming to her rescue. "She's female, and we're wired to care, but she's free to hook up with other guys, too."

"Not all women are looking for a husband," Evie said.

"I know," Daphne said. "I didn't mean it like that. When I was single, I could never sleep with a guy who might be hooking up with other women. Forget jealousy. I would've been too insecure, thinking he was comparing me to his other hookups. Don't get me wrong. I'm secure with Jock. I *know* he loves my muffin top and every single stretch mark, but if he'd been with other women when we were dating, I wouldn't have been able to do it."

"For the record, you're gorgeous, Daph, and I'm with you on this," Mia said. "I don't think I could do it."

"Hooking up is definitely not for the faint of heart," Izzy said.

"You'd know," Dixie said. "You've been hooking up with Jace's brother forever."

Izzy shook her head. "Jared is on my shit list at the moment, but I'm here for the makeup sex."

"I've never been a one-night-stand girl, so this might be a weird question, but, Mads, do you feel like he respects you?" Amber asked a little bashfully. "And do you respect him?"

"Yes. I think we mutually respect each other and the fact that neither of us is looking for more than what we're doing. But like Izzy said, hooking up is *not* for the faint of heart. I've definitely had pangs of jealousy."

"Do you talk or just have sex?" Amber asked.

"We talk and we laugh a lot. We don't talk about each other's lives or make plans, and I'll admit that took some getting used to, but I *like* hooking up with Tobias," Madigan admitted. "I've never been with anyone who made me feel as sexy and wanted as he does, and it's been this way since the first time we got together. Sex is *fun* with him, and our dirty texts make it even more thrilling. With him, I want to be dirty, and I *like* discovering that naughtier side of myself."

"Maybe I need a hookup guy," Steph said.

"You must feel really safe with him, Mads," Chloe said.

"I *do*. I can *try* or *say* anything without worrying that he's going to judge me or run his mouth about it." Her phone vibrated, and she pulled it out of her pocket. "Speaking of my dirty devil…" She opened the text, and another stick-figure drawing appeared. They were in the water, the girl's legs wrapped around the guy's waist. Her pulse quickened as a second text bubble popped up with a real photo of a pond or a cove. Tobias had caught part of his guitar, one jeans-clad leg, and his bare foot resting in the sand. Heat spread like wildfire up Madigan's chest. How could that little flash of him make her heart race? Another text rolled in. *Care to join?*

She quickly typed, "*Yes!*" and within seconds a GPS link appeared. Adrenaline surged through her, and she looked up from her phone, catching the girls watching her with bated breath.

"I'm jealous of that look in your eyes," Steph said.

"Just how dirty *is* that text?" Starr asked.

"Dirty enough, obviously," Marly said, and Madigan didn't even try to deny it.

TOBIAS GAZED OUT at the secluded cove he'd stumbled across a few weeks ago, listening to the peaceful sounds of crickets. The cove had become his go-to spot to write and clear his head, and tonight of all nights, he needed to be there. He'd had a difficult visit with his grandfather, and he was struggling to come to grips with the fact that his grandfather was on a permanent downhill slide. Witnessing his decline was eating away at him, and he'd thought the serenity of the cove would help, but it was too quiet.

Too lonely.

He'd never minded silence or loneliness until Madigan's nervous chatter, sassy banter, and sensual pleas began filling those voids. He'd texted her an hour ago, and he was starting to wonder if she'd decided to blow him off. Maybe the drawings were too cheesy. He wondered if she'd mentioned him to her friends. Had they talked her out of seeing him? He wondered a lot of things about her. Personal things he shouldn't care about.

But he couldn't help it. She'd already gotten under his skin.

He picked up his guitar and began playing "Elderly Woman Behind the Counter in a Small Town" by Pearl Jam. As he sang about a hauntingly familiar face he couldn't place and life catching up with him, the sweetest voice he'd ever heard joined in.

He turned as he played, seeing an angel who was usually disguised as a woman who wasn't looking for more than a good time but was now dressed to kill in a sinful leather outfit. Her bare feet gave her a hint of innocence, and she was beaming at him as she sang, her voice carrying in the air so electrified, he didn't know how they weren't going up in flames.

He stopped strumming, his body aching for her, his mind wanting her smile, her laughter, and the way she made real life disappear too damn easily, and his fucking heart…

No. He couldn't go there.

Kicking himself in the ass, he turned those thoughts to safer ones, eyeing her lasciviously. "Damn, Blue Eyes. Is book club code for sex club?"

"No. Keep playing. Finish the song."

"You want me to concentrate on a song when you're dressed like that?"

She dropped the blanket and towel she was carrying and touched his shoulder as she lowered herself to the sand beside him. "*Please?* I like hearing you sing."

"You like torturing me."

He leaned in for a kiss, and she whispered, "That, too."

She smelled like summer sins and winter fires, and the combination was as intoxicating as her pillowy lips and the sensual slide of her tongue against his.

"*Play*," she said softly.

He couldn't deny her, and as he played, they sang about recognizing breaths and memories and being stuck. Their voices escalated, singing about wanting to scream, and when they sang about both of them being there, he felt the comfort of those words, of her *presence*, in his core. Their voices softened as they sang the chorus about fading hearts and memories.

Madigan looked at him a little dreamily as he strummed the last chord, and damn, that was another look he wanted to see more of.

"What a great song," she said softly.

"My grandfather used to play it."

"He must be a cool grandpa if he likes Pearl Jam. Is he still around?"

"Yeah." He set the guitar down and leaned in for another kiss. "Good to see you, Blue Eyes. I thought you might've changed your mind."

"Sorry I took so long. I couldn't just ditch my friends."

Chalking up *loyalty* to another thing he dug about her, he

fingered her spiked leather collar, his dick hardening at the possibilities of what this show of leather might mean. "I'm curious about these friends." He dragged his finger along her jaw, down her neck, and traced the swell of her breasts, which were practically spilling out of her leather bustier. "Did they dress the part, too?"

"We always do. It makes it more fun."

"In that case, I'd like to request you read more of those kinds of books." He opened one of the six silver buckles running down the center of her top.

Her eyes sparked with desire. "That makes two of us."

"And maybe a story about a French maid." He kissed her jaw. "And a lingerie model." He brushed his lips over hers. "And a hot girl in a sexy *skort* on a Barbie mobile."

"A skort hardly compares to lingerie."

"You obviously haven't looked in the mirror when you were wearing one." He lowered his lips to hers in a long, passionate kiss that had her hands pushing into his hair. Taking her down to her back, earning the moans that drove him wild, he intensified his efforts. *God*, he'd missed her. How was it possible to miss her taste, her voice, the feel of her touching him, when he'd left her house at three that morning?

He ran his hand up her outer thigh, beneath her miniskirt, and squeezed, loving the moan slipping from her lungs into his. He pushed his fingers under the slim strip of her thong riding high on her hip. "I want to touch all of you at once."

"I believe you promised me some sexy water play," she said so sweetly, it contradicted the leather clinging to her curves.

"That I did." He kissed her again, deeper, more possessively. He brushed his lips over hers, holding her gaze as he unlatched another buckle on her bustier. "You're wearing this another night when we're indoors, because I've just added several games to our to-do list."

"And I've got the toys to play."

"*Christ*, Blue Eyes." *I like you way too much.* He reclaimed her mouth, chasing away the thought as he wrestled with her collar, and then with the rest of her clothes. "Too many damn buckles." She giggled at his frustration, and he bit her shoulder. "You're going to pay for that laugh."

"I'm counting on it," she challenged.

When he finally rid her of the leather and whipped off her thong, he flipped her over in the sand and smacked her ass.

"Hey!" She turned over, grinning from ear to ear, sand covering her gorgeous tits and enticing stomach. "I'm going to laugh at you more often."

"*I'm* counting on it."

He stripped off his clothes and swept her into his arms, sprinting toward the shore. She shrieked, clinging to him as he went chest-deep in the frigid water.

She buried her face in his neck, shivering, her legs tightening around his waist. *"Coldcoldcold!"*

"I'm about to fix that. Give me your mouth."

Their mouths came together in a frenzy of deep, devouring kisses. He wrapped one arm around her, grabbing her ass, and pushed two fingers into her pussy, earning a loud, salacious moan. Water sloshed over their chests as she greedily rode his fingers. He kissed her rougher, his body burning, aching, *throbbing* despite the cold water. He withdrew his fingers, aligning the head of his cock to her pussy, and broke the kiss. "I need to be inside you." Their eyes locked, mutual desperation pulsing between them. "Are you on birth control, or do I need to pull out?"

"I'm covered."

She crushed her mouth to his, and he drove into her. Bolts of pleasure seared through him at the feel of her tightness enveloping him. He held her there, the heat of her pussy radiating through his cock to every iota of his being. Holy fucking hell, he'd never felt anything so perfect and intense.

"*Ohmygod.* Tobias..."

Her pussy clenched, and her eyes found his, the astonishment in them burrowing right to the center of his chest. He tightened his hold on her, not wanting the incredible sensations to end.

"Don't fucking move."

"How can it feel this good?" she asked on a whimper.

He didn't respond. He couldn't. There was no explanation, and when her inner muscles squeezed again, tight, hot, and so fucking good, his restraint snapped on a groan, and he took her in a brutal kiss as they began to move. She used his shoulders for leverage, slamming down on his cock, meeting his every thrust with a squeeze and rock of her own. The buoyancy of the water allowed her to ride him faster, their bodies to slide easier. They feasted on each other like they'd never get enough, fucking like animals, moaning, crying out, nails digging into flesh, teeth marking territory. Raw lust and visceral appreciation for the beautiful, sensual woman riding his cock twisted together inside him like venomous snakes battling, his greediness for *her* consuming him.

He needed *more* of her, *all* of her, and he pushed his finger between her ass cheeks, teasing over forbidden territory. She rode him faster, breaking their kiss as she sank down, his finger breaching the tight rim of muscles.

"*Yes—*" she cried out, pleasure-drenched eyes snapping to

his as she rode his finger and cock, lasting only a few thrusts before she arched back, moonlight spilling over her face and breasts as "*Tobias—*" sailed from her lips.

Fucking glorious.

Her pussy squeezed so tight, he abandoned all restraint, their cries of ecstasy splitting the still night. As happened every time they were together, his climax felt endless, dredged from the depths of his soul, lasting long after she went limp in his arms. When the last of its clutches released him, he was dazed, blissed-out, and he held her tight, kissing her shoulder as she nuzzled against his neck.

"Jesus, Blue Eyes. We're fucking dangerous together."

He felt her smiling against his skin. "We were made for this exact moment, right here, right now. Together."

He stilled, steeling himself against the voice in his head that wanted to agree with her and the bone-deep pain it caused. "Don't say shit like that. You know where we stand."

"I...I know," she said softly, lifting her head to look at him. "I wasn't asking for more."

He couldn't tell if the shadows in her eyes were hurt or acceptance of reality, but either way, he had to be clear with her. "You sure? Because if you're catching feelings, we've got to end this."

"I'm not," she said sharply. "That's the last thing I want. I just meant the sex was amazing, and we fit together perfectly. This kind of pleasure is a first for me."

"Good, because you're a sweet girl, and I don't want to break your heart."

With an expression of pure resilience, she said, "You can't break a heart that you don't own."

Her earnest words hung between them. The thought of her

with anyone else made him crazy. He wanted to claim her, but he had nothing to offer other than a rap sheet and a promise that one day soon he was going to drive off the Cape and never return. But he wasn't leaving yet, and he didn't want to think about any of that negative shit. Shoving it down deep, he said, "You're shivering. Let's get you out of the water and warmed up."

"It's not just because I'm cold. Don't let this go to your head, but you kind of rocked my world." She slid down his body, and as they waded toward shore, she peered up at him with a devastating smile.

His chest constricted, and those unwanted thoughts tried to creep back in, but he kicked the motherfuckers to the curb and put a chain on the fucking door, refusing to get sucked into the darkness when all the light he could ever ask for was right in front of him.

"Too late. It's already gone to my head." He hauled her over his shoulder and slapped her ass again. She squealed with laughter as he carried her out of the water and set her on her feet in the sand. He reached for the towel to dry her off, and she crossed her arms, shivering harder. He wrapped the towel around her, and then he gathered her in his arms. "Your lips are blue."

"Then you'd better kiss me." She went up on her toes, looking so sweet and sexy, he wanted to build her a fucking fire and stay there all night.

He lowered his lips to hers, and she snaked her arms around his waist, pressing her cool, bare breasts against him.

"*Mm.* You're nice and warm."

"You keep rubbing your naked body against me, and things are going to heat up real fast."

Her smile widened. "Put it in your pants, Sir Broodiness. I'm still coming down from my last orgasm."

He chuckled as he dried her off and grabbed his T-shirt, shaking off the sand. As he slipped it over her head, she said, "I have clothes."

"Leather and water don't go well together."

He helped her put her arms into his shirt and towel dried the rest of her, all the way down to her feet. She stepped into her thong as he spread out the blanket, then sat on it, watching him as he dried off and put on his boxer briefs and jeans. He lowered himself to the blanket and pulled her back against his chest. When his arms circled her, she melted against him with a sated sigh, and he added that sound to the growing list of things he shouldn't want more of.

"Better?"

"Much. How did you find this place? I've never been here before."

"I was cruising around, exploring the area, after work a few weeks ago, and I ended up at the dead end where you parked. I saw the overgrown path and got curious. It's a great spot, isn't it?"

"Yeah. Very private. Do you come here often?"

He pressed a kiss to her neck. "You sound like you're trying to pick me up."

"Maybe I am." She shifted so she was sitting sideways between his legs and could see him. "So? Do you?"

"Fairly often."

"Do you always walk down random paths?"

"If I feel like it." He'd always craved the open road, but now he appreciated different aspects of his freedom in ways most people never thought about.

"What's your favorite thing to do?" she asked casually.

He cocked a grin.

She leaned her shoulder into his chest. "Besides *that*."

"Being out on my bike, or in a place like this, where I can hear myself think."

"Do you like hanging out at the Salty Hog?"

"It's a'right."

"I've never seen you drink much."

He shook his head. "I like to keep my wits about me."

"I've never seen you pick up anyone there, either."

"That's not why I go there."

"Why, then?"

She asked it earnestly, like she really wanted to know, so he gave her the truth. "I'm not much for attention. A place like that allows me to blend in. Take in life from the periphery. You're there a lot. What do you like about it?"

"Everything. My aunt Ginger and uncle Conroy have owned it forever. I basically grew up there. I like that it's laid-back, and as much as I hate being watched all the time, I like that it's safe. Do you have more places like this where you can take me?"

"Maybe." He hadn't thought before answering and realized he didn't have any special places other than his childhood haunts, and he wasn't taking her there.

She rested her cheek against his chest, and they sat in silence for a while. It was nice being with her like that, listening to the sounds of nature, letting go of his thoughts, and just enjoying the comfort of her.

"How long have you played the guitar?" she asked.

"A while."

"Did your grandfather teach you?"

"Yeah, after my mother died. He taught me all her favorite songs. The one I was playing when you got here was one of them. She used to sing it to me a lot."

"Aw, I love that. What else did she sing?"

"Just about everything. 'When You Come Around,' 'Free Falling,' 'Interstate Love Song,' 'Faithfully,' and a bunch of other oldies. What about you? How did you learn to play?"

"I taught myself when I was twelve so I could teach Zander to play."

"Isn't he older than you?"

"Yes, but he has dyslexia, and when he took lessons, he got frustrated trying to read music, so I learned and taught him."

"To read music?"

"No, but we found ways around that. He's incredibly talented, and he plays by ear."

"That's impressive, and your helping him is impressive, too."

"No, it's not. That's what you do for family, like how you helped your sister."

And then hurt her in the worst way possible.

"We all help each other," she said. "Zeke basically walked Zander through every assignment when he was in school to make sure he passed. He even went to community college his first year just to stick around and help Zan, to make sure he graduated."

Her voice was thick with admiration, and Tobias liked getting that glimpse into her family. "Zeke sounds like a good guy."

"He's the best."

"What's he into?"

"He's a nature lover and a fact hoarder. I swear his brain is one big encyclopedia, and he's unbelievably patient. At least most of the time. He doesn't do well with bullies."

"What do you mean? People bully him?"

"No way," she said. "I'd hate to see the fool who tried to bully any of my brothers. Zeke was a special ed teacher until someone made a comment about the kids and he beat the shit out of him and lost his job. Now he works with Zander and our father at our family's renovation company."

Tobias took note of what she said, and all he could think about was that Zeke was lucky the guy didn't die. How fucked up was that?

"Anyway, Zan and I write songs together."

"I remember him mentioning that the night we met. Play me one." He reached for the guitar, lifting it out of the case.

As he handed it to her, she leaned around it and grabbed his notebook from the guitar case. "What's this?"

He snagged it from her, his chest knotting up. "Shit. You don't need to see."

"Sorry. I know we're not…I didn't mean to pry."

She started to get up, but he pulled her back down between his legs, belting one arm across her. "It's not that. I don't share it with anyone." He didn't know if it was the deflation of her tone or the emotions rattling the chains of the dungeon, or both, but he wanted to give her some kind of explanation so she would see that it wasn't just her. "I write to get over shit and figure things out."

She peeled his arm off her and turned so she could see him again. "Lots of people have diaries. I do the same thing, but with songs."

Her gaze was soft, her voice compassionate, unraveling the knots in his chest. "It's not a *diary.*"

"Then what do you call a guy's diary?" she asked playfully. "A journal?"

"It's just a notebook. I've got dozens of them. I've been writing since I was a kid."

"Since your mom died?" she asked sweetly.

"Yeah."

"That's a good thing, Tobias. You didn't have to go all gruff and mysterious on me."

"Sorry. I'm not used to people touching my stuff." He put the notebook back in the case and handed her the guitar. "Are you going to play me a song, or what?"

She moved next to him and began strumming a tune, swaying to the beat with a mischievous glint in her eyes as she sang. *"Just sittin' here with a guy I screwed."*

They both laughed.

"He's mysterious, sexy, and a little bit rude."

He shook his head, loving her sense of humor.

"It's a good thing he's great in bed, because I can't get into his head." She smirked. *"But he's not here to stay, no, no, no. This broody boy just wants to play, play, play."*

He took the guitar, both of them laughing as he pulled her into a kiss. "You're pretty cool, Blue Eyes."

"I like hanging out with you, too, broody boy. But I am curious about how long you think you'll be sticking around."

"Long enough to get you back into that leather outfit and to my place, so we can live out a few dozen of our darkest fantasies."

"Oh, *goody*. I have a bag full of toys in my Jeep. Maybe you'll meet Mistress Madigan tonight."

He uttered a curse and hauled her into a deep, passionate kiss. "I look forward to being a *very* bad boy."

THEY STUMBLED INTO his apartment in a rush of messy, urgent kisses and rough, greedy gropes. Tobias had never been this gluttonous for anything in his life. Every time they were together, he wanted more of her. His hands moved over her leather fuck-me outfit, knocking her bag from her shoulder to the floor, their mouths fused together.

She pushed out of his arms, cheeks flushed, lips alluringly pink and swollen from the force of their kisses. "Wait." She spun around, bending at the waist to fish in her bag. Her miniskirt rode up, and he ran his hands up the creamy expanse of her legs, teasing between them. She swatted at him, giggling. "Hold on a sec."

"You want me to hold on, baby?" He reached around her, running one hand up the front of her thigh and between her legs, his other palming her breast, as he rocked his stone-hard cock against her ass.

She giggled, trying to push his hands away, and turned with handcuffs dangling from her fingers. "I could handcuff you to the bed."

His entire body tensed. "No fucking way. No cuffs."

"Then we'll save these to use on *me*." She turned, rooting around in the bag again, and spun around with a whip in one hand and a feather tickler in the other, the sexiest temptress he'd ever seen. "I'll just..." She flicked her wrist, and the whip snapped. She yelped, dropping it like she'd been burned. "That's out. Nope. No way. Too scary."

He laughed.

"We'll stick with this." She looked at the tickler with the

cutest curious expression. “It looks like a feather duster.” She stuck her ass out, waving the tickler, sexy and playful. “Maybe we should save it for the French maid costume.”

“Fuck the toys. I just want *you*,” he growled, hauling her into his arms and crushing his mouth to hers.

Chapter Eight

IF MADIGAN SNUGGLED any closer to Tobias, making those sweet little noises in her sleep, he was going to lose his mind. He liked this too damn much. *All* of it. Fucking her senseless, holding her as they drifted off to sleep, naked and sated, and waking before dawn to the feel of her trying to burrow beneath his skin. He hadn't slept through the night in three years, and he wasn't sure he'd *ever* slept as hard as he had last night.

What was it about last night?

He'd thought, or had convinced himself, he'd just wanted more sex with Madigan, but now he realized he'd been wrong. Holding her like this struck a chord he hadn't wanted, much less known was missing. As dawn rolled in, he was consumed by an inescapable desire for more of *her*. More of her sexy mischief, sweet giggles, and alluring glimpses into a life he could never be part of.

He'd fucked up last night.

Every time they'd been together, he'd ended the night telling her—reminding himself—that it'd been fun, but it wouldn't happen again. But last night he couldn't even force himself to step up and say it.

This was *it*. The end. No more dicking around.

He had to distance himself before he got in any deeper.

Before he broke the heart of a woman who deserved nothing but beautiful things and amazing sex. A woman who deserved exactly what she said she didn't want. Love, a ring on her finger, and a promise of forever.

She stirred in his arms, stretching like a cat, her supple ass grinding against his erection. Another sleepy, sensual, addicting noise slipped from her lips. That just might be the second-best sound he'd ever heard. The first being when she cried out his name in the throes of passion.

He ran his hand down her hip and kissed her neck.

She stilled and abruptly flipped over. "*Shit.* I slept over? I'm sorry. We're not supposed to—"

She pushed to her feet, and he grabbed her wrist, shocking himself. He should let her go, let it end. But he wasn't ready. He needed *more*. Just one more hour, one more fuck, a thousand more insane kisses.

He tugged her down to her hands and knees on the futon mattress, her luscious mouth close enough to lick. "The damage is already done."

Her gaze slid to his eager cock, and she licked her lips.

"You want to suck it or ride it?"

A needy, breathy sound fell from her lips. So fucking sexy.

"Are you wet for me, Blue Eyes?" He reached between her legs, his fingers sliding through her wetness.

She closed her eyes, a moan slipping out.

"Eyes on me, beautiful." When her eyes opened, he licked his fingers. "Sweet as honey."

Her tits heaved with her heavy breaths, and the hunger in her eyes had him reaching for her. "Get your pretty little ass over here and ride me until you cream on my cock."

A LONG WHILE later, after she'd come twice and he'd come once, her hands were pressed to the shower wall as he drove into her from behind, warm water raining down on them. The image of her riding him, her tits bouncing, eyes locked on him as she came, was etched in his mind. Just as this image would be. He clutched her hip in one hand, his other snaked around her, dipping to her clit. He'd learned to read her body, knew exactly what she needed and when to push for more.

"Tobias... Oh God—"

She cried out as her orgasm crashed over her, her pussy pulsing around him. He stayed with her, pumping and grinding as they rode out her pleasure. Unwanted emotions trampled through him. He tried to fuck them away, thrusting harder, taking her rougher, but it only drove them deeper, until he felt them taking root, sparking a storm that tried to rip those roots to shreds. Conflicting emotions pummeled him as she came down from the peak, her shoulders dropping, the tension in her body easing, as she panted out, "*So good.*"

He thrust harder, pumping up that storm.

This was it. It had to be the last time he'd ever be buried deep inside her. The last time he'd feel her come or hear the excruciatingly erotic sounds spilling from her lungs. Suddenly a selfish bastard, he was going to make damn sure she would feel him for days and think of him every time someone else touched her, wishing they could make her feel as good as he did. But he knew nobody would ever be able to, because she was fucking right when she'd said they were made for each other. Made for *this.*

He moved his hand from her hip to her ass, massaging the soft globe, rubbing circles over her clit with his other hand.

Her head fell back with a breathy, "*Yes.*"

He slid his fingers down the crack of her ass, teasing over her tightest entrance. She arched, pushing back against his finger. "*Tell me* you want it," he said gruffly, needing to hear her.

She looked over her shoulder, blue eyes boring into him. "I *want* it," she panted out vehemently. "I want your finger inside me while you're fucking me."

Fuuck. He pushed his finger past the tight rim of muscles, and "*Oh God, Tobias*" fell from her lips as her pussy clamped around his cock. He groaned, fucking her faster with both dick and finger and pushed his other hand lower, rubbing her clit with his palm as he fingered the seam of her pussy, feeling his cock moving in and out of her.

"You feel so fucking good. So *tight.*"

She clawed at the tile wall, and he moved his fingers back to her clit, quickening his efforts as fire spiked down his spine. She went up on her toes, and with the next thrust, they both lost control, untethered sounds echoing off the walls as they came, hard and loud, until they had nothing left to give. He turned her trembling body in his arms, their hearts hammering out the same frantic beat. Warm water beat down her back, and a full-on war waged in his head.

When their breathing calmed, she tilted her face up, her eyes moving from his face to his necklaces.

"You never take these off, do you?" she asked.

He shook his head.

"Where'd you get them?"

He was just about to shut her down, sever their ties, but decided to give her this small piece of himself. "The silver chain with the silver angel wing was my mother's." His mother had worn two of them, and she'd given them to him and his sister about a month before she'd died. *So you know I'm always with you, and you're always with each other.* "My grandfather gave me the leather one with the silver circle when I first moved away from home." *I don't know what it means, but I feel like you're supposed to have it.*

Madigan traced the silver circle with her finger, water droplets beading on her beautiful face. "A circle means so many things. Wholeness, unity, evolution. But yours is connected to leather, which is a symbol of power and protection, and those fit you perfectly. Did you know that silver manifests the main Moon principles? Connectivity, reflection, sensuality. I think you're all those things, too."

She blinked up at him through her long lashes, her trusting eyes twisting a knife in his chest. *She's been kissed by the moon and sung to by the stars...don't be actin' a fool.*

He'd already acted a fool, allowing himself to get lost in her, and she was going to get hurt because of it. It took all his willpower to give her one last kiss and take a step back, reaching for the bodywash. He needed to disengage, to wash off the proof of their connection and switch on a colder attitude, but he longed to bathe her, to caress her skin, and cherish her just this once. To treat her how she deserved to be treated.

He poured bodywash into his hand and did just that, taking his time, memorizing the feel of her soft, luscious body, which felt so different from when they were lying down. His hands slid along her hills and valleys, and as he washed away the bubbles, he peppered her freshly cleansed skin with kisses, murmuring, "You're beautiful, Blue Eyes…so soft and feminine." She made the sweetest, most appreciative sounds, trailing her fingers through his hair as he worked his way down her body. This was a type of nirvana he'd never known, and he wanted so much more of it, he knew he'd made a mistake. By the time he was done bathing every inch of her, he was hard again. He had a feeling even if he fucked her a million times, he'd still be hungry for more.

"Your hands feel so good," she said softly. "I'll wash your hair if you wash mine."

Fuck. He wanted that more than he wanted his next breath, which was why he refused himself the pleasure.

"No time. *Sorry.*" He forced himself to quickly wash up and step out of the shower, leaving her to tend to her own hair. He dried off and wrapped a towel around his waist. As he brushed his teeth, wiping the steam from the mirror, Madigan began singing.

"Whoooaaa."

God, her voice…It got to him every damn time she sang.

He was so fucked.

She sang about counting down the hours until they saw each other again and his touch being like a drug. Her sultry voice drove that knife deeper. He leaned his palms on the counter, blowing out a breath, his head falling between his shoulders as she sang about him being like a cigarette, a shot of liquor, and how she craved him, followed by a long, melodic, "*Yeah.*" When she sang about when they kissed, he lifted his gaze to the mirror, the steam swallowed his image, and her sweet voice threatened to steal his resolve.

He strode out of the bathroom, refusing to get any more

caught up in the angel who effortlessly drew him from his darkness. He put on boxer briefs and jeans and headed into the kitchen for coffee. There was a knock on the door. He raked a hand through his wet hair and went to answer it, thinking some dumb bastard had the wrong apartment.

He pulled the door open, and his chest iced over at the sight of Blaine standing on his doorstep, with Zander and five other large men standing behind him, arms crossed over their black leather vests, seven motorcycles lined up in the lot, blocking his bike in. Tobias squared his shoulders, hands flexing as he shifted on his feet, readying for a fight.

"I told you to stay the hell away from Madigan," Blaine said threateningly.

"As far as I can tell, she's a grown woman capable of making her own decisions."

Madigan's singing rang out behind him. *"It feels good to—"*

Tobias's gut fisted as she came to his side, her happiness shut off like a switch as she stalked past him wearing her leather miniskirt, one of his T-shirts tied at her waist, and a furious scowl.

"What the hell are you all doing here?" she asked with annoyance.

"Saving your ass," Blaine said sharply.

She scoffed. "I don't *need* saving, Blaine. What is wrong with all of you? Go *home*."

Blaine stepped toward her, and Tobias stepped onto the porch, inserting himself between them.

Blaine glowered and turned angrily to Madigan. "Then you know this son of a bitch, Tobias Fucking Riggs, killed a man and just got out of prison three months ago?"

Fuuck.

The color drained from Madigan's face, and she turned to Tobias, chin trembling, looking young and vulnerable with her wet hair, face void of makeup. "Is that true?"

The fear and disbelief in her eyes gutted him. There were a hundred things he wanted to say to plead his case and give Blaine hell for coming after him. But he knew she was better off without him, and if Madigan were his sister, he'd do the same thing, or worse. He forced himself to look into the eyes that had held such immense trust, now shattered beyond recognition, and confirm her worst fears. "Yes."

The air rushed from her lungs, and she gaped at him, eyes glistening with tears, her devastation nearly taking him to his knees.

"Madigan," he said gruffly, unable to hold back.

"*Don't*," she seethed, fury hardening her features. "I guess I should have listened when you warned me to stay away from you."

Tobias ground his back teeth, furious with himself for getting caught up in her and with her fucking brother for acting like he was better than him. But he told himself to let her go as Zander and a rough-looking guy with ice-blue eyes came to her side.

"Leave me alone," she snarled at them. "I've got to get my stuff."

"I'll get it," Tobias bit out.

"You've done enough," she fumed, and stalked past him into the apartment.

Blaine reached for his arm, and Tobias plowed forward, going chest to chest with him, sending him down the steps. "Back the fuck off. You got what you came for."

The others moved in, but Blaine held up his hand, stopping

them.

"You got *anything* to say for yourself?" Blaine barked.

"Why bother?" Tobias narrowed his eyes. "Sounds like you've got me all figured out."

"Sure as hell do." Blaine held his gaze. "You go near Madigan or the Salty Hog again, and it'll be the last time you go anywhere."

Tobias leaned closer, seething, "You think you know me, but you don't know shit. Be careful tossing threats like that around."

"It's not a threat. It's a promise."

"Then that makes you a worse man than me."

"You can stop your pissing match," Madigan said as she plowed between them, bag in hand. She turned a scathing look on Tobias. "I'm not stupid enough to go back for more."

As she stalked toward her Jeep, Blaine pointed to the largest of the other men and the guy with ice-blue eyes who had stepped up with Zander. "Tank, Maverick, you keep eyes on this asshole." To the others he said, "Let's go," and like little soldiers, they headed for their motorcycles.

Madigan shot those men death stares as they mounted their bikes and hollered out her window, "Do *not* follow me."

They paid her no mind, following her out of the parking lot like the fucking Secret Service guarding the president. Madigan's voice echoed in his mind. *There's something special about the president's daughter.* When it came to her, it was the fucking truth. He watched her Jeep disappear around the corner, feeling like his heart was being ripped from his chest.

How the hell had that happened so fast?

He turned away, trying to escape the pain, but the jagged edges of it all—being outed, Madigan's devastation, the hatred from the men she adored—tore at him.

Tank and Maverick stared him down like they wanted to tear his head off.

He closed the distance between them, getting right in their faces. "You think I'm such a piece of shit that I'd *ever* hurt her? None of you fucking know me. But if you want a piece of me, come and get it." He banged his fists on his chest, hoping they'd beat him so he could feel something other than the torment ravaging through him. "Go ahead. Give me your best shot. Fucking *take* it."

They stared at him, stone-faced.

"Fucking pussies." He stormed inside to do what he should have done a month ago and furiously packed his shit.

Chapter Nine

MADIGAN STRUGGLED TO see through the blur of tears and fury as she sped down the road, hoping to lose her brothers and cousins. The traffic light up ahead turned yellow. She gripped the steering wheel so hard her knuckles blanched and floored it, flying through the yellow light. Relief flooded her, but her victorious glance in the rearview showed five motorcycles speeding through the intersection. *Damn it.* They stuck to her like flies on shit, and that's exactly what she felt like. *Shit.* Why couldn't they just let her wallow in her anger and misery alone?

Blaine's voice slammed into her. *Then you know this son of a bitch, Tobias Fucking Riggs, killed a man and just got out of prison three months ago?* She'd seen the truth in Tobias's eyes before he'd even opened his mouth.

An angry sob bubbled out as she turned down the street that led to hers, the roar of motorcycles close behind. She saw Baz and Gunner fall back from the others, and she knew damn well they were going to take up residence a block away from her cottage. They probably had more Dark Knights posted at strategic locations in the woods around her house, just far enough away that Madigan couldn't see them but close enough to keep her safe. Her chest ached at the thought that Tobias was someone she needed protection from. She felt so stupid. She'd *seen* the red flags with him. He'd warned her away, and she'd *still* plowed forward like she had a reservation at Heartbreak Hotel, and she'd be damned if she'd miss it. But at the same time, she couldn't believe the one man who made her feel free and safe had *killed* someone. How was that possible? Wouldn't she have felt that kind of evil energy? Felt it in his touch? Seen it in his eyes? *Something.*

Tobias's face flashed in her mind, that now-familiar tug she'd felt since the very first time she'd seen him slicing like a knife.

She turned down her street and into her driveway, throwing the Jeep into park, hoping to make it inside before her bodyguards got to her. But when she climbed out of her Jeep, Blaine and Zeke were already climbing off their bikes. Zander must have hung back to stand guard at the end of her road. She hurried up to the front door.

"Madigan," Blaine called after her.

She ignored him, trying to hold her shit together as she unlocked the door.

"Mads!" Zeke ran up behind her.

"I *can't*," she said without turning around and rushed inside, locking the door behind her. Her heart raced as she leaned her back against it.

"Come on, Madigan," Blaine said through the door. "It had to be done."

"Go *away*," she shouted through her tears, chest aching.

"You know I won't leave you," Blaine insisted.

She heard him and Zeke arguing. Zeke was trying to convince him to give her space, but Blaine wasn't giving an inch.

How did such a great morning turn into *this*? Her brothers' argument escalated, and something inside her snapped. She threw open the door, seething at Blaine. "Why can't you leave me alone? Haven't you done *enough*?"

Blaine stepped forward. "I know you're pissed, but—"

"*No.* No *buts.* What you did was fucked-up. I'm your *sister. I'm* the one you should have come to, *not* Tobias."

"I *warned* him," Blaine fumed.

"You warned *me*, too," she shouted. "And so did Tobias. *I'm* the one who pushed to get together with him. It was *my* decision, and confronting him should have been mine, too. When are you going to understand that I'm *not* a child? How did you even know I was seeing him?"

"Gunner saw Kent at the gym this morning," Zeke, always the calm to her brothers' storms, explained. "Kent told him you came by the shop to have lunch with Tobias and that you two looked *cozy*. Gunner called Blaine, and Blaine looked into the guy. It didn't take much to find out the truth."

Fresh tears slid down her cheeks, the truth hurting more than it had the first time, which made her even angrier at herself. "You should've given *me* the chance to end things *my* way. You humiliated me."

"You didn't answer your damn phone," Blaine said gruffly.

Zeke shot him a narrow-eyed stare, turning a softer gaze on Madigan. "We were worried about you, and maybe you have a right to be pissed. I'm sorry, but we love you, and we'll take the heat of your wrath to keep you safe."

She snapped her mouth shut, emotions swamping her. She turned away, pushing her door as she stepped inside.

"*Mads*," Blaine said.

It was all she could do to close and relock the door before

her legs gave out, and she crumpled to the floor in an agonizing heap.

MADIGAN WASN'T ONE for pity parties.

After a good, hard cry, disgusted with herself for falling apart and for allowing herself to get hurt again, she scraped herself off the floor and tried to pull herself together. She changed into sweats and a tank top and threw her hair up in a bun. She debated burning the T-shirt of Tobias's she'd worn home and had even held it over a flame on the stove.

But she couldn't do it.

He'd killed someone. Taken a *life*.

She should be able to burn that shirt and walk away.

What was wrong with her that she couldn't hate him?

How did this happen? He'd warned her, and he'd been just as clear about not wanting to share his life as she'd been about not wanting more than a little fun. And she *didn't* want more. Or at least she hadn't. She hadn't expected that with every kiss, touch, and laugh, every stolen moment, quiet confession, and mind-numbing orgasm, he'd been weaseling his way into her stupid heart. But she needed to get him *out* of her heart.

He was a killer.

Why couldn't she believe it?

She was in denial. That's what this was. Denial.

Her phone buzzed for the millionth time. The damn thing had been buzzing like a vibrator on speed all morning. She silenced it and threw herself into work.

She spent the morning trying to outline therapy plans for

two new clients she'd picked up at LOCAL. But after a few hours of creating plans, being dissatisfied, and starting over again, she gave up. It didn't help that Blaine knocked on the door every half hour, trying to get her to talk to him, or that she couldn't stop thinking about Tobias and continually vacillated between being angry—at herself, at him, and at her brothers—frustrated with her inability to have walked away from Tobias in the first place and sad because even now, with as hurt and angry as she was, her thoughts kept scrambling back to the look in Tobias's eyes when she'd asked him if what Blaine said was true. She'd seen confirmation, but she'd also seen regret and about a hundred other emotions she'd been too shocked to decipher.

Even with his confession, she still couldn't believe it. She needed proof, and after pacing her living room for forty-five minutes, she forced herself to search *Tobias Riggs* online. The headlines gutted her anew. KEVIN "NAPALM" ARLO KILLED BY UP-AND-COMING FIGHTER TOBIAS RIGGS. There was a picture of Tobias standing next to an MMA fighting cage. His hair was short, the tips bleached blond, his face was clean-shaven, and he was smiling like he was on top of the world. He looked so different from the brooding—*broken?*—man she knew, she didn't believe it was him. She couldn't stomach reading the article and closed her laptop, shoving it across the table.

She'd thought she was getting to know him with the little bits and pieces she'd learned about him, but she hadn't even known he was a fighter. She looked up at the ceiling, missing Ashley. "I really wish you were here right now." Tears streaked her cheeks.

With her mind reeling and her heart in pieces, it took nearly two hours for her to regroup and find her footing again. She was emotionally exhausted, and in the hours since, she'd tried to read a manufacturing and distributing proposal she'd received earlier in the week for her expansion, but she was too distracted to retain the information and spent the rest of the afternoon watching movies, doing yoga, trying—and failing—to come up with new card designs, staring into her empty pantry, and experiencing every emotion known to man. She heard motorcycles come and go and ignored every knock at the door, which brought an onslaught of other emotions she didn't want to deal with.

Evening found her sitting on the dining room floor with a notebook on her lap, working on ideas for cards again. She heard her front door rattling. Still not in the mood to speak to her brothers, she shouted, "Go away," just as the door opened, and her mother peeked her head in.

"Sorry to use my key, but if I don't show proof of life in the next ten minutes, your brothers will break down the door. I'm just dropping off homemade mac and cheese. Is it okay if I come in?" Before she could respond, her mother held up a pint of Ben and Jerry's Half Baked ice cream. "I thought you might want this, but if you're not hungry, I can give it to one of them."

"I'm starved." Madigan moved to stand.

"Relax, honey. I'll heat you up a plate of mac and cheese."

Her mother joined her a few minutes later, handing her the promised plate. It smelled delicious, and she knew it would bring comfort, which she needed now more than ever as the simple act of her mother lowering herself to sit beside her on the floor made her heart ache. Her parents had raised her to be cautious, to watch her back, ask questions, and make smart decisions. When she'd gone to Spain, she'd spent weeks getting to know Alejandro and had thought she'd asked all the right questions. But the truth was, she'd been too starry-eyed over him to remember what she'd learned under the tutelage of her streetwise parents and protective brothers. She hadn't thought to clear away the leaves that had willingly fallen from the tree and dig into the dirt for the ones that had already been stepped on. Alejandro had known just how to sweep her off her feet, and she'd believed his lies, which had made his deceit even more painful. She'd gotten carried away with Tobias, too, caught up in how good she felt when she was with him, and she'd trusted him despite his shutting down their conversations. Under her mother's worried gaze, embarrassment at her recklessness set in.

"Are you okay, honey?"

"I will be," she said with more confidence than she felt, and ate a forkful of mac and cheese.

"I know you like to wrap up your hurts and kick them to the curb like they never existed, but this was a big blow. Do you want to talk about it?"

Madigan shook her head, eating another bite.

Her mother picked up the notebook she'd been writing in. "I see you've been busy."

"I was trying to come up with new ideas for cards."

Her mother read aloud. *"Roses are red, violets are blue, my brothers suck, and so do you."* She glanced at Madigan and read another. *"Secrets are like lies. Thanks for making me cry."* Her mother set down the notebook and touched her hand. "Oh, honey. I don't think these are going to go over too well."

Madigan put down the plate, unable to eat, hurt and anger clawing their way to the surface again, and spewed out, "I'm just so *mad*. I feel stupid. I can't believe Tobias *killed* someone. I know it's true, but I can't see him doing it." Tears slipped down her cheeks.

Her mother embraced her. "It's okay, honey. You should feel that way."

"No, it's *not.* I trusted him. He made me feel safer than I've ever felt with a guy, and I totally let my guard down in a way I swore I never would. And I know he's guarded, but he was slowly opening up to me, which I knew was hard for him, but I never in a million years would've thought…I should've sensed *something.*"

"You can't blame yourself, honey. Deception comes in all shapes and forms."

"But that's just it. I *want* to feel deceived and lied to, but he *didn't* deceive me or lie about his background." She dried her eyes, frustration taking the forefront. "He said he wasn't the kind of guy I should be with, and he was honest about not wanting to get tied down. But I wasn't looking for a relationship, and I was *so* drawn to him. I felt something between us that was deeper than chemistry, like we were supposed to meet, so I went for it, which you probably don't want to hear, but it's true. I *wanted* to be with him, Mom, and I didn't care if he didn't get along with his family or was leaving town soon, because our connection was that intense."

Her mother's expression turned even more serious. "Were you falling for him?"

"No." Madigan shook her head, refusing to go there.

"Are you sure? Because I know you, baby girl. I see how you look at Maverick and Chloe, and Tank and Leah and the girls, and Gunner and Sid. As much as you claim not to want a relationship, I think that heart of yours might have other ideas."

"It doesn't," she insisted, refusing to explore the ache in her heart that had been tugging at her all day. "I wasn't secretly hoping we'd fall in love and ride off into the sunset. I thought he was mysterious and intriguing and maybe even the most beautiful man I've ever seen. And yes, I *liked* that he was elusive, a little gruff, and not a people pleaser. I mean, look around us. That's the kind of men I grew up with. And then I dropped my Vespa off at the auto shop not knowing he worked there, and when I told him I was going to take an Uber to work, he drove me so I wouldn't get into a car with a stranger, and he waited to drive me home afterward."

"That's *interesting.*"

"That's not all. When I invited him in after he drove me home, he didn't accept. I found out why the next morning when my Vespa was in my driveway. He'd fixed it and dropped it off later that night because he knew I wanted to drive it on the Fourth."

Her mother looked intrigued. "That was thoughtful of him."

"That's what I'm saying. He did the kind of things Dad taught the boys to do. If we were at his place, he'd follow me home to make sure I got there safely, and he sent me texts to let me know he was thinking about me." *Many were dirty, but still.* "But I *saw* the red flags, Mom. I noticed how he shut down when I asked about certain things, but I never would have guessed that *this* was what he was hiding. I'm pissed at him for getting close to me and not telling me what he did, and I'm angry at myself for disregarding the red flags, but I am furious with Blaine and the guys. I can't believe Dad let them go after Tobias like that instead of making them come to *me* first. I can handle my own messes."

"We know you can. But, honey, your father didn't know what the boys were up to, and he's not happy with the way this went down. Apparently, as soon as Blaine heard Tobias had a record, he went off half-cocked and rallied the others. Your father looked deeper into Tobias's conviction—"

"I don't want to know the details. I *can't*. It's too much. I can't even believe…"

Her mother gave her hand a gentle squeeze. "It's okay, sweetheart. I understand. You can rest assured your father has given Blaine and the others a piece of his mind. He's been sitting outside your house all day."

"What do they think is going to happen? That Tobias is going to try to kill me? Because he'd never do that, and trust me, he's had ample opportunities."

"Your father is out there for *you*, honey. You might be all grown up, but you'll always be his little girl. When you hurt, he hurts."

"Is he disappointed in me? I'm probably the only person who could grow up with someone as all-seeing as him and have no clue that I was with a killer." Tears welled in her eyes, and her voice cracked as she choked out, "I can't believe he killed someone."

Her mother's brows slanted. "Honey, Tobias isn't a cold-blooded killer. He got in a bar fight protecting his sister and threw one unlucky punch that killed the man."

Madigan blinked several times in disbelief. "*What?* I don't understand. Is that even possible?"

"Apparently so. It was only one punch. They were in Vegas, and he was sentenced to five years for manslaughter but only served three."

"But Blaine made it sound like he…" Anger roared inside her, and she shot to her feet. "I'm going to *kill* him." Seeing red, she stormed out of the house and spotted Blaine pacing by his motorcycle, talking on his cell phone. She sprinted off the porch, past her father and Zeke.

Blaine turned around just as her hands connected with his chest, shoving him backward.

"What the hell is wrong with you?" she shouted, shoving him again. "He got in a *bar fight* protecting his *sister*, and you made it sound like he *murdered* someone in cold blood. That could've happened to any one of you. Maverick could have killed that asshole who attacked Chloe, and then what? Would you have gone after him, too?"

"It's our *job* to protect you." Blaine stepped closer, looming over her. "And you went sneaking around with a guy you knew *nothing* about after we told you he was trouble and to stay away from him."

"That was *your* opinion. *I* decide who I spend time with, *not* you," she fumed.

Blaine got in her face, nostrils flaring. "We lost Ashley because we didn't watch her closely enough. Do you *really* think we'd take a chance on losing you, too?"

She stopped cold, struggling to drag air into her lungs, tears welling. "Don't you *dare* use her death against me." She spun around on shaky legs, nearly barreling into Zeke and her father, and pushed past them.

"Mads," Zeke called after her.

She kept walking.

"Where are you going?" Blaine hollered.

She turned, tears streaming down her cheeks. "To see Tobias, and don't try to stop me. I'm going to tell him I'm sorry my brothers are assholes and *if* he'll still talk to me after being humiliated in front of his whole neighborhood, I'll listen to *his* side of the story and make my own fucking decision about whether I want to see him again."

"Don't bother," Blaine said flatly.

"Go to hell." She headed for the house.

"Tobias is *gone*," Blaine hollered.

Madigan froze.

"He packed his shit and took off minutes after you left," Blaine said. "Tank and Maverick followed him almost to Rhode Island before turning back."

Gutted, she stared at the ground in disbelief. He was *gone*? Just like that? She wasn't even worth an explanation? The ache in her chest magnified as that jarring reality sank in, but she closed her eyes, refusing to give in to the pain. She squared her shoulders, refitting the armor that had melted off under Tobias's heated gaze, and turned around one last time, meeting her father's disheartened gaze. "Now you know why I traveled and stayed away for so long." She shifted a steely gaze to Blaine. "I hope you're happy, because I'm sure as hell not."

Chapter Ten

THREE DAYS, FIVE new stories, endless frustration, and too many tears down. How much more did Madigan have to endure until she felt normal again?

She reminded herself that the first three days after a breakup were the worst.

But we didn't have a relationship, so we didn't really break up.

She gripped her Jeep's steering wheel tighter, mentally and physically exhausted. Between work, dodging her brothers, who she still couldn't look in the eyes without getting upset, taking calls and texts from well-meaning friends and family, and her own neurotic need to run through every scenario possible with regard to Tobias, her emotions had run the gamut. She wished she could turn her brain off, but even in the few hours she'd slept each night, Tobias was front and center. Sometimes they were wrapped up in each other's arms, but mostly she relived the awful confrontation with him and her brothers and woke up feeling sick.

But she was done wallowing, and as she drove toward LOCAL, she vowed for the hundredth time to pull her shit together. She was looking forward to seeing her grandfather and working with two new clients.

Her phone rang, and Marly's name appeared on the screen on the dashboard. Marly had shown up Sunday morning with muffins and coffee and had understood when Madigan had begged out of a long visit. She'd called a couple of times each day, and knowing Madigan didn't want to talk, she'd say things like, *Still breathing? Good. Just checking*, and then she'd hang up. Madigan couldn't ask for a better friend.

She answered the call. "Hey, Mar."

"Hi. I know you don't want to talk about it, but have you heard anything from you-know-who?"

Madigan's chest tightened. "No, and I still don't want to talk about it."

"Okay, just tell me this. Have you texted him yet?"

"*No*, and I told you I'm not going to. I refuse to chase a man who got all up in every inch of my body and left town without as much as a goodbye."

"He's probably afraid of your brothers."

Tobias's gruff voice traipsed through her mind. *Your brothers and their wolf pack don't scare me.* "No, he's not. It shouldn't be a big deal. He never planned on staying in town anyway, and we were just messing around."

"Then why are you avoiding your brothers like the plague?"

"Because of what they did and how they did it, and now I'm left with so many unanswered questions that I'll never know the answers to, thanks to *them*."

"But if not for them, you may never have known anything."

Madigan sighed, knowing she was right.

"Blaine's going insane, Mads, and I swear Zeke is planning an intervention."

"I know. I've listened to their voicemails." She'd briefly spoken to Maverick when he'd shown up at LOCAL before her shift Monday to apologize and to Zander when he'd brought a pizza as a peace offering later that night, but she hadn't given either of them more than three minutes. She couldn't. She'd had to escape before getting too upset.

"How long are you going to punish them?"

"I don't know. Maybe I'll send them Christmas cards."

"*Mads…*"

"I *want* to forgive them, especially after what Blaine said about Ashley." Her throat thickened. "But I get too upset when I think about how everything went down." She stopped at a red light. "Maybe I'm just so mad at myself, I'm turning it on them. I don't know. I hate feeling like this."

"You must've really liked Tobias to be this conflicted."

"It's stupid. He's shown me where I stand. Obviously the connection I thought we had was all in my head." The light changed, and she turned the corner. "Can we *not* talk about him? I promised myself I'd stop thinking about him."

"Okay, then I'll tell you about the date I have this weekend."

Glad for the change of subject, she jumped on it. "You have a date?"

"Yes, and if you'd stop hiding out, you could have been with me in P-town last night when I ran into Dante."

"You're going out with Dante?" Madigan was surprised. "I knew you thought he was hot, but I didn't know you were into him like that."

"Neither did I. But we hit it off last night. See what you miss when you don't hang out with me?"

"I wouldn't have been good company, but I'm happy for you. Be sure to ask him a zillion questions before falling into his bed, and be specific, like, *Have you killed anyone?*" Madigan knew Dante well, but she was beginning to wonder if she ever really knew anyone at all.

"I already did. He's never been in prison, never married, no STDs, and no little ones running around, as far as he knows."

"Damn, you're good, Mar."

"I know, right? We're going to the Hog Saturday night to watch your performance, and I was hoping you'd join us for a drink afterward."

Madigan knew she'd probably see at least one or two of her brothers and cousins, and dealing with them was the last thing she wanted to do. But she was going to be performing anyway, and she needed to get past this ridiculous heartache. "Okay. One drink."

"Yes!" Marly exclaimed. "I know just how to get you-know-who off your mind, too."

"Don't bother saying I should find another guy, because I'm done with all that. I've decided to fast-track the whole cat-lady thing, adopt a houseful of cats, and forget men altogether." She pulled into the parking lot of LOCAL, doing a quick visual sweep of the parking lot, looking for her brothers' truck and motorcycles, but the coast was clear. "Mar, I've got to go. I just got to LOCAL, and I want to see my grandfather before I start work."

After ending the call, she gathered her things and made her way inside to her grandfather's apartment. Her father answered the door, throwing her for a loop. How had she missed *his* vehicle? She'd been avoiding his calls, too, which wasn't fair, but she wasn't ready to have a conversation with him about the situation with Tobias. He was wearing a black T-shirt, worn jeans, and his black biker boots, which meant he hadn't come from work, and he'd ridden his motorcycle. His expression was so serious, people would be intimidated, but not Madigan, because when he looked at her, all it took was a second for those ice-blue eyes to turn warm as a summer's sky.

"*Dad.* Hi. I wasn't expecting to see you."

"Hi, darlin'." He pulled her into an embrace. "I've been worried about you."

"I'm fine."

He drew back, holding her by the shoulders. "That's what you said when you came back from Spain. Then you hid out in your bedroom and emerged months later with an attitude bigger than Boston and a business plan. So, tell me, baby girl, are we about to lose you to traveling again, or are you conjuring up your next business venture?"

She was always floored by how well her parents knew her.

"*Robert,*" her grandfather barked from the other room. "Leave that girl alone, and let her come in here and give her grandpa a hug."

Madigan smiled at her father as she slipped past without answering, but he snagged her bag from her shoulder. "Dad, that's my work stuff."

"Uh-huh." He followed her into the living room. "Then you won't mind if I take a look inside."

She and her grandfather exchanged guilty glances.

"You think I don't know you two are in cahoots?" Her father reached into the bag and pulled out a candy bar, waving it at them.

"That's *mine,*" Madigan lied. She brought her grandfather a candy bar every week, but what her grandfather hadn't yet figured out was that she put a sugar-free candy bar in a regular wrapper, so she had to keep up the ruse. "I get hungry between clients."

"Give her back that candy," her grandfather insisted. "She's a growing girl and needs her nourishment."

Her father pointed the candy bar at him. "You ought to be ashamed of yourself, swindling your granddaughter into bringing you this crap."

Her grandfather grumbled something indiscernible.

"Dad, I just told you it's mine."

He strode over to her, shaking his head. "You should know better than to lie to your old man. Just for that…" He ripped open the candy bar and took a bite.

"Rotten bastard," her grandfather said with a shake of his head.

Madigan set down her puppetry case by the couch, watching as her father made a disgusted face and began inspecting the candy wrapper. He glanced at Madigan, and she arched a brow, watching as her silent message set in.

He shook his head, tossing her a wink as his expression turned disgruntled, and he thrust the rest of the candy bar toward her grandfather. "You're right, Pops. I shouldn't be so greedy."

Her grandfather grabbed the candy bar. "Damn right. Respect your elders." He motioned to the armchair. "Now sit your ass down and let me visit with my granddaughter."

Madigan sat on the couch as her father settled into the chair, and her grandfather enjoyed his treat. When he finished eating, she said, "I take it Dad told you about Tobias?"

"Yes, as did each of your brothers and a few of your cousins who filed in here over the last few days."

Madigan rolled her eyes. "I swear they gossip more than the ladies in this place."

"It's not considered gossip when it's about family." Her

grandfather set the empty wrapper on the coffee table and sat back, crossing his arms. "I heard you gave Blaine hell."

"He deserved it. They all did."

"Maybe so, but they've been raised to watch out for family," her grandfather said.

"Not like that," her father interjected. "What happened was a tragedy, and that young man paid the price for it, but he was protecting his sister, and I respect that. Madigan was right. Any one of us could've been that guy any number of times." He turned a compassionate gaze on Madigan. "I wish it hadn't gone down that way, sweetheart, and I know your brothers regret it."

"I know they do, and I don't want to talk about it. You asked me if I was going to start traveling again, and the truth is, I have spent countless hours debating it these last few days. I miss traveling, and I miss my freedom."

"You're not a runner," her grandfather said.

"Grandpa, *you* ran away, and look how good things turned out for you." Her grandfather had run away from home at seventeen to escape an abusive situation, and he'd met the love of his life a year later. They'd raised a beautiful family free from abuse.

Madigan's situation wasn't abusive, but at times like these, it was oppressive.

"I wasn't running away from someone I loved," her grandfather said.

"I don't *love* Tobias," she said adamantly. "That's not what we were. We didn't even have a real relationship."

Her grandfather waved a hand dismissively. "Yeah, yeah, so I've heard. But don't fool yourself. You two had some kind of relationship, and you do love your brothers. You'd be running from them, too."

"I don't want to talk about them."

"Then let's talk about you and Tobias. You two trusted each other enough to share parts of yourselves," her father said without a hint of judgment. "That matters, honey. A lot." He leaned his forearms on his legs, but his eyes never left hers. "Running away won't help you heal from the hurt of his taking off."

"I *know*. Apart from feeling like I'm under everyone's thumb, I love being here, and I'm not going to let some guy ruin everything I've worked so hard to build. So you can relax. I'm sticking around for now, and I'm going to focus on expanding my business. I just wanted you to know I was seriously considering it."

"That's my girl," her father said. "Just be careful you don't take on too much at once. Unfinished business has a way of catching up with people, and if you're not careful, it can bite you in the ass."

"I think it already has," she pointed out. She and Tobias were about as unfinished as two people could get.

"Then maybe you'll get lucky," her grandfather said with a wink, "and it'll set you free."

MUCH LATER, MADIGAN left her first client's apartment, pleased with how the initial meeting had gone and excited to work with the kind, elderly woman. She made her way to her next client's apartment and knocked on the door, where she heard a singsong voice calling in response, "*I'm coming.*"

A petite woman who looked to be about Madigan's mother's age answered the door. She had beautiful thick dark hair, a friendly face, and warm hazel eyes. "Hi. You must be Madigan."

"Yes. Are you Elsa?"

"That's right. Please come in." She stepped aside, and as Madigan walked in, she said, "Thank you for accepting Hank into your program. The timing couldn't be better."

"Why is that?"

"Hank's grandson had been living nearby and visiting a few times each week, which Hank really looked forward to. But he's just moved away, and I think this will give Hank something else to look forward to."

"I hope so. As I'm sure you know, changes in schedules can be quite disruptive. How has Hank taken the news about his grandson's move?"

"They've always been very close, and in moments of clarity, which are few and far between these days, he's quite distraught over it. I guess in a way, where this is concerned, his waning cognition is a blessing in disguise."

"Well, maybe I can help. Puppetry can help bring out and deal with emotions that are hard to communicate."

"I sure hope so."

"I have some paperwork that I ask caregivers to fill out." She withdrew the documents from her bag and handed them to Elsa. "It's helpful for me to have a list of names of people he might bring up from the past or present, their relationships to him, and if you know anything about familial pets, childhood stories, or events, good or bad, that might come up during our sessions, that information will help me to decide which puppets to bring."

"Sure. Why don't I introduce you to Hank, and I'll get started on the paperwork while you two get to know each other." Elsa lowered her voice. "He's having a rather difficult day."

"I understand."

"He might snap at you."

Madigan nodded. "I'm used to it. Alzheimer's can steal the warmth from the sweetest of people and enhance it in others. We'll be just fine."

Elsa let out a relieved breath and led her into the living room, where Hank was pacing by the patio doors. "Hank? You have a visitor."

Hank Pettazzoni turned, angry eyes moving between Elsa and Madigan. He had wispy white hair, heavy jowls, his skin mapped with wrinkles and age spots. Before Elsa could introduce her, Hank smiled, and in the space of a few beautiful seconds, the smile reached his eyes, washing away the anger. "Carrie, do Nonno a favor, will you, please? Bring me my guitar." He pointed past Madigan to a guitar leaning against the wall.

"He thinks you're his granddaughter," Elsa said softly. "Nonno is what his grandchildren call him."

"No problem." Madigan retrieved the guitar and handed it to him. "Here you are, Nonno. Will you play me a song?"

"Only if you'll sing with me." He sat on the couch and patted the cushion beside him.

Madigan sat down. "I'd be happy to if I know the words."

He settled the guitar on his leg and leaned closer to her, lowering his voice. "If you forget, Toby will remind you when he gets home from the store with your daddy."

Madigan's pulse quickened as the names registered and "*Tobias?*" slipped out like a hopeful secret.

Elsa said, "Yes, his grandson."

As Hank sang "Elderly Woman Behind the Counter in a Small Town," Madigan was thrown back to the cove, to Tobias's gravelly voice, and the peaceful look in his eyes she'd glimpsed for only a few seconds before he'd focused on her. The moment their gazes had connected, she'd felt a gust of energy so intense, she was sure they'd gotten caught in a sudden electrical storm, her every heartbeat an explosion of heat lightning, every breath magnetic, drawing her to him.

His grandfather nudged her with his knee, pulling her back to the moment. She struggled to keep her emotions in check as she joined him in singing about love and memories fading away, her mind trickling back to when Tobias had driven her to work. Had he come to see his grandfather that day? Had he moved there to be near him, just as she had with her grandfather?

Could Marly have been right? Had her brothers scared him away from the one place he longed to be? Her attention was drawn to a framed photograph on the wall of a teenage Tobias in a boxing ring, wearing headgear and shorts, eyes dancing with excitement, his gloved hands in the air like he'd just won the match. To the right of that picture was another of a skinny little Tobias at six or seven standing between his mother and a little girl who looked to be about three or four. *Carrie?* He was holding their hands and looking adoringly up at his mother.

Sadness swamped her. She longed for answers she'd never get and ached for the little boy his grandfather remembered and for the man she wanted to know better.

As the song came to an end, she forced herself to make a painful, mental correction *not* to long for the man who had driven away without giving her a second thought. Instead, she ached for the starry-eyed girl who'd sworn she'd never get swept away again and for the romantic-hearted woman who had gotten caught up in the gusty winds of the wrong man.

Chapter Eleven

MADIGAN PLOWED THROUGH the second half of the week writing music to go along with her new stories, which were filled with as much anger as sadness, puppeteering at two birthday parties, negotiating distribution and merchandising for the Mad Truth expansion, and then falling into bed and overthinking every word, glance, and touch she and Tobias had shared, until she could no longer keep her eyes open.

She'd been stupid to let her guard down, and it pissed her off that she was still thinking about him despite her determination to get back to normal. Tobias was probably out there winning over some other woman's reluctant heart with his mysterious broodiness and innate ability to drive her wild. Would she have blue eyes, too? Would he call *her* Blue Eyes?

Despite herself, she glanced toward the bar from her perch on the stage, secretly hoping to see Tobias standing there, those brooding eyes watching her. Forcing herself to look away, she played harder, sang louder, pushing away the frustration as the last of her story flew vehemently from her lips toward the crowd at the Salty Hog. *"I won't break, won't break, won't break. Not from heartache, heartache, heartache. I've already danced with the devil, and the devil's got nothing on me."* She strummed lighter, singing softer. *"The dirty-bastard devil's got nothing on me."*

Applause rang out, and seated patrons shot to their feet, blowing her away as they cheered, calling out for more.

"Way to go, Mads!" Blaine shouted.

Her chest tightened as she looked over the crowd, past Marly's table, where she and Dante were clapping, and found Blaine standing by the windows with Zeke and Zander, the three of them chanting her name, fists in the air. She was still angry, but carrying the anger and hurt was exhausting, and she *missed* them. It was too much to try to deal with in front of a bar full of people. Tearing her gaze away, she pushed to her feet and thanked the crowd, wishing she hadn't made eye contact with her brothers and stirred up all the annoyance she'd been trying to ignore.

She left the stage and headed into the back room to put her guitar away. Her phone vibrated in her pocket, and she pulled it out, reading her mother's message. *Grandpa's coming for breakfast Sunday at 8am. Join us?* Madigan sent a quick reply saying she'd be there.

"That was a great set," Blaine said from behind her, sending her emotions reeling.

She pocketed her phone and zipped her guitar case. "Thanks."

"I'm sorry for pissing you off, but this silent treatment needs to end."

She turned to face him, trying her best to remain calm. "See, Blaine, this is where you're wrong. You don't get to decide what I'm allowed to feel."

"I'm not trying to. But you're shutting us out like you did when you came back from Spain. We know bad shit went down there, and we *still* don't know what it was."

Her stomach knotted. "And you never will, because it's none of your business."

"You're our *sister*. Anything that hurts you *is* our business."

She rolled her eyes.

"I'm not asking what happened back then," he fumed. "Just *tell me* what I can do to fix things now, because I fucking hate this. We all do."

"Then maybe you shouldn't have barged into my life, guns loaded."

His eyes narrowed. "We've been over this. We were worried about you."

"I hear the words coming out of your mouth, but they make no sense. Tobias was *protecting* his sister."

"So was I."

"From *what*? Tobias wasn't a threat to me."

"He rubbed me the wrong way, and think about it, Mads," he pleaded. "He got close to you without revealing his shit. That's just *wrong*."

"That's *my* body, *my* decision." She planted a hand on her hip. "I'm sure you don't tell every woman you mess around with everything you've done in your life."

"That's different. I've never killed anyone."

Her hands fisted in frustration. "I'm not doing this with you."

"Because you know I'm right," he said firmly.

"It doesn't matter if I *wish* he'd told me or not. He was opening up to me, and I was okay with it happening slowly. That was *my* decision to make, not yours to judge."

Blaine's eyes remained stern, but his tone softened. "He didn't fight for you, Mads. Why are you fighting for him?"

That stung, but she somehow managed to keep her composure. "I'm not fighting for him. I'm fighting for myself. I love you, and I know you mean well, but I don't need to be under your thumb anymore." She grabbed her guitar case. "Now, if you'll excuse me, I promised Marly I'd have a drink with her and her *date*."

She swore Blaine grimaced, but instead of lightening the air and teasing him about making his move before he missed out, she left the room with her chin high and her heart heavy. Making her way toward Marly, she tried to temper the sting of his words—*He didn't fight for you*—and drag herself out from under the frustration and grief that came from arguing with the brother she loved. But she *had* to stand up for herself.

Marly and Dante were talking quietly as she approached. Marly looked beautiful in a vibrant floral cap-sleeved low-cut dress, and Dante was as handsome and real as ever. The man didn't dress up for anyone. His brown hair looked finger combed, his scruff unmanicured, and his faded T-shirt looked like an old favorite. But the smile in his eyes told Madigan he was into Marly.

"There she is." Marly got up to hug her. "We were just talking about how much we loved your set."

"Thanks."

Dante stood, bending to kiss her cheek. "You nailed it, Mads." He pulled out a chair for her.

"Thank you. That last song was a new one. I was a little worried about how it would go over."

"The Dirty-Bastard Devil?" Marly raised her brows. "It was darker than your usual stuff, but *so* good."

"What—or *who*—inspired it?" Dante asked.

Madigan glanced at Marly, nearly missing the slight shake of her head, indicating she hadn't told him about Tobias.

Relieved, she said, "Years of dating the wrong guys."

Starr sidled up to the table to take their orders. "I've got something special on tap for you tonight, Mads." She nodded across the room to three good-looking guys standing by the dance floor. The tallest of them lifted his chin. "He's been trying to get your attention all night. I did some recon. He's here from Florida for a week with his brothers, there's no ring on his left hand, and he seems nice."

"In that case," Madigan said, "I'll just have iced tea, nonalcoholic, please." Tired and drunk was never a pretty combination.

"Okay. Coming right up."

After Starr went to fill her order, Madigan mustered a smile for Marly and Dante. "So, how's the big date going?"

"I couldn't ask for better company." Dante looked appreciatively at Marly.

Marly gazed dreamily at him, and as they told Madigan about the restaurant they'd gone to and the walk they'd taken through the nearby galleries, they shared intimate glances, finished each other's sentences, and laughed when they said the same things at the same time. Madigan couldn't help being a little jealous. Her mother was right. Her heart did have other ideas, because it was tiptoeing down a painful path, wondering if she and Tobias would have ever gotten that far. They might not have been looking for a relationship, but her father and grandfather were right, too. The trust they shared was in and of itself a type of relationship.

She stayed for one drink, as promised, hoping she wasn't a downer for Marly and Dante. She hugged them, thanked them for a fun time, and went to get her guitar.

Her uncle sidled up to her as she left the back room. "Hey,

kiddo. How're you holding up?"

"I'm fine, Uncle Con."

"*Mm-hm.* Fine in female-speak means you're not, but you don't want to talk about it. That's okay."

"Aunt Ginger taught you well," she said with a smile.

"That she did. I've been keeping my nose out of your business, but you know if you need a place to escape to while you sort out your feelings, or if you just want to bend our ears, Ginger and I are here for you."

"I know. Thank you." She started to leave but stopped herself and said, "It's times like these that I miss Ash the most."

"I know, darlin', but she's still with us. Blaine told me you gave him hell, and I'd bet Ashley's cheering you on."

Laughter bubbled out past the lump forming in her throat. "I can't believe Blaine told you."

"He's having a rough time. He knows he jumped the gun with Tobias, but he didn't like finding out that you didn't know about Tobias's past."

"But that's on *me*, not Tobias. I knew he had secrets, and I could've walked away. Tobias *tried* to get me to, but I saw something in him, and I felt something between us that I wanted to explore, and never once did I feel unsafe with him."

"I don't think you would've been with him if you did, and I don't think Blaine does either." A compassionate smile appeared on his handsome face. "Right or wrong doesn't go very far when it comes to the people you love. If you ask me—which you didn't, but I'm going to give you my two cents anyway because I love you both and hate to see you at odds—Blaine wasn't there to protect you when you studied overseas, and he doesn't want to miss something and see you get hurt again."

"He told me that, and I appreciate you trying to help." She

glanced toward the bar, where Blaine sat drinking a beer, her heart aching. "We'll figure this out at some point. It's just…" *I'm still too hurt.* "I really have to go." She gave him a quick hug and wove through the crowd, trying not to let her guilt weigh her down.

She pushed through the door and into the muggy night. As she descended the steps toward the parking lot, the scents of the sea brought memories of July Fourth, when she'd stumbled upon Tobias playing his guitar. *You stalking me again, Blue Eyes?* She swallowed against the emotions rising within her. How could she miss him *this* much? Maybe she should have joined Blaine at the bar and drank herself into oblivion. Maybe then she'd forget the way Tobias had looked at her like he couldn't look away and touched her like he couldn't get enough.

God, I'm such a loser. Just let him go already.

She slid her arms through the straps of her guitar case so it rested on her back and glanced at the woods as she crossed the parking lot. It was hard to believe that less than two weeks ago they'd given in to the raging passion between them right there in the trees. Arousal flared hot and bright inside her with memories of his rough hands groping her as they lost themselves in each other. She could still feel the bark of a tree abrading her palms.

Why did she do this to herself?

Her phone vibrated, startling her from the memory. There was only one person she wanted to talk to, and she knew it wasn't him, so she ignored it. When she reached her Vespa, her phone vibrated again. Annoyed, she pulled it out of her pocket and stared at Tobias's name on the screen in disbelief, pulse quickening, mind racing as she debated not reading the text. But she could no sooner leave it unread than forget him. With a shaky thumb, she opened the message, and a picture of a peach appeared. A lump lodged in her throat.

He was thinking of her.

Another text popped up, and a whole line of peaches appeared. She inhaled a ragged breath, her heart pounding. For the first time in a week, she felt a spark of hope, but she didn't know if she should cling to it or run from it.

"That was a hell of a performance, Blue Eyes."

Tears sprang to her eyes as Tobias stepped from the shadows of the tree line, and her heart cracked open.

MOONLIGHT ILLUMINATED THE tears slipping down Madigan's cheeks, each one cutting Tobias deeper, but *God,* for the first time in a week, he felt like he could breathe. He wanted to take her in his arms and never let her go, but he knew he'd be lucky if she stuck around long enough to have a conversation. *Please don't tell me to fuck off.*

Madigan lifted her chin, not bothering to dry her tears, eyes narrowing. "You disappear for a week, and that's what you open with?"

He stepped closer, too drawn to her to stay away. "Isn't that where we started?"

A sad smile tugged at her lips, but it didn't last. "You left me high and dry, like I meant nothing to you—which is fine, because we weren't anything anyway, but it was still a shitty thing to do."

"I know, and I'm so fucking sorry. I thought I was doing the right thing by leaving. I caused a shit show with your family, and you didn't need more of that. I drove for three days, trying to get as far away from you as I could. Trying to forget you and the pain I know I caused. But I couldn't stop thinking about you, and I couldn't stay away knowing I'd hurt you. I'm so damn sorry, Blue Eyes." He stepped forward, but she stepped back. He took the gut punch and held his hands up in surrender. "I just want to talk."

Her lower lip trembled, and she swiped at her eyes, her strong will winning out. "You were in prison, and you were a fighter, and I had *no* idea about either of those things. I thought I was getting to know you, but I'm not sure I knew you at all."

"You didn't know my background, but you sure as hell were getting to know *me*."

Turbulent, conflicting emotions warred in her eyes. "Why'd you come back?"

"Because I never should have left. You deserve to hear the truth directly from me."

"I *know* the truth."

"You know what the media reported, but you don't know the whole story. Can we please go someplace to talk? That's all I'm asking for. I promise I won't try anything."

She looked over her shoulder at the restaurant.

"I'm not afraid of your brothers, Madigan. That's not why I left. I left to keep from causing you more trouble. If you want to tell them I'm here, go right ahead. I don't give a damn what anyone thinks about me, except *you*, and I'm not leaving until you've heard the whole truth."

He thought he saw the longing he felt mirrored in her eyes, but it was shadowed by too many other emotions to be sure. "I don't want to talk here."

"Where, then? Your place? My apartment? Someplace public if you're scared to be alone with me. I'll go anywhere you want."

"Your place. I'll meet you there."

Chapter Twelve

TOBIAS PACED HIS living room. He'd thought he was prepared to tell Madigan everything, but now that she was there, sitting on his futon with heartache written all over her, he hated himself even more for leaving. He'd hoped to make this as painless as possible for her, but he knew that wasn't a possibility.

"I'm not sure where to start. Do you just want to know how I landed in prison, or—"

"I want to know *you*, Tobias, not just about what you did."

Thank God. "Then I'll start with the basics. I grew up in Bourne, and I had a great life before my mother died. My sister and I were close, and she could be a pain in the ass, but I'm sure I was to her, too. My father is a district manager with a computer company in Hyannis. He was a good father when I was a kid, and my mother worked at a restaurant part time while we were at school. She was laid-back and loved music and baking. She sang all the time, and there was always something delicious waiting for us after school. My grandmother died of ovarian cancer, and by the time my mother was diagnosed, her cancer had already metastasized." He paused, trying to stall the emotions creeping up his chest. "She wasn't afraid of anything other than not being there for us. You'd think she'd get regular checkups because of that. She told my father she did, but..." He shook his head trying to escape the pain that stirred. "I guess she thought if she didn't know about it, it wouldn't kill her."

"Oh, *Tobias*," Madigan said softly.

"It's okay. I accepted it a long time ago. People make bad decisions, and the rest of the world is left to live with them." He knew that all too well. "Anyway, as you can imagine, after she died, things pretty much sucked. I told you how anxious Carrie was, but that was just the start of it. Our mother's absence left a gaping hole in our lives. The house was too quiet, my father was resentful that she'd lied to him and hadn't taken care of herself, and I think my sister and I felt that way too for a while. Her death felt like a living, breathing thing in the house that we couldn't talk about around my father because it upset him, which made it worse. My father did his best to hold us together, but he worked a lot, and I took care of Carrie."

"Did you and Carrie talk about your mom?"

"Yeah, and that helped some, but Carrie is four years younger than me, and she was only nine. I didn't know if I was doing the right thing because she'd get so upset."

"Is that when you started writing?"

He nodded. "My grandfather stepped in when he could, teaching me to play guitar and refusing to let us forget a single thing about our mother. I listened to all of his stories, but like you, I found it easier to write than to share what I was feeling. He's been my savior in a lot of ways, consistently supporting my decisions, even when my father didn't." Guilt for leaving his grandfather tightened in his chest.

"Your grandfather is Hank Pettazzoni, right? He lives at LOCAL?" Madigan asked softly.

"Yes."

"I just started working with him. Did you ask Elsa to get him into my program?"

He nodded, relieved that she'd taken him on as a client. "The first time we met. Thank you for working with him. How is he?"

"Good. We only had one introductory meeting so far. He thought I was Carrie, but he played his guitar for me, and when I showed him my puppets, he thought one looked like you and told me all about his grandson who wrestled and boxed and took great care of his little sister. I'm looking forward to working with him."

Tobias smiled. "He came to all my high school wrestling and boxing matches. He's the reason I came here after I got out of prison, but I'll get to that. I want you to know how things evolved."

"I appreciate that."

"My father pushed hard for me to go to college, but I wasn't into it. I was never great at school, and my grandfather tried to make him understand, but he didn't get very far. I had worked at an auto shop while I was in high school, and I went full-time after graduation. I knew I didn't want to be a mechanic forever, but I had no idea what I wanted to do, and my father rode my ass about it every day, which didn't help his side of things."

Her brows knitted. "Not everyone is meant to go to college."

"He didn't see it that way. The guy who owned the auto shop took me under his wing, teaching me everything he knew. A few years later he suggested I get my ASE certificate, and once I did, he told me I needed to move on."

"That doesn't make sense."

"I didn't think so either, but it did. He said I was too good to stick around and get paid peanuts, and he hooked me up with a guy who owned a shop in New Jersey servicing high-end cars. His friend offered me twice what I was earning. It was a no-brainer to head to Jersey and start to build my life."

"How did your dad take it?"

"He wasted no time letting me know how much of a disappointment I was."

"That's awful. And Carrie?"

"It had been me and her against the world for so long. She wasn't very happy about me moving away, but she understood, and she still had our grandfather nearby. But she made me promise to call her every week."

Madigan smiled. "I'm glad she was supportive."

"Me too. I kept my promise, and she'd come stay with me some weekends, which was cool. I'd been working in Jersey for about a year and a half when I met Kevin Arlo, the guy…" He couldn't stomach saying *The guy I killed.*

"I know who he is." She held his gaze, which was a lot more than his sister, father, or ex had done.

"He was in town for a fight and came into the gym where I was working out. He saw me sparring and struck up a conversation. He was a few years older than me, making his way up the professional circuit. He said he was impressed with my fighting and asked if I'd ever considered doing it professionally. As a kid I'd dreamed of being a fighter, but my father didn't approve of me being on the high school wrestling and boxing teams, so I let that go. I went to see Kevin's match, and he asked me if I wanted to give it a try. He said he'd mentor me and get me in with his coach. I was twenty-two with nothing tying me down. He was the kind of guy who could pump you up about anything—he was loud, aggressive, and so full of positivity about the sport, it was impossible not to want to be part of it. I took him up on the offer and gave my notice. Two weeks later I moved to New York to train, and I was *good.*"

"Did you enjoy it?"

"I fucking *loved* it. I felt like I'd finally figured out where I belonged and had a future I could count on."

"Do you miss it?" she asked carefully.

"Hell yeah, and the camaraderie with other fighters and coaches that went along with it," he said honestly. "But that part of my life is over, and I lost a lot getting there. My father stopped speaking to me, but by then I'd accepted that short of getting a college degree and working in an office, there was no way to win his approval."

"That's so sad. I can't imagine one of my parents turning their back on me."

"It is what it is. Things might have been different if my mother hadn't died, but you can't live in a world that isn't real."

"Was he that way with your sister?"

"Not at first. I mean, he had trouble with her anxiety, but he was supportive of her when she went away to college. She and I saw each other as often as we could. I kept in touch with my grandfather, and he and Carrie came to a few of my fights. After Carrie graduated, she came to stay with me in Jersey and got a job as a dietitian at the hospital. I was seeing a girl named Michelle, and she was practically living at my place. They got along well, and Kevin and Carrie had gotten to know each other through her visits. I knew they were attracted to each other, but nothing had ever happened between them. A few months after Carrie moved in, Kevin asked if I'd be cool with him asking her out."

He stopped pacing and crossed his arms, a buffer between the awful feelings mounting inside him and the beautiful woman watching his every move. "He was my closest friend. He was seven years older than her, which I wasn't crazy about, but I trusted Kevin and I knew she was wild about him, so I let it happen. I *know* how that sounds to you. It wasn't my decision to make; it was *hers*. But I could've stopped it, and I wish like hell I had."

"No you couldn't have," Madigan said firmly. "That's what big brothers don't seem to understand. You guys aren't all-powerful. If a woman wants something to happen, it's going to happen."

"I don't think that's true. He respected me enough to ask, and if I had told him I didn't want him to see her, he would have backed off."

"That's only half the equation," she said empathetically. "You just said your sister was wild about him. Do you really believe she wouldn't have eventually acted on that? Women are strong, Tobias, and if she's anything like me, then telling her something can't happen just makes her want it more."

"She is strong, and maybe you're right. But I still wish I had tried to stop it from happening."

"Why?"

"Because of all the shit that went down. But there's something else you need to know before we get there." He sat beside her, so she would see that he wasn't running from the truth, and he held her gaze. "One night when we got home from a club, Carrie made a joke about me and Michelle getting married since she was there all the time. Michelle grabbed on to that comment and wouldn't let it go. We were young, I was twenty-four and she was twenty-two, and I didn't know a damn thing about love, but she was sweet, and I was happy enough. I thought she loved me, so two months later the four of us went to the courthouse, and Michelle and I got married."

Madigan sat back, eyes widening. "You're *married*?"

"*No.* I was married for less than a year."

"Do you have kids?" she asked cautiously.

"*No*, and I'm sorry I didn't tell you about her, but you asked if I was married, not if I'd ever been married—"

"Guess that'll teach me to be more specific," she said sarcastically.

"It wasn't about the question, Madigan. You and I weren't supposed to be anything more than a good time."

She lowered her eyes.

"But we both know we were never just that."

She lifted her eyes in silent confirmation.

"I was with Michelle for months, and I never once felt for her what I've felt for you since our very first kiss. I tried to keep my feelings for you in perspective. I was used to being alone, and I liked it that way. But then you came along, a gorgeous, sassy, confident woman who didn't take any shit. When we were together, it was the only place I wanted to be, and when we were apart, I just wanted to be with you. But I've got nothing to offer, and every night I told myself it would be our last night together. Only I couldn't stop seeing you. I didn't *want* to stop. And when I left town, every fucking minute away from you was torture."

The anguish and strength in her expression didn't confirm or deny that they were on the same page. "What happened with Michelle?"

Fuck. Was this it? Was she just gathering facts so she could have closure and be done with him? He rubbed his hands together, his chest constricting. He had to get through this. She deserved to know what happened, and then he could figure out the rest.

"Carrie got pregnant three months later, and she moved in with Kevin. My father turned his back on her, which was really hard on Carrie. I reached out to him, trying to fix it for her, but he wouldn't talk to me. Anyway, she had me and Kevin, and I thought she'd be okay, but then I started noticing little changes in her. Sometimes she was too quiet, and she'd say she was sad about our father, or she had morning sickness that sometimes lasted all day. She always had an excuse, and they all seemed reasonable. She used to tell me everything, and when she stopped, I asked her about it, and she said I didn't need to know every detail of her life. Michelle said I had to let Carrie grow up and live her own life, which I'm sure you can appreciate."

She nodded.

"It made sense to me, too. She was an adult, living with the father of her child. But then I started noticing Kevin's moods ramping up. He was more aggressive when he was in the ring, and he'd fly off the handle at some of the guys. And when we'd get together with Michelle and Carrie, he was even more upbeat and outrageous, which I now know was his way of distracting me from the changes in my sister. Then he had a match in Vegas, and we all went to cheer him on. When we were walking into the hotel, Carrie tripped, and I caught her by the arm. She cried out, and it was too loud and painful for the way I had touched her. When I lifted her sleeve, I saw bruises. She said she'd forgotten to eat the day before and had passed out and Kevin had caught her the same way I had, by the arm. Something didn't sit right with me, and I tried to pull her aside and talk to her, but she clammed up. I asked Michelle to try to talk with her, but she thought I was overreacting."

"I don't like where this is going," Madigan said anxiously.

"It's not pretty. Do you want me to stop?"

"No, go on."

"That night Kevin won his match, and we all went to a club to celebrate. Carrie didn't drink, of course. I was never a big drinker, and Kevin hadn't been either, as far as I knew, but that night he drank a lot. He made a comment about a woman at the bar, and I could see how much it hurt Carrie. She excused herself to go to the bathroom, and when Michelle went with her, I gave Kevin hell for it. He wasn't normally like that, but like I said, things had seemed off lately. Anyway, the girls came back, and I could tell Carrie had been crying. Kevin made a big show of apologizing and blamed it on the beer. I suggested we take off, but it was his big night and he wanted to stay, so I went to get us waters, figuring it was time to cut him off. When I got back to the table, he and Carrie were gone. Michelle said they got into an argument, and Carrie had gone to the restroom again. Michelle got up to follow her, but Kevin said he'd make sure she was okay."

His pulse sped up, just as it had that night when the hair on the back of his neck had stood on end. "Something felt off, so we went looking for them. The place was like a maze, and before we even got to the bathrooms, I heard my sister tell someone to get their hands off her, and I looked in the direction of her voice. Kevin had her by her upper arms. It took a second, maybe two, for the fear in her eyes to register, and he threw her back against the wall and locked his forearm against her throat. She was fucking *pregnant*. I didn't think, and I didn't hesitate. I just grabbed him by the back of his shirt and tore him off her. He cocked his fist, and I let mine fly, but he turned away, and I caught him in the side of the head."

Bile rose in his throat, the sickening crack of bone against his knuckles coming back with a vengeance. "It all happened so fast." He covered his fist with his hand and lowered his eyes. "You *never* hit someone in the side of the head. The skull is thinnest there, and there's an artery…He went down like a ton of bricks, and I *knew*…" He closed his eyes, tears burning, and blinked them away. "People were fucking cheering me on. My sister was on her knees beside Kevin, hysterical, Michelle was screaming at me, and I couldn't fucking move." He felt a crushing weight on his chest as if he were right back there. "I don't even know how to describe what I felt when the fear in my sister's eyes registered and he threw her against that wall." He gritted his teeth. "God only knows how many other times he'd done it, but he was also my *best* friend, and he wasn't moving. He wasn't breathing. My friend was *dead*, and my sister…" He looked away, trying to pull himself together as he choked out, "I'd *killed* the father of her child, and she told me flat-out she was done with me. After I was arrested, Michelle put my shit into storage and had me served with divorce papers."

TEARS WELLED IN Madigan's eyes, her heart breaking for him. She knew the devastation of losing a best friend, but to be the one who had killed them, even if that best friend wasn't who he'd thought he was? To carry that burden for the rest of his life? To be abandoned by the sister he'd practically raised and had tried to protect? The wife who took vows for better or worse? What the hell was wrong with those people?

She studied his profile. His jaw muscles bunched, his lashes damp with tears he refused to let fall. He looked defeated, but at the same time like he was ready to go to battle. He looked beautifully, treacherously broken. Her gaze traveled down the bulging veins in his neck and along the tension-riddled muscles in his arm to his hands, which were fisted so tight, she knew his fingernails had to be digging into his palms. She'd slept with this man, knew every inch of his body intimately. He'd put those strong hands on her, and she'd never once been afraid. She'd been livid about his leaving without a word, but now all she wanted was to ease his burden. Well, that and give his ex-wife and sister hell for not standing by such a loyal, protective man.

He cocked his head, eyeing her with the same determined expression he'd had every night before they'd gone their separate ways, when he'd tell her to have a good life or to take care of herself. The look that said he'd been through hell, and he would get through this, too.

"I'm so fucking sorry, Blue Eyes. If I could change my past or go back and start over with you and tell you everything, I would do it in a heartbeat. I won't blame you if you never want to see me again."

Her father and grandfather were right. This unfinished business *had* bitten her in the ass, but as she covered his hands with hers and said, "I'm not going anywhere," it was also setting her free.

Chapter Thirteen

MORNING TRICKLED IN like the sun peeking over a mountain, bringing into focus the feel of Tobias's chest rising and falling beneath Madigan's cheek as they lay on the futon, the rugged scent of man and musk curling around her. His arm lay heavily across her back, his big hand palming her hip. They'd opened the futon last night, and she must have fallen asleep while they were talking, because they were still fully dressed.

They'd both been emotionally drained, but Tobias had gone on to tell her that his father hadn't returned his calls when he'd been arrested, and they hadn't spoken in years. When he'd told her that his sister had completely cut him off, his grief had been as raw as an open wound, and Madigan had felt his pain as her own. That pain had eased a little knowing his grandfather had stuck by him, but it was driven deeper when he'd told her that he'd learned of his grandfather's cognitive decline while he was in prison.

She traced the lines of his stomach through his T-shirt, and he covered her hand with his, pressing a kiss to the top of her head. He'd kept his promise and hadn't even tried to kiss her last night. She shifted so she could see his face, resting her chin on his chest. He looked exhausted, but his lips tipped up on one side in a crooked smile that tugged at her heartstrings.

"Did you sleep at all?"

He shrugged one shoulder. "With one eye open in case you left."

"I wouldn't have snuck out without saying goodbye." The second the words were out, his smile faded, and she regretted saying it.

"I'm sorry, Mads." He ran his hand through her hair. "I'm so fucking sorry for the way I left."

"I didn't mean that as a dig."

"It's okay if you did. I deserve it. You have every right to be angry. I wasn't sure you'd ever want to see me again, and I appreciate you hearing me out."

"I wasn't sure, either. I felt betrayed, hearing about your past from my brothers. But you didn't betray me. We agreed that we were just having fun, so that was on me, and part of the reason it hurt so much was that I was with someone who had secrets once, and when I found out, it broke me. Hearing yours from my brothers sent me right back there."

His eyes narrowed. "The guy in Spain?"

She nodded. "What I didn't tell you about him—and what nobody else knows—is that I fell for my professor, which is bad enough but not the worst of it. I didn't know he was my professor at first, and when we realized I was going to be in his class, we knew we had to keep things on the down low. I didn't mind, and he was really good at it, which should have clued me in. He knew where we could go without running into the people he worked with. He was several years older than me, handsome, smart, and *so* romantic. He had an apartment by the university, and he literally swept me off my feet, taking me to see the sights, to music festivals and soccer games. We spent lazy days at the beach and ate at amazing restaurants and cafés. I was drunk on the culture and high on him. And then one day I went exploring outside the city with my roommates, and I saw him holding an adorable baby and kissing a beautiful woman. They turned out to be his son and his wife. There was a reason he was adept at keeping our relationship a secret. His family lived outside the city in a nearby town. Who knows how many other students' beds he'd charmed his way into."

"*Shit*, Madigan. What did you do?"

"I felt like a fool, so I came home and cried into my pillow. I shut everyone out and swore I'd never let myself get hurt like that again."

"Why didn't you tell your brothers about that asshole?"

"Because I was ashamed. They'd warned me about guys like him since I was old enough to look at boys as more than pains in my butt, and I walked right into it. We talked *all* the time about our lives and what we wanted in the future, but I never thought to ask him if he was married. That's why when I found out what you'd done, I nearly lost my mind. I wanted to hate you for not telling me, but I couldn't because we didn't have that kind of relationship, and I was furious at my brothers for not coming to me first. They're still paying the price."

"They were just trying to protect you."

"I know, but you didn't set out to kill anyone. You protected your sister. I'm glad you told me everything. I never could have imagined there was so much behind that one punch. The way Blaine said it that morning at your place made me think you were a cold-blooded killer."

"If I was, I would've gotten convicted of more than involuntary manslaughter and sentenced to more than three years."

"How was I supposed to know that?"

"You couldn't have. But that asshole didn't break you, Mads. He might've taken you to your knees, but you pulled yourself up and created your own empire of puppets and cards and musical stories."

"It's *hardly* an empire."

"You're a world traveler. Isn't that what you said?"

"Yeah."

"I know you're here for your grandfather—which is cool, by the way, that we both ended up here for our grandfathers. But when are you packing up and traveling again?"

"I don't know. I came back for my grandfather, but then Maverick got married, and now he and Chloe are trying to start their family, and Tank and Leah got married, and they have two little girls and a baby on the way, and at some point, Gunner and Sid will get married and start a family, too. I want to travel, but I'm not sure I want to miss being part of all that."

"That's understandable. I'd give anything to meet my niece," he said solemnly.

"You could reach out to your sister."

He shook his head. "I won't put her in that position. She told me where I stand, and respecting her decision is the least I can do."

She wanted to tell him things could change, but she could see how drained he was, so she remained quiet. As good as it felt to have him open up to her, she didn't know what it meant or what his plans were. "When we met, you said you weren't sticking around. Is that still true?"

"I tried to leave, and look where I am. Staring into the eyes of an angel I don't deserve."

Her heart filled up. "Why would you say you don't deserve

me?"

"Because I lost everything, Mads. I've got nothing but some shit in storage and a small pile of money in the bank from before my life exploded. I have no career, no future. I lost my job because I took off and didn't show up for work, and I don't even know what I want to do for a living. Thank God I didn't turn in the keys to my apartment. I've got nothing to offer you, Blue Eyes."

"Believe it or not, I didn't like you for your job or this castle." She grinned.

"Are you making fun of my digs?"

"No. I like it here. But you know you can get another job, and I'm not trying to minimize how awful it must be to find something you love doing and then lose it, but at some point I'm sure you'll figure out a new career. Although I will miss seeing you on that skateboard thing rolling out from under a car. That was hot."

"Skateboard thing?" He arched a brow as he threaded his fingers into her hair, gently pushing it away from her face. "*God*, I missed you, Blue Eyes."

"Is that why you haven't kissed me yet?"

He rolled her onto her back, gazing deeply into her eyes. "I haven't kissed you because I want you to be sure you want to be with me. I don't want to fuck this up, and I don't want you to regret being with me ever again."

"I don't regret it."

"But you *did*. I saw it in your eyes when Blaine told you what I'd done."

"You're right, but that was before I knew the whole story, and more importantly, before I had time to think rationally and realize you didn't owe me an explanation." She reached up and pressed her hands to his scruffy cheeks. "You listen to me, Tobias Riggs. *People make bad decisions, and the rest of the world is left to live with them.*"

"Did you just quote me?"

"Yes, but let me finish. Those same people can learn from their mistakes, and that means you and me. I want to be with you, but only if we can be honest with each other on every level."

"Madigan, I want to be with you, and I promise that you know everything now. I hated keeping it from you, and I will never put you in that position again. But that conviction will be on my record for years. People will continue to find out about it. It'll hinder my chances for employment, and a lot of people won't be as understanding as you are."

"The heck with them. Maverick beat a man to a pulp for hurting Chloe. Did you know that?"

"No."

"He did, and Zeke beat up a guy for talking shit about disabled kids. Ashley took the drugs that killed her because of some jerk at school talking shit about her, and Tank tracked him down and beat him unconscious. They could have killed any one of those people, and that's just a sampling of the things that go on with Dark Knights families. They're *protectors*, and you are, too, so don't you dare minimize that part of yourself. I know how much it hurts to lose your best friend, and it sucks that it ended the way it did. But if you hadn't stepped in, you don't know if your sister would have survived the night. Or if she did, when it would happen again. You'd never forgive yourself if he put her in the hospital, or worse."

"Jesus, Mads," he said uneasily.

"It's true. You need to face those facts. I know you're consumed with guilt. I get it. But someone has to show you the other side of things. The awful *what ifs*. What if she lost the baby at his hands or if he'd hurt the baby?"

"I can't think about that."

"I know, but you have to hear it, so one day you can try to move past it and figure out your future."

"Moving past it isn't even a consideration. One of the reasons I don't have a clue about what my future looks like is because I can't see past the crushing guilt of what I've done. I can't just pretend like it never happened. This will stick with me forever."

"I don't mean pretend like it never happened. I meant finding a way to forgive yourself so you can move forward. You might want to talk to a professional about how to deal with everything you've been through. You *deserve* to be happy and have a future and a career you love, and if we're together, I will have your back no matter what people say, because protecting your sister was honorable, even if it ended tragically. You've paid the price for that, Tobias, and you're right—everything that's happened is a part of you now. But that conviction is *not* who you are. Do you hear me? It doesn't define you, and you shouldn't let it."

He lowered his forehead to hers, his hair falling forward. "You really are my angel."

"You of all people know I'm more devil than angel."

"You're no devil, Blue Eyes." He brushed his lips over hers, rasping, "You're my wicked angel."

His mouth covered hers in a deep, hungry kiss, his tongue sweeping and *possessing*, lulling her into him with a fierce and seductive rhythm, until she felt it in every beat of her heart, every breath she took. She tugged at his shirt, and he drew back, eyes blazing.

"Once we're naked, I can't promise to go slow."

"I don't *want* you to."

She pulled his mouth to hers, and seconds later they were tearing at each other's clothes, teeth gnashing, laughter bubbling out as their clothes went flying, until they were finally, blissfully naked. He came down over her, his thick cock nestled against her entrance, his chest hair tickling her nipples, and those gorgeous eyes drilling into her. It was all right there, the *want* and *need*, the inescapable fire between them. The weight of his body felt deliciously familiar and unbelievably good as her arms circled him, and his fingers threaded into her hair, cradling her head with both hands as their bodies came together. She clung to him as he filled her so completely, they both released sounds of shock and pleasure.

His head dipped beside hers. "Christ, you feel like *home*."

Her heart didn't have time to catch up as his mouth covered hers and they began to move. Their kisses and movements were deep and rough, their passion too strong to temper, but then he found a way, slowing them down to a sensual, erotic beat and keeping them there. Her senses reeled and her ability to think fell away as he intensified their kisses, thrusting harder, lifting and angling her hips, taking her impossibly deeper. She spread her legs wider, wanting everything he had to give.

"I'm addicted to kissing you," he said against her lips, and took her in another intoxicating kiss. "To fucking you." His words scorched through her as he sank his teeth into her neck, grinding against her clit, sending fire rocketing through her.

"Tobias—"

He drove into her faster, harder. "That's it, baby. Come on my cock."

God, what he did to her.

Reclaiming her mouth as she hit the peak, he lifted her hips again, slowing his efforts, dragging his cock in and out of her excruciatingly slowly, hitting that magical spot with laser precision. She bucked and moaned, and when she came down from her high, he rewarded her with more dirty talk. "Your pussy feels so good. I need to taste it." He moved down her body, nipping, licking, and sucking, until she was writhing and begging for more, on the verge of release. His talented mouth devoured her, his fingers strumming her clit like they were made for it. Heat raced from the tips of her fingers to the ends of her toes, gathering in her core. She felt like the strings of a guitar, pulled too tight, ready to snap. He must have sensed it, because he clutched her hips, an eager growl rumbling up his throat as he took her clit between his teeth, and the world spun away. She cried out, caught in the throes of another orgasm, and he rose up, driving his hard length into her in one thrust.

Her eyes flew open with the immense pleasure. *"Again."*

"That's it, baby." He thrust hard and fast. "Squeeze my dick. Make me come."

She was lost in a world of sensations, his filthy words spiraling through her, his magnificent cock working its magic. She grasped at his arms, his back, his head, wherever she could find purchase. His thighs tensed, and his next thrust hurled them both over the edge. Then his mouth was on hers, feasting ravenously, hips grinding and rocking, hands groping, as they rode out their pleasure in a symphony of guttural moans and greedy pleas.

When they finally came back down to earth, they lay with their bodies tangled, a sheen of sweat between them. "Jesus, Blue Eyes. What have you done to me?"

"I could ask you the same thing."

He kissed her softly. "It's seriously never been like this."

"For me, either," she panted out. "Maybe we should try it again to see if it was real or we imagined it."

He buried his face in her neck. "Thank you."

"For the sex?"

"No. For seeing something in me I had forgotten existed."

Chapter Fourteen

TOBIAS FOLLOWED MADIGAN through her parents' middle-class neighborhood and parked at the end of a long driveway beside a large two-story home with a wide front porch, gabled roof, and a breezeway leading to a multicar garage that appeared to have an apartment above it. As he climbed off his motorcycle, he noticed Madigan staring at the motorcycles and cars in the driveway. He set his helmet on the seat and went to her, giving a short rap of his knuckles on her helmet.

She tugged it off and turned with worried eyes. "It was just supposed to be my parents and grandfather, but everyone is here, including my brothers and Maverick's wife, Chloe. You don't have to come in."

He knew he was walking into a spider's web. Nothing about this was going to be easy, but they'd talked about that when he'd asked if he could come with her this morning to speak with her parents. He wasn't sure going in there would help the situation with her brothers, but if leaving had taught him one thing, it was that he'd do whatever it took to be with her. "I told you if we're going to be together, I'm not hiding anything from your family. We started off on the wrong foot, and I want to rectify that. Facing them all at once just speeds things up."

"Or brings it to a screaming halt," she said sarcastically. "Are you sure you want to go in there?"

"Are you sure you want to be with me?"

"*Yes,*" she said adamantly.

He ran the backs of his fingers down her cheek, so damn thankful for her forgiveness. "Then let's do this. I'll say my piece and take off to see my grandfather so you can have time with your family."

As they made their way up the driveway, he could feel Madigan steeling herself for whatever came their way, and he was right there with her. "You okay?"

"I will be." She pulled open the door, and as he followed her into the kitchen, the smell of bacon, eggs, and something freshly baked surrounded them, throwing Tobias back to his childhood. A woman with the same mahogany hair as Madigan, who could only be her mother, was standing at the stove, transferring bacon from a pan to a platter as Zander, wearing his black leather vest, snagged a slice and a tough-looking man with slicked-back silver-and-black hair and tattooed arms strode into the kitchen with Blaine, their serious eyes landing on him. Both men were also wearing their leather vests.

"Hi," Madigan said, her nervousness coming out in her clipped tone, drawing the attention of her mother and Zander.

"What the hell is he doing here?" Blaine snapped.

"What the hell are *you* doing here?" Madigan challenged.

The older guy glared at Blaine and Madigan. "That's *enough*."

Zeke, Maverick, and a tall, thin blonde came into the kitchen, their curious gazes landing on Tobias as two dogs trotted past them, heading for Madigan. Zeke and Maverick were also sporting their vests, magnifying Tobias's feeling of being an outsider to their closely knit family.

"Way to ambush me, Dad," Madigan said, petting the dogs. "I thought I was having breakfast with you, Mom, and Grandpa."

Dad. Tobias mentally ticked off what he knew about her father. He was president of the motorcycle club, owned a renovation company, had raised four overprotective sons and a fierce daughter, and his brother and sister-in-law owned the Salty Hog.

"This rift has gone on long enough," her father said sternly. "We all know tomorrows aren't guaranteed. It's time to get this shit sorted out."

Tobias added, *smart man* to that list.

"Fine." Madigan lifted her chin. "This is Tobias, and he's going to be in my life. So you all better get on board with it, or you'll have me to deal with."

Forget fierce. She was a force to be reckoned with. Not that he needed her to stand up for him, but damn it felt good to be appreciated and wanted.

Blaine's eyes narrowed, locking on him.

Tobias held his stare, wishing once again that he'd never left town. Only this time it was because he didn't want Blaine thinking he'd left out of fear. He didn't want to be the first to look away, but he knew the pecking order and shifted his attention to her father, holding out his hand. "Tobias Riggs, sir. I believe I have some explaining to do."

"The name's Rob, but you can call me Preacher, and we'll get to that explaining." Her father shook his hand. "This is my wife, Reba, and I believe you know my sons, Blaine, Maverick, Zeke, and Zander." As he said their names, each nodded in turn, except Blaine, who still had a death stare locked on

Tobias. Preacher motioned to the pretty blonde. "And this is Chloe, Maverick's wife."

Before Tobias could get a word out, Reba said, "Welcome to our home, Tobias."

She opened her arms and embraced him, and hell if it didn't bring a wave of emotion. It felt like forever since he'd been greeted that warmly. Her friendly, easy demeanor reminded him of his mother.

"Nice to meet you, ma'am. I'm sorry for intruding on your morning."

"Don't be silly. Any friend of Madigan's is always welcome here." She glanced disapprovingly at Blaine and returned a soft smile to Tobias. "I hope you're hungry, because we've made a feast."

"Thank you, but I'll just say my piece and let you and your family be."

"Oh, heavens no," she said with a laugh. "I made enough food for an army. Surely you can spare half an hour to eat."

As she hugged Madigan, whispering something that made Madigan smile, Zander stepped forward, hand extended. "Guess you realized my sister's performances don't suck after all."

Tobias shook his hand, glad for the levity, although his nerves were still pinging. "I never thought they sucked. She's got the voice of an angel, and her stories hit hard. They're just too good to be rushed."

"There is a lot of truth in that statement," Zeke said. "It takes balls to walk in here after the way we treated you."

"Zeke, *language*," Reba said sharply.

"Just stating a fact, Mom," Zeke said.

"Y'all didn't scare me off. I only left to save Madigan any more grief," Tobias said evenly.

"When we went to your apartment, we didn't know Madigan was there," Maverick explained. "And we didn't know the full story. I'm sorry for both."

Tobias gave a curt nod. "I have a sister. I get it."

"Yeah, I imagine you do," Maverick said.

"It's nice to meet you, Tobias. I've heard a lot about you," Chloe said, a secret glance passing between her and Madigan.

"Hopefully it's not all bad."

"It's definitely not," Chloe said.

"Chloe runs the book club I'm in," Madigan explained.

The image of Madigan walking down the path in that sexy leather outfit flashed in his mind, and from the blush reddening her cheeks, he had a feeling she was thinking about their night of debauchery, too.

"What the heck is going on? I go to the bathroom and everyone disappears," an old man said as he came into the kitchen.

"Grandpa, this is Tobias Riggs." Madigan looked up at Tobias with reverence he wasn't sure he deserved, but he soaked it up like the sun. "Tobias, this is my grandfather, Mike Wicked."

"It's nice to meet you, sir." Tobias offered his hand.

Her grandfather's brows slanted, wise eyes that looked like they'd seen their fair share of trouble openly appraising him. "Well, if it isn't Mr. Unfinished Business."

"*Pop*," Preacher warned.

Her grandfather paid him no mind, serious eyes boring into Tobias as he lifted a slightly crooked finger and poked him in the chest. "You tell me one thing, Tobias Riggs. Are you going to bite my girl in the ass, or are you going to set her free?"

"Grandpa!" Madigan looked appalled.

"If Madigan is into that, I'll happily oblige, sir, but if you think I'm walking away, you're sorely mistaken" came out before he could check it.

Zander said, "*Damn*," while Madigan, Chloe, and her mother tried to stifle laughs. Blaine looked like a bull ready to charge, and Maverick uttered, "*Shit*," and stepped in front of Blaine.

Tobias wasn't worried about Blaine, but the two older men were sharing some sort of silent exchange, matching deep Vs etched between their serious eyes. Just as he opened his mouth to try to smooth things over, the two of them burst into laughter.

Preacher clapped him on the back. "What do you say we go eat?"

Relief barreled through Tobias. "If you don't mind, I'd like to say what I came to say first."

"Go right ahead, honey," Reba said.

Blaine shifted on his feet, and Tobias didn't miss the annoyance in his expression. Ignoring it, he said, "Thank you. I'll try to keep this brief. Madigan said you're aware of the circumstances that led to my conviction, but what you may not know is that my best friend, Kevin Arlo, the man I didn't set out to kill but *did*, manhandled my pregnant sister. I was a fighter, and I knew better than to hit anyone in the side of the head. Especially the man who had mentored me and offered me a future I should have been able to count on." He swallowed hard against the emotions coming at him. "But it happened, and I lost everyone I loved with the exception of my grandfather. His cognition is failing, and I came here when I got out of prison to be near him. But I wasn't planning on sticking around, and I didn't intend to get caught up with anyone while I was here." He glanced at Madigan, watching him with appreciation and deep affection, and felt that knot in his chest he'd tried so hard to ignore when he'd left. "Certainly not a woman as special as Madigan. But you all know how great she is. She's smart and tough, and when she's nervous, she rambles incessantly. It's just about the cutest thing I've ever seen."

His gaze moved over her family, taking in the compassion in her mother's eyes and the knowing glance passing between Maverick and Chloe. He was sure they'd felt that pull, because he could feel something similar between them. "We weren't supposed to have the kind of relationship where you share your baggage, but as we got closer, I wanted to tell her everything, but I couldn't." He looked at Madigan again, and there was no containing his feelings. "How do you tell the most beautiful soul you've ever met, a woman who brings light into your darkness, that you've taken a life?" He turned back to her family, noticing her father and grandfather nodding. "It didn't seem fair, and I tried to end it so she wouldn't suffer because of my past. But no matter how many times I tried, it never stuck. I couldn't go a day without seeing her. I was going to try to end it again the morning you guys showed up. You made it easier, because after seeing the pain she felt, I never wanted to cause her pain again. But from the second I drove away, I wanted to come back. I felt like I had left the best part of myself behind. But Madigan *wasn't* mine, and I believed she was better off without my past hanging over her head."

"Then why the hell did you come back?" Blaine snarled.

Tobias met his stare. "Because she deserved to hear the truth from *me*, and there are not enough miles in this world to make me forget your sister."

"So, what? Now we're just supposed to pretend all is well?" Blaine asked. "That you didn't lie to her?"

"He *never* lied to me," Madigan snapped. "What is wrong with you?"

"The answer is *no*, Blaine. We're done pretending." Tobias held Blaine's gaze, speaking firmly. "We're leading with honesty and giving this thing between us a shot. I've got nothing to hide. I know what I've done, and I'll carry the weight of that to my grave. I know I don't have much to offer at the moment, and Madigan knows that. I lost my self-respect when I drove away from her and I lost my job when I left town. Now that I've got Madigan back, I'll be pounding the pavement tomorrow looking for a new job. Any other questions?"

"*No*," Preacher said authoritatively, shooting Blaine a dark, silencing look. "We appreciate your candor, Tobias."

"Yes, we do. That couldn't have been easy," Reba said, handing a platter of bacon to Zander and one of eggs to Zeke. "Now, let's go sit down and enjoy a meal, shall we?"

As her family shuffled dutifully toward the dining room, Blaine remained by the counter, arms crossed, and Preacher walked over to him. "I believe your mother said we're sitting down to breakfast." He jerked his head in the direction of the dining room, and Blaine reluctantly strode past Tobias into the dining room.

Tobias hiked a thumb toward the door. "I should just—"

"No, sir, you shouldn't," Preacher said. "When my wife offers you breakfast, you say thank you and you eat until you're stuffed, or she'll feel like she wasted her time in the kitchen."

"Sounds like my mother. But with all due respect, that was a lot for everyone to process."

"And they'll deal with it." Preacher looked at Madigan. "Our daughter brought you into our home, and she stood her ground when she told us to get used to you being around. If you walk out that door now, Blaine wins."

"Oh, *hell no*," Madigan said, taking Tobias's arm and dragging him into the dining room.

THE TENSION BETWEEN Blaine and Tobias hung over them like a rain cloud on the verge of bursting, keeping Madigan on edge during breakfast. Thankfully, her mother kept the conversations light, steering them away from the topic of family, and her grandfather kept them entertained with stories about his last visit with Junie and Rosie and the *stories* they'd drawn on his arms. Tobias joined in where he could, asking questions and commenting as if Blaine wasn't throwing visual daggers in his direction. Madigan told them about the new puppetry and storytelling gigs she had coming up, and when Maverick told them about the sculpture he was working on for the Dark Knights' annual Suicide-Prevention Ride and Rally, Tobias listened intently, asked questions about the event and Maverick's work. It wasn't until her brothers, with the exception of Blaine, started joking around and Tobias joined in that Madigan felt like she could finally breathe again. In those joking moments, she saw glimpses of the man she had a feeling Tobias had tried to bury right along with his friend.

Everyone helped clean up, and as they got ready to leave, Madigan's mother pulled her aside. "I'd say that went well."

"What am I going to do about Blaine?"

"Nothing. You go on with your life, and those two will figure it out." Her mother nodded in the direction of Tobias, talking with her brothers by the kitchen door, save for Blaine, who had gone outside with their father and grandfather. "That man can handle himself. He's been through a lot, baby girl, and got the hard edges to prove it. But he's got a tender heart. I might have swooned a little when he was talking about you."

"Me too." Warming with the memory, Madigan lowered her voice. "I really like him, Mom. But he's lost so much. His sister, his father. He has a niece he's never met. He lost the career he loved *and* his best friend. I want to help him with all of it, but I don't know how."

"Oh, honey, you already are," her mother said with the confidence of someone who knew something Madigan didn't.

"See ya, Mads. We're taking off." Zander waved from across the kitchen.

"Go," her mother said with a smile.

"Bye, Zan. See ya, Zeke," she said, heading over to Tobias as they went out the door.

"Hey, Blue Eyes. Maverick and Chloe want us to go out with them sometime." Tobias ran his hand down her back.

She leaned against him, craving the contact. "Sounds good to me."

"Good. I'll look at our calendars and text you," Chloe said.

"We'd better take off," Maverick said. "We're meeting up with my brothers and some of the guys in an hour to ride out to Plymouth. You two want to come?"

"Thanks, but I need to go see my grandfather," Tobias said.

"Another time, then," Maverick suggested.

After a round of goodbyes, they walked out with Maverick and Chloe. Her father and grandfather stood with their arms crossed, watching Blaine drive away on his motorcycle. After saying goodbye to Maverick and Chloe, her father looked at Tobias and said, "Can I get a minute?"

"Yes, sir." He stepped aside with her father, and Madigan craned to hear their conversation.

"You ever work in construction?" her father asked.

"Yes, sir. For about a year and a half when I was in Jersey."

"Any good with a hammer?"

Tobias cleared his throat. "I'd like to think I am."

"Think you can work with Zeke and Zander?"

"I don't see why not."

Madigan's heart was so full, she could barely hold her tongue.

"If you're interested, we could use a hand." Her father went over the pay and benefits. "But I won't cut you slack for seeing my daughter."

"I wouldn't respect you if you did."

Madigan's grandfather elbowed her, startling her from her eavesdropping, and gave an *attaboy* nod as her father handed Tobias a business card and told him to be at his shop at seven o'clock the next morning.

As they said their goodbyes, Madigan hugged her father and couldn't resist whispering, "Thank you for helping him."

He hugged her tighter, speaking quietly. "If you two stop seeing each other, he gets to keep the job if he wants it. He's lost enough for one lifetime. Understand?"

Her heart filled to the brim as she nodded.

"Thank you again, sir. You won't be disappointed." Tobias shook her father's hand.

"Then cut the *sir*, and go with Preacher," her father said.

Tobias agreed and offered a hand to her grandfather. "It was a pleasure meeting you, sir. My grandfather also lives at LOCAL."

"I know all about Hank Pettazzoni, and I'm sorry for what

he's going through," her grandfather said.

"How?" Madigan asked.

"Your old man might be the badass biker with connections far and wide, but I've got my network, and I know you're working with Hank." Her grandfather winked at her and looked at Tobias. "Madigan is excellent at what she does. I'll make a point to meet Hank and that sweet nurse of his." He eyed Preacher. "You and I need to have a talk about live-in help. I could use a beautiful woman on the daily."

"Christ, Pop." Preacher shook his head. "We'll see you kids around."

As they headed inside, Tobias walked Madigan to her Vespa. "Your grandfather's a trip."

"That he is," she said with a smile. "Was that awful for you?"

He pulled her into his arms, gazing down at her intently. But there was something new in that intensity. A hint of new light peeking in. "I don't think anything could be awful if I'm with you. You've got a great family, and honestly, I'm relieved they know the truth. I hate hiding things from anyone, but especially from you and the people in your life."

"Thank you. I appreciate that, and I'm sorry about Blaine."

"Don't be. He loves you, and it's going to take time."

"So…I guess I'll see you around?" she said awkwardly.

A low chuckle rumbled out. "Where are you heading?"

"Home, I guess."

"Come with me to see my grandfather."

"Don't you want time alone with him?"

"I want time with him, but I've been alone long enough. No more hiding, remember? And you should probably make sure there aren't any conflicts of interest with you doing therapy with a resident when you're sleeping with his grandson."

"Chloe's the director of the facility. I think we can work something out."

"No shit? She is?"

"Yes, but I'll be sure to talk with her and Elsa, and assuming Chloe and Elsa are okay with it, if your grandfather has a lucid moment when I'm with him, I'll speak to him about it, too."

"Thank you. But what if Chloe feels there is a conflict of interest?"

"Well, then either we stop sleeping together, or I work with him on my own time, not through the facility."

"I'll take option number two, please." He leaned down, kissing her. "After we see my grandfather, do you think you'll have time to go bed shopping with me?"

She cocked her head. "You're buying a bed?"

"If I'm sticking around, I'm sure as hell not sleeping on that hard-ass futon. What do you say?"

"Hm..." She tapped her jaw, pretending to mull it over. "Do we get to christen it?"

He brushed his lips over hers, whispering, "Only if you're a very good girl."

"How about if I promise to be a very *bad* girl?"

"Keep talking like that and I might have to take you over my knee."

Her body ignited. "That's a shame. I was thinking you'd want me *on my* knees."

He tightened his hold on her, and she felt his hard length pressing into her belly. "Get on your Barbie mobile," he growled. "We're going to my place first."

"My place is closer," she taunted as he strode to his motorcycle.

He straddled his bike, the fire in his eyes blazing a path between them.

She'd never driven home quite so fast.

Chapter Fifteen

AUGUST ARRIVED WITH sweltering heat and too many tourists, but as Tobias put the last of his tools away and wiped the sweat from his brow, he knew better than to bitch about the little shit. He was with a woman he adored, and he loved being able to treat her to dinners and kiss her whenever he felt like it. He had a job he enjoyed, and he had his freedom. Life was pretty damn good. He grabbed his water bottle from the grass and guzzled it down just as Zander ran out the front door of the carriage house they were renovating, laughing his ass off. Zeke was on his heels and swatted the back of his head. Tobias chuckled.

It was hard to believe that nearly two weeks ago he'd been nervous about taking a job with Madigan's father and brothers. He hadn't wanted to accept a handout, but he'd needed the work and wasn't about to let his pride stand in his way. He'd always miss fighting, but it felt great to be doing something physical again, and Preacher was tough but fair. He expected them to work hard and treat each other, and their clients, with respect. Tobias had been pleasantly surprised when they'd put him to work without any animosity. He'd known things were going to be okay halfway through his first day, when Zander started singing "Like a Virgin" and had turned it into a song about Zeke. They'd quickly roped him into the banter, and that amicable friendship had continued ever since.

He was glad, because there was nothing better than being with Madigan, free to openly adore her, treat her to dinners, and kiss her whenever he felt like it. They'd gotten lucky during their visit after breakfast with her family, and his grandfather had experienced a brief period of lucidity. He'd told embarrassing stories about when Tobias, aka *Toby*, was young, charming his way into Madigan's heart so deeply, they were having dinner with him tomorrow night. But Tobias felt lucky on many fronts. With the exception of Blaine, who was keeping his distance and staring him down, Tobias was enjoying the friendships he was building with her brothers and cousins. They'd had dinner with Maverick and Chloe last week, and he'd learned more about their families. Maverick had lost his mother to suicide when he was young, and Chloe's mother sounded worthless. The three of them had bonded over their losses and heartaches. It was a strange thing, connecting over bad situations, but he was realizing that everyone had things to overcome and baggage to carry. And it wasn't so much about how much baggage a person had, but how it was carried, and while he'd thought he needed to carry his alone, he was realizing that having others to lean on was a hell of a lot healthier and more enjoyable.

"Hey, douchebag," Zander called out as he and Zeke made their way across the lawn.

Zeke swatted the back of his head again. "Show some respect."

Zander dropped to one knee with a smirk. "Tobias, sir, king of kings, would you care to join us this evening at the Salty

Hog, where we will imbibe vast quantities of alcohol?"

Tobias and Madigan had hung out with her brothers and cousins at the Salty Hog after she'd performed last week, once over the weekend, and again Wednesday night after the guys' motorcycle club meeting. Tobias had met a number of other Dark Knights, including Cuffs, a cop, and Justice, an attorney, both of whom seemed like good guys. They'd tried to sell him on becoming a Dark Knight, raving about the members and the chapters in other states. There was a lot more to them than he'd imagined, including what sounded like a brotherhood like no other. As appealing as that was, considering Blaine had left the table whenever Tobias had shown up, he wasn't about to invade an angry lion's territory.

"Don't be an ass, Zan," Zeke said as Zander pushed to his feet.

Zander splayed his hands. "I am who I am. What do you say, Tobias?"

"Thanks, but I'm taking Mads out tonight, and since we're getting off early, I want to surprise her at the park. She's putting on a puppet show for a kids' camp." Last night they'd put together goody bags for the kids with the makings for a toilet-paper-roll puppet and a Madigan's Magic Puppetry business card, which had a picture from one of her puppet shows and her website address. Of course he'd immediately checked it out.

"So take her to the Hog," Zander suggested.

"Dude, he's probably sick of us and wants to take her someplace special," Zeke said.

"In other words, he's pussy-whipped." Zander smirked.

"That's our sister you're talking about," Zeke reminded him. "Ignore him, T. The last time Zander did anything other than chase pussy was…Oh, wait, he never has."

Zander scoffed. “I don’t know what you’re talking about. I don’t chase pussy. Women flock to me.”

They were still talking shit half an hour later when Tobias climbed onto his motorcycle and headed home to shower. He and Madigan spent about half their time at his place and half at hers, and they had more than christened his new bed. He loved their lazy nights together as much as he liked going out. They watched movies and played guitar. It seemed like Madigan was always working on new stories, new cards, new puppetry ideas, and he enjoyed hearing about them and brainstorming ideas with her.

They’d stayed at his place last night, and her scent lingered in the apartment. *Summer sins and winter fires.* They’d mastered the summer sins, and he was looking forward to winter fires. On the beach and in the bedroom.

After showering, he went into the bedroom and spotted Madigan’s ereader plugged in on her side of the bed. They were staying at her place tonight, and as he reached for it, it struck him that for more than three years, he hadn’t thought about tomorrow, much less a future, but with Madigan he found himself looking forward to things to come.

He woke up every day grateful to have his angel in his arms and went to bed most nights worshipping every inch of her. He wanted more of that, but he wanted more of many other things, too. Like watching Madigan perform and hanging out with her friends and family. Her cousin Gunner and his fiancée, Sid, had told them about an adoption event coming up for their animal rescue, and Madigan’s eyes had lit up. He didn’t know anything about the event, but he looked forward to going to it with Madigan. He wanted more breakfasts with her messy hair and his T-shirt billowing around her, when they forwent food and devoured each other, more dirty texts that left him salivating for her, and evenings spent learning all the little things from her growing-up years that made her who she was, then falling into each other's arms, insatiable for a deeper connection, which sometimes came in the form of simply holding each other and sharing whispers in the dark.

Just wanting *more* was a miraculous feeling he never thought he'd have again.

He put on his boots, grabbed his keys and Madigan's eread-er, and looked for his guitar. Remembering he'd left it at her place, he headed out. Twenty minutes later he was making his way through the park, and spotted Madigan's puppetry booth surrounded by a group of mesmerized children. He'd seen her with her professional cap on, answering emails and talking on the phone, and he'd seen her perform musical storytelling at bars and local cafés, but *this* was a first. He stood off to the side, listening to the story about friendship she told through the puppets. He'd learned that she had more than a dozen puppets, all of which were incredible, with big eyes and expressive faces.

Today she was using a dark-skinned, dark-haired girl pup-pet, a crazy-haired redheaded girl puppet, and a blond, freckle-faced boy puppet. Each puppet had a distinct voice and personality, but it was Madigan's effervescent storytelling that had the kids gasping and laughing and calling out to the puppets. When the puppets sang a snappy little tune with a repetitive line of *I'm your friend, you're my friend, let's be everyone's friend*, they encouraged the kids to join them, and Tobias found himself tapping his foot to the beat.

After the show, the kids clapped and jumped to their feet as the puppets waved and blew kisses. The camp counselors helped the kids form a line, and Madigan came out from behind the booth to give each of the kids a goody bag. Many of the children hugged her, and they all left with smiles on their faces. As the counselors ushered the kids down a path, Madigan went behind the booth to put her puppets away, and Tobias headed for his girl.

"How much for a private show?"

"Tobias!" She popped to her feet, brightening the entire fucking sky.

"Hey, Blue Eyes." He bent to kiss her.

Her gorgeous eyes trailed down his short-sleeved black button-down and jeans. "Wow, you look great. What are you doing here?"

"Bringing you these." He pulled the bouquet of flowers he'd bought for her on the way there from behind his back.

Her eyes widened. "Oh my gosh, they're beautiful." She went up on her toes, pressing her lips to his, and he deepened the kiss, earning one of her enticing moans.

"Missed you," he said, and went back for more, taking his fill and leaving her breathless and a little hazy eyed, which he loved.

She sighed dreamily. "You sure know how to greet a girl. What are the flowers for?"

"I told you I'm doing things right this time."

She smelled the flowers. "I *like* the way you do things, but I still have to shower and get ready."

"I'm in no hurry, babe. I wanted to catch you in action. You really have a gift for making a difference."

"You saw the show? What did you think? Was I too chatty? The kids were so cute, weren't they? I love it when they shout things, and I know I shouldn't encourage calling out, but they're so full of excitement…"

He couldn't fit a word in edgewise as they put her things away, but he didn't mind. She was so passionate about everything she did, and her excitement was contagious. When they finished putting everything away, she finally took a breath, her gorgeous eyes flicking up to his. "Sorry I'm such a talkaholic."

"*Stop.* You're adorable, your show was amazing, and I love your rambling." Before she could say another word, he took her in another long, slow kiss.

She met his eyes with a playful glimmer, whispering, "*Again.*"

She didn't have to ask twice.

MADIGAN GRABBED THE beautiful flowers Tobias had given her and brought them to her nose, inhaling their scent for the dozenth time. She hadn't been given flowers by anyone since Alejandro, and everything that scoundrel had done was tainted with betrayal. Tobias had been back for almost two weeks, and she was loving the way their lives were coming together. But between work and their relationship, she hadn't had time to review and finalize the distribution and merchandising contracts for her expansion. She'd hoped to squeeze it in before their date tonight, but as she watched Tobias climb off his motorcycle, the idea of spending even a minute of their time together on work went out the window.

Tobias always took her breath away, but in that black button-down, he was striking. She wanted to grab that shirt with both hands and rip it off him, sending those buttons flying so she could get her mouth on his skin. He set his dark eyes on her, closing the distance between them, his every step sending currents of heat rolling through her.

"Keep looking at me like that, Blue Eyes, and we're not going to make it to dinner."

She ran her teeth over her lower lip, mulling that over.

He must have seen the lust in her eyes, because he hauled her into his arms, giving her ass a squeeze. "I'm taking you out, beautiful. We're doing this right, remember?"

She hooked her finger into the waist of his jeans and licked her lips. "I know how to do it *right*."

He ran his hand up her back, tangling his fingers in her hair the way she loved and tugging her head back, his eyes blazing into hers. He lowered his face so close to hers, his breath warmed her lips. "Don't tempt me with that mouth of yours. You know how I like to fuck it."

A shiver of heat shot through her. "Okay, that's just not fair. You can't talk like that and then deny me the chance to follow through."

"Sure I can." He backed her up against her Jeep, bending his knees so his cock aligned with her center, and rocked against her. The friction was maddeningly arousing. "I'm going to love driving you right up to the edge without touching you."

"Good luck trying." She was being snarky, but the man got her wet with dirty texts. She knew exactly what he was capable of, and she looked forward to whatever he had planned.

He dragged his tongue along her lower lip. "Wear a dress tonight, and skip the panties."

Her nipples pebbled at his naughty request and the feel of his hot mouth trailing kisses to her ear.

"I'm going to make you so wet, you won't be able to think straight." He traced the shell of her ear with his tongue, and a needy sigh escaped. "Are you going to wear panties?"

"*No,*" she said breathily.

"Good girl." He took her in an excruciatingly deep kiss that sent lightning through her core, rendering her legs useless. "Let's go, Blue Eyes. We've got a date to go on."

He stepped back, and she remained against the car, trying to catch her breath.

A slow grin spread across his face. "This is going to be fun."

Needing a cold shower, Madigan forced her legs to move. She was going to lose her mind well before dinner if he kept this up. She headed into her bedroom and into the closet to pick out a dress. When she came out to set her little black dress on the bed, Tobias was leaning against the bathroom doorframe shirtless, legs casually crossed at the ankle, and the shower was running. Had he changed his mind? A shiver of heat scampered through her.

"I thought you already showered."

"I did." He strode toward her.

"Then what are you doing?"

Without a word, he undressed her, shrouding them in a cloud of desire so thick, it prickled over her skin like hot needles with every piece of clothing he peeled off. When he sank to one knee, taking off her embarrassingly damp panties, she tingled with anticipation. He rose slowly, his mouth trailing so close to her skin, she ached for its touch. His hot breath coasted up her inner thighs, her sex, stomach, and torso, lingering between her breasts, making her pant and her sex clench needily. When he finally lifted his face, that tempting mouth a whisper away from hers, and said, "I'm going to watch you shower," her mouth went dry.

Sweet baby Jesus.

"Let's go, angel."

The endearment made her heart sing, but her body was strung so tight, she could barely breathe. He motioned for her to lead the way, the heat of his stare burning through her. Why was this so freaking hot? They showered together all the time. They got naked all over her house and his apartment. But this taunting, this *longing*, heightened all her senses. Her stomach pulled tight, every inhalation of his potent scent bringing a wave of desire.

She reached into the shower to feel the water. It was luxuriously warm, but under Tobias's scalding gaze, she knew that water would boil. She moved to make it colder and felt his bare chest against her back as he lowered her arm.

"Sorry, baby. No cold shower tonight."

Scintillating sensations chased over her at his gravelly insistence. But two could play at this game. As she stepped into the shower, he leaned his ass against the counter, casually crossing his ankles, and said, "Leave the door open."

"I was planning on it." She stepped under the warm water and tipped her face up.

"Face me," he said gruffly.

She turned, and his hungry gaze slid to her breasts. *Look your fill, dirty boy.* She put bodywash in her hands and began washing herself, caressing her breasts, arching her back, making the sexy noises she knew he loved. His jaw tensed, and she held his gaze as she slid her fingers between her legs.

"*Don't,*" he demanded.

"Why not?" She continued rubbing her finger over her clit, breathing heavier.

He pushed from the counter, standing right outside the shower, his broad frame soaking up the steam. "Because tonight we play my way. *Hands off.*"

"You're cruel." She narrowed her eyes, continuing to touch herself, sliding her finger along her slick pussy and over her clit. She trapped her lower lip between her teeth, her gaze never wavering from his.

"Not cruel, angel." He grabbed her wrist, leaning in until he was *right there.* Water peppered his face, his hungry eyes drilling into her. "All I want is to bring you pleasure. I've thought about making love to you all day. Getting my hands and mouth on you, tasting your come, hearing your pleas." His gaze dropped to her mouth. "I've conjured scenarios with your greedy hands and that fuckable mouth on me that I'd like to play out later. But if you aren't enjoying this, then by all means, make yourself come. But know *this.* I won't stand by with idle hands, and I *won't* touch you. If you're doing *you,* I'll do me and come on those pretty tits of yours."

She. Couldn't. Think.

"What's it going to be, Mads?" He leaned in further, the sensual scratch of his whiskers abrading her cheek, sending lust slithering through her as he rasped in her ear, "Do you want to play this out and get my hands, my mouth, and my cock on you? *Inside* you? Everywhere you want them? Or are you calling the game now with nothing more than a show?"

"*Both*" rushed from her lungs. "I want both. Can we do this now and then start over?"

He leaned back, desire blazing in his eyes and a cocky grin on his lips. "No can do, sweetheart. My game, my rules."

He released her hand, but she was frozen in place, thinking about him jerking off while she touched herself. She wanted that. She wanted *him.* She wanted *everything.*

Chapter Sixteen

MADIGAN HAD NEVER been called patient, but as she watched Tobias eat another oyster, she deserved a freaking award for it. His eyes were as wicked as the devil himself as he put his lips up to the shell and the oyster slid onto his tongue, eliciting a sensual sound, giving her visions of his mouth between her legs. She couldn't squeeze her thighs tightly enough to quell the ache *or* the wetness seeping between them. When his tongue darted out, licking his lower lip, flames sparking in his eyes, she was *this close* to throwing everything she'd ever known about herself to the wind, saying *fuck it*, and straddling him right there at the table.

Why did she have to be so greedy? This was the *worst* idea ever. She should have gone with the shower show, because she wasn't sure she'd survive a whole night of him taunting her. He'd reserved a quiet table in the corner of a fancy restaurant and was sitting so close to her, electric currents pulsed in the air around them. The man was a walking aphrodisiac. But eating oysters, when he'd spent the last hour bringing her to the brink of madness with nothing more than taunting looks and seductive whispers?

He was *temptation personified.*

He put his hand on her thigh, his long, hot fingers creeping under the edge of her minidress. "Don't you want to eat something?"

He'd ordered an array of her favorite seafood, which they were sharing, along with a pasta dish that was to die for. She'd taken a few bites, but the only thing she wanted in her mouth was the sex god whose fingers had just slid into the wetness on her upper thigh. That slow grin that made her belly tighten slid into place, and she stifled a moan. She should have brought her vibrator. He'd never know if she excused herself to do a little *self-care* in the ladies' room.

"I sure do," she said, and knowing how much he loved her mouth, she made a slow, sensual show of licking her lips. *"Desperately."*

He squeezed her thigh, eyes igniting.

That's right, big guy. I'm going to make you just as lust crazed as you make me. She angled her body toward him, forcing his hand to her inner thigh, and arched a brow. His finger moved in slow circles through the wetness there, so close to where she needed him, she inched forward on her chair, but he pressed his fingers into her flesh, refusing her.

"There's plenty of food just waiting for you." He nodded toward the table.

She'd break that will of steel if it took all night. Plucking a breadstick from the basket, she leaned her elbow on the table, resting her chin on her thumb with her fingertips touching her cheek, blocking the view of her mouth from other patrons as she ran her tongue over the end of the breadstick.

His eyes narrowed.

A little giddy at his reaction, she dragged her tongue along the length of the breadstick. "*Mm.* Big and salty. Just how I like it."

His grip on her thigh tightened.

She inserted the breadstick slowly into her open mouth, pushing it all the way back to her throat, and he uttered a curse. She withdrew it and did it again, wrapping her lips around it. His chest rose with his heavy breaths. She licked her lips, loving the way his jaw tightened, and started over, doing everything slower this time. His fingers inched closer to her center, their heat radiating through her, making her even wetter. When his gaze dropped to her breasts, she realized she was breathing just as hard as he was, and she was too wet, too turned on. On the brink of an embarrassing disaster.

She dropped the breadstick on a plate and leaned closer, whispering, "I need to get cleaned up before I embarrass us both."

She pushed to her feet, doing her best to walk on wobbly legs toward the bathroom. She pushed through the door, and a second later *he* blew through behind her, taking her by surprise as he turned the lock, his expression feral.

"*Tobias*," she said breathily, all *want*, no warning.

"The only thing cleaning up your sweet pussy is going to be my mouth." He lifted her up and set her onto the counter, shoving her dress up to her waist and spreading her legs wide. He held her there, his dark eyes looking their fill, turning her on even more before meeting her gaze. "So fucking wet and so damn beautiful."

She couldn't look away, didn't want to miss a second of the ravenous beast she'd unleashed as he lowered his mouth, feasting on her like the hungry wolf he was. She clawed at the cold sink, arching at the exquisite sensations racing through her. His whiskers abraded her thighs, making her want *more*. She fisted one hand in his hair, rocking against his eager mouth as he fucked and sucked and grazed his teeth in the most titillating devouring she'd ever endured. His salacious sounds and gratified groans took her higher. Emotions stacked up inside her until her heart felt like it was going to explode right along with the rest of her. A thousand pinpricks blazed through her like wildfire, her climax clawing just out of reach.

"Don't stop."

He took her clit between his teeth, pushing a finger inside her and stroking that magical spot like a detonator, hurling her into ecstasy. She bit down to keep from crying out, digging her fingernails into his shoulders as her orgasm gripped and soared, ravaging her entire being. She bucked and moaned, clinging to him until she had nothing left, and she lay back, boneless and euphoric. "*Ohmygodohmygodohmygod,*" she said in one long breath.

Tobias grinned, his lips wet with her arousal. He took his time lapping it up before gathering her in his arms.

She rested her cheek on his chest. "I like your games."

"We're not done here." He lifted her chin, dragging his thumb across her lower lip. "I want your sexy mouth on my cock."

"So do I," fell from her lips as she slid off the counter. She had a fleeting thought about where they were, but it was no match for the desires pounding through her as she opened his jeans. She tugged them down to his ankles and pushed him back against the wall. "Get *lower*. I want to be on my knees."

He sank lower, and she hiked her dress up to her waist and knelt, taking his beautiful, thick length in her hand, then proceeded to lick and suck and tease as he bit out curses, his hands fisted in her hair. Everything he did, every noise he made as she took him to the back of her throat, sucking for all she was worth, turned her on. She was lost in his pleasure, drenched between her legs again, and she never wanted to be found. But she had a surprise for him. Slowing her pace, she stroked him tighter, feeling him swell in her hand.

"*Fuck,*" he bit out. "I'm going to come so hard."

She withdrew his cock from her mouth. "One sec." She began unbuttoning the front of her dress.

"What are—"

His words were lost as she unhooked the front of her bra, pulling the cups, and her dress, to the sides, baring her breasts. The lust in his eyes nearly did her in as she said, "Finish *on* me." She reached between her legs, working her clit. She was so close to coming, it wouldn't take long.

"*Christ*, Blue Eyes." He fisted his cock. Their gazes locked as he pumped fast and tight, eyes brimming with emotions so deep, she wanted to bottle them up and keep them forever. She bit her lower lip, her eyes flicking between his big hand wrapped around his dick and those captivating eyes. Shaking with need, trying to stave off her orgasm, she pleaded, "*Tobias, I'm so close.*"

"Now, baby. *Now—*"

Her climax consumed her as he came in hot spurts all over her breasts, jaw tight, eyes never leaving hers. He was a glorious sight, enraptured by her, by *them*, branding her from the outside as he had from the inside, and she knew at that moment, *his* was all she ever wanted to be.

THEY STUMBLED OUT of the restaurant twenty minutes

later in hysterics. After cleaning themselves up, they'd found two women waiting to use the restroom. They'd left the remaining food uneaten, paid their bill, and headed straight out the door. Even with the embarrassment, Madigan wouldn't trade that experience for anything.

"We're going to be banned from that restaurant." Tobias wrapped his arm snuggly around Madigan's shoulders and kissed her temple.

"It could have been worse."

He looked at her doubtfully as they made their way to her Jeep. "How's that?"

"We could have found my mom or my aunt waiting outside the restroom."

"Aw, *shit*. I'm in enough trouble with Blaine. I don't need the rest of your family hating me." He unlocked the passenger door and gazed down at her. "I'm crazy about you, Mads, but I really hate what's going on with Blaine. I never wanted to cause trouble for you."

"I don't like what's going on with him, either, but he's acting ridiculous. You came back and owned up to everything. He's got no reason to be against us. Whatever hair he has up his ass will eventually work itself out. It always does. This is how he argues. You should have seen him with Maverick when they were younger. My parents fostered Maverick before they adopted him, and my mom said that Blaine wouldn't give him the time of day. He was asserting his dominance as the alpha brother or something. But what matters is that he got over it, and he'll get over this, too."

"I hope you're right." He glanced back at the restaurant. "I guess we suck at eating out."

"Actually, I think you excel at *eating out*, and from what I just experienced, I'd say I'm not so bad at sucking."

He chuckled. "As true as that is, tonight was supposed to be a romantic date, and then I got carried away at your place. It doesn't take much when I'm with you. The looks you were giving me when I got off my bike got me all worked up."

"I *like* getting you worked up, and you don't have to take me out to a fancy dinner to romance me. I think it's romantic when we sit on my back porch and play our guitars, or have coffee together in the morning. You came to see my puppet show. *That's* romantic, and bringing me flowers?" She wound her arms around his neck. "You're the king of romance right now, Mr. Riggs, and I'm totally and unabashedly into you."

"I'm crazy about you, too, Blue Eyes." He pressed his lips to hers. "But I'm not done romancing you. What do you think about a walk by the ocean?"

"If you include an ice cream cone, I'd be into that."

They stopped at Emack and Bolio's on their way to the beach, left their footwear in the Jeep, and walked along the shore. A cool breeze swept off the water, and Tobias reached for her hand. His was so big, it swallowed hers, his rings pressing against the sides of her fingers. It was a good feeling. Comforting and oddly familiar even though this was the first time they'd held hands. "I haven't held hands with anyone since Spain."

"Does it bring up bad memories?"

"No. Holding hands with Alejandro was nothing like this. When I look past the heartbreak, I see the cracks in our relationship. It was very one-sided. I was blindly infatuated with him. I felt high but not grounded, if that makes sense."

"It does. Do you think you're blindly infatuated with me?"

"That would be impossible," she said. "I mean, maybe at first, when I saw you across the bar and felt that inescapable thrum of electricity. But I've thought about *everything*. The red flags, ignoring them, the way my heart went crazy every time I saw you, and still does. I thought about how broody you were and what it might mean. I definitely went into this with my eyes open, and then we were dropped into a pool of reality wearing concrete boots. There's no blind anything on my side. What about you?"

"I coasted through my relationship with Michelle, letting it happen around me. I haven't done that with you. I made sure of it. I've forced myself to make every decision. Even the bad ones were made consciously."

"I guess that's good." They walked in comfortable silence as they finished their ice creams, listening to the waves kissing the shore. "Can I ask you something about prison?"

He nodded, and she felt his walls going up, but she was curious about a few things.

"Was it as bad as it is in movies?"

"I guess that depends on the movie. It sucked. It was scary, demeaning, boring, and lonely as hell."

"Did people try to…?" She didn't know how to ask the question.

"Make me their bitch? No. I was in for killing a man with one punch, and word spreads fast behind bars. I wasn't someone they wanted to fuck with. But I got in a few fights over stupid shit. Nothing major. It was really just hundred-hour days and month-long nights of overthinking everything that had happened."

"Did anyone visit you?"

He shook his head. "Michelle divorced me, as I told you, and my father and sister weren't speaking to me. My grandfather was going to come out early on, but I told him not to. I didn't want him traveling all that way just to see me behind bars. I thought we'd catch up after I got out. He was such a strong presence in my life, such a strong man, it never crossed my mind that I wouldn't get a chance to try to make it up to him."

They'd had dinner with his grandfather last week, and Madigan had gotten approval to continue working with him. "He loves you unconditionally. I don't think you have anything to make up to him."

"He believed in me when nobody else did, and I hate that I let him down."

She stepped in front of him, so she could have his full attention. "I can't imagine that your grandfather will find fault in protecting your sister. I bet if you caught him in a lucid moment and told him how you feel, he'd tell you that you need to forgive yourself so *you* can heal."

His arms circled her, and he held her close. He didn't say a word, just kissed the top of her head. But she felt his struggle between wanting to heal and feeling like he didn't deserve to.

"Thank you." He put his arm around her, keeping her close as they continued walking down the beach. "What else do you want to know?"

"Everything."

He smiled and shook his head. "Of course you do."

"Did you reach out to your sister during those three years?"

"I wrote to her every week for two years, and my letters were returned unopened with *Return to sender* scribbled on the envelopes."

She was crushed for him. "Oh, Tobias. I'm so sorry."

"That's life."

"Have you tried to contact her since you got out?"

"No. She has a good life with her daughter, and I don't want to fuck it up."

"How do you know she has a good life?"

"Because I've checked on her," he said sharply.

"Sorry. I don't mean to pry."

"Yes, you do, and it's okay, Mads. I'm not upset with you. I don't want to leave you in the dark about anything. I miss her, and it's just hard to talk about."

"I understand. But three years is a long time. Maybe she's changed her mind."

He stepped in front of her this time and took her hands in his, his expression serious. "Mads, I know this all comes from your heart, but can you please just let it go?"

"Yes. I'm sorry. I just know how much she means to you, and I wish things could be different. But I'll stop."

"Thank you." He draped his arm around her shoulders again, and she felt his relief. "Tell me how your shopping trip with Steph and Sid went."

They'd gone shopping for gifts for Tank and Leah's baby. "We had so much fun. You should see all the stuff we bought for the baby."

"Did you get one of those musical things that hangs over a crib?"

She laughed. "You mean a mobile?"

He squeezed her butt, smiling down at her. What a beautiful sight that was. "Listen here, Miss *Skateboard Thing*."

She giggled. "I guess we're a perfect pair. But no, I didn't get a mobile. My aunt has dibs on the nursery decor. I got one of those books where you read the story and it records your voice, so the baby can always hear Auntie Mads, and a stuffed rabbit, and the cutest onesies, and…" Her heart sank. "Oh my gosh. I'm rambling on about baby gifts after what we just talked about. I'm so insensitive. I'm sorry."

"Mads, I asked you, and please don't do that. Don't shut down your happiness because of my shitty situation. I want to hear about what you bought for the baby, and I want to hear it with that joy in your voice that brings me so much happiness."

"Really? It doesn't upset you?"

"Not at all."

"*Well,*" she said sheepishly. "You could send your sister the stuffed rabbit for your niece."

"*Madigan,*" he warned.

"I'm letting it go. I promise."

He hugged her against his side. "I wish I could make things right, but at least I've got you, and you make everything else better than right."

"Even with my big mouth?"

"Maybe even *because of* your big, sexy, adorably chatty mouth." He leaned in and kissed her senseless.

Chapter Seventeen

TOBIAS PARKED THE work truck behind the shop on Monday afternoon. They'd gotten as far as they could on the renovations until the rest of their supplies were delivered after lunch. Zeke and Zander had invited him to have pizza with them, but Tobias had something more important he needed to do after swapping the work truck for his motorcycle.

As he headed inside, he gazed up at the Cape Renovations sign above the back door and felt a sense of pride that Preacher not only trusted him with his daughter but also with his clients and one of his vehicles. He and Zeke and Zander made a good team. He'd missed having friends to shoot the shit with. It was a strange and wonderful feeling to go from years of days blurring together to the first few months after getting out of prison, when the days of the week didn't matter because he was just so damn happy to be free, to looking forward to evenings and weekends with Madigan. He'd been surprised to realize he looked forward to work every day, too.

He went into the office to hang up the truck keys. Reba's door was ajar, and he heard Preacher talking low and Reba giggling, followed by sounds of kissing, more low voices, giggling, and kissing. *Shit.* It was no wonder Madigan was so openly affectionate. When they met at the shop in the mornings, Reba greeted each of them with a special comment or a hug and a smile as bright as her daughter's. Tobias had noticed how touchy-feely she and Preacher were with each other and how they made a point of saying goodbye with an *I love you* and a kiss every time they parted ways. He wanted that with Madigan, and he hoped her eyes never stopped lighting up when she saw him.

A man is only as good as he makes the people around him feel. His grandfather had drilled that into his head when he was young. No truer words had ever been spoken, which was why he was on a mission to make things right with Blaine.

Tobias quickly hung up the keys, and his phone vibrated with a text. He stepped out of the office and into the hall as he pulled out his phone and saw Madigan's name on the screen. He opened the message and *Thinking of you* appeared. Another message popped up, a picture of a card that had five gold stars across the top and *EXCELLENT PENIS. HIGHLY RECOMMEND* beneath. He chuckled as he thumbed out, *I'll see your five stars and raise you five more. Mesmerizing Mouth. TEN Stars. Can't wait to revisit.* He added a devil emoji and sent it off.

"Tobias."

Startled, he pocketed his phone and looked up, meeting Preacher's serious gaze and Reba's sweet smile. "Hey, Preacher. Reba."

"Hi, sweetheart," she said. "You look a little harried. Is everything okay?"

"Yes, I was just"—*sending your daughter a dirty text*—"on my way out."

"I'll walk out with you." Preacher leaned in to kiss Reba. "Love you, darlin'."

"Love you, too. You boys have a good afternoon."

"Everything go okay this morning?" Preacher asked as they headed outside.

"Sure did. We made good time. The rest of the supplies should be delivered by one thirty, and we'll be back at it." Tobias nodded to an old black Trans Am parked by Preacher's truck. "Whose ride is that?"

"She's mine. Reba got sick of her taking up space in the garage, so I had her towed over this morning."

"It doesn't run?"

"Nah. I've been tinkering with her, trying to figure out why. It might be about time to rebuild the engine."

"I can take a look at it if you'd like. I've been working on cars since I was a teenager."

Preacher crossed his arms. "You wouldn't mind?"

"Are you kidding? That's a dream car right there. It'd be an honor to work on it."

Preacher looked at the car with reverence. "She was my first car. I bought her when I was seventeen."

Tobias smiled, shaking his head. "At seventeen I was walking two miles to and from work each day. I'd be happy to take a look. I've got something to take care of right now, and I'm having dinner with Mads and my grandfather tonight, but I could take a look tomorrow after work."

"I'd really appreciate that. How's your grandfather doing?"

Tobias shrugged. "About as well as can be expected. He's got Alzheimer's, and he has more bad days than good, but he's still here, and I'm thankful for that. Mads is working with him this afternoon."

"That's a rough road. If you, or he, need anything at all, you let us know."

"Thank you. I appreciate that. Well, I'd better get going. I don't want to be late coming back and piss off the boss."

"Smart man," Preacher said with a nod as Tobias headed over to his motorcycle.

TOBIAS MIGHT NOT be able to fix his own shitty situation with his family, but he sure as hell could try to make things right for Madigan. He walked into Cape Stone, his gaze sweeping over impressive stone fountains, pillars, fireplaces, and other design displays as he made his way through the showroom. Maverick was on the phone at the counter and lifted his chin in acknowledgment.

Tobias nodded and took a few steps away just as Blaine came out a door in the back. His hair was tousled and his expression casual—for about three seconds before he spotted Tobias closing the distance between them, and it iced over.

Blaine crossed his arms, looking a lot like his old man, except he looked down his nose at Tobias. *"Riggs."*

Tobias wasn't dissuaded. "You got a minute?"

"For?"

"A conversation."

Blaine's jaw clenched. "We've got nothing to converse about."

"Is Madigan no longer important to you?" It was a dig, but he needed to shake Blaine up to get him to talk.

Blaine glowered but didn't respond.

Tobias drew his shoulders back. "I'm not going anywhere, Blaine. You can give me five minutes now, or I'll come back every day until you do."

"Don't be an ass, Blaine," Maverick bit out as he walked past them.

Blaine's eyes never left Tobias, but his jaw tightened. Neither said a word, uncomfortable silence stretching between them. Tobias was determined not to back down. He'd made this mess, and he was going to clean it up.

"Five minutes," Blaine said curtly, and strode into an office.

Tobias followed, closing the door behind him. Blaine stood with his arms crossed and the same unforgiving expression. "I care about your sister, and I understand that you don't think I'm good enough for her."

"You lied to her."

"I *didn't*, but you already know that."

"You slept with her without coming clean about being in prison," he seethed.

"You're right, because *that's* what our relationship was at that point."

Blaine's hands fisted.

"I have a sister, too. I know what you're feeling right now, and I'm sorry, but all I can do is be honest with you. That's how Madigan and I *started*, but she got under my skin, and I'm crazy about her. I came back *because* I was crazy about her, and I wanted to do right by her. I've got nothing to prove to you, and I'm not going to try," he said firmly. "But for *Madigan*, I will spend every day making up for the hurt I caused."

"How do we know you don't have more skeletons in your closet?"

"Maybe you don't, but I'd imagine your cop friend has already checked me out. All I'm asking is that you don't make Madigan pay for my mistakes. She fucking worships you, man, and you're treating her like she's an outcast. Like she isn't smart enough to make her own decisions or grown up enough to use her body however she sees fit. Your sister is the fiercest, smartest, and most loving woman I have ever met, and that's partially because of you. You've taught her to take care of herself." He paused, letting that sink in. "I lost my sister when I was trying to protect her, and I never saw it coming. I wouldn't wish the guilt or sadness that causes me every damn day on anyone. But you've got your eyes wide open. Tread carefully, Blaine, because some wrongs can't be made right."

MADIGAN HELD THE cat puppet while Hank stroked its fur, recounting the story of how his childhood pet, Lazy Cat, had gotten his name. He'd been highly agitated when Madigan had arrived for their session, and he'd thought she was his mother. It had taken some doing, but she'd finally found the right approach to pull him out of his agitated state and into more pleasant memories. Their session time had already ended, but Tobias would be there soon, and she was hoping his grandfather's mood would remain upbeat. Hank was always happy to see Tobias, whether he mistook him for his younger self, his brother John, or as he had last week, his father, but she hoped to help him stay as far from sheer agitation as she could.

"John pokes him," Hank said in a conspiratorial whisper.

"He does?" Madigan asked with surprise. "How do you think Lazy Cat feels about that?"

"He doesn't know. He's too fat to feel it. Watch." He poked the cat puppet, and Madigan made the puppet yawn, as if it was oblivious to his finger.

As he told her secrets and stories from his youth, Madigan thought about how much she loved working with him and with the other residents there at LOCAL. When she'd arrived for work today, Chloe had been waiting for her. That wasn't unusual. They often caught up throughout the week, but this time Chloe had asked if she'd be willing to work more hours to accommodate more residents. Apparently they were starting to put together a waiting list for her services. Madigan loved the idea of helping more people, but she'd already put the wheels into motion for her new merchandising line, and she was behind on making it happen. She'd told Chloe she'd have to think about it and had been trying to figure out how to fit everything in.

"Where is John?" Hank asked, drawing her from her thoughts. "He didn't go fishing without me, did he? That little bugger."

"No. He went down to the corner store." Madigan knew his brother used to go down to the corner store when they were young, because Elsa had gathered even more information from her own parents about Hank and their family, and she'd shared it with Madigan after their last session. There was a knock at the door, and Madigan's pulse quickened as Elsa answered it. She heard her filling Tobias in on what they were doing.

"I hope he doesn't lose your money this time," Hank said, stroking the cat. His face brightened when Tobias walked into the living room carrying a large bag from his grandfather's favorite restaurant. "Speak of the devil. What's in the bag, John?"

"Dinner. Are you hungry?" Tobias glanced at Madigan, affection and gratitude fighting for space in his overly broody eyes.

"Do you have enough for Lazy Cat?" his grandfather asked with a chuckle.

"I think we might," Tobias said tightly.

She wondered what was going on with Tobias, but she continued playing the part of his grandfather's mother. "I don't think it's a good idea for Lazy Cat to eat human food. How about if I put her down for a nap while we eat?"

"More for us that way." Hank pushed to his feet and walked over to Tobias, lowering his voice as he said, "Knucklehead."

"Want me to give you a knuckle sandwich?" Tobias retorted, earning another chuckle from his grandfather as he went with Elsa into the kitchen.

Madigan went to Tobias. His small smile as he drew her into his arms was everything. Now that she knew how many times he'd reached out to his sister and how many letters were returned, each one another slap in his face, she understood how deeply rooted those shadows in his brooding eyes were. That made moments like these, when Tobias could see that his grandfather was able to be at peace even with the awful disease that was rapidly stealing him away, even more important.

"Hey, Blue Eyes. How was he today?"

"Good." She caressed his cheek, feeling his tension, and went up on her toes, pressing her lips to his and remaining there for an extra beat, until she felt that tension start to ease. Only then did she sink back to her heels. "The question is, how are you?"

"Better now, angel. Much better now."

Chapter Eighteen

MADIGAN THUMBED OUT a text to Marly as she left the Scullery Maid, a hole-in-the-wall tavern located about an hour away from Harwich, where she'd just met with the owner about a musical storytelling gig. *Remind me not to wear a short skirt if I get the gig. Did this week seem excruciatingly long to you? TGIF!* She added a celebration emoji and sent it off.

She loved dives like the Scullery Maid, despite a few seedy customers. The vibe was totally different from most of the places she played. Places like this were usually packed with people who were so excited to see good entertainment, their enthusiasm pumped her up to play for them.

As she climbed into her Jeep, she checked her email, taking note of the messages from the distribution company that she still hadn't gotten back to. She didn't need to open it to know they were waiting for her to review and sign the contract. Her phone rang, and Chloe's name appeared on the screen. *Shoot.* She really needed to make a decision about expanding her hours, too. Where had the week gone?

"Hi, Chloe."

"Hi. How are you?"

"Crazed, but good. You?"

"It's been a long week, but Justin and I are taking Shadow and Sampson on a long walk on the beach tonight, and we *all* need it." Shadow and Sampson were the dogs they'd adopted from Gunner and Sid's rescue. "Are you sure you're okay? We saw Blaine last night, and it sounded like you two aren't making any headway."

Madigan had thought he might reach out to her after rudely leaving the table last week at the Salty Hog when she and Tobias had arrived. But he hadn't, and it was breaking her heart. "No, but I'm playing at the Hog tomorrow, and I'll talk to him then."

"He won't be there. He and Justin are meeting with a new big-wig client on Martha's Vineyard, and the only time the guy could meet was tomorrow evening."

Madigan sighed. "Sunday he'll be riding with the guys, and then I'll be at Leah's baby shower. I guess I'll try to talk to him after that if the shower ends early enough. You know how it is when we all get together."

"If it gets too late, maybe you can catch up with him early next week. I've just never seen him like this. He's always given you a hard time about wearing skimpy clothes or trying to meet guys, but this is a little weird, isn't it? It's going on so long. Justin said I shouldn't worry, that this is how Blaine deals with things. But I'm worried for both of you."

"We'll be fine." Although Chloe was right. It had gone on for so long, she wasn't so sure they would be fine. "Marly thinks he's acting this way because he's never had to deal with me getting serious with a guy."

"It's times like these I'm glad I don't have brothers."

"Oh, but Mrs. Wicked, now you have *many*."

"I know, right?" Chloe said. "I love them all, even though

Blaine's being a butthead. Anyway, have you given any thought to working more hours? I know you've got a lot on your plate with your Mad Truth expansion, and I'll totally understand if it's too much. I'm not trying to pressure you."

"I really want to do it, but I'm still trying to figure out how I can fit everything in. Can I give you an answer sometime next week?"

"Of course. Did you see the announcement about the next book club meeting on the forums? We just posted it last night."

Shoot. She hadn't made it past chapter four. "No, but I'll look tonight." Another call buzzed through, and she glanced at the screen. "Chloe, Marly's calling, and I know she has another date with Dante in about an hour. Can I call you right back?"

"No need. Tell her I said good luck."

"Will do." She took a deep breath as she answered Marly's call. "Hey, Mar, I just hung up with Chloe. She said good luck on your date. Can you hold on a sec?"

"Yup."

She put on her seat belt, started the Jeep, and waited for Bluetooth to pick up the call before driving out of the parking lot. "Okay, I'm here."

"You're in for a long drive. Dante just called and said Route Six is moving at a snail's pace."

"*Great,*" she said sarcastically. "Tell me some good news. How are things with Dante?"

"Wonderful, which Blaine hates, by the way. Dante and I saw him at the Hog the other night, and Blaine wouldn't even look at me. So if you want to pin your brother's face to the dart board, I'm totally down for a game."

"I'm sorry he's being a jerk." She pulled onto the highway and behind a long line of slow-moving traffic. "But I'm glad things are good with Dante. Does that mean you've let him get past second base?"

"No. We're still taking things slow, but I really like him. He's thoughtful and funny, and he *doesn't* drive a motorcycle."

"Right, *all* the sexy things that women look for." Madigan rolled her eyes even though her friend couldn't see it. "He's also a freaking hot rock star who's totally into you."

"I'm totally into him, too."

"Then why can't he get you in the back of his *band van*?"

"I'm just being careful. Sex confuses things."

"I don't know, Mar. I couldn't have taken things slow with Sir Broodiness if I'd wanted to. I still can't. I see him and I turn into some sort of feral sex kitten, all claws and rampant desire." They both laughed, but Madigan's amusement was short lived. "I'm a little worried about where my head is lately. One day I'm a girl boss ready to take on the world, and the next thing I know, I'm all swoony and weak kneed. When did I become *that* girl?"

"What are you talking about? You're still a girl boss."

"Not like before. Tobias has a hold over me. My feelings for him are all consuming. I've never felt like this."

"It's the five-star penis, isn't it?"

"There is *that*, but I'm serious. I told you, *feral cat over here*. But it's *everything* about him, Mar. Sometimes I just want to put work and everything else aside and spend every second with him."

"Come on," Marly said with disbelief.

"I'm not kidding. Last night I was working and he was cooking, fully dressed in jeans and a T-shirt, and I stared at him for half an hour. *Stared* at him, Marly, like a ridiculous teenager, drunk on the barefoot man in my kitchen. What *is* that? And when he plays guitar, I might as well forget trying to do anything else, because he gets this faraway look in his eyes, and his voice goes all soulful, and I'm just *gone*. Don't even get me started on the way he looks at me and loves everything I do. He even helps me come up with ideas for puppet shows, which should inspire me to do more, not less. But I swear it's like my drive to do more has just fizzled out, and we haven't even been together that long. Am I making a mistake? Because you can tell me. I need to know so I'm not walking around with blinders on."

"Take a breath, Mads," she said gently. "It sounds to me like you guys are crazy about each other."

Madigan's heart thundered, fear prickling her limbs. "It's too much too fast, isn't it?" She felt a jolt of panic. *Please tell me it's not.*

"Only you can answer that. Deep down, in your heart of hearts, what do you feel for him?"

"*Everything.* I love being with him, and when we're not together, it makes me happy to think about him. I love holding his hand and seeing him smile. I love the way my heart races every time I think of him and the way he holds me tight in the mornings and inhales so deeply it's like he wants to fill his senses with me and never let me go."

"Geez, girl. I want that."

"I *know*. But it's even bigger than that. I want to make everything in *his* life good, and I wish I could fix things with his sister, but I know he has to do that on his own, when he's ready."

"What if he never is?"

"I can't think about that. She left a gaping hole in him that I don't think anything or anyone else could ever fill." She paused, readying to spill more of her feelings. "I feel so much for him, it scares the heck out of me. What if there's another shoe hanging above us, and it just hasn't dropped yet? I don't want to get hit on the head with it."

"I'm pretty sure he'd catch it before it hit you."

Madigan smiled. "That doesn't even make sense. It would be *his* shoe dropping."

"Yeah, well, I'm getting dressed for my date and trying to be smart at the same time. It's not that easy. All that matters is that Tobias isn't an A-hole who crushed your heart, and as far as I can tell, Sir Broodiness is doing all he can to heal your heart, not hurt it."

Madigan sighed. "He totally is. But I'm supposed to be expanding my business, and that whole process has stalled because I'd rather be with him than look over contracts and meet with attorneys and accountants."

"Who wouldn't?" Marly said lightly. "Besides, you can afford not to work and live off just your greeting card income. Do you really need to expand right now?"

"I can't just rest on my laurels. I'm twenty-five."

"Girl, you have *three* jobs. You'll never rest on your laurels. But you finally have someone that makes you want to slow down and enjoy life rather than working all the time. That's a *blessing*, not a mistake, and my vote is that you enjoy it."

She stared at the slow-moving cars ahead of her, thinking about all of the hoops she'd been jumping through for the last few years to *keep from* slowing down enough to become—*or realize?*—she was lonely, and she remembered the call she'd gotten from her father two days ago. Her father wasn't one to gush, but Tobias had been checking out his car for him, and they'd spent a lot of time together, and her father had used words like *good man* and *careful thinker* and had said that it might be a good idea for Tobias to prospect the Dark Knights to give him a sense of belonging and family. A few of her brothers, cousins, and friends had mentioned the same thing over the last couple of weeks, and she was glad they were bonding with him, but her feelings were so deep, she'd never survive it if they broke up and she still had to see him all the time. Not that she thought that would happen, but there was no holding back her fear as "What if I get hurt?" slipped out.

"Oh, you *will* get hurt," Marly assured her. "All relationships come with some amount of heartache. How else can you learn and grow? But don't worry. If he ever breaks your heart, I'll be there to help you through it, and Blaine will spend his life trying to slaughter him."

"Marly."

"Hey, he's *your* brother. Why are you freaking out about all of this right now? Because you're a little behind on your self-imposed conquer-the-world deadline?"

Because I think I'm falling in love with him. "Because I'm sitting in traffic and have nothing better to do."

THE SUN HAD dipped from the sky by the time Madigan finally got home, and she was relieved to see Tobias's motorcycle. She'd called to let him know traffic was horrendous, and they'd agreed to meet at her place, but she should have been there forty minutes ago. At least she'd made good use of the time and had finally figured out what to do about her work situation.

She climbed out of her Jeep and was greeted by the low, husky sound of Tobias's singing "…*And learn to reconnect with the life…I'll be trying to catch up on all my memories.*" She followed his voice along the side of the house, stopping at the edge of the backyard to listen. He was sitting in the screened porch, playing his guitar. There was a backpack at his feet, and he was looking down at an open book on the table as he sang. Even from at least thirty feet away, she could *feel* his energy. It was mournful *and* hopeful, and that hope was beautiful. She stood there, unnoticed, listening to the end of one song and the beginning of another, his voice escalating with the upbeat tune.

As she stepped out of the shadows, he was so intent on the book and singing, he didn't notice her making her way to the porch.

"It'll all make sense like it did. I'll connect the dots again…I've been hurting like a kid. And nothing hurts like thinking you'll never be present…"

The emotion in his voice was so raw, it brought a lump to her throat. She'd experienced the gut-wrenching pain he was singing about, the horrific ache of knowing she'd never see Ashley again. She never would have thought to describe it as hurting like a kid, but that was *exactly* how she'd felt after Ashley died. She opened the door to the screened porch, and he looked over, his broody eyes filling with warmth.

"Hey, Blue Eyes."

He held out his hand, and she went to him, noticing the backpack was full of unopened letters and the book on the table wasn't a book after all. It was the journal he kept in his guitar case. He took her hand, pulling her into a kiss and guiding her to sit beside him on the wicker love seat.

TOBIAS WAS CONSUMED with emotions from the memories he was singing about, but none were stronger than the relief of seeing Madigan. "Traffic sucked, huh?"

"There were two accidents. Sorry it took so long. What song were you playing?"

He shrugged. "I guess I'll call it 'Tonight.'"

"You just wrote it?" She couldn't hide her astonishment.

He shook his head and tapped the open journal. "I wrote it a long time ago, but it wasn't a song. It was a letter to Carrie that I never sent."

"And you made it into a song?"

"Yeah. At your show the other night, you told the story that I now realize was about when you saw Alejandro with his family. That's got to be a hard story for you to tell. But you do, over and over again. Your strength blows me away, angel."

"Thank you," she said softly, humbly.

"I remembered what you said about how putting your words to music was what helped you finally get all those awful feelings out, so I thought I'd give it a try."

"And?" she asked hopefully.

"It helped. I've been at it for quite a while."

"Tobias, that's wonderful." She hugged him. "And *you* blew me away with your words. Your description of hurting like a kid is so accurate. That's exactly what I felt after losing Ashley. All I wanted to do was crawl onto my mother's lap and let her make things better."

He swallowed hard, hating that he unknowingly stirred hurtful memories. He set down his guitar and took her hand. "I didn't mean to make you sad."

"It's okay. I'm glad I heard it. I want to know what you felt like then and what you feel now. But I had my mom. I could go to her anytime I wanted for a hug or so she could tell me that we'd get through it." Tears welled in her eyes. "But you couldn't."

"It's okay, babe." He hugged her. "I was fine."

"How could you be *fine*? You lost your mom, your dad wasn't there for you as you got older, and then you lost everything else. It must have been awful going all those years without anyone to hug you or hold you or tell you they loved you."

"My grandfather and Elsa told me."

"But still. I miss Blaine and it's only been a few weeks." She wiped her eyes, glancing at the backpack. "Are those the letters you sent to your sister?"

"Yeah. I was going to try putting one to music, but…" He shook his head. "I'm not there yet."

"That's okay."

"Every time I look in that backpack, the same questions hit me. Why didn't she come to me when he was hurting her? I was always there for her. *Always.* I took every phone call, every text. I talked through hundreds of problems with her." He reached into the front pocket of the backpack and pulled out a Mad Truth About Love card. "She gave me this when she moved in with me."

He handed her the card and watched her reading the words he'd long ago memorized. WE MAY NOT ALWAYS SEE EYE TO EYE was printed on the front of the card, and inside, PROBABLY BECAUSE YOU'RE FREAKISHLY TALL, BUT I STILL LOVE YOU.

As she silently read his sister's note, the words played out in his mind.

Big Bo, thank you for always being there for me and for letting me move in with you. I promise to rearrange your shelves, nag you about laundry, bore you with stories of the guys I go out with (yes, I WILL be dating, so get used to it!), and basically annoy the heck out of you. We're going to argue, so you might as well accept that I'm going to win every time and give up now, and don't you dare leave the toilet seat up or I'll put itching powder in your sheets. She'd drawn a smiley face. *Seriously, I have no idea what I'd do without you.*

I love your ugly face, Carrie.

Madigan met his gaze. "She sounds funny and sweet, and she obviously adored you."

"She is and she did. She gave me this one when she moved in with Kevin." He withdrew another Mad Truth card and handed it to her. On the front was, I SMILE MOST OF THE TIME BECAUSE YOU'RE MY BROTHER. Inside, on the left was, SOMETIMES I PUNCH THINGS FOR THE SAME REASON, and on the right, BUT I LAUGH EVERY SINGLE DAY BECAUSE YOU'RE STUCK WITH ME.

"I came up with this card for Blaine," Madigan said solemnly without looking up, and then she read his sister's note.

Big Bo, you really are stuck with me forever, so don't think just because I'm moving in with Kevin, you're going to get a reprieve from me bugging the heck out of you or driving you crazy with my babbling. That's NEVER going to change. You'll always be my rock, my sounding board, and my favorite person. But you should be used to that by now.

Love, your amazing sister, Carrie

Madigan looked at him. "This makes me so sad."

He nodded. "That's what I'm saying. She trusted me with everything. Why wouldn't she trust me with the most important thing—what Kevin was doing to her?"

"Maybe because of the same reason I still haven't told anyone but you the truth about Alejandro being married. Because she was ashamed. It's hard to face the people who have spent their lives protecting you when you fail to protect yourself."

"But I'd never hold that against her. She was a fucking *victim*, and I had no clue. The guy was my best friend, and I didn't even see what was right in front of my face. That kills me."

"You *did* see it, but she covered it up. You can't fault yourself for trusting her, but I wish you could tell her how you feel. Maybe then things could get better. I can't tell you how much I hate that you're hurting and that you two aren't talking."

"You don't have to tell me, because I'm in the same position with you and Blaine."

"I don't want to talk about Blaine right now."

If anyone understood the need to avoid hurtful topics, it was Tobias. He tried to lighten the mood for both of them. "Maybe we should set Blaine and Carrie up on a date."

"Maybe we should write a song about it."

"Setting them up on a date?" he asked with amusement.

"No. How we feel about each other's situations. We could write it together." She shrugged. "It might help both of us."

That wasn't a bad idea. He picked up his guitar and began strumming the tune to "Paint It, Black," and sang, "*I see my girl hurting, and I want to take it all back. Wash away the hurt, and start over again.*"

Madigan chimed in, singing, "*I want to shake your sister until she lets you in. I have to bite my tongue, make the anger go away.*"

They both smiled, and he felt the darker emotions giving way. He began playing the chorus. "*I want to take it, take it back. Back to a clean slate that can't be misconstrued.*"

Madigan broke in. "*I wanna make her listen, wanna make her see, that you did it out of love, and it was an accidental tragedy. She needs to let you in, let you in, let you in.*"

They played and sang, their lyrics going from serious to lighter, changing subjects at their whims, until they realized they were singing about being starved and eating pizza. They both laughed as he set down his guitar and lifted Madigan onto his lap, gazing into her smiling eyes. "Why don't I go pick up some dinner for us while you go through that contract you've been putting off?"

Her brows knitted. "How do you know I've been putting it off?"

"I've got eyes and ears. I know I've been distracting you from important things, and don't even try to deny it. You have a business to run, and you told me you were expanding it. I don't want to screw that up for you."

"I decided to put off the expansion."

"But you were so excited about it. Why would you put it off?"

"Because I was only expanding to keep myself busy in the evenings, and now that we're together, I don't want to be that busy."

"Mads, you can't change your life because of me. I want to help you accomplish your dreams, not hold you back."

"You're not holding me back. Chloe wants me to take on more clients at LOCAL, which I'd really like to do, and that's going to eat up more of my free time."

"This doesn't feel right. If I hadn't come along, you wouldn't be distracted from the things that are important to you. What if I help you? I'll keep you on task instead of distracting you. Hell, you can put me to work. I'll do whatever you need. I can make phone calls, stuff packages. You name it, and I'll be happy to do it. Just don't put off the things you're passionate about."

"That's the point. I'm passionate about us. Can't you see my smile?" She pointed to her pearly whites.

"I'm serious, Mads."

"I know. That's why I'm smiling. I know you'll do whatever it takes to support me. But I promise you that I've been thinking about expanding for a while and only put the wheels into motion because I couldn't stop thinking about *you*."

He narrowed his eyes. "Be *honest* with yourself, Mads."

"I *am*. I needed something that would keep me super busy, and expanding a business takes oodles of time."

"Oodles?" He kissed her. "You're so fucking cute. Can't you start small?"

"Yes, but my brand is big, so if I start small it will only end up exploding in my face."

"There has to be a way."

"There is. I commit to the extra time with Chloe, because working with the residents makes me happy, and we continue monopolizing each other's time in fun and filthy-dirty ways, and see where we are in a year."

Was she seriously thinking that far ahead about them? "Why a year?"

"Because that's the *shortest* length of time I'm willing to go before thinking about giving up time with you for something as unimportant as selling hoodies."

Her words hit him right in the center of his chest, and he reveled in it. But he was serious about not letting her put off her dreams because of them. "Six months."

"A year, but there's a caveat. An *option period*."

He arched a brow, loving the sneakiness in her eyes.

"If in a year we're still as happy as we are now, I have the option to delay expansion for another year."

He wound his arms around her. "And what happens if you're happier then than you are now?"

"Then the option period is extended to two years."

"And if you're even happier in two years?"

"The extension period doubles every time it comes up."

"So, basically, if we're happy, you might never expand your business?" He smacked her ass. "You're a shrewd businesswoman. But I'm not signing that deal."

Her brows knitted. "Why not?"

"Because you have three careers, and you love to travel. You're not going to be satisfied year after year without something new going on in your life. So here's the new deal. Six months, and every time you delay, I'm taking you on a trip."

"Tobias, you don't have to do that. Traveling is expensive, and—"

He silenced her with a kiss and caressed her cheek as their lips parted. "Don't you worry about what it'll cost. You're my girl, and I'm going to make damn sure that you don't miss out on doing the things you love and are passionate about."

"You drive a hard bargain, Sir Broodiness."

He rocked his hips. "Want to find out just how hard?"

"I thought you'd never ask."

Chapter Nineteen

MADIGAN AWOKE SUNDAY morning to the sounds of birds chirping, the feel of Tobias's hard body against her back, one strong arm wrapped snuggly around her, his warm hand cupping her breast, and an overwhelming sense of peace.

She'd wondered if she'd regret delaying the expansion of her business. If she'd wake up itchy to take back what she'd said. But when she'd woken up yesterday, she hadn't felt an ounce of regret. She'd thought it might hit her later, but as the day had progressed, she played devil's advocate, trying to imagine what it would be like to launch a new line, the excitement of creating the line, the thrill of seeing new products hit the market, and the rush of her brand blowing up anew on social media, but regret had never come. Even in the hypothetical, she longed for those hours she'd miss with Tobias. As she lay with the man who she wanted even more of, memorizing the steady and sure beat of his heart against her back, she knew she'd made the right decision. Nothing was more luxurious than the cocoon of his body, and no business or amount of wealth compared to the beauty of being adored by him.

She'd miss him today.

He was going to work on her father's car while she and the

girls were preparing for Leah's baby shower at Ginger and Conroy's house. Between morning preparations and the baby shower, which was at five o'clock, she was coming home to work and inform distributors and manufacturers of her decision. If the baby shower was over early enough, she was going to track down Blaine and see if she could mend that rickety fence.

Tobias inhaled deeply, his hold on her tightening. He caressed her breast, his fingers playing over her nipple, bringing rise to prickles of lust that always seemed to be lingering between them. She closed her eyes as he rubbed his scruff along her cheek, kissing her there as he rocked his arousal against her bottom, turning those prickles to full-on flames.

"Morning, angel."

She'd never tire of hearing that sleepy, gravelly voice. She turned in his arms, and he ran his hand down her back, palming her ass. "Morning, broody boy."

She touched her finger to his lips, and he captured it between his teeth, hunger flaring in his eyes. "What time are you meeting the girls?" He kissed the edge of her mouth, sliding his fingers between her legs, making a low, sinful sound as they slid through her wetness.

"*Ten*," came out breathy. "What time are you meeting my dad?"

He brushed his lips over hers, whispering, "Same," and took her in a spine-tingling kiss. He drew back, holding her gaze as his fingers dipped into her center. She gasped, clinging to him as pleasure radiated through her core. His lips curved up greedily, and he rolled her onto her back, his gaze traveling slowly down the length of her. Her body sizzled beneath his heated gaze.

"Look at you, so beautiful." He leaned down and slicked his tongue over her nipple.

"*Tobias,*" she pleaded.

He did it again and nipped at the swell of her breast. She inhaled sharply, a needy sound escaping. "Let's make you come, baby girl." He dragged his fingers along her slickness, slowing to massage her clit just long enough to make her ache and writhe, before those fingers slid lower and pushed into her pussy, expertly stroking that magical hidden spot. Her eyes closed, her hips bucking off the mattress as pleasure streaked through her.

"Eyes on me," he rasped.

She forced her eyes open, and he repeated the same exquisite torture, teasing, dragging, massaging, and dipping inside her again, over and over until her heels dug into the mattress, and her back bowed off the bed. "I can't take it. *Please,*" she begged.

His mouth captured hers in a deep, passionate kiss as his fingers pushed into her, and his thumb worked her clit, sending scintillating sensations racing through her. She tried to focus on just one—the feel of his fingers fucking her, just his thumb making her tremble, or his glorious tongue wreaking havoc with her mouth—to ground herself as the world spun around her, but as always happened with Tobias, she was too lost in *them.* She gasped for breath as those sensations engulfed her, sending her soaring into a crescendo of erotic pleasure, and just as she opened her mouth to cry out, he shifted, driving into her in one hard thrust.

"Ohgodyes!"

His mouth came down over hers roughly as he pounded into her, and she rocked and bucked, her nails digging into the flesh of his ass. He made a guttural noise, rolling them over so she was on top, riding him with reckless abandon. He clutched her hips, driving deep, and holding her there as he gyrated. Exquisite pressure mounted inside her, throbbing beneath her skin, her clit aching.

"Give me your mouth," he demanded, and feverishly devoured her.

His fingers dug into her flesh as they feasted on each other, chest to chest, the angle of their bodies providing tantalizing friction exactly where she needed it. Heat pulsed through her limbs, fire engulfed her core, and she squeezed her inner muscles, knowing it would drive him wild. His cock jerked inside her, and just when she was about to come, he rolled her onto her back again, still buried deep.

"I don't ever want to stop," he growled, and his mouth covered hers in a slow, sweet kiss, heightening every sensation, making her crave every thrust.

They moved in perfect sync to the same languid rhythm, growing hotter, needier, as he murmured against her neck. She was too swept up in them to make out his words, and he laced their fingers together, kissing her light as a feather, his cock sliding in painfully slowly and intoxicatingly deep. She gasped on every withdrawal, holding her breath as he filled her until he was buried to the hilt and gave an extra thrust. Her breath rushed from her lungs, and she lost all sense of time and space, spiraling over the edge and taking him with her. He held her tight, growling her name like a prayer as they rode out their mutual release.

They lay spent, tangled in each other's arms, hearts hammering, bodies slick and sizzling. He touched his forehead to hers, his hair falling around their faces the way she'd come to adore.

"God, Blue Eyes," he panted out. "How can one person

change so much, so fast?"

Her heart squeezed, and she whispered, "Two people."

"It's all you, angel. You've got some kind of magic in that heart of yours, and I don't want to imagine a single day without you by my side."

"Then don't." As she drew his mouth toward hers, she said, "Because I don't want to, either."

MADIGAN RODE THAT high all morning as she worked with her mother, her aunt Ginger, Chloe, and Sid, preparing for Leah's baby shower. Music played from an old-fashioned radio that had been in the exact same place on Ginger's counter for as long as Madigan could remember, and she and Chloe were belting out "My Heart Will Go On" as they mixed ingredients for chocolate-chip muffins and sugar cookies. Her mother was making pasta salad and chatting with Ginger, who was layering lasagna, and Sid was rolling meats for the charcuterie board.

The oven timer went off, and Sid said, "I've got it," around a mouthful of meat. She looked cute in cutoffs and a Wicked Rescue T-shirt as she opened the oven and the smell of brownies filled the room.

"*Mm-mm,*" Ginger said. "Nothing smells better than freshly baked brownies."

Madigan grinned. "Tobias does."

"Does he?" her mother asked, sharing an approving smile with Ginger.

"You're crazy," Sid said. "No man smells better than this." She popped a piece of a brownie in her mouth.

"I love how Justin smells, but I might have to agree with Sid on this one," Chloe chimed in.

"I'm telling you, Tobias smells rugged and delicious," Madigan insisted. "You should smell him sometime."

Sid wrinkled her nose. "No thanks. I've got enough manly smells with Gunner around, and not that I don't like the way he smells, but come on, *brownies*?"

"Your loss." Madigan poured more chocolate chips into the batter.

"I was going to ask how things were going between you two, but I guess that answers my question," her mother said.

"I think it's safe to say your baby girl is smitten with her broody beau." Ginger winked at Madigan.

They were all looking at her, and after the morning she and Tobias had shared, she was bursting at the seams to talk about him. "I totally *am*, and it's terrifying and wonderful, and I am ridiculously happy."

"Really? Because we couldn't tell when you were at the Hog the other night. You guys practically acted like strangers," Sid teased, eating the rest of the brownie.

"Strangers who couldn't keep their hands off each other," Chloe said with a smile.

"Do you blame me?" Madigan asked. "I swear when we kiss, the entire world disappears."

"Forget smitten, you're a total goner," Sid said.

"I *am*. I know we got a bumpy start, but it made us stronger."

"Reality has a way of doing that," her mother said.

"I think it's wonderful." Ginger added another noodle to the lasagna. "I liked Tobias the first time he sat at my bar. He has a quiet strength about him, and I have to say, I love the way he looks at you, Mads."

"So do I. I love everything about us, and that's the reason I decided to delay launching the Mad Truth merchandise line and take Chloe up on working a few more hours at LOCAL." Madigan began spooning dough onto a cookie sheet.

"You *are*?" her mother said excitedly. "Oh, darlin', I'm so glad. I was worried you were taking on too much and leaving no time for fun."

"Our residents will be *thrilled*," Chloe exclaimed.

"I'm happy about it, too. I love working with them, and I know it's the right decision." She heard several car doors close and looked out the kitchen window. Blaine's and Baz's trucks were parked out front, and Blaine was walking toward Gunner and Baz. Her pulse quickened. "What are the guys doing here? I thought they were going riding."

"They are. The tables and chairs for the party were still at Tank's house from the wedding, and they picked them up so Tank could stay home and help Leah with the girls," Ginger explained.

Madigan wiped her hands on a towel. "I'll be right back. I want to talk to Blaine."

Her mother grabbed her wrist as she walked past. "Go easy on him. He's having a hard time."

"So am I." She headed out the door, making a beeline for her brother.

"Hey, gorgeous," Baz said as she approached.

She tried to smile, but she was on a mission and she was nervous.

"Mads? Do I need my referee shirt?" Gunner asked.

"I hope not," she said more to herself than to him. When she and Tobias had talked about his sister on Friday night, she'd realized that Blaine had already told her what his problem was the night Tobias had left town, but she'd been too angry to hear it.

Blaine busied himself taking chairs out of Baz's truck bed, not looking up at Madigan as she approached, which pissed her off. But as her father had said, there were no guarantees of tomorrow, and she wasn't wasting another day.

"Come on." She took Blaine by the wrist, tugging him away from the others.

Blaine yanked his arm free. "What the hell?"

"We need to talk, and I didn't think you'd want to do it around Baz and Gunner, but if you're good here, I am, too."

He eyed their cousins and nodded toward the side yard. She followed him over, her nerves pinging. Blaine stopped by a tree and crossed his arms, looking at her expectantly.

She didn't know where to start, but when she opened her mouth, words came easily. "I appreciate how you've always protected me, and I understand why you got so mad when you found out that I was sneaking around with Tobias. But I'm an adult, Blaine, and I shouldn't have to sneak around in the first place. So many of you guys pick up women all the time, and those women are someone's daughter or sister, and you don't see me giving you hell."

"You *know* I'm not like that," he said evenly.

"I could argue that point, but I won't because that's *your* business."

"Madigan, if you're going to tell me to back off and not protect you, don't bother. Protecting you is part of who I am, and I don't *want* to change it."

She softened at that. "I don't want you to. But walking away when Tobias and I come into a room is bullshit. He's an amazing man, and I'm pretty cool, too. We don't deserve to be treated like that."

His jaw tightened.

She kept her tone even, not angry, but firm. "You humiliated me when you showed up at his apartment. I know you acted on instinct, and that wasn't your intent, but you had no right to barge in the way you did. But I also realize that we didn't grow up in a family where those boundaries exist, for each other or for anyone else we love. We were brought up to always have each other's backs, and sometimes that means stepping in where we don't belong and hurting someone in the process. That was your one hall pass, Blaine. You don't get another, so think before you act next time."

He nodded curtly.

It wasn't an apology, but she saw one in his eyes. "I know you don't think anybody will ever be good enough for me, and I can't fix that for you, but I think I finally understand why this particular situation has gotten so volatile. In your eyes, I'm a ticking time bomb, aren't I?"

His brows slanted. "What does that mean?"

"It means that when I came back from Spain, you begged me to tell you what happened, and I was so ashamed, I couldn't. But after talking with Tobias and learning that the man he accidentally killed, his best friend, was hurting his sister, it opened my eyes. She didn't tell Tobias that Kevin was hurting her. He saw the bruises, and later that night he witnessed his friend pushing her against a wall, and *that's* why Tobias threw that fatal punch. I don't want *that* to happen to you or Tobias or anyone else. So I'm going to tell you what happened in Spain, because I think if I hadn't kept that secret, you wouldn't be digging your heels in every time I show my independence."

She swallowed hard, hoping this helped. "I fell hard for a guy while I was there, which I think you know, but the reason I was so messed up was that I found out he was married."

Blaine's nostrils flared. "Who the fuck is he?"

"That doesn't matter. What matters is that I didn't tell you because I was so disappointed in myself, I couldn't survive seeing that same disappointment in your eyes, or anyone else's." Tears burned, but she willed them not to fall. "The only people who know the truth are you and Tobias."

"I wouldn't have been disappointed in *you*," he said angrily. "You were just a kid. I would've gotten on a plane and torn that asshole apart. I'd like to do that right now."

"I know you would, and part of me would like you to. But a bigger part of me doesn't want what happened to Tobias to happen to you. I was a kid, and kids do stupid things. I didn't realize that what happened to Ashley would have an impact on how you saw me and the things I did until you said what you did the night Tobias left, but I was too angry to hear it. Ash is always on my mind, too. She was my best friend, and I wish she had told me what was going on with her. I would have tried to talk her through it, and maybe that night would have ended differently. But we can't go back and undo things that have happened. We can only learn from the past and try to do better in the future. And what I've learned from all of this is that when you couple your worry with my secret, it makes *me* the ticking time bomb, and you're continually trying to clear a path so I don't get tripped up and go off."

The muscles in his jaw bulged, his eyes narrowing again.

"I love you for that, Blaine, but what happened in Spain is *not* your fault. What happened to Ashley is *not* your fault. You can't be everywhere I am, but the man that I'm crazy about?

The man who spent three years behind bars for protecting his sister? I'm pretty sure he'll be there for me when you're not, and that should make you feel good, not angry." She swiped at a tear sliding down her cheek.

"Aw, *hell*, Mads. Don't cry." He pulled her into his arms. "I'm sorry I've been a dick, but every time I look at him, I remember how crushed you were when I told you what he'd done, and it pisses me off that he hadn't told you himself."

She pushed from his arms. "I told you that was on *me*."

"I get it," he snapped. "But I can't help it."

"Well, you need to, because you're making me choose between the two of you, and you're making it uncomfortable for everyone else, and that's not fair."

"I don't want you to fucking choose. You're with him, and this is *my* shit. I was eight when you were born, and I've been watching out for you ever since, and it's really fucking hard to just hand over the reins to some other guy. But the last thing I want is to lose you."

"I love you, Blaine, and I get it, but if you keep treating him this way, you *will* lose me, because that whole protective, no-boundaries thing is part of who I am, too." Knowing she had to come across just as strong as him, she headed back inside with her heart in her throat, hoping she was doing the right thing.

Her mother was waiting by the kitchen door. "I saw you two hug, but you don't look happy. Are things better?"

"I don't know," she said honestly. "I think we're getting there, but sometimes I think it would be easier if we were brought up like other families, where brothers and sisters stay out of each other's business."

"Oh, honey, your brothers love you."

"I know, and I love them, but this is *hard*. I just want him and Tobias to get along."

"Want me and Chloe to have Gunner and Maverick take Blaine out and beat him into submission?" Sid offered.

"No," Madigan said solemnly. "Not when one wrong punch can lead to tragedy."

"We could kidnap him and leave him in the desert until he agrees to get along with Tobias," Chloe suggested.

"You're not borrowing our Wicked Rescue van," Sid said.

"Darn it," Chloe complained.

"There's always waterboarding," Sid suggested.

They all looked at her like she'd lost her mind.

"I think you've been watching too many action movies," Madigan said.

"We can do what we used to do with the boys when they were young and lock them in a room until they get along," Ginger suggested.

"It's a wonder they all made it out alive," Sid said.

Madigan's mother picked up the plate of brownies and held it out toward her. "How about we just have some brownies and let the guys figure it out?"

BEFORE LEAVING FOR their ride, Blaine, Baz, and Gunner strung twinkling lights around the backyard. Madigan had hoped Blaine might seek her out, but he hadn't, and by the time she and the girls finished preparing the food and went outside to decorate, they were gone.

Now it was almost after six, and the baby shower was in full swing. Ginger and Conroy's backyard was bustling with happy chatter and little-girl giggles. Green and yellow balloons danced from long strings tied to the backs of chairs, and pink and blue lanterns hung from the trees around the edge of the yard. Tables were draped in yellow tablecloths, and children's books were stacked as centerpieces, each topped with a stuffed animal for Tank and Leah's new baby.

On the table with the gifts was a jar for guests to guess the name of the baby. Madigan would bet everything she had that most of those guesses included the names of Leah's father and brother, Leo and River. But Leah was giving nothing away as far as names went.

Leah looked beautiful and ready to *pop* in a blue maternity top and stretchy white skirt. She was sitting on the patio in a comfy armchair that Madigan and Steph had carried outside for her, looking over the tattoo bear—a cute stuffed bear with no fur—Madigan's mother had given her, reading off what everyone had *tattooed* on it with permanent marker. Junie sat beside her, still as could be, while Aria Bad, who worked at Tank's tattoo shop, drew a picture on her arm of a cat surfing, and Gia Galant, another tattooist at Wicked Ink, made up a story about the surfing cat.

Marly was gushing about Dante to Evie, Sid, and Cait Weatherby, who used to work at Wicked Ink but had recently fallen in love and moved to Silver Island to be with her fiancé. Across the yard, Steph, Chloe, and Starr were chatting with Junie and Rosie's daycare provider, Corinne, and some of the other waitresses Leah had worked with at the Salty Hog, while Rosie and Starr's daughter, Gracie, played a few feet away with some of the other guests' kids.

They'd played games and eaten a feast, and now Madigan's mother was flitting from one group to the next, doting on everyone, while Ginger cut the cake and Madigan handed out slices.

Madigan picked up the last two plates and forks and carried them over to Aria and Gia. "That cat is adorable. I'm just going to leave this here, and you can eat it when you're done drawing." She set a plate on the table beside Aria, who was as petite and slim as Gia was curvy and tall.

"Thanks, Mads." Aria smiled up at her, her long dirty-blond hair cascading over her shoulders. She wore a silver hoop in one nostril and a gray-and-black sleeveless dress, which showed off her colorful tattoos.

"My girl Aria has *mad* drawing skills," Gia said. She was all legs, with flawless brown skin, and a plethora of tattoos. She held out her hand. "I know that corner slice is for me."

"Yes, my frosting-loving hottie, it is." Madigan handed it to her.

"Thanks." Gia scooped frosting onto her finger and licked it off, looking like a vamp in her tight red minidress. "When are you going to bring your new man by the shop so I can check him out?"

"You mean so you can give him the third degree?" Madigan raised her brows. Gia was as protective of her friends as Madigan's brothers were.

"Maybe." Gia ate a bite of cake.

Leah leaned forward and picked up Aria's plate. "I'm afraid this is going to melt, so I'll just…" She ate a forkful.

"*Mama*, that's for Awia," Junie complained.

Leah giggled. "Pregnant mamas are allowed to have seconds."

"Don't worry, Junie, we have plenty more for Aria," Ginger assured her.

"I'm not that hungry anyway," Aria said.

"You didn't eat much tonight," Madigan said, wondering if she was just being her shy self, not wanting to be a bother. Aria had social anxieties and tended to try to blend into the background rather than stand out.

"I think I'm still full from last night's dinner," Aria said softly. "Zeke dragged me out for pizza with some of his friends, and it was so good, I swear I ate as much as he did."

Madigan and some of the other girls were pretty sure Aria had a crush on Zeke, who was a few years older than her. He'd tutored her when she was in school and had been watching out for her ever since.

"What happened *after* dinner?" Gia asked as Marly, Evie, and Sid joined them.

Aria ignored the question.

"Let me guess," Gia said. "*Raven* was there."

"Uh-huh. They're really good together," Aria said sweetly.

"Are you talking about Zeke?" Sid asked.

"He's the only one going out with Raven," Marly pointed out.

"Wait. Zeke brings you on his dates with her?" Evie asked.

What the heck is my brother thinking?

"*No*, just when there's a group of people going," Aria explained.

Gia looked at her disapprovingly. "What did I tell you about letting him bring you as his third wheel?"

"We're *friends*, and I like being with him. *Them.* I like being with them," Aria insisted.

"I like being with Uncle Zeke," Junie interrupted, and the relief on Aria's face was evident. "We explore together, and he teaches me things."

In an effort to rescue Aria from any further questions, Madigan said, "Uncle Zeke loves hanging out with you, too, Junie."

"Okay, Junebug," Aria said. "I just have to fix this line, and then you're done."

"Great, then who's ready for some diaper pong?" Madigan asked loudly.

There was a flurry of activity, and as the adults headed over to the diaper pong table, Rosie yelled, "*I play!*"

As Rosie and Gracie ran over, Gracie shouted, "Me too!"

Rosie peered down at the drawing on Junie's arm. "Pwetty cat."

"Her name is Rufus, and she surfed all the way from Cape Cod to Hawaii to save her little brother from a meanie," Junie explained.

"*Rufus?*" Madigan's mother asked with an arched brow.

"She's a very progressive cat," Gia said.

As everyone gathered around the table, Madigan thought about how Blaine was like Rufus. She knew he'd travel around the world to keep her safe, and she hoped he would find a way to overcome his issues, because if she had things her way, Tobias would be in her life for a very long time.

Chapter Twenty

TOBIAS WALKED INTO the Salty Hog and was surprised by how busy it was for a Sunday evening. A group of about twenty people was drinking and carrying on around two tables that were pushed together, and nearly every table in the place was occupied.

He headed over to the bar, hoping Madigan was having a good time at the baby shower. She'd texted earlier to say she'd talked to Blaine and even though she hadn't gotten far, she wasn't giving up.

Neither was Tobias.

One way or another, he was going to get through to her brother.

He spotted Conroy at the other end of the bar, helping a customer, and the other bartender, a brunette, was also busy with customers. He took the only empty stool at the bar, and as he grabbed a menu, a guy bumped into his back. He turned around, meeting the glassy eyes of a thirtysomething dude.

"Hey, man, watch where you're going," the guy said as he stumbled away.

Tobias didn't have the patience to deal with assholes today. He shook his head and turned back around, surprised to see

Conroy's friendly face.

"Gotta love when guys get together with their frat brothers a decade after college and act like they're still nineteen years old." Conroy revealed his dimples. "How're you doing, buddy?"

"A'right. You?" Tobias asked.

"Doing great. Hated to miss our ride today, but someone's got to hold down the fort while my beautiful old lady throws a hen party." He wiped down the bar. "What can I get you?"

"A cold beer and a burger would hit the spot, thanks."

"You've got it." Conroy went to place his order and came back with a frosty mug, which he promptly filled. "You and Mads should come riding with us sometime."

"I'll keep that in mind. Maybe after I'm done fixing Preacher's car."

Conroy put a napkin down and set the frosty mug on it. "I heard you were doing that. I've got an old bike in my garage that Ginger has been after me to fix up, but between this place, the grandkids, and the new baby coming, it doesn't look possible anytime soon."

"I'd be happy to take a look at it."

"I was hoping you'd say that."

"Are you excited about Tank and Leah's baby?"

Conroy pressed his palms to the bar, eyes dancing with elation. "Excited doesn't begin to describe how much we're looking forward to it. We never thought we'd see the day Tank opened himself up to anyone, and Leah and the girls bring nothing but joy into our lives."

"I've heard a lot about Junie and Rosie. I hope to meet them someday."

"We'll make that happen," Conroy said with a nod. "Those girls are really something. They call us Gingy and Connie, and it's the cutest damn thing. Wait until you see them. Junie's got red hair and Rosie's is brown, and they're as different as kids can be…"

As Conroy raved about his granddaughters, Tobias's mind wandered to his sister and niece. He had no idea if his father had been there for Carrie when she was pregnant, or if he'd made her suffer alone. He didn't have it in him to ask Elsa, because it would only piss him off if his father hadn't been there for Carrie.

"I wonder what they'll call you," Conroy asked, but before Tobias could respond, he was called away to help another customer. A little while later he brought Tobias his burger, and they talked for a few minutes before Conroy got pulled away again, and the place got even busier.

It was weird eating dinner alone after weeks of eating with Madigan. He pulled out his phone and texted her a peach emoji and a heart. *A fucking heart.* He'd never been a texter, much less a guy who used emojis, but everything was different with her. He'd sell his soul to fix things with Blaine, but he wouldn't do the one thing he knew would fix it. He wouldn't walk away from the woman he was falling wildly and passionately in love with.

He couldn't believe he'd admitted how he felt to her that morning. *I don't want to imagine a single day without you by my side.* He hadn't planned on saying it, but when they'd been making love, it had been impossible to satisfy his insatiable desire for her. No matter how deep he took her, he hadn't been able to get close enough. It was only afterward, when he'd gazed into her eyes, that he'd realized the closeness he craved was to her heart, and when she'd said, *Then don't…Because I don't want to, either*, time had stood still, and he'd known he was falling hard and fast, and he never wanted to stop.

There was a commotion behind him. He pocketed his phone and looked over his shoulder, seeing three young guys plowing through the crowd, their tattooed arms around scantily clad blondes. He turned back to the bar, ordering another beer from the female bartender, and looked up at the baseball game on the television.

The three couples pushed their way up to the bar. The girls were hanging all over their men, giggling, and kissing them. The tallest of the guys, wearing a black bandanna tied around his dark hair, squeezed between the couple sitting to Tobias's right and flagged down the female bartender, ordering a round of beers. The couple vacated their stools, and two of the giggling blondes slid onto them.

Tobias wondered if youth and stupidity made them oblivious to everyone around them, or if they were just assholes.

The heaviest guy hiked a thumb over his shoulder, speaking in a thick Southern accent. "I'm gonna hit the head."

"Me too," Bandanna said, and leaned in to tongue-fuck the woman on the stool beside Tobias. "Don't you go anywhere, baby."

She rolled her eyes, but he'd already walked away.

"Wait up, John. I need to pee, too." The heavyset guy's girlfriend hurried after him.

The other couple had their tongues down each other's throats.

It seemed like all the rowdies were out tonight. Tobias looked up at the television. The blonde leaned closer, pushing her shoulder into his arm. He glanced at her out of the corner of his eyes.

"'Scuse me. Can you give me that menu?" She pointed to

the menu on his other side.

He handed it to her, turning his attention back to the television.

"Have you eaten here?" she asked. "What's good?"

He didn't know if she was talking to him or her friend, who was taking a breather from her tongue-fucking.

She bumped his shoulder again. "Hey, handsome. I'm talking to you."

"Sorry, *what*?"

She turned on her stool so her knees touched his leg and leaned her elbow on the bar, rested her chin on her palm, fluttering her long fake lashes. "You're a grumpy one. Is your team losing or something?"

"No." He looked up at the television, and she tapped his arm.

When he glanced at her, she smiled. "Have you eaten here?"

He nodded.

"What's yummy?"

"The burger was good."

She cocked her head. "See? Was that so hard?"

Time for me to go. He put cash on the bar to pay for his bill and pushed to his feet, bumping into Bandanna's chest. "Sorry, man."

Bandanna stepped closer, eyes wide and chaotic like he'd done coke in the bathroom. "Were you talking to my girl?"

Come on, dude. Don't be a dick. "Just answered her questions, man. She's all yours."

"No shit she's all mine." He bumped his chest into Tobias's. "What's wrong—can't get your own woman?"

Tobias's hands curled into fists. He had a good four inches on the asshole, but the guy wasn't worth losing his temper over.

"I suggest you back up."

"Did you hear that?" Bandanna said to his buddies as they moved behind him. "This douchebag thinks I need to back up."

"I agree with that guy." Blaine's voice sounded before Tobias saw him cutting through the crowd with Tank, Baz, Maverick, Gunner, Zeke, and Zander on his heels. They flanked Tobias in their black leather vests, cold eyes set on the three assholes. "I believe the man told you to back the fuck up."

Tobias was shocked, but he didn't let it show. He didn't need to be saved, but *damn*, to be on this side of the intimidation was a fucking rush. Almost as much of a rush as stepping into the ring.

Tank, a mountainous, intimidating beast when he *wasn't* angry, stepped forward, cold dark eyes locked on Bandanna, muscles bulging, baring his teeth as he seethed, "This is *my* family's bar. You either sit down and shut your mouth, or get the fuck out of here."

Eyes locked on Tobias, Bandanna fumed, "This isn't over."

"You're even dumber than you look." Like a grizzly picking up its prey, Tank grabbed him by the collar, lifted him off his feet, and pushed through the crowd with the asshole dangling above the floor.

Tobias and Blaine charged forward, pushing the guy's buddies toward the door, with Madigan's other brothers and cousins on their heels. The three blondes followed their men out the door, calling Tobias and the Wickeds *pricks*. Tobias stood with Blaine and Tank on the deck outside the door with the rest of the guys behind them, watching the troublemakers drive out of the parking lot.

"Well, that was fun. Let's go," Tank said, and he and the other guys headed down the steps toward the parking lot, with the exception of Blaine, whose serious eyes were trained on Tobias.

Tobias realized that Blaine might have thought he was causing trouble, too, and said, “Sorry about that. But you didn’t need to step in. I would have walked out before I caused a scene in your family’s bar.”

“I believe you would, but that’s not how we roll. Nobody rides alone in this family, and you’re with my sister, which means we’ll have your back even when you don’t need it.”

It took a moment for Tobias to process that, and the emotions it stirred, but he knew an olive branch when he saw one and didn’t take too much time thinking about it. “I appreciate that. Can I buy you a beer?”

“Nah, you’re coming with us.” Blaine took his arm, leading him to the stairs.

Tobias stilled at the top of the steps as motorcycle engines roared to life. Even though Blaine had talked about having his back, he wasn’t going to blindly follow him. “Where?”

For the first time, Blaine cracked a grin. “We’re crashing the baby shower.”

Tobias raked a hand through his hair, shaking his head in disbelief and amusement. “You sure you want me there?”

“What do you think happened tonight? That we used our Spidey senses about trouble happening at the Hog and made a quick detour on our way to the shower? We came here to get *you*,” Blaine said evenly. “Don’t look so shocked. My sister’s crazy about you. If I don’t bring you, she’s going to kick my ass. Now, are you coming or what?”

“Yeah,” Tobias said, a little dumbfounded.

“Don’t think this means I won’t watch your every step.”

As they descended the stairs, Tobias said, “I’d expect nothing less.”

TOBIAS FOLLOWED THE guys off the beaten path and down a dark dirt road to a dead end. There definitely wasn't a baby shower around there. As the guys turned their bikes around, backing them up to park in a line, like they'd done it a million times before, he wondered if he'd been played. Could Blaine be that good an actor? He didn't think any of the other guys had it out for him, but they were blood to Blaine, and he was merely Madigan's guy.

Fuck.

He waited for them to finish parking and turned his own bike around, parking a good distance away from the others. *Just in case.* He didn't want to fight anyone, and he sure as hell didn't want to fight men he'd come to respect. But as he took off his helmet, eyeing the seven tough bikers, he mentally puzzled out which ones he could take. Any way he cut it, he knew he'd take a beating.

A truck rumbled down the road, the headlights blinding him as he climbed off his bike. He watched as the truck turned around, and when it was facing the way it had come, the headlights flashed.

"Let's go," Tank called out, and the guys fell into step, heading for the truck.

"Riggs." Maverick waved him over.

Utterly confused, and relieved, Tobias headed over. Tank stood by the tailgate as Baz and Zeke climbed in, and Blaine jogged up to the driver's side door to speak to whoever was driving.

"Hey, man." Gunner clapped Tobias on the back. "Glad

you and Blaine aren't at each other's throats tonight."

"About damn time," Maverick said as he followed Zeke into the back of the truck.

"Madigan is going to lose her shit when she sees you," Zander said.

"They're all going to lose their shit when they see us." Gunner climbed into the truck bed.

Tobias still had no idea what was going on. "What's the deal with the truck?"

"You can hear our bikes a mile away. They're used to Con's truck," Zander explained, and followed Gunner's lead, climbing in behind him.

Tank stepped in front of Tobias and said, "I'm real sorry about the shit you've gone through and for the way we came at you. We've all lost people we loved. If you need an ear, Leah and I are here for you."

Tobias's emotions were taking a beating tonight, and he couldn't be more grateful. "Thanks, Tank. I appreciate it."

Tank nodded curtly and motioned for Tobias to climb into the truck. He did, and Tank waited for Blaine to climb in before joining them and closing the tailgate. Maverick banged on the hood of the cab, and the truck rolled down the street.

On the way, Tobias learned that Conroy was driving, and Justice, Cuffs, and Sid's father, who went by the road name Colonel, were at the Salty Hog in case those assholes came back. Preacher and his father were meeting them at Conroy and Ginger's house with a gift for Tank and Leah's girls. They were like a well-oiled machine. The way they had each other's backs and the respect for their hierarchy were impressive. Tobias felt proud and grateful to be included.

Preacher and Mike were waiting at the end of Conroy's

street in Preacher's truck, and they pulled out in front of Conroy. Both men cut the headlights as they rolled up to the curb in front of Conroy and Ginger's rambling two-story, situated on a sweet piece of private property.

The guys shushed each other as they all jumped out, and Tank, Baz, Blaine, and Zeke hopped into the back of Preacher's truck, lifting a child's pink ride-on truck with massive wheels and all the bells and whistles. They handed it down to Preacher, Conroy, Zander, and Gunner, and Tobias saw a big stuffed bear in the driver's seat wearing a Dark Knights T-shirt.

Holy shit. Now, that's a gift.

Tobias wished he'd known he was coming. He didn't have a gift for the shower, but he was glad to be there, and when he saw Madigan's Jeep in the driveway, he felt himself smiling. He couldn't wait to see her.

Mike sidled up to him and said, "Glad you and Blaine got your heads out of your asses."

Tobias didn't know what to say to that, so he simply nodded.

"Zeke installed a camera on the front of the truck and rigged the remote control up to Tank's phone," Zander whispered.

Preacher put his finger over his lips, shushing them.

The little pink truck led the way toward the backyard, followed by Preacher, Conroy, Mike, and Tank, who was controlling it with his phone. Tobias and the others trailed behind.

As they neared the backyard, the girls' happy voices filled the air. It sounded like they were having a great time, and Tobias noticed that all the other men were smiling just as hard as he was. Preacher, Conroy, Mike, and Tank stopped before reaching the back of the house, and they all joined them, waiting in silence as the little pink truck made its way around to the corner of the house.

"What is *that*?" Madigan's voice rang out, and Tobias chuckled.

Zander elbowed him, and he snapped his mouth closed.

"Aw, that's the cutest!" another girl said, and suddenly a cacophony of curious female voices sounded, their words indiscernible.

"Mama! Look!" a little girl shouted, and Tobias could tell by the cadence of her voice that she was running.

"That's Rosie. She's a wild one," Zander whispered.

"*Wosey*, don't!"

Blaine said, "That's Junie, our little redheaded rule follower."

"Me *wide*! Me *wide*!"

"That'd be Gracie, Starr's daughter," Zander said as a pack of women came around the side of the house, little-girl voices and squeals still ringing out in the yard.

Leah stood with her hands on her hips. "Who's getting yelled at?"

Tobias heard the others mumbling and sensed movement, but his eyes were riveted to his blue-eyed girl. The women giggled, and Blaine cleared his throat, catching Tobias's attention. He realized all the other guys had stepped back in answer to Leah's question, except him and Blaine, and Blaine was hiking a thumb at *him*.

"*Me?* What? *Wait.* What?" Tobias looked around, and as everyone cracked up and began talking at once, he realized Blaine had used him as a scapegoat. But he didn't care, because Madigan ran to him, launching herself into his arms, pressing her pillowy lips to his.

"I can't believe you're here," she gushed. "How did this happen?"

"They showed up at the Hog to get me."

"What about Blaine?" Madigan asked with confusion.

"I think it was his idea."

Her eyes dampened, and she looked across the grass at her brother, who was watching them with a smile on his face. She mouthed, *Thank you*, and he nodded.

Reba and Preacher looked over with warm expressions, and Reba put her hand over her heart. Ginger was hugging Conroy, Gunner had a lip-lock on Sid, and Maverick and Chloe were holding hands as everyone headed for the backyard.

The three little ones were squished into the pink truck. Rosie, a sprite of a girl with light brown skin and puffy golden-brown pigtails, was standing on the passenger seat wearing a pretty yellow sundress, shouting, "Papa Tank! Look what Uncle Blaine got me!"

"He got it for *us*, Wosie," Junie corrected her, her adorable face surrounded by red spiral curls as she clutched the steering wheel.

The little blond cutie crouched between them, saying, "I dwive. I good dwiver," had to be Gracie.

Reba and Ginger introduced everyone, and then Ginger said, "We were just about to open presents."

"You go ahead. I'm good here," Zander said, cutting himself a slice of cake. He eyed Starr. "Want to lick my frosting?"

"You're such a child." Starr shook her head.

Zander smirked. "Give me ten minutes, and you'll not only take that back, but you'll be begging for more."

"*Zander*," Reba chided.

"Ten *minutes*?" Starr scoffed. "That's hardly worth getting undressed. Any woman would beg for more."

Everyone cracked up, and they gathered around to watch Tank and Leah open presents. Junie and Rosie helped tear the wrapping paper off each gift, and everyone *ooh*ed and *ahh*ed as tiny onesies and baby toys were unveiled.

"I feel bad," Tobias whispered to Madigan. "I didn't get them a gift."

"Yes, you did. They're opening it now."

Leah opened the box in her lap and pulled out a stuffed bunny, several adorable onesies, the book Madigan had read and recorded, and a handful of colorful baby toys. She and Tank looked at them with love in their eyes, and as Tank gave an appreciative nod, Leah said, "Thank you, Mads and Tobias. I love all of it."

Rosie followed her parents' gazes to Tobias, seeing him for the first time. Her eyes brightened. "Is that big boy over there *Toe*?"

Christ. His heart was really getting hammered tonight.

"Yes, honey. That's Aunt Madigan's boyfriend, Tobias."

"He's *mine*, too!" Rosie exclaimed. "Wight, Toe? Wight?"

Madigan grinned up at him, and everyone else was watching him, too.

"Sure thing," he said, and wondered if Madigan and her family could tell that his mind was tiptoeing back to the niece he'd never met and the sister he missed.

"Yay!" Rosie yelled. "You can buy me candy, and presents, and—"

Tank scooped her up, holding her over his head with a serious scowl, but she just grinned down at him. "Cheeky, what'd I tell you about asking for presents?"

"Not to do it." Rosie never stopped smiling. "I forgot. I won't do it again."

"Yes, she will!" Junie called out, causing more laughter.

Rosie giggled, and Tank kissed her cheek and lowered her to the ground, giving her bottom a playful swat. She ran over to Tobias and wrapped her arms around his leg, beaming up at him with sweet big brown eyes. "I'm sorry I asked for presents. Will you still be mine?"

Damn, she was adorable. He hoisted her into his arms. "Sure, as long as you listen to your Papa Tank."

She threw her arms around his neck and kissed his cheek, immediately scrunching up her nose. "You're prickly like Papa Tank."

"No one's as prickly as Papa Tank," Baz said.

And with that, Tank took the prickly comment as praise, and he and Leah went back to opening presents. When they were done, the ladies made everyone play baby shower games, including Tobias, as if he'd been part of their group forever. Even Blaine joked with him a few times. Reba doted on Tobias just as she did everyone else, asking if he wanted more of this or that. They ate and drank and laughed so much, for a little while, Tobias forgot his troubles.

But later, after many of the guests left, when it was just the two families gathered around a bonfire, and he sat with Madigan between his legs, her back against his chest, his love for her growing with every passing minute, thoughts of his sister returned. As he looked at the love surrounding him—couples and longtime friends sharing lounge chairs, as he and Madigan were, little girls curled up in their grandparents' laps—he wondered if his sister had *this*. He knew she had friends. He'd seen her climb out of a car full of women one day when he was checking on her. But did her little girl cuddle in her grandfather's lap? Did their father look at her with as much love in his eyes as Preacher and Conroy looked at their kids? He sure hoped so.

As everyone talked, he looked at Leah sitting between Tank's legs, his hands caressing her swollen belly, and he felt a pang of guilt. He often wondered what would have happened if Kevin didn't die. Would he have gotten help? Become a better man for Carrie and their baby? Tobias had robbed her of any chance of that, and that was a hard pill to swallow.

"Hey, Tobias, do you miss fighting?" Gunner asked.

"Yeah, I do. A lot."

"Think you'll ever go back into it?" Sid asked.

"No." He shook his head. "I love the sport, and I wish I could find something in the field, but I won't fight again."

"Can you train other fighters?" Evie asked from her perch on a chair with Baz.

"I don't know, but to be honest, I don't want to be responsible for some other guy going through what I went through."

"That's understandable," Preacher said. "Have you thought about teaching women self-defense?"

"No, but that's an interesting idea." Tobias mulled that over.

"Diesel Black, one of our Nomad members, started a training program in Peaceful Harbor, Maryland," Preacher said. "Reba's brother, Biggs, is the president of that chapter, and they do a lot of work with women's shelters. Diesel's fiancée, Tracey, was attacked after work one day, and after she and Diesel got together, they decided to help other women learn to protect themselves. They've been teaching part time for several months, and they've helped a lot of women."

"That sounds like something I could get behind, and it would allow me to still work with you, which I'm really enjoying."

Madigan looked up at him and smiled. "I'd take your class."

"Me too," Chloe said, and the other girls agreed.

"I could hook you up with my buddy Brock," Maverick suggested. "He owns a boxing club in Eastham, and his wife, Cree, is a good friend of mine and the daughter of a Dark Knights family in Biggs's chapter."

"I appreciate that, but I don't know the first thing about starting that type of business. I'll have to do some research first. I have been wanting to join a gym. I'll have to check that one out."

"Why don't we connect you with Diesel and Tracey? They can tell you everything you need to know about the business end, and you're dating one hell of a businesswoman, who can probably also offer some guidance." Preacher winked at Madigan.

"I would love to help." Madigan turned so she could see him. "Diesel and Tracey are really nice."

Several of the guys cleared their throats, and Madigan looked at them with irritation. "What?"

"I don't know that I'd classify Diesel as *nice*," Blaine said.

"The man doesn't speak. He grunts," Baz added.

"*Boys*, be nice." Reba looked at Tobias and said, "Diesel is a lot like Tank. He's hard and gruff, and in some ways, he's like you, too. A man of few words."

Tobias nodded. "Sounds like we'll get along just fine."

"If you're serious, I could also hook you up with my buddy Cory's older brother, Bastian," Gunner offered. "He's a vigilante of sorts. Families hire him to get their friends and relatives out of bad situations. He's helped a lot of people find their way to safety."

"I'd really like to look into teaching self-defense, and I'll think about your buddy Bastian," Tobias said. "Preacher, if you don't mind, I'd appreciate an introduction to Diesel and Tracey."

"I'll make it happen this week."

With the exception of brief periods of time, when his first boss at the gas station had mentored him toward a better life, and later when Kevin had opened the door to fighting, Tobias had felt like he'd had to fight for everything he'd ever gotten. He couldn't believe Madigan's family was trying to help him, despite the way things had started and the tension between him and Blaine. He'd thought that being with Madigan and having a job he enjoyed were more than he could ever ask for. But the support from Madigan's family? That brought a level of happiness he'd never expected…and a dose of guilt that weighed heavily on his shoulders.

TOBIAS HAD BEEN unusually quiet when Madigan had taken him to get his motorcycle after the baby shower, and as they walked into her place, he still seemed sidetracked. She wondered if her family had been too much for him. They could be overwhelming. He seemed excited about the idea of teaching self-defense, but after a dozen goodbye hugs and *let me knows*, maybe he was just being nice and he felt pushed.

She rubbed his back as she toed off her sandals and he untied his boots. "I hope you don't feel pressured into talking with

Diesel and Tracey."

He set his boots aside, rising to his full height. "I don't. I want to talk with them. I like the idea of helping women learn to protect themselves."

"You didn't think my family was too pushy?"

"No, angel. Your family is amazing. They're exactly what family should be. They share and fight and love." He gathered her in his arms. "I've never in my life had as much support as they gave me in just a few hours. It was a little overwhelming, but I appreciate their help, and I'm glad things are heading in a better direction with Blaine. To be honest, he shocked the hell out of me tonight."

"He surprised me, too. I'm so glad he's finally coming around. But if it's not my family, then what am I picking up on? Something feels off."

"That's because you already know me so well."

"Why? Did I do something?"

"Yes. You *exist*, which makes my life a million times better than I ever imagined." He pressed his lips to hers.

"*Tobias*," she said with as much gratitude as frustration, hugging him. "If it's not me, what is it?"

"It's *me*. When we were sitting around the fire, listening to Gunner and Sid talk about their recent rescues, Zeke's stories about the kids he's helping at the community center, Baz talking about the surgery he's doing on that dog tomorrow, and Leah going on about the mural Tank had painted in the nursery, Junie was curled up in Conroy's lap and Rosie in Reba's, and your brothers were loving on their significant others. Your parents were sneaking kisses, and Con and Ginger were whispering like teenagers, and all I could think about was how lucky I am and how I don't deserve it, because I ruined any chance Carrie had at that." He turned away, pacing. "I don't know what to do with the guilt, and I don't want to bring you down because of my shit. I don't even know if my sister *had* a baby shower. But I do know that I fucked her over, and maybe you're right and I saved her from a worse fate, but that doesn't take away the guilt. When Tank was talking to Leah's belly, I was thinking that Carrie never had that."

"Then go see her. *Talk* to her."

"I told you what she said." He shook his head and sat on the couch in the living room, leaning his elbows on his legs.

Madigan sank to her knees in front of him. "Everyone says things they don't mean. What's the worst that can happen?"

"I can't risk making her hate me even more."

"What do you think she's going to say?" Her mind raced as his anguish filled the long silence stretching between them. She wanted to ease his pain, to get him to really talk about what he thought might happen, and an idea formed. "I'll be right back."

She went to get two of her puppets and lowered herself to the floor in front of him again.

"What're you doing, Blue Eyes? Puppets can't fix this."

"How much do you trust me?"

A slightly crooked smile appeared. "Explicitly."

"Good, then just go with it. We're going to play devil's advocate and figure out what you think might happen." She handed him a girl puppet and showed him how to use it.

He looked at the puppet. "I'm feeling a little emasculated."

"It's good for you to explore your feminine side." She wanted to know what *he* thought his sister would say. "I'm going to be you, and you'll be Carrie. We'll pretend you've just knocked on her door." She held up her bearded puppet.

"I can't go to her house. It's an invasion of her personal

space."

"Oh. I didn't think of that. Where would you go see her?"

"I don't know."

"Okay, well, you can think about that, and just for conversation's sake, we'll say you knock on her door, but it's not her house. It's a door that's out in a field. Neutral territory."

He nodded.

"So I knock, as you, and you open the door." Using the puppet, she pretended to knock on the door, and his puppet pretended to open it.

"*You*," he said accusatorily with the puppet, and pretended to slam the door in Madigan's puppet's face.

Madigan's puppet was quick to catch the door and peer around it. "Carrie, wait, please. I just want to talk."

"I have nothing to say to you."

"Then just listen, please. I'm sorry. I wish I hadn't punched Kevin. I wish I had known what was happening to you, and more than anything, I wish I knew how to fix things between us."

He swallowed hard. "You *can't* fix it. You killed the man I loved, and I hate you for it." He turned his puppet away from hers.

"*Wait.* I know I can't bring him back, and I'll carry that guilt for the rest of my life. But can we please try to talk? I miss you. I want to get to know your daughter."

He shook his puppet's head and pretended to turn and slam the door.

Madigan sighed. "She might do that, but she might not, and I could have been totally off with what you'd say. Let's try swapping puppets." They traded puppets, and she hoped now he'd be able to really tell her what he felt. "You knock on the door."

His puppet stared at the space where Madigan had pretended to knock on the door for a minute before finally knocking. Madigan pretended to open the door. "Tobias…?" she said cautiously.

"Hi, Carrie." He swallowed hard.

"What are you doing here?"

"I needed to see you."

Madigan wanted more than anything to play out only a positive situation, but she didn't think Tobias would continue playing along if she made it too easy, and she needed to get there. To hear his worries. "I told you to leave us alone."

"I know, and I'm sorry. I'll only take a minute of your time. I just want you to know how sorry I am that I messed up your life. I'm sorry I killed Kevin. I'm so fucking sorry for everything, and I don't expect you to forgive me." His voice cracked. "But I *miss* you, Care. I miss you so much it hurts, and all I want is to make things better."

Madigan's puppet wiped her eyes, and she sniffled, blinking away her own tears because Tobias's agony was palpable, and as much as she knew he was expecting a harsh response from his sister, she didn't have the heart to play one out. "I miss you, too. Do you want to sit down and talk?"

"More than you fucking know," he said angrily, and tore the puppet off his hand, dropping it on the couch. "I can't do this, Mads. I'm sorry. I know you're trying to help, but puppets *can't* fix this. Don't you get it? She *knows* I'm out of prison and she hasn't reached out. She doesn't want to talk to me."

It took everything she had to push past the pain in his eyes. "Maybe she's scared, too." She set down her puppet and went up on her knees, putting her arms around him. "I know puppets can't fix it, but maybe *you* can by just knocking on a door and letting her know you'd like to talk."

He shook his head. "I can't do that to her."

"I know you're afraid trying will hurt her more, but what about *you*? You're suffering, too, and you deserve to get closure one way or another."

"I'll be fine. I'll figure it out." He met her gaze, his sadness hanging between them. "I'm sorry. We had such a great night, and I'm dragging you down."

"No, you're not. You're letting me into the dark places where you keep your hurt, and I want to be in there with you. A girl who was kissed by the moon and sung to by the stars must possess a *little* ray of sunshine, doesn't she? I'm going to be right by your side, making sure you can find your way out of that dark place, no matter how long it takes."

His arms circled her, and he lifted her onto his lap. "God, Blue Eyes, you're so full of hope. I used to be like that, and I miss it."

"It's never too late for a second chance. We found ours, didn't we?"

Chapter Twenty-One

MADIGAN LOVED SEPTEMBER. She loved the slight dip in temperature, the crisper air and anticipation of fall colors, and the way days began bleeding into nights earlier than during the summer. Most of her friends hated losing that daylight, but she'd always loved it. Sundown was when so many of the good parts of life happened. When families and friends got together and the stress of the day fell away. In the three weeks since Blaine had begun accepting Tobias's presence in their lives, he no longer avoided them when they were out. Madigan had noticed not only changes in Tobias because of it but also in herself and others.

But so much had happened over that time, it seemed everyone was riding high.

Leah had given birth to a beautiful, healthy little boy, Leo River Wicked, just days after her shower, and everyone was in love with him. Tobias had spoken with Diesel and Tracey, and he and Madigan were heading to Maryland next weekend to sit in on their self-defense classes and go over programs and the business structure. With the exception of when they made love, Madigan had never seen Tobias so passionate. There was new light in his eyes, sparks of hope and excitement, and when he talked about the classes, she could tell they had given him purpose.

That new light had drawn others to him. After fixing her father's Trans Am and Conroy's old bike, Justice had roped him into fixing one of his old cars. Tobias had told her he liked giving back to the people who had rallied around him. But it was his camaraderie with the guys that had her smiling every time they were out with them. Two nights ago, after her gig at the Salty Hog, she'd heard Gunner and Zander trying once again to convince him to prospect the club. But he'd said he had too much on his plate to take on anything new.

She wondered if some of that was the unresolved issues with his sister, but she knew it was also partially her fault. In addition to working a few more hours at LOCAL and the two of them visiting their grandfathers every week, she'd gotten the gig at the Scullery Maid, and her beautiful beau came to every show. He wasn't thrilled about her playing for rowdier crowds, but he'd never ask her not to. The rowdier customers really enjoyed her shows, which made them even more fun for her. She loved seeing Tobias in the audience, looking at her like she was his whole world. Even though she knew she couldn't, and shouldn't, be. They both needed room in their hearts for friends and family, and she hoped one day he would find his way back to his family and prospect the club, because she knew both would be good for him.

Their days were busy, but they still made time for fun. Sexy texts and brainstorming cards had remained their *thing*. In the evenings, after her musical gigs and gatherings with family or friends, they usually played guitar, read, walked on the beach, or talked. He'd asked a million questions about her stories, and as he'd put more of his letters to music, he answered her questions, too. She hadn't finished the book for her last book club meeting, but this month she was making better headway. They cooked dinner together, did laundry, and did a dozen other typically mundane things that weren't mundane at all when they were together. When they fell into bed at night, sometimes they just lay in each other's arms talking or just *being*, and other times they spent hours fucking or lovemaking and doing every exquisite thing in between.

What they *weren't* doing was talking about the situation with his sister.

Tobias hadn't mentioned it since the night of the baby shower, and Madigan hadn't pushed. He knew she was there if he wanted to talk. But she worried about him holding all that sadness and regret in.

She glanced at their joined hands between their seats in the Jeep, and her heart beat a little faster. They were on their way to see baby Leo before her evening gig. She was almost as obsessed with Tank and Leah's new baby as she was with Tobias. When they'd gone to see Leo the first time, Tobias had been as enamored with him as she was, and holy smokes. She'd thought seeing him with Junie and Rosie, who now called herself *Toe's girl*, had made him even more irresistible. But seeing her man with a tiny baby in his arms had done all sorts of crazy things to her. Images of him holding, loving, and protecting *their* baby had taken root in her heart, and she didn't even want children any time soon.

Unfortunately, she'd also sensed his mind whirling with guilt, and she knew any hope of that kind of future with Tobias was tentative at best. She would be okay with not having children, but she'd never be okay with the man she loved—and she did love him, with everything she had—never getting out from under the guilt he carried. She'd asked if spending time with Leo and the girls was too much, and she'd never forget his response. *It doesn't matter if it is. I want a life with you. I want this life with you, and there's nothing I won't do to make sure it's the best it can be.*

At the time, she'd thought, *Except face your sister.*

Now, as she drank in the face she saw in her dreams, the arms that always made her feel safe, and the hands that made her body sing—and had brought him a lifetime of guilt—she wondered if he'd ever be able to truly move forward.

He glanced over, catching her staring. "Like what you see, Blue Eyes?" He winked, stirring the butterflies that had taken up residence inside her.

"More than you know." They hadn't said those three special words yet, but she felt his love in every look, touch, and kiss. She felt it in his pained expressions when she knew he was thinking about his family, and in the moments when she found him sitting with his guitar in his lap and a faraway look in his eyes. It was in those moments when he reached for her and held her so tight that they felt like two sides of the same heart.

"I GET IT!" Rosie shouted, and darted out of the living room to get a diaper and a onesie for Leo.

Junie ran after her, shouting, "He's *my* baby!"

They'd been at Tank and Leah's for an hour already, and the girls had been in constant motion. Tank and Leah looked exhausted and happy as Madigan cradled baby Leo in her arms. Even though she'd seen him several times since he was born, she still couldn't get over how beautiful and tiny he was. His skin was a shade lighter than Rosie's, his nose broad, like Leah's, and he had the thinnest layer of feathery pitch-black hair like Tank's. His fingers were long, his skin as soft as velvet, and his little lips were perfectly bowed. And Madigan couldn't get enough of the way he smelled like love and joy and everything good in the world.

"I don't know how you stand it," Madigan said. "All three of your babies are so freaking cute."

"It's good to see the girls are still helping with the baby," Tobias said.

"I thought they'd get bored of it by now," Leah said. "But they're all about taking care of him. They even pretend to nurse their dolls when Leo nurses."

"That's so cute," Madigan said.

"But they're still little kids. They scream and climb all over the furniture," Tank said in a way that showed just how much he adored them. "The other night we found them sleeping in the crib with Leo."

"Yikes," Madigan said. "Isn't that dangerous?"

"I guess it could be. Rosie was on one side of him, Junie on the other, their arms draped over his stomach. They were both fast asleep." Tank nodded toward the baby. "This one was wide-eyed between them, legs kicking. That's the first time he wasn't crying when he woke up."

Leah reached for Tank's hand. "We have our hands full, but we're too blessed to be stressed."

Tobias ran his hand lovingly down Madigan's back, and she hoped one day he'd feel that way about his life.

"We got 'em!" Junie shouted as the girls sprinted into the room.

Tank scooped them up like footballs, one under each arm, and they squealed and kicked, giggling up a storm. "Papa Tank!" Junie hollered, clutching a onesie, and Rosie waved a diaper. Leah was smiling so hard she glowed, and Tank had never looked happier. It was such a magnificent sight, Madigan hoped Ashley and River were out there somewhere witnessing it.

"*Toe!* Save me!" Rosie shouted.

Tobias laughed. "Sorry, Rosie, but I'm no match for your Papa Tank."

"Yes, you *are*," Rosie insisted.

"No, he's *not*," Junie said sharply. "Nobody's stronger than Papa Tank."

"That's right, Twitch," Tank said as he set them down.

Junie ran to Madigan, gently petting Leo's head. "I love my baby."

"He loves you, too," Madigan said.

"He's not *yours*, Junie." Rosie scrambled onto Tobias's lap and hooked her arm around his neck. His thick arm circled her tiny body, and he kissed her head, causing Madigan to melt a little.

"Leo is *all* of ours," Leah said. "Just like you two are."

Rosie whispered loudly to Tobias, "Aunt Mads is a baby hog like Papa Tank."

"She sure is." Tobias stroked a hand down Madigan's back again.

"Are you gonna have babies?" Junie asked.

Madigan almost came to his rescue, but she wanted to hear his answer.

"Not today," he said, giving nothing away.

"We're gonna have more babies," Junie announced.

Madigan and Tobias looked at Leah.

Leah shook her head. "Don't look at *me*. I'm not letting that man anywhere near me for at least a year."

"You know you can't keep your hands off me." Tank leaned down and kissed her. "And we make beautiful babies."

"He's right about that," Tobias said.

"And they'll be just as beautiful if we wait a year to have another," Leah said with a sweet smile.

Tank looked down at Madigan. "Okay, baby hog. Give me the little man."

She nuzzled against the baby's cheek, whispering, "I love you," and handed him to his daddy.

Tank brushed kisses on Leo's forehead, cradling him against his massive chest as the girls followed him over to the changing table.

"Do you guys want to stay for dinner?" Leah offered. "Ginger and Reba keep bringing over the most delicious meals. We can't possibly eat them all."

"Thanks, but I have a gig at the Scullery Maid," Madigan said. "We really have to get going."

"Since when are you working at that shithole?" Tank asked.

"Papa Tank said *shit*," Rosie shouted from her perch on a stool beside Tank, holding a diaper at the ready.

"*Wosie*," Junie chided from her stool on Tank's other side as she pulled baby wipes out of the container. "You can't say that word."

Rosie's smile never faded as she said, "Sorry, Papa Tank."

"Me too, Cheeky." He shot a serious look over his shoulder at Madigan. "How long have you been working there?"

"Two weeks, and it's *fine*, Tank."

"Don't worry. I've got her back," Tobias reassured him as he and Madigan got up to leave.

"And who's got yours?" Tank asked, turning back to the baby.

"Tank, they're fine," Leah said.

Madigan hugged her. "Your girls are never going to be allowed to leave the house."

"Sure they are. As long as he's with them." Leah hugged Tobias. "I'm so glad you came by."

"Let us know if you need anything," Tobias said.

"Are you leavin'?" Junie asked.

"Yes. I have to get to work," Madigan said as she and Tobias went to hug them goodbye. "But I promise to visit again soon."

"Can Toe stay?" Rosie flashed a hopeful grin.

"Not this time, honey," Leah said.

"Little man is clean." Tank lifted baby Leo off the changing table and laid him on his chest. Leo's adorable little face scrunched and turned beat red as he strained to poop, and Tank uttered a curse, sending the girls into hysterics.

THE SCULLERY MAID *was*, as Tank had said, a *shithole*, with paneled walls, an old wooden bar and tables that had names and dates scratched into almost every inch of them, crooked pictures and neon beer signs decorating the walls, and a crowd that went ballistic for Madigan's performances. She'd played there only three times before tonight, but she'd been so impressive at her first gig, word had spread fast that Madigan Wicked was a phenomenal musical storyteller, and she'd drawn a full house ever since.

Blaine and Zeke had shown up twenty minutes into Madigan's set. Apparently Tank had texted them. At first Tobias had wondered if Tank didn't trust him to protect Madigan, but when he'd said as much to Blaine, her brother had simply shaken his head and said, *Brotherhood, man. We've got you.*

Now Blaine and Zeke were at a table talking with a couple of women, and Tobias sat at the bar nursing a beer, his attention riveted to the stage, admiring the woman who had stolen his heart, nurtured his soul, and become his best friend. As Madigan sang about drowning in bad decisions and finding her way to the surface, he realized that was exactly how he'd felt when he met her. Everything about them was unexpected. Madigan made him think about things he'd spent too long running from and feel things he hadn't thought possible. He no longer felt as though he were drowning or fighting to reach the surface. But as happy as he was with the direction he and Madigan were going and the life they were building, he couldn't shake the feeling of being at risk of sinking again under the weight of the guilt riding on his shoulders.

"I know that you don't wanna lose
What you know about who you are."

He'd learned about all of her stories and the thoughts and emotions that had driven them to fruition, and although he enjoyed them all, this one was a favorite. She hadn't written it about anyone in particular but rather about every person who walked the earth. She claimed everyone heard something different in the story, and he believed that because she'd written it in such a way that made it easy to insert oneself into it. He'd heard her sing it in many different ways, and she was so talented, it made just as big of an impact whether she sang it low and thoughtful, as she was now, or loud and aggressive.

"This is the hard part, knock you on your ass
And onto logically challenging shit."

When he'd come back to town to face Madigan with the truth about his past, he'd thought that would be the hardest part, but that was only the first step. Thanks to Madigan and her family, he was finally reconnecting with the focused, forward-moving guy he'd once been. Unfortunately, coming into his own again magnified the parts of himself that were missing, leaving him unsettled. He was still trying to figure out how to handle that, but he knew one thing for sure. If he was ever going to be the man Madigan deserved, he had to figure out his shit sooner rather than later.

"I wish I had the answers, but I don't, so let go of it
Revert a little primally and learn to reconnect with your life.
And I'll be trying to catch up on all my memories.
It's clearer every day, but it was harder before I had a clue..."

He'd had three hard years to think about how clueless he'd been when he was growing up, thinking he'd known about life and its hardships. He hadn't a clue back then, and it wasn't just the death of his friend or prison that had brought that to light or changed him. It was Madigan. She'd taught him more about life and love in a couple of months than he'd learned in all the years before, and thanks to Madigan and her family, he was beginning to see a future for himself. A future he wanted *with* Madigan.

But he was still a broken man.

He'd been thinking about what Madigan had said about

reaching out to Carrie, but as badly as he wanted to try to bridge that gap, fear of fucking up his sister's life even worse than he already had stopped him at every turn, making the future he longed for so far out of reach, he wasn't sure he'd *ever* get there.

Madigan's voice escalated to match the quickening beat, drawing him from his thoughts. He looked around the bar, and it seemed nobody else could take their eyes off his mahogany-haired girl, either. She looked edgy and gorgeous in a silk black-and-silver spaghetti-strap top, dark skinny jeans, and those sexy black leather boots she wore so often. She was nearly shouting, pouring all her emotion into the story. People shot to their feet, punching their fists in the air to the beat. Tobias pushed to his feet, craning to see over the crowd.

"It's almost unreal how the world's so beautiful.
It's like a steal the way we get to experience."

Madigan's voice softened, singing so quietly the din of the crowd silenced. Her eyes found Tobias, dancing with that special light meant solely for *him*, and hell if he didn't feel a thrum of heat right down to his bones.

"The feelings I feel when I am right next to you.
Or in the car singing the feelings out loud."

As she strummed the last chord, applause and whistles rang out. His chest swelled with love, and in that extra beat in which she held his gaze, her smile spoke louder than all the patrons' cheers put together.

He finished his beer as she thanked the audience and announced her next gig. The bartender, a thick-chested sandy-haired guy, said, "Hey, man. Tell her I said thanks for another awesome show."

"Will do. See ya, buddy." Tobias weaved through the crowd, trying to spot Madigan, and caught a glimpse of her just as she slipped through the crowd heading toward the staff break room, where she'd stowed her guitar case. As he rounded the stage, he got caught in a throng of customers getting up to leave their tables.

"Sorry," one of the guys said.

Tobias gave a tight nod. When he finally got past them, he headed for the hall that led to the break room. "*Get your hands off me!*" Madigan's panicked voice hit him before he turned the corner and saw her struggling against a tall dark-haired man who had her pinned to the wall. Fire exploded in Tobias's chest. Fueled by rage and love and he had no idea what else because he couldn't think, couldn't see beyond the blaze of red as he tore the asshole off Madigan, his fist connecting with bone, sending the guy flying into the wall with a thud, his body dropping limply to the floor, filling the narrow hallway. The edges of Tobias's vision blackened and blurred, memories impaling him. *The thud of Kevin's lifeless body hitting the floor. People cheering for a fight. Carrie's uncontrollable wails. Sirens. Shouting. No pulse. Chaos. Futile efforts to revive him. Desperate words burning, pleading, screaming in Tobias's mind. It's not real. It can't be real. Get up. Get up, man. Come on.*

"Tobias, *please...*"

"Dude, he's okay."

"*Tobias*, let him go."

The demand sounded far away. Strong hands gripped Tobias's shoulders, shaking him as reality slowly started to come back into focus, and he realized he was kneeling on the floor, leaning over Madigan's assailant, fists clenched in his shirt, shouting, "*Get up. Get up, man.*" Blood streamed from the guy's nose, coating his lips, chin, and cheek, and he was trembling. *Trembling*. He wasn't dead. He wasn't Kevin.

"Tobias, *please* look at me."

Tobias's heart cracked open as he lifted his gaze, meeting Madigan's teary eyes. He blinked several times, trying to clear the past from his mind. Zeke was crouched by the guy's head. Blaine was holding Tobias's shoulders, and they were all trying to coax him back to the moment.

"He's okay," Madigan said anxiously. "You have to let him go."

She tried to pry his fingers from the guy's shirt, as Blaine pulled Tobias backward. "Let 'im go, man. We've got 'im now."

Tobias released him, and Zeke dragged the guy up to his feet, slamming him against a wall and barking something in his face, but Tobias was still drowning in the aftermath of…*what?* A panic attack? A flashback? What the hell was happening to him?

"You're okay, man. I've got you." Blaine helped him to his feet. "Look at me, Tobias."

He tried to focus on Blaine, but too many emotions were tearing through him.

"It's okay," Madigan said softly. "You're okay."

"No, *I'm* definitely not okay. I can't protect you with this shit in my head." He looked at her attacker, studying his face, and then the pieces fell into place. *This isn't over* slammed through his mind. *Fucking Bandanna.* Fury burned through his fog, sending him charging past Zeke.

"Tobias!" Madigan cried.

Ignoring her plea, he grabbed the guy by the shirt, seething,

"How did you know I was with her? How did you know we were here?"

The guy's panicked eyes widened, words tumbling fast through blood-streaked lips. "My buddy saw you and called me."

"We had eyes on him for two weeks after that first incident," Zeke said. "He never came near you or Madigan."

Blaine inserted himself between Tobias and the bloody asshole. "Back off, Tobias. Zeke, get that asshole out of here *now.*"

As Zeke dragged the guy out of the room, Tobias fumed, pacing.

"It's okay, man," Blaine reassured him.

"No, it's fucking *not* okay. When he hit the ground, I thought he was Kevin. I don't get it. I got in fights in the pen, and that *never* happened. What the hell was that?"

"In prison you weren't protecting someone you loved," Blaine pointed out. "*Your sister. Mads.* I think *that's* your trigger."

"You have to find a way to deal with what happened and forgive yourself, or it'll always haunt you," Madigan pleaded.

"She's right. Just look at all the shit I was holding in. It nearly ruined my relationship with Mads and everyone else." Blaine stepped into Tobias's path, stopping him from pacing. "You gave me damn good advice that I took too long to follow. Now it's my turn. Don't waste another day, man. You've got to face your demons, or they'll eat you alive and ruin every relationship you ever have."

Madigan's song came back to him. *When you realize you're the source of your pain, will you make enough adjustments to make a change?*

His heart thundered, anxiety flaring in his chest at the prospect of facing his sister.

This is the hard part, knock you on your ass.

The hope and plea in his angel's blue eyes told him he needed to do this, or walk away forever.

He headed for the door.

"Tobias, where are you going?" Madigan asked shakily.

"To face my demons."

"You need keys to the Jeep." She grabbed her bag and rummaged through it.

Blaine put his keys in Tobias's hand. "Take my bike. I've got Mads."

Chapter Twenty-Two

TOBIAS'S CHEST FELT like a tangle of red-hot barbed wire, tightening with every breath. He looked in the rearview mirror as he drove into Bourne. The two motorcycles that had been tailing him for the past forty minutes were still there. *Nobody rides alone in this family…We'll have your back even when you don't need it.* Emotions stacked up inside him as the bridge came into view.

How could he ever have thought putting a bridge and any number of miles between him and Carrie could dull the pain of her absence in his life? He gripped the handlebars tighter. His jaw tightened as he turned off the main road and made his way to the residential neighborhood.

It was late, most of the houses dark.

Was he *too* late?

The double meaning had him slowing to a crawl down his sister's street. The picket fence came into view, and his hands were sweaty as he pulled up to the curb. A glance in the mirror showed the other two motorcycles hanging back. He was surprised at how their presence gave him strength, and he wondered if that came from good old-fashioned peer pressure—he couldn't back down with two guys watching his every move—or the support of the men who had become an important part of his life. The men who had stood up to him to protect the woman he'd come to love and then had taken the time to get to know him and not only accepted his past, but were helping him to build a future he could be proud of.

His heart thundered, making it hard to hear his own thoughts as he looked past the fence to the tiger lilies that had lost their blooms and the vibrant blue and white hydrangeas flanking the front steps. Carrie had planted their mother's favorite flowers. His sister's younger voice cut through the thunder. *I hate when the lily petals shrivel up and die, and all that's left are ugly stems and leaves. I wish they could stay pretty forever.*

He gritted his teeth as his mother's voice sailed through his mind, as soft as a whisper. *It's a shame you only see dead flowers and ugly stems. I see brave flowers that made room for new seed pods, and strong stems putting all their energy into nourishing those pods.* She'd crooked her finger, beckoning Tobias and his sister closer, as if she were sharing a treasured secret. *Don't be fooled by your beautiful petals. The part of you that people have to search deeper to find—the inner strength that learns and heals and grows—that's where your true beauty lies.*

But no one can see that, Carrie had insisted.

Sure they can, swee' pea. They see it in everything you do and hear it in every word you say. But the thing that matters is that you *know it's there.* Their mother had taken their hands and looked at them for a long moment, eyes full of love and what Tobias now knew had been hope for their futures she'd miss. *Promise me that when something seems too big or scary, you'll remember what I'm telling you right now.* They'd promised without hesitation. *There is nothing a beautiful soul can't do, and you are the two most beautiful souls on this earth.*

Tobias swore he felt her squeezing his hand and looked down at his fingers curled tightly around the handlebars. He unfurled them and pressed his palms to his thighs. He'd faced men twice his size, ruthless murderers who would have taken his life without a second thought, and had never been as scared as he was right then. But in prison he hadn't had anyone waiting on the other side of those fights for him other than his grandfather, and at the time, he hadn't been sure his presence in his grandfather's life would do more good than harm.

Now he knew better.

Now he had Madigan, and her family and friends, and he understood that even if he played a different role in his grandfather's life, it was still an important one.

Now he had a *life* and a future he desperately wanted hanging in the balance of this perilous night.

He climbed off the bike, gathering his courage like a cloak. The living room curtains were open, a spray of light spilling in from a hallway. Three years was a long time. *What ifs* came at him from all directions, each one a rapid-fire bullet, making it hard to breathe. Madigan's voice broke through the noise, coaxing him through the gate. *I know puppets can't fix it, but maybe you can by just knocking on a door and letting her know you'd like to talk.*

His sister walked into the living room, and he stilled, his heart beating so hard he was sure she could feel it pulsing in the air. She was talking on the phone, smiling, wearing shorts and a T-shirt. She picked up a stuffed toy from the floor and tucked it under her arm, oblivious to his presence. A dozen thoughts came at once. Did he have the right to intrude in her life? Would she even open the door if she saw it was him? Should he turn around and leave…?

But a dozen other thoughts carried him to the front door—his love for his sister, for the niece he'd never met and the family he'd lost. His love for Madigan and the future he wanted with her. His need to apologize, to ask for forgiveness even if he didn't receive it. His conflicting feelings for the best friend he'd lost…and the monster he hadn't seen. He needed to make this right, to show Carrie that all men were not animals.

He stood at the door with his heart in his throat, throwing out one last prayer that she wouldn't slam it in his face, and finally forced himself to knock.

His sister's face appeared in the sidelight window, eyes widening, brow furrowing.

Please open the door. Please give me a fucking chance.

The door opened slowly, and then she was standing before him, worry thickening his throat as she opened her mouth to speak. He couldn't bear the thought of her telling him to leave, or worse, so he held up his hands and cut her off.

"I know you don't want me here. Please just hear me out. I'm sorry for ruining your life. I'm sorry for hitting—*killing*—Kevin. I never meant for that to happen. I loved him like a brother, and when I saw him push you…the bruises. I couldn't…I lost it. I *love* you." Tears slid down her cheeks, drawing his own as he poured his heart out. "Seeing him…I couldn't just let it happen. I wish I'd never met him and had never introduced you two. It's *my* fault he got to you, and I don't expect you to forgive me, but I miss you every fucking day, and I will do *anything* to make it up to you. I know that's selfish. This shouldn't be about me or what I want. But it was always *us*. You and me against the world, and when I lost you, I—"

"Felt like you lost the one person you could always count on?" she said, hushed and angry as she stepped out of the house, pulling the door closed behind her.

"*Yes.* I know I fucked up everything."

She wrapped her arms around her middle, like she'd done as a little girl when she was sad or mad or scared. *Fuck.* Was she scared of him?

"You *did*," she said through a river of tears, her words gutting him anew. "You fucked up a lot of things."

"*Carrie—*"

"You killed the man I *loved*," she seethed, his plea lost to her vehemence. "That messed me up in ways I can't even begin to describe. You killed my baby girl's father."

"I didn't *mean* to. He turned his head," he said with tears wetting his cheeks, anger bleeding from his soul. "He was a *fighter*. He knew better than to turn his head."

"He did. I know that now, but back then I didn't know the difference between what you meant to do and what happened. I was twenty-two, a *pregnant*, hormonal mess, and the man I'd have given my life for had died at the hands of the only other man I'd have done *anything* for."

That jagged knife twisted in his heart, enveloping him in an agonizing blur of pain and sorrow. "I'm sorry" fell lamely between them, and he turned to leave.

"After Mom died, you promised to always be there for me," she said sharply. "And you *were*, Tobias."

He froze.

"You were there when Dad was a dick and when I was homesick at college and cried all night. You were there for me after graduation, when I wasn't sure I'd ever find a job or if I even knew how to be an adult."

Those memories brought more pain.

"Of course you were there for me when you found out the awful truth about Kevin."

He closed his eyes against those painful memories. *Breathe. Just fucking breathe.* He turned around, taking in the tears streaking her cheeks, her lower lip trembling.

"It wasn't your fault, Tobias. It was *mine*. I should've left him the first time he hurt me, or told you what he was doing, but I was so in love with him, I was in denial. I was young and stupid, and Dad had basically disowned me when I got pregnant. I had you, but you were training all the time and just getting started with a real career and a life with Michelle. You'd taken care of me forever, and I didn't want to be a burden anymore."

"You were *never* a burden."

A small smile appeared, but the despair in her eyes remained. "I know that now. I'm ashamed to admit this, but loving Kevin wiped away everything Mom and Dad, and even you, had ever taught me. I didn't even know that was possible, and his death took the end of my rope and unraveled what was left of the person I'd been."

Tobias clenched his jaw. "How did I miss the signs?"

"Because he was smart, and I was lost. I didn't even see it or believe it until I was so mired down in it, I used his own words to rationalize the abuse. It took me a long time after he was gone to seek therapy, and then it took me two years to fully understand what I'd been through and forgive myself enough to really start moving forward." She looked up at him. "I'm sorry for villainizing you and returning the letters and for all of the horrible things I said. I'm sorry I didn't reach out to you when you got out of prison, but I was scared you'd never forgive me."

"Forgive you? I *love* you, and I never blamed you for hating me."

"I didn't hate you. I hated myself." She touched the angel-wing charm hanging around her neck. "You saved me and allowed me to save my little girl. Lynnie Loo is the purest, most beautiful soul on this earth, and if anyone ever hurts her like Kevin hurt me, it'll be me behind bars."

"Don't say that," he demanded. "It never goes away, Care."

"You have to let it go. I learned that, and it's not easy, but it's important. He hurt me a lot, and I'm at fault for covering it up. But I will do whatever I can to try to make up for all the pain I've caused you."

All the emotions he'd been holding back broke free, and he wrapped her in his arms. "Having you and Lynnie Loo in my life is all I need."

He held her as she cried, both of them choking out apologies, forgiveness, and long-missed love. They stayed there, embracing on the porch, until her tears stopped and his racing heart calmed, and as he stepped back, she looked over his shoulder with confusion in her eyes.

He followed her gaze to Madigan standing at the open gate, her hand over her heart, tears glistening in the moonlight, and his chest felt like it might explode. "*Mads*, what are you doing here?"

"Did you really think I was going to let you do this by yourself? Nobody in this family rides alone."

She ran to him, and he saw Zeke, Zander, and Blaine walking down the road. He really wasn't alone anymore, not in this. Not in anything. He drew her into his arms, his heart pounding so hard, he could barely think as he gazed into her eyes, and "*God*," came out on a sigh. "I love you so damn much, Blue

Eyes."

She looked up at him with fresh tears. "I love you, too."

He knew she cared about him. He'd felt it in everything she did and said, but still his heart nearly stopped as she said it. She could have any man she wanted, and she chose *him* above everyone else despite his faults, flaws, and painful past.

"I take it this is your girlfriend?" Carrie asked, snapping Tobias back to the moment.

"*Shit.* Where is my head? Sorry. Care, this is Madigan, and she's more than my girl. She's my angel. She's the reason I'm here."

"That's not true," Madigan interjected hastily. "I mean, he calls me angel, but he's here because he loves you, and he loves your daughter. I'm just the one who wouldn't stop nagging him to knock on your door."

"I'm so thankful that you didn't," she said.

"Are you guys going to be okay?" Madigan asked.

Carrie looked at him, happiness and hope rising in her eyes and in his heart as they said, "We will be," at the same time.

TOBIAS LOOKED AT the adorable toddler sleeping with her arm around a stuffed moose. Several strands of dirty-blond hair lay on her pudgy little cheek. Her eyelashes were as blond as blond could be.

"She's beautiful," he whispered. "Just perfect. I'm so sorry I wasn't there for you."

"Believe it or not, Dad really stepped up after I moved back to the area." As they left her daughter's room, she pulled the door behind, leaving it ajar. "He said he got lost after Mom died, and he's more like he was when we were kids, only different. He's lost that shine in his eyes, but it's still in his heart. I guess none of us will ever be the same, but he's a wonderful grandfather."

Tobias got choked up. "That's good."

"He talks about you and about his regrets. He has a lot of them. I think he'd like to see you if you're willing to talk to him."

Tobias looked across the living room at Madigan, who was talking with Zeke at the entrance to the kitchen, thinking about what she'd said the night of the fireworks. The night everything changed between them. *I don't think a person can have too many people who love them in their life.* "I'd like that."

Blaine walked out of the kitchen and said, "You live here alone?"

"With my daughter. Why?" Carrie asked.

"You've only got that one lock on the kitchen door. You should have a dead bolt," Blaine said, heading over to the front windows.

"What's his deal?" Carrie whispered to Tobias.

"He's a big brother." He shrugged, smiling as she rolled her eyes.

"When we have time, I want to hear *all* about you and Madigan, but for now…" She lowered her voice to whisper, "Her brothers are cute. Are the other two single?"

He chuckled. "They're all single. What's wrong with Blaine?"

"As of tonight, I already have one overprotective man in my life. I don't think I can take another."

Zander came out of the kitchen carrying a box of iced animal crackers. "Hey, hot stuff, is it okay if I have a few of these?"

"Dude, show some respect." Zeke snagged the box from his hands and shoved Zander back into the kitchen as he flashed a coy grin at Carrie. "Excuse him. He left his manners at home." He handed her the box of cookies. "You might want to lock these up."

She waved away the box. "It's okay. Lynnie doesn't mind sharing. Can you stick around? I'll put some coffee on."

"We sure can," Blaine said, catching a side-eye from Zeke as they followed Carrie into the kitchen, and Madigan made her way over to Tobias.

"Should I be worried about them with my sister?"

"Probably," Madigan teased. "I'm so happy for you. How does it feel to be here?"

"Surreal. Tonight I got to tell the two most important women in my life that I love them." Gathering her in his arms, he touched his forehead to hers and said, "And that's all because of you. With you, I found a new family, and because of you, I'm getting my family back. You really are my angel."

"Your *wicked* angel?" She wound her arms around his neck.

As he lowered his lips to hers, he said, "Yes, Blue Eyes, but you're so much more than that."

Epilogue

MADIGAN WRAPPED A towel around herself after her shower and tiptoed through the bedroom, taking one last look at Tobias, fast asleep on their bed with one arm arced over his head, the other lying across her pillow, the sheet bunched low on his waist. Her love for him bubbled up inside as she studied his handsome face. Gone were the tension lines that used to remain as he slept. It had been two months since he'd reunited with Carrie and almost as long since he'd moved in, and Madigan still couldn't get enough of him. She loved getting to know the more relaxed Tobias, the one who shared more openly, laughed more often, and loved with everything he had.

She loved *loving* him and being loved by him, in all its shapes and forms.

She tiptoed out of the bedroom and headed into the kitchen. The ceramic tile was cold on her bare feet as she turned on the coffee maker and gazed out the window. Colorful leaves skated along the grass in the gusty November wind, whipping around the old truck Tobias had bought for work. She couldn't believe it was Thanksgiving already. They had a lot to be thankful for, and on top of that list was Tobias's reunion with his family. This would be the first holiday Tobias would celebrate with his sister in three years and with his father in far longer than that. Madigan's parents were hosting dinner, and she was excited to bring their families together again. They'd had fun at the Dark Knights' Trunk or Treat event on Halloween. She and Tobias had dressed up as Sandy and Danny from *Grease*, and Tobias had two permanent appendages—Lynnie and Rosie—and he'd loved every minute of it.

Things were going great between him and Carrie, and although things weren't perfect with his father, they were working on it. His father seemed genuinely proud of him for the man he'd become, and Madigan was glad about that, because she'd never met a better man than Sir Broodiness, who wasn't quite so broody anymore.

Tobias had started teaching women's self-defense classes at Brock's gym, and every class was booked solid. Madigan, Carrie, and their friends were taking the classes, too, and she was pretty sure that several of his other students were there because of the studly instructor. But she wasn't worried. Her man had eyes, among other things, only for *her*.

She opened the fridge, and as she reached for the eggs, strong hands slid around her from behind, holding her against a *very* hard, very familiar body.

"Did you shower without me?" Tobias nipped at her neck.

"I wanted to surprise you with breakfast in bed." She set the eggs on the counter and turned in his arms, her heart fluttering at the lustful look in his loving eyes. He was shirtless, wearing black boxer briefs and a wicked grin.

"Mm." He leaned down, kissing her slow and deep, grinding his hard length against her belly. He tasted of mint and happiness. He ran his finger along the edge of her towel and gently tugged it off. It puddled at her feet, and those hungry

eyes drank her in, making her heart race and her body flame. He made a low, rumbling noise as he backed her up against the counter. "Looks like my Thanksgiving breakfast is served."

Yes, please.

"I have a lot to be thankful for." He cupped her jaw, brushing his thumb along her lower lip. "I'm thankful for these sinful lips and the kisses they give." He pushed his thumb into her mouth, and she closed around it, licking the thick digit. "And for this beautiful mouth, which rambles adorably and sucks exquisitely." When he withdrew his thumb, a moan slipped out.

"Love those sounds you make," he murmured against her skin, kissing a path down her neck and dipping his head to slick his tongue over her nipple, making her ache for more. "I'm thankful for your gorgeous breasts and the loving heart behind them."

Holding her gaze, his hand slid over her thigh. "And for these legs that squeeze me when you ride my cock and hold you up when I take you from behind." He dragged his fingers along her wetness. "Think your family will know I'll be thinking about bending you over the dinner table all night?"

A whimper escaped, and she bit her lower lip. "Now I'll be thinking about that, too."

He brushed his lips over hers, whispering, "Good," and dipped his fingers inside her, then withdrew, teasing over her slickness again. Her eyes closed with the titillating sensations skittering up her chest. "Eyes on me, beautiful." She opened her eyes, and he did it again.

"*Tobias*," she pleaded.

"There are not enough words to describe how thankful I am for your tight pussy, which allows me to truly become one with you."

His dirty-talking romantic side always did her in. He lowered his mouth to hers in a mind-numbing kiss as he pushed his fingers inside her, making her gasp with pleasure, and proceeded to stroke that hidden spot ever so slowly, until she was mewling and trembling, aching for more. He nudged her legs open wider with his knee. "Spread your legs, baby. Your man has an appetite for the sweetest thing on this planet."

A slow grin spread his lips as he dropped to his knees, guiding one of her legs over his shoulder. His eyes remained trained on hers as he dragged his tongue along her sex and then feasted roughly, driving her out of her mind with his talented mouth and strong hands. *"Tobias—"* He quickened his efforts on her clit. *"Don't stop. Oh God..."*

She writhed against his mouth, arching and pleading. He pushed his fingers inside her, licking exquisitely, and then his mouth reclaimed her sex, and those wet fingers moved to her bottom, teasing over the forbidden spot that only *he* had ever touched. *"Yes..."* She clung to his shoulders, shaking, her thoughts frayed as he worked her to perfection, taking her right up to the edge and holding her there. He devoured, teased, and taunted until she was barely holding on to her sanity, a stream of indiscernible pleas spilling from her lips. When he pushed the tip of his finger into her ass, she lost it, crying out as she rode his mouth, nails digging into his skin, hips bucking, her moans filling the room. He stayed with her, feasting, fucking, and driving her wild, until she collapsed, dizzy and sated, against him.

"Christ, baby, I love watching you come." He lifted her chin, kissing her slow and sweet and leaving her breathless. "I love *everything* about you. I hope you know how special you are."

She looked at him through half-mast eyes as he rose to his feet. "How could I not? You show me every day." *In so many ways.* He brought her flowers, watched her performances, kept her safe without being overbearing, encouraged her every endeavor, and loved her so completely, she'd gone from not believing in love herself to never wanting to see a day without him in it.

"Now it's my turn," she said, dragging her nails, and her lips, down his chest and biting his nipple. He cursed, and that sexy sound spurred her on. She did it again, and he inhaled sharply. His dark eyes bored into her as she wet her hand with her own arousal and fisted his cock, giving it a tight tug as she lowered herself into a chair.

He stepped closer, and she smiled up at him. "*Don't* come in my mouth. I want to feel you come inside me."

"Such a naughty girl." He ran his fingers over her lips, and she bit the tips, earning a low growl.

She released his fingers and brought his cock to her mouth, gliding her tongue over the broad head, loving the flames in his eyes. As she took him in her mouth, he tangled his hands in her hair and pumped his hips. She squeezed him tighter, her hand following her mouth as she quickened her efforts. His muscles tensed, and she knew he was close. She saw him eyeing the table and knew what he was thinking seconds before he withdrew and pulled her to her feet, bending her over that table. He gave her ass a playful smack, and a surprised squeak fell from her lips. God, she loved their sexy times. She looked over her shoulder, their eyes connecting sharp and searing as she said, "*Again.*"

"Gladly." He caressed her ass, then smacked it again, harder this time, sending enticing prickles racing through her.

"*Fuck me*," she urged, but he was already there, gripping her hips and driving his cock into her tight heat, sending pleasure barreling through her. She gripped the edges of the table, craving his power, the lustful sounds he made, and the way he took her right over the edge.

As she came down from the peak, he withdrew and lifted her onto the counter, his mouth claiming hers roughly and devouringly as he drove into her, burying himself to the hilt. She cried out, and "*Fuuck*" fell from his lips, but he didn't slow down. He thrust and she rocked, meeting every pump and grind as he pounded into her. Their bodies took over, hands and mouths groping, kissing, nipping, and biting.

"*Harder*," she begged.

She clung to him as he pulled her off the counter, her legs clamping around his waist. He turned, and her back hit the wall. Using it for leverage, he took her harder, deeper, until they lost control, sounds of pleasure filling the air and love filling their hearts.

REBA AND PREACHER'S house was buzzing with love, laughter, and more family than Tobias ever imagined having in his life. His family, Madigan and her extended family, and Sid's father, were all there. He and Madigan had spent the afternoon with his grandfather, who was having a fairly good day, and though they'd considered bringing him to dinner, they worried it would be too overwhelming. They'd made the right decision. As joyful and wonderful as it was to be around so many good people, it was also loud and chaotic.

Gunner and Blaine carried platters of biscuits and mashed

potatoes out to the table, and Zander snagged a biscuit, shoving it into his mouth, as he hurried away.

"Dude, really?" Blaine hollered.

"What?" Zander splayed his hands with cheeks full of biscuit and laughed.

Carrie was holding Leo, chatting with Chloe, Leah, and Sid, and she glanced at Blaine.

He winked, his irritation at his brother forgotten.

Carrie shook her head and turned away, but not before Tobias noticed a light blush on his sister's cheeks. He'd never tire of seeing her smile and hoped one day she'd find love like he and Madigan had, a love that didn't shy away from the difficulties of life, of which there were many. He and Carrie and his father had shared deep conversations that had led to tears, laughter, anger, and every emotion in between. He was sure they had more to come, but he knew Madigan would be there for him every step of the way.

Tobias looked at his beautiful girl sitting on the floor beside Milo, playing her guitar and singing a song about a friendship between a frog and a girl who met in a meadow and gathered all the other animals and children for a Thanksgiving feast. Junie sat on Grandpa Mike's lap, fascinated. Buster lay between Rosie and Lynnie as the girls absently petted him, hanging on Madigan's every word. Lynnie leaned down and kissed the dog's head every few minutes. She was sweet-natured, and although he and Madigan had a long way to go before they'd be ready for the next step, much less a family of their own, he hoped one day they'd have their own children and raise them to love openly and stand up for the people around them.

"I don't know how she comes up with this stuff, but she's definitely got a gift," Tobias said to Zeke and Baz as the three of them headed into the kitchen to help carry more food to the table. Reba, Ginger, and the girls had made enough food to feed six families.

"You know the correlation between frogs and Leah's brother, don't you?" Baz asked.

Tobias shook his head. "No. What is it?"

"Before River died, he took the girls to the creek, and he told them a story about eating frogs and growing a family of them in his stomach," Zeke explained. "Now every time they see or hear about a frog, they remember River and feel like he's with them."

"That's wonderful." Tobias looked at Madigan as he carried a platter of green beans out to the table. She always knew how to bring a little extra love into people's lives. She glanced over, smiling as she sang, and his heart beat a little faster. How was it possible to love someone so much that he missed her when she was just across the room?

"She's got a beautiful voice," his father said, sidling up to him.

Walter Riggs had aged a lot in recent years. His hair was more silver than brown, he had fine lines around his eyes and mouth, and carried a bit more weight around the middle. But the kind-hearted father Tobias used to know was trying to make a comeback, and for that Tobias was grateful. His father had apologized more than was necessary, but thanks to a therapist they were seeing together, Tobias had realized he wasn't innocent in the deterioration of their relationship. He hadn't realized how much he'd blamed his father for his mother's death, as if he should have checked up on those supposed doctor appointments. Apparently he'd buried those feelings early on, but they were working through them now, and their relationship continued to grow stronger.

"She does," Tobias agreed.

"She reminds me of your mother with that light in her eyes." His expression warmed. "What did your mom used to say about you and Carrie? Kissed by the stars?"

He smiled with the memory. "She'd say we'd been kissed by the moon and sung to by the stars."

"That's it. She always had those special sayings, and she knew just when to bring them out."

The longing in his father's voice and the faraway look in his eyes made Tobias realize that if he missed Madigan when she was right across the room, it was no wonder his father had nearly lost his mind when he'd lost the love of his life.

"Your mother would have liked her."

"Yeah, I think she would have." He turned to the man who had caused him so much grief, had unknowingly made him stronger, and was pointedly trying to repair the damage he'd done, and he filled with gratitude. "I'm really glad you're here, Dad."

His father's face brightened. "Me too, son, and I have a feeling your little lady had a lot to do with that."

"She has a lot to do with everything good in my life."

Conroy and Preacher came out of the kitchen, each carrying a platter with a turkey on it, and Preacher said, "Who's ready to eat?"

There was a rush of chaos as the four families settled around the two long tables that ran from the dining room into the living room.

"You know it's been a good year when your Thanksgiving table gets a little bigger, and for that I'm more than grateful," Preacher said. "Thank you all for allowing us to be part of your holiday. Each of you has added something valuable to our lives."

Masking his words with a cough, Zander said, "Except Zeke."

Preacher glowered at him. "How about we go around the table and share what we're thankful for. I think we'll start with you, Zander."

Zander set a flirtatious gaze on Carrie. "I'm thankful for the gorgeous new face across the table."

Zeke swatted him, Blaine glowered, and Carrie grinned.

"Moving on," Preacher said, and one by one they shared what they were thankful for.

Tobias had been counting his blessings all day, most of which were right there in front of him. At this time last year, he was behind bars, with no foreseeable future and feeling like he'd be alone for the rest of his life. Now here he was, overflowing with reasons to be thankful, starting with the blue-eyed beauty sitting beside him.

"I'm thankful for Toe," Rosie announced. "And Lynnie Loo, and Junie, and my baby—"

"*Our* baby," Junie reminded her.

"Baby!" Lynnie squealed, and pointed to baby Leo from her perch between Tobias and Carrie.

"That's right, sweetheart," Carrie said.

Carrie was an amazing mother. She was patient, and she doled out the same lessons their mother had taught them, with just as much gentleness and enthusiasm.

Rosie bounced in her seat. "Papa Tank, it's your turn!"

Tank had one arm around Leah, and the other cradled baby Leo. "I'm thankful for my sweet girls, my loud-crying little man, my patient, gorgeous wife, and all the other people who put up with me in this world." He kissed the baby's forehead. "I'm also thankful for not getting blown up this year."

There were murmurs of agreement. Tobias had heard the story about Tank saving children from a burning building and the terrifying life-changing events of that night.

"Blown up?" Carrie asked. "Did I miss something?"

"Let's just say that last year was a tough Thanksgiving, and we're all thankful Tank is still with us," Conroy said.

They continued going around the table, mentioning loved ones and successes. When they reached Maverick, his eyes glowed with pride as he pulled Chloe close and said, "We're thankful for the baby we have on the way," inciting cheers, congratulations, and toasts.

As the excitement calmed, Reba said, "Dibs on babysitting," and everyone laughed.

"Way to steal our thunder, man." Gunner shook his head.

Everyone looked at Gunner and Sid expectantly.

"Is Sid pregnant, too?" Ginger asked hopefully.

"Good Lord, *no*," Sid said flatly, causing more chuckles. "We don't need more babies. We have enough of the four-legged variety. We finally chose a wedding season."

"A wedding *season*?" Madigan asked.

"Yes. We want to get married next summer, but we haven't decided on a date yet," Sid explained. "And I guess that's a good thing since Chloe's pregnant. Chloe, when are you due?"

"Mid-June," she said. "But first babies can be late, so give or take a week, I think."

"Okay, so no June wedding. Anyone else have summer plans?" Gunner asked.

Everyone shook their heads.

"July or August it is, then," Gunner said.

"Summer weddings are beautiful," Ginger added.

Madigan rubbed her hands together with a mischievous look in her eyes. "Does this mean we can start planning?"

"Yes, please," Gunner said. "If Sid has it her way, we'll just pop into the courthouse with no fanfare and come out married."

"Now, that sounds like my Sidekick," Sid's father said with a wink.

"What can I say?" Sid sipped her wine. "I'm low-maintenance."

"A low-maintenance woman? What the heck is that?" Preacher teased, and Reba swatted him.

Everyone laughed, and they continued making their way around the table, sharing what they were thankful for. Tobias's turn was nearing, and there were several things he wanted to say to Madigan's family and to his, but there were also private things he wanted only Madigan to hear. Someone made another joke, and as laughter rang out, he leaned closer to Madigan and whispered, "Thank you for accepting me with all of my faults and flaws." She looked at him with so much love in her eyes, everything else faded away, and his heart poured out. "Thank you for helping me find myself, my family, and my purpose and for opening my eyes and my heart, which allowed me to focus on becoming the best man I can possibly be. Thank you for *choosing* me. If I get nothing else in this life but eighty more years with you, I'll be a rich man."

"I love you, Tobias, and I'll always choose you."

"I hope so, because I still have strides to make before I'll be worthy of your hand, but I'm going to marry you one day, Blue Eyes, and I'm going to make your life so damn good, you'll never regret a second of it."

"I'd marry you tomorrow and never regret it," she said with tears in her eyes.

His throat thickened, and he drew her closer. "I love you, baby, and I appreciate that, but I don't want to rush. You're too important to me. Remember July Fourth, when you sang to me about how I was *unwritten* and *totally undefined*?"

She nodded.

"When I get down on one knee, I want us both to know exactly who I am and what lies ahead. I want to be a man you can be proud of in every sense of the word, and then we'll write all our pages together for the rest of our lives."

Tears streamed down her cheeks. "I want *that*."

"I want to find that, too."

Tobias turned at the sound of his sister's tearful voice, and everyone was looking at them, the women dreamy eyed and the men nodding approvingly. Tobias cleared his throat. "Sorry. I didn't mean to interrupt."

Preacher held up his glass in a toast. "Here's to more of those kinds of interruptions in our lives."

"Hear, hear," Grandpa Mike said.

As everyone lifted their glasses, Madigan said, "Here's to singing too fast and being called out for it by the broodiest biker at the Salty Hog."

"That's only because Tank wasn't there," Blaine said, and everyone laughed.

Tobias gazed into Madigan's eyes, so full of her, more truth poured out. "That night changed my life, angel, and I wouldn't have it any other way." As he kissed her smiling lips and more cheers rang out, he thanked the moon and the stars and his mother above, all of which he was sure had a hand in bringing his wicked angel into his life.

Ready for More Wickeds?

Blaine Wicked is used to women doing what he says in and out of the bedroom, but what happens when he falls for the one woman who won't submit to his wicked ways? Find out in the next insanely sexy, deeply emotional Dark Knights at Bayside romance.

Meet Johnny Bad

This rock star's life has just imploded. Can unexpected love save him?

A Braden + Bad Boys After Dark Crossover Novel

What happens when a rock star with no plans of settling down finds out he has a teenage daughter, his manager is embezzling, and the woman he's hired to design his tour wardrobe is breathing fire? Come along for the snarky, emotional, and insanely sexy ride as Jillian and Johnny get caught up in a storm that just might be bigger than both of them.

Fall in love with DARE WHISKEY

The Whiskeys: Dark Knights at Redemption Ranch series

She's the only woman he's ever loved and the one he could never have…

Years after losing one of their best friends to a dare gone wrong, Devlin "Dare" Whiskey continues to live up to his name, endlessly testing fate, while Billie Mancini buries the best parts of herself. Billie is beautiful, tough, and determined not to go back to the adrenaline-driven lifestyle she once craved like a drug and now fears like the devil. But Dare is done watching her pretend to be something she's not and takes on his most important challenge yet—showing the woman he loves that some dares are worth the risk.

Love Melissa's Writing?

Discover more of the magic behind *New York Times* bestselling and award-winning author Melissa Foster. The Wickeds are just one of the many family series in the Love in Bloom big-family romance collection, featuring fiercely loyal heroes, sassy, sexy heroines, and stories that go above and beyond your expectations! See the collection here:
www.MelissaFoster.com/love-bloom-series

Free first-in-series ebooks, downloadable series checklists, reading orders, and more can be found on Melissa's Reader Goodies page.
www.MelissaFoster.com/RG

More Books By Melissa Foster

LOVE IN BLOOM SERIES

SNOW SISTERS

Sisters in Love
Sisters in Bloom
Sisters in White

THE BRADENS at Weston

Lovers at Heart, Reimagined
Destined for Love
Friendship on Fire
Sea of Love
Bursting with Love
Hearts at Play

THE BRADENS at Trusty

Taken by Love
Fated for Love
Romancing My Love
Flirting with Love
Dreaming of Love
Crashing into Love

THE BRADENS at Peaceful Harbor

Healed by Love
Surrender My Love
River of Love
Crushing on Love
Whisper of Love
Thrill of Love

THE BRADENS & MONTGOMERYS at Pleasant Hill – Oak Falls

Embracing Her Heart
Anything for Love

Trails of Love
Wild Crazy Hearts
Making You Mine
Searching for Love
Hot for Love
Sweet Sexy Heart
Then Came Love
Rocked by Love
Our Wicked Hearts
Claiming Her Heart

THE BRADEN NOVELLAS

Promise My Love
Our New Love
Daring Her Love
Story of Love
Love at Last
A Very Braden Christmas

THE REMINGTONS

Game of Love
Stroke of Love
Flames of Love
Slope of Love
Read, Write, Love
Touched by Love

SEASIDE SUMMERS

Seaside Dreams
Seaside Hearts
Seaside Sunsets
Seaside Secrets
Seaside Nights
Seaside Embrace
Seaside Lovers
Seaside Whispers
Seaside Serenade

BAYSIDE SUMMERS

Bayside Desires

Bayside Passions

Bayside Heat

Bayside Escape

Bayside Romance

Bayside Fantasies

THE STEELES AT SILVER ISLAND

Tempted by Love

My True Love

Caught by Love

Always Her Love

THE RYDERS

Seized by Love

Claimed by Love

Chased by Love

Rescued by Love

Swept Into Love

THE WHISKEYS: DARK KNIGHTS AT PEACEFUL HARBOR

Tru Blue

Truly, Madly, Whiskey

Driving Whiskey Wild

Wicked Whiskey Love

Mad About Moon

Taming My Whiskey

The Gritty Truth

In for a Penny

Running on Diesel

THE WHISKEYS: DARK KNIGHTS AT REDEMPTION RANCH

The Trouble with Whiskey

For the Love of Whiskey

SUGAR LAKE

The Real Thing

Only for You

Love Like Ours

Finding My Girl

HARMONY POINTE

Call Her Mine

This is Love

She Loves Me

THE WICKEDS: DARK KNIGHTS AT BAYSIDE

A Little Bit Wicked

The Wicked Aftermath

Crazy, Wicked Love

The Wicked Truth

His Wicked Ways

SILVER HARBOR

Maybe We Will

Maybe We Should

Maybe We Won't

WILD BOYS AFTER DARK

Logan

Heath

Jackson

Cooper

BAD BOYS AFTER DARK

Mick

Dylan

Carson

Brett

HARBORSIDE NIGHTS SERIES

Includes characters from the Love in Bloom series

Catching Cassidy

Discovering Delilah

Tempting Tristan

More Books by Melissa

Chasing Amanda (mystery/suspense)

Come Back to Me (mystery/suspense)

Have No Shame (historical fiction/romance)

Love, Lies & Mystery (3-book bundle)

Megan's Way (literary fiction)

Traces of Kara (psychological thriller)

Where Petals Fall (suspense)

Acknowledgments

I hope you enjoyed Madigan and Tobias's story. Music plays a large role in many of my stories, and as a musical storyteller, music plays a large part in Madigan Wicked's life. As an author, I am restricted from using lyrics in my novels without consent from the artists, and I am forever grateful to my son Jake Foster (musician Blue Foster) for not only allowing me to use his lyrics in my stories but for also performing Madigan Wicked's song "Kiss Off" so I could share it with readers. You can find "Kiss Off" on Spotify and all other major music-streaming services.

I'd also like to thank Lisa Filipe for "too blessed to be stressed." I'm sure many of you have heard that saying before, but I had not until Lisa mentioned it when I was running late for my deadline on this book. That saying resonated so strongly, and it now has a permanent home in Tank and Leah Wicked's life as well as my own.

If this was your first Wicked novel and you would like to read the books that came before it, start with Justin and Chloe's story, A LITTLE BIT WICKED. You might also enjoy reading The Whiskeys: Dark Knights at Peaceful Harbor, featuring the Wickeds' cousins. Start that series with TRU BLUE.

Please note that the Wickeds is just one of the series in the Love in Bloom big-family romance collection. All my books can be enjoyed as stand-alone novels, without cliffhangers or unre-

solved issues, and characters appear in other family series, so you never miss out on an engagement, wedding, or birth. You can find information about the Love in Bloom series here:
www.MelissaFoster.com/melissas-books

I offer several free first-in-series ebooks, which you can find here:
www.MelissaFoster.com/LIBFree

If you'd like a peek into my writing world, I chat with fans often in my fan club on Facebook.
www.Facebook.com/groups/MelissaFosterFans

Follow my social pages for fun giveaways and updates on what's going on in our fictional boyfriends' worlds.
www.Facebook.com/MelissaFosterAuthor
Instagram: @MelissaFoster_Author
TikTok: @MelissaFoster_Author

If you prefer sweet romance, with no explicit scenes or graphic language, please try the Sweet with Heat series written under my pen name, Addison Cole. You'll find the same great love stories with toned-down heat levels.

Many thanks to my faithful assistants, Sharon Martin and Lisa Filipe, for somehow managing to deal with me and all of my craziness, talking me off ledges, keeping me on track every day of the year without fail, and for the million other things you do for me. Most importantly, thank you both for honoring me with your friendship. I have great appreciation for my incredible editorial team, Kristen Weber and Penina Lopez, my meticulous proofreaders, Elaini Caruso, Juliette Hill, Lynn Mullan, and

Justinn Harrison, and my last set of eyes, Lee Fisher. My work would not shine without all your help.

As always, heaps of gratitude go out to my family and friends for your endless support and patience.

Meet Melissa

www.MelissaFoster.com

Melissa Foster is a *New York Times*, *Wall Street Journal*, and *USA Today* bestselling and award-winning author. Her books have been recommended by *USA Today's* book blog, *Hagerstown* magazine, *The Patriot*, and several other print venues. Melissa has painted and donated several murals to the Hospital for Sick Children in Washington, DC.

Visit Melissa on her website or chat with her on social media. Melissa enjoys discussing her books with book clubs and reader groups and welcomes an invitation to your event. Melissa's books are available through most online retailers in paperback and digital formats.

Melissa also writes sweet romance under the pen name Addison Cole.

CPSIA information can be obtained
at www.ICGtesting.com
Printed in the USA
BVHW051324281122
652930BV00004B/22

9 781948 004718